What people are saying about
**Luisa Buehler**

### The Scout Master: *A Prepared Death*

"The plot is large and complicated but surprisingly easy to follow; a tribute to Luisa Buehler's writing skill and style. The pace is not frantic but it moves along nicely. Although advertised as a cozy, T*he Scout Master* carries heavyweight impact providing much more action than I had expected. This book scores a few stars on my personal scale."

–MyShelf.com

"This is an exciting-fast paced thriller that readers will thoroughly enjoy. ...the audience will root for the heroine to survive the many attempts on her life and hope she gets to kick butt. She is a warm and caring character who is a true heroine because she perseveres in spite of her fears."

–Harriet Klausner

### The Station Master: *A Scheduled Death*

"Cutting-edge cozy. *The Station Master* is filled with long-buried secrets, elaborate twists, and nail-biting suspense. Buehler and Marsden just keep getting better and better."

–J.A. Konrath, author of
*Dirty Martini*: A Lt. Jack Daniels Thriller

### The Lion Tamer: *A Caged Death*

"...a curious heroine, a handsome husband, a dashing ex-lover, and a skeleton or two...engaging...romance and mayhem vie for her attention–much to a reader's satisfaction and delight!"

–Sharon Fiffer, author of The Jane Wheel Mysteries

### The Rosary Bride: *A Cloistered Death*

"...a stylishly written novel evocative of Barbara Michaels and Teri Holbrook. Luisa Buehler presents a fascinating cast of characters, an engrossing tale of old wrongs, long-kept secrets, and murder."

–Denise Swanson, author of the bestselling
Scumble River Mysteries

Luisa Buehler

# The Lighthouse Keeper:
# A Beckoning Death

Book Five

*A Grace Marsden Mystery*

**Echelon Press, LLC**

THE LIGHTHOUSE KEEPER: A BECKONING DEATH
A Grace Marsden Mystery
Book Five
An Echelon Press Book

First Echelon Press paperback printing / December 2007

Echelon Press, LLC
9735 Country Meadows Lane 1-D
Laurel, MD 20723
www.echelonpress.com

ISBN 1-59080-564-X
978-1-59080-564-0
Library of Congress Control Number: 2007933587

PRINTED IN THE UNITED STATES OF AMERICA

10 9 8 7 6 5 4 3 2 1

## ❧ Dedication ❧

To my best friend from third grade, Joan Mitchell Hamilton and her husband, Dave Hamilton. Thank you for allowing me the use of your cottage for the setting and inspiration for this book. Thank you to Colleen, Ken, Debbie, Bob, Laurie, and Garry for allowing me to cast you as suspects, heroes, and villains. You are all heroes to me.

A loving thank you to Gerry and Kit for their continued support and encouragement in spite of missed dinners and extra chores.

# Chapter One

"It's behind that wall."

My brother's whisper brought Joan and me to his side. We'd climbed up to the lantern room in the old lighthouse over an hour ago, ostensibly to take notes and measurements.

"I don't hear anything."

"There can't be anything *behind* these walls, Marty–they're made of three-foot-thick stone. *Behind* is out there." Joan motioned toward the windows.

"There it is again. Hear it?"

I heard a faint scratching.

Joan shook her head. "I didn't hear it. If it's anything, it has to be coming from downstairs. Sound displaces in lighthouses…something about the cylindrical shape."

Marty started down the stairs. Joan shook her head and smiled. "It's probably an island rat," she whispered.

"Yuck. The brochure said nothing about rats, island or otherwise." I referred to my childhood friend's letter inviting me to Christian Island for a visit. "And while we're on that page, couldn't you and Dave have waited to sell at the end of the season? Who visits the island in January?"

"People live here year round. It's only us 'cottagers' who can't cope in the dark months. Besides, you get a better price when people are freezing and longing to have their own cottage by May. It's all about marketing, Gracie."

I smiled and grumbled at my oldest friend. We'd been through elementary and high school together.

"Hey. Down here. I found something." We hurried to the main gallery. Marty crouched on the floor next to the only furniture in the room, a small built-in bookcase. The Christian Island lighthouse had been vacant since 1922, and the iron from the lantern room had been cut up for scrap during World War II. Joan's group hoped to replace the Dioptric lantern by 1999 as part of the restoration.

"If this is supposed to become a historical marker and museum, where is the furniture–in storage? The bareness does show off the old timber and beams' architectural style."

"Whatever furnishings had been here were 'liberated' by islanders or cottagers years before. I have it on good authority that if you take tea with some of the families on the island, you'll be sipping from and probably sitting on items from here."

"Maybe the keeper took away his things when the lighthouse shut down."

"No. It's a safe bet that the last lighthouse keeper didn't take anything, besides his own life."

# Chapter Two

The hair on the back of my neck stiffened. "Someone died here?"

Joan recognized my discomfort. "Yeah, well sort of. I mean, his family found him and rushed him to the mainland, but with the ferry running late because of the storm that came up he didn't make it."

"So, he didn't die here." I don't know why I pursued that distinction. "Right?"

"They're pretty sure he died at the landing, but technically no one checked his pulse while they were in the lighthouse."

"Sounds to me like you're splitting hairs, Joan, trying to build a possible ghost story around this place to suck in...uh, attract more tourists." My brother smiled at his long-time nemesis.

"Martin Morelli, are you accusing me of fabrication for profit for a non-for-profit cause?" Her blue eyes sparkled with humor at the chance to spar with her childhood adversary.

"Yes, and I think it's brilliant. Nothing pulls them in faster than a haunted house. Right, Gracie?"

Of my four brothers, Martin, the youngest, bore the title of 'least sensitive' with nonplussed acceptance. The reason I came to Canada dovetailed perfectly with a chance to visit my old friend, but my fervent hope to dispel the memory of the last two months looked less likely to happen.

Joan smiled and nodded her head. "The committee for restoration and revitalization thinks so. We're going to do more research, get some photos, and do a display of the history of the lighthouse keepers through the years."

"Have any others died here?" Marty's voice sounded like he'd asked for ice cream.

"No, not that we can tell. But we're hopeful about the second keeper, Burton Havilland. Details are sketchy."

"Would you two stop; do you hear yourselves?" I shook my head and started for the door.

"Wait, Gracie. I want to show you what I found. The scratching I heard came from behind the bookshelf, which is an unusual design. It's built in two pieces, one inside the other. The bottom's been chewed out, and that's what clued me in to the design. There's a double wall, so if one knew to yank or pull on something," he motioned for Joan to take the other side, "one could probably slide this front piece out."

The small edge didn't allow for a good grip. Their fingertips slipped from each angle they tried. I stood squarely in the middle of a round room, smiling at the juxtaposition. The room seemed colder than when we'd first entered, the temperature must be dropping. I zipped up the jacket I'd let hang open. My fingers pulled a length of clothesline from my pocket and slowly slid the rough texture across my palm. I hurried to loop the line end over end and through to complete one pattern, then another, and another. Cold cramped my fingers, but I continued per the plan to do ten before I could stop. The air condensed in the small space and rolled around at our feet. *How odd. I've never seen that. Must be an anomaly in round rooms.* The interior fog rose to waist high.

"Joan, this is the oddest fog I've ever seen. Does it happen often?" The cloud climbed and circled around our heads. Joan and Marty's figures grew dim even though they stood a scant ten feet away. The sharp cold held my feet to the floor and crept up my legs, forcing the blood and muscle to harden. A feeling of dread skimmed my spine in a way that made me cry out as a figure turned toward me—wild, tortured eyes, sunken into a drawn face surrounded by tufts of matted gray hair. His gaze held mine, then he purposely looked at his hands thrust deep into the shelf. He lifted his forearms against the wood and turned to me again; then the mist covered him.

"Gracie, are you alright?" Marty shook my shoulder.

"Grace, you're scaring me. What's wrong?" Joan stood next to me. When had they approached?

"Where's the fog?"

"What fog? You asked me that before. When I turned around,

you were rooted to this spot staring at me. Only I got the feeling it wasn't me you were seeing."

I could feel a deep flush on my face and yanked at my zipper. The cool air rushed at my neck and I welcomed the natural crispness that cleared the eerie daydream from my mind. "Whew, I guess I overheated or something," I offered.

"More like overreacted to something." My brother's concern shone in his eyes.

One way to find out, I thought, and approached the bookcase dead center. "Have you tried this?" I reached deep into the case and lifted my arms against the top. The shelf shifted slightly under the pressure, and I felt rather than heard a latch open. I gripped the wood with my palms and pulled slowly. Did I imagine wisps of long-imprisoned air escaping to curl around my head on their path to freedom? The smell of desiccated air filled my nose and the shelf unit slid effortlessly across the smooth floor until I felt a catch stop it.

"How did you know…never mind." My brother's voice sounded strained.

Marty and Joan leaned in from each side. "There's something there." Joan's voice quivered with excitement. I felt Marty push forward and reach into the space. He carefully handed out a long narrow box and reached in again. This time he held an oilskin-covered packet the size of an 8 x 10 frame. Joan eagerly accepted it. "This is great. Maybe there'll be pictures and notes."

Marty straightened, holding a long thin fillet knife gingerly between two fingers. The blade gleamed intermittently between spaces of silver and smears of a brown stain. "I'm no expert, but I think the dark stuff is blood."

"It's a filleting knife. Blood wouldn't be unusual, it's not like it's a knitting needle." I didn't want the experience in the mist to be anything more than fatigue from a long drive and nerves from a tumultuous sendoff.

Joan and Marty stared in silence, and I read the message in my brother's eyes. He knew the demons I'd been fending off; he'd some of his own. I'd accepted Joan's invitation as a way for my youngest brother and me to clock out from the daily grind and change our pace and focus. Marty's wife Eve left him the day after Christmas, offering reconciliation only when he stopped self-medicating and sought counseling for his potential addiction.

"Should we put it in a bag or something? You know, for prints?" Joan's voice sounded serious. What had been a smiling, excited face now fell with concern.

We had sapped the joy from her discovery. Why couldn't anything happen lately in my life without a hidden agenda, motives, or murder. Murder? Who said murder? My mind begged off the question as soon as I thought it. Too much death had smothered my life this past year; too many tragic circumstances and desperate people. Always, feeling the fugue that lured me, embroiled me beyond my control.

I shrugged. "It does seem odd that someone would hide it. Maybe we should handle it carefully and take it over to the mainland tonight, turn it over to the police in Midland."

Joan nodded. "I've a plastic shopping bag in the car. I'll get it."

Marty pushed the bookshelf back into its sleeve. "Nifty design; great hiding place. That reminds me, how did you know the secret of the bookcase?"

"Geez, Marty. You make me sound like Nancy Drew."

"I got dibs on being your chum, George," Joan called from the doorway and handed Marty the bag. He wrapped the knife in it.

"It looks like rain's coming. I brought more." As we wrapped the box and packet, I wondered if you could lift fingerprints from oilskin.

A clap of unexpected thunder startled me, and I lurched against the bookcase. Lightning sliced sideways across the still sunny sky.

"Let's go. These storms come up fast." Joan stood near the doorway. Another clap of anger filled the room and vibrated through the floor. In the eerie silence I heard a dull click and felt a weight against my leg; I stepped away and the bookcase slid slowly toward me.

# Chapter Three

A length of brilliant light slashed through the room and filled it with energy and danger. Joanie's hair stood straight out from her head, and the air tingled against my face like hundreds of pulsating cells.

The concussion of the strike threw us to the ground. Smoke filled the air and the bookcase, charred and cleaved by the lightning, burned into the stone.

"Oh my gosh. Oh no." Joan's voice grew stronger; she moved closer to me.

I grabbed her arm and turned her away from the bookcase. "Too much smoke, let's get out of here." A coughing jag seized Joan as we pushed toward the door. Fresh air and cold rain pelted us as we emerged from the lighthouse. Smoke followed us, but lost density and toxicity in the open space.

"Marty!" He hadn't followed. "Marty!" My scream brought a muffled response from the interior. Was he hurt? I dropped to my knees and crossed the threshold at a fast crawl. The lower strata provided easier breathing; I could see Marty crouched, one hand covering his mouth and nose, the other swinging his jacket at the bookcase, smothering the last fingers of flame licking at the dry wood. The wind that had encouraged the flames now swept the swirls of smoke from the area. I stood and screamed at my brother, "Are you crazy? What the hell's the matter with you?"

"Geez, Gracie, relax. I had it under control."

"Control? We get hit by lightning and you have it under control?" I sputtered for words I didn't have. My eyes filled with tears from the churning fear I'd felt. He saw my distress.

"I'm sorry, Sis. I knew I could put it out. C'mon, don't cry." He put his arms around me and snugged me close. "Didn't know you cared. I mean, you used to tell me to go fly a kite when it stormed." I smiled at his childhood recollection. "Or was that go fly a kite in traffic?"

I laughed and punched him in the arm. "I don't care, I'm supposed to watch out for you; Dad said so." I repeated my mantra from years before. "I hated having to be responsible for you. Glenn would sit and read and watch television. You had to climb trees and fences and disappear on your bike." I punched him again.

"Oww. Stop that."

"Who you gonna tell?"

"You were a pain in the ass, Marty. No sympathy from me." Joan smiled and suggested we leave before anything else happened.

"Thanks for putting out the fire; it would have been sad to lose her to a fire, but sadder to lose you."

"Aww, you do care." Marty snagged Joan with his other arm and pulled her into our group hug. "Yeah, like having two older mean sisters." He let go and stepped back before either of us could smack him.

The rain soaked us before we covered the twenty yards to the car. The short ride to the cottage held no comment or banter.

We changed into dry clothes and reconvened at the small kitchen table like three kids ready to investigate the 'treasure' of Christian Island Lighthouse.

Joan spread out the flaps of the oilskin and smiled at the contents. "This is great. Photos, letters…omigosh, what a find." She carefully slipped one letter from its envelope, smoothing it out on the tabletop.

> *Dear Child,*
>
> *I read your last letter with great concern and sadness. The weight of married life can seem unbearable at times, but your duty and your vow must outweigh your personal feelings. Some men can be demanding in their proclivities and the number of demands does seem excessive. Your husband has not turned out to be the man we expected for you, but that is of no matter. The marriage is sealed, as is your fate with Mr. Havilland.*
>
> *The children you bear will bring you comfort. It is my experience that, after the third child, that type of husband often stays away from home more and more seeking his ribald pleasures in more suggestive surroundings. Soon,*

*my dear, you will be mistress of your home. Take to his bed when he demands, it is your duty, but a crying child nearby has a devastating effect on his desire to prolong the encounter. Do not avoid conception; children are all that make life worth living.*

*Your loving Grandmother,*
*Mrs. Arthur Pantier*

"Yuck. That's the worst advice I've ever heard. Can you believe this drivel?"

I lifted the envelope from the table. "Mrs. Burton Havilland. Is the letter dated?"

"Uh, yes, 18 November 1881. Wow, this letter is over a hundred years old." Joan pulled a Ziploc plastic bag from her drawer. "I think I'll keep it unfolded in here." She slid the letter and envelope into the clear bag.

"I bet she read and reread that letter, by the looks of those deep creases."

"Yeah, she probably couldn't believe her Gran sold her down the river," Marty snickered. "Any other letters with rousing encouragement?"

"Marty, think about it. It's not like she had any choices. She married the lighthouse keeper on a small island. They depended on the ferry to bring their food, household needs, mail, everything."

"Weren't there natives or something living on the island?"

Joan rolled her eyes. "The Beausoleil First Nation settled Christian Island in 1856. They wouldn't have interacted with them."

"Great choice–be at the beck and call of the lighthouse keeper twenty-four/seven or have enough kids to keep him at arm's length."

"The second option never happened; the Havillands were childless. So she must have endured him until the accident that killed him."

All three of us looked at the wrapped knife.

"I told you it looked like blood."

"And I told you that's crazy. Burton Havilland died when the gun he was cleaning discharged and caught him in the chest. The family tried to get to him to the mainland, but the weather had come up and the ferry wasn't running."

"The ferry wasn't running when the last lighthouse keeper needed medical attention either. What's with that?"

Marty made a good point, but I was curious about something else. "What family? I thought they didn't have kids."

"Amelia's brother, Joshua, visited several times a year, but stayed the longest after the harvest on their family farm in Lafontaine."

Marty lost interest in the genealogy. He picked up the long piece of wood and jumped with excitement. "Hey, look at this. This part has carving on it. Maybe the lighthouse keeper was a woodcarver."

Joan reached for it. "That wouldn't be unusual. Long hours on watch, long *boring* hours." Joan ran her hand over the cut wood. "It's not much of a design."

I reached for it. "Maybe he wasn't finished and he–"

"Kept it hidden when he wasn't working on it?" Marty grinned. He took it back and ran his thumb over the pattern. "Looks like my woodcarving merit badge attempt. He wasn't good."

"He wasn't finished. That's a geef box. People on the island carved them. They're used to hide little treasures or keepsakes." Dave Hamilton stood in the doorway, his light brown hair swept low on his forehead in a 'Beach Boys' style. Dave loved the water and the outdoors. Bright blue eyes gleamed from a weather-ruddy face. He held a small grocer's box in one arm and a paper sack of groceries in the other.

Marty stepped up to relieve him of the box.

"Thanks. Put it on the counter by the sink." He shifted the bag toward Joan. "I'm a bit muddy, don't want to step in." He slipped out of his shoes and pulled his poncho over his head. "There's a blow coming; caught the last ferry 'til the weather tuckers out." He hung the glistening garment on a peg and pushed the mat under the hem to catch any drips.

"Stranded on the island? When do the lights flicker and go out?" Marty's attempt at a Christie plot brought laughter from our hosts.

"Not likely, mate. We invested in a generator that keeps us

warm, lighted, and microwave-ready."

Joan emptied the contents of the bag into various cabinets and checked the box for anything perishable. Two butcher-paper-wrapped items went into the fridge and the produce went into the sink for a good wash.

"Coffee in the middle of the day?" Dave poured himself a cup.

"You know Grace…she can't go for more than a few hours without the stuff. We were soaked, and before she even changed into dry clothes she had the pot going."

Dave took a sip and smiled. "Hmm, the good stuff. Thank you, ma'am," he held his cup up in a toast. "Can I pour one for you?"

"A refill would be great."

"He's in heaven when you're here. Colleen is the only other one who inhales the stuff."

"Happy to make your day, Dave," I toasted back with my cup.

"Did you make it to the lighthouse before the storm broke?"

"We most certainly did. Better yet, we found a secret cabinet and emptied it in the nick of time." Joan filled her husband in on the lightning strike and Marty's foolhardy success in putting out the fire.

"I'd hate to have to explain to your Dad, Marty, how you, either of you, were injured on my watch. Be a pal and don't do anything else dangerous."

"Tell her," Marty looked at me. "She's the one always finding dead bodies. Up until a week ago she had a cast on her wrist from some nutcase in a robe who threw a brick at her."

Joan and Dave's eyes widened. I waved my hand in dismissal. "He exaggerates." My mind hurried to find a diversion. "Aren't you going to show Dave the letter and…"

"The murder weapon," Marty chimed in.

Dave's eyes not only widened, his eyebrows shot up under his hair. He looked at Joan with a glance that assigned guilt for the connection firmly on her side. Joan shrugged. She'd known my family since we'd moved to Berkeley and I met her in the third grade at St. Domitilla.

I glared at Marty. This trip was supposed to be R & R from the weird, the bizarre, and the dead. He stood there, apparently aware of his size twelve shoe in his mouth, and mumbled around the leather, "Okay, okay. We found a hidden knife with what could be blood on it."

Even stated simply, it didn't sound good. Dave unwrapped the knife and stared at the blade. "This is a beauty. Looks like a genuine Polecat. I think they only made these in the thirties or forties. I can check my catalogs."

"Then Amelia's in the clear. She'd hardly be wielding that fifty years before it was made." Joan sounded relieved.

Dave smiled and nodded. "Modern science clears her too. This wrap isn't oilskin like the other," he pointed at the tabletop. "It's plastine, an early cousin to plastic."

"So two people knew about the secret cabinet: Amelia and whoever hid the knife."

"Why would whoever hid the knife not take the letters?"

"Why would Burton hide a piece of wood?"

Dave reached for the wood. "Because a geef may be a hiding place in a hiding place. The odd-sounding name is not Indian. A Dutch commerce ship sailed into harbor in the 1860's and befriended the Indians. Geef is Dutch for gift. The name stuck and island boys learned to carve at their father's side; a skill passed on." Dave indicated the thin grooves running the length of the wood. I hadn't noticed them. "A long strip is carefully removed and then the inside of the wood is hollowed out in different ways for different use. When the hollowing out is completed, the carver cuts a groove on either side and a corresponding groove on the piece removed that now becomes a lid." Dave held the wood lengthwise against his body and worked his thumbs against the carved part. "The lid," he kept pushing at the pattern, "should slide easily." He stopped. "But it doesn't. Too much humidity, the wood is swollen."

Dave continued to work the wood. "Got it. I felt it move." His voice reflected our excitement. He slid the top slowly, each inch resisting giving up the secret. A quarter open, it seemed to snag. "C'mon, baby, open. Little more...that's it." The wood separated and Dave held the top free from the bottom. A long narrow bone lay in a smooth, oiled hollow.

A crash of thunder stopped the conversation and the lights flickered with the lightning strike.

"Sounds close. You may get to see the generator in use." Dave's words barely reached our ears before the room plunged into darkness. I heard him move, and as my eyes adjusted I could see him at the kitchen counter. In the next instant I heard a click, and the darkness split for a strong beam of light. "Ray-o-Vac police model; keep one in every room." Dave tapped Marty on the shoulder. "Come with me."

Joanie spoke up. "While the menfolk rub two wires together for light, let's relax. Can you see well enough to get down to the couch?" A flash of lightning conveniently illuminated the two steps leading to the small family room. We both giggled at the intervention. I chose the couch and Joan moved in next to me.

"We haven't had much time alone since you arrived, and by tomorrow this place will be Grand Central, so what gives?"

Joan could always sense my moods. As children, she could tell when my obsessive-compulsive behavior peaked and she'd suggest a game that would accommodate rather than exclude me. I remember being 'it' and having to count to 100 by twos and then by fives. Most of the kids lost interest and came out of hiding.

I shrugged. "I needed to unwind. Life has become complicated."

She raised her eyebrows.

"More complicated," I continued with a smile. "Harry's been preoccupied with Will, rightfully so," I hurried to add. "Dad's found a woman he's interested in; first one since Mom died."

"So you're feeling that the center of the universe has shifted from you to somewhere else with the two men who mean the most to you?"

"Geez Louise, you make me sound like a whiny kid."

"Nah, just a human one. Both guys bailed on you at the same time. Speaking of men who matter most…"

I raised my hand, palm out. "Don't go there. Ric is pursuing a certain police officer from Lisle."

"In one of your letters you said he moved in with Lily."

"That was for medicinal purposes only."

"Is that what they're calling it now?" Joan's smirk lifted my mood. "You have Will on weekends, right?"

"That's changed. Lily bought a loft in the River North area with plans to remodel it into a gallery. She intends to live in Karen's and Hannah's B&B, if they ever agree on anything. The house in Pine Marsh is on the market. Hannah wanted to move the twins out there, but Karen wouldn't budge on that issue. I think that move would have torn apart their mar…relationship."

"So where's Will in all of this?"

"Right now Harry and Will are in England visiting the Marsdens. Will starts at a new school in Woodridge in two weeks. He'll be living with us from now on. Lily gets him on weekends."

"Whew, no wonder you needed a break. The Hamilton cottage over the next two weeks will be fun, relaxing, and worry free. Give you time to gear up for your new life as a full-time mom."

The lights came on then, and in that instant of illumination the look on Joan's face showed concern belied by her cheery voice. I knew she was wondering how her 'center of attention, spoiled by all the men in her life, brothers included' best friend could handle the enormous selfless task of being someone's mom. I didn't blame her; I wondered the same.

Dave called out from the sliding door, "We're going to check out the other cottages, see if anyone's here and if they need help."

They stood on the deck just visible by the splash of light from the kitchen. In their ponchos and boots they reminded me of two action figures. I watched until they walked into the darkness, only two bobbing beams preceding them on their mission. A voice crackled behind me and I jumped.

Joan laughed and apologized, "Sorry." She pointed to the walkie-talkie on the table. "He's checking the channel." She lifted the radio and responded.

"Boy, a generator, walkie-talkies, big flashlights, search and rescue mission–I'll never get Marty home. This is like playing make believe for real."

Her dimpled smile heightened the gleam in her clear blue eyes. "You can be in charge of the radio if you want."

"That's okay. I'll just go *'kersh, kersh*, over,' if I need them." I held my hand up to my mouth pretending to hold a radio and used my thumb to 'operate' the key.

"You always did hear a different drummer, didn't you?"

"Several, sometimes all at once." We burst into laughter and impulsively hugged each other. "God, it's good to be here. I can't believe it's been three years."

"Would have been less, but you missed reunion last year. I'd have skipped reunion to spend the summer in England, but no one asked."

I loved her sense of humor. Spending two weeks with Joanie on her island was just what the doctor ordered. I had left the prescription for antidepressants that he really had ordered back home in Pine Marsh. Marty and I were flying solo from our spouses and med-free from our demons.

"I don't know about Dave, but Marty will be hungry when he gets back from 'patrol.' Maybe we should make dinner?"

"Your brothers were always hungry. I made lasagna on Russell Street and lugged it over before you arrived. I have two casseroles in the freezer; the rest of the food for our stay is coming with the Christian Island regulars." Joan peeled the foil back from a pan and invited my approval.

"Looks good."

"It better be. It's your dad's recipe. Everyone up here who eats it raves about it. They can't figure out the difference. It's the ricotta cheese and homemade sauce."

"Gravy," I corrected automatically.

Joan grinned. "Homemade gravy. I had the devil of a time getting ricotta up here. They carry it in Barrie's Finer Foods now."

She tucked the pan into the small oven and set the egg timer. "I have some plastic bags in the fridge with salad stuff. Make what you want."

I busied myself preparing lettuce, tomatoes, pepper, and onion for a tossed salad as my thoughts drifted for the first time in hours to the figure I had glimpsed in the lighthouse. I had hoped whatever sensitivity toward restless spirits I'd discovered this past year would be local, but after today I feared my susceptibility extended beyond my own backyard.

"Hey, what's this?" Joan stood at the table unwrapping the oilskin packet. She placed more than a dozen small squares on the table. "Looks like photos of rocks and terrain, only they've been cut up."

"Like one of those scramble square puzzles, the ones with teapots or cats and you have to match the edges." I shivered at the thought. For someone with OCD, the thought of not being able to complete a pattern sent tremors to my fingertips. I pulled a length of cord from my pocket and fingered the tight strands.

Joan glanced at my hands and back at the pieces. "Let's keep this until tomorrow. Debbie is a puzzle fiend. We'll put her on it." She carefully slipped the pieces into another baggie and put everything on the counter.

"You'd better rewrap that or someone might wash it tomorrow." I nodded toward the fillet knife left on the counter.

The sliding door opened and Marty and Dave slipped in, closing it quickly. "Whew, it's still blowing sideways out there."

"That didn't take long. Everyone's generator up and running?"

"There are no other cottagers on the island. We checked them all on this side and didn't see any lights across the water from those. The only lights are from Band Council families–the only legitimate residents of the island."

"Ha, no other hearty mainlanders?" Marty asked.

"Most mainlanders would call us foolhardy, not hearty. They don't come out in January, but it's been so mild and we won't have the cottage in May. Hope our idea to have a last fling doesn't turn south with the weather."

"For starters, if this weather doesn't blow out by morning the ferry won't be coming across."

"No use worrying about that now. We'll see about the weather in the morning, and make some calls. Let's eat."

A flash lit up the deck. The figure standing on the other side of the glass door stared at us through dark holes, his face full of rage.

# Chapter Four

My scream shared airtime with a shattering clap of thunder. I pointed at the door...dark again. "Someone's out there. A man, a face." My voice quaked and I sucked in deep breaths to calm myself.

"He may need help and saw our lights on." Dave moved toward the door.

"No!"

Three heads swung toward me, all with eyebrows raised waiting for the explanation of my outburst.

"He didn't look friendly. He looked evil, maybe even dead." I hadn't meant to say that part out loud. My mind registered three distinct expressions: horror, concern, and excitement.

Marty put his arm around me. "Hey, take it easy. The storm's got you spooked." I nodded and let him walk me to the nearest chair.

Dave had stepped away from me and closer to the sliding door, apparently feeling safer with whatever was out there. He shook his head. "Probably a Band Council elder. They look a little rough around the edges. I'll be right back." He slipped into his poncho and picked up the heavyweight flashlight. Marty moved to join him, but Dave raised his hand. "No need to come with. I know most of the islanders. Be right back." He flipped up the hood and stepped outside.

Joan stood at the counter still holding the paring knife she'd been using to cut up a pepper. Her eyes gleamed with conspiracy, and I wondered at her enigmatic smile. I could tell she wanted to talk to me, alone. My curiosity at her behavior would have to wait; Dave returned smiling.

"Mystery solved. Found old Joe up at the driveway. Says he wasn't on the deck, but I'm sure he's been curious about why a cottager is here. He didn't want to admit he was a peeping Tom."

I wasn't convinced. The figure I saw wasn't trying to hide and peep in; he was staring straight at me. He wanted to be seen. Each set of eyes looked to me for acceptance. I summoned a megawatt smile from my repertoire—one recipient believed it.

Dave steered the dinner conversation sharply away from the events of the day and concentrated on planning the next week. Six more people would be arriving tomorrow, swelling the residents to ten adults threatening to burst the cottage at the seams. He laid out the accommodations. "You and Marty will have the bunks in the little room. Whoever sleeps on top can step on the freezer chest to get up there. Debbie and Bob will have the second bedroom, and Colleen and Ken and Laurie and Garry will get the pull-outs in the pit." He smiled and waved his fork at the family room.

Dave and Joan's room was an addition reached by walking outside to the deck and down a few stairs.

"In the summer, we pitch a tent and couples take turns in the tent. More privacy."

Joan smiled, and I wondered if Marty felt as much a fifth wheel as I did. This trip originally included Harry, before Will. I mentally pushed those thoughts away. It would be a "hoot," as my transplanted best friend would say, connecting with my little brother, traipsing around an island away from work and life back home. *Some hoot*, my brain responded and my OCD mind checked off the events: *almost struck by lightning, pulled into a fugue-like state by some restless spirit, and visited by the same spirit mistaken for a peeping Tom. Oh joy, only thirteen more days to go. Thirteen? I don't like that. Don't be silly, you were born on the thirteenth. Yeah, see how well that's worked out.*

"Earth to Grace." Joan waved her hand in front of my face. "Where do you go when you get that way? I'd love to be able to do that when I'm in front of my class. Serve them right if I zoned out."

"Joan, they're grade one," Dave sputtered with laugher.

Joan smiled. "They are a sweet bunch. Okay, not with them but it still looks like a good place to go."

I forced myself to look focused on the here and now. *A good place to go. If she only knew.*

After we cleared and cleaned up quickly, Dave suggested we conserve some power by using the hurricane lamps. Joan and I positioned four large candles inside glass chimneys throughout the living room. The glow from the flames illuminated enough area to make it cozy. Again I thought of how Harry should be with me, and how satisfying snuggling with him would feel about now. Dave filled the belly of the Franklin stove and pleasant warmth permeated the room.

The storm blew itself out about midnight and the night turned clear and crisp. We bundled into our coats and pulled chairs out from the overhang. Marty and Dave competed at naming the constellations, two scouts verbally pushing and shoving. Dave proved more accurate, but he conceded this wasn't Marty's night sky. I leaned back and stared at the firmament, marveling at the hundreds of stars I could see in this remote sky. A sense of calm filled me and I relaxed, content to be a small cog in a larger view.

"Think about it, guys. Probably twelve percent of the stars we're seeing have already gone nova. Dead and they don't know it."

So much for calm. My brother was a jerk sometimes.

# Chapter Five

The morning bore no resemblance to its cloudy predecessor. Marty and I woke early and made our way through the cabinets to find coffee, tea, and appropriate pots. My brother decided to turn to tea under Joan's insistence of its intrinsic healing potential. I personally thought he still had a smidgen of the crush he'd had on her when we were kids.

"Hey, Sis, about yesterday. How did you know how to open the cabinet?"

Marty's eyes held no teasing expression. He'd realized, later than my older brothers, that answers about family problems or issues come to me unbidden and mostly unwanted. He stirred sugar into his tea. "I mean, did you think it or dream it while you were in that kind of zone you go to?"

"You mean the 'where have you been and why do you go there' place in her head?"

Joan's voice startled us. She provided the distraction I needed. I nodded toward Marty. "You've a tea convert."

Joan's face lit up and she hurried to Marty's side. "Which did you choose? Hmm, good choice for clarity and calmness. Lovely way to start the day." She smiled at my brother, and I knew by the pink tops of his ears that he was ten years old again and madly in love with his sister's Olivia Newton-John look-alike best friend.

"Hello, hello."

Cheery voices hailed from the driveway. The sounds of car doors opening and closing, and coolers rolling across the gravel reached my ears. Joan held open the back door and six people, each carrying a box or suitcase or cooler, marched up the stairs like ants bringing food to the picnic in reverse *modus operandi*. Joan directed people to rooms, food to freezer or fridge, and nonperishables to the kitchen table.

Introductions took a few minutes before the newcomers stowed their personal gear. Dave took the guys down to the water to show them one of the canoes he wanted to sell. Joan offered us beverages and muffins…anxious to share our discovery, but always the good hostess. A drum roll seemed to be in order as we crowded in at the Formica table. I sat quietly and watched her glow with excitement while she recounted our adventure. She didn't mention the knife.

"We haven't had time to study the puzzle. It seems to be several similar photographs of the same scene, but in slightly different locations in the same general area. They've been cut into small squares, twenty-four of them."

"Hello. Look at the back of these." Colleen turned over several pieces. There appeared to be small, cramped writing, a few sentences filling the small box. Some pieces were blank. "Maybe it would be easier to match the writing."

"The sentences don't carry over. I've read three blocks so far and they don't seem connected to each other. I think you have to get the picture together and then the back will make sense."

"Laurie, you're quiet. I thought you'd be all over this."

We turned expectantly to her. She appeared thoughtful. "I'm sorry, Joan. I'm a little stunned at finding another letter from Amelia."

We all sat up and took notice. "Another letter?"

Laurie nodded, pushed her shoulder-length hair behind her ears, and sat straighter in her chair. Her gray eyes leveled the group with an expression of part defiance, part trepidation. "Amelia Havilland was Garry's great-great aunt."

Joan clapped her hands together like a child on her birthday. "Oh, that's wonderful. We can get more information about her for the museum. Why didn't you tell me she was family? You know I've been working on this lighthouse project."

Debbie grinned, "Everyone knows." We chuckled and nodded knowingly. Once Joan caught an idea, there was no going back. I might be obsessive-compulsive; she was just plain obsessed.

Laurie's smile didn't reach her eyes. "We don't talk about Amelia."

"Why, was she the black sheep of the family?" Joan held up the letter. "Her grandmother's response made me wonder how pitiful Amelia's letter home must have been. Her husband sounded horrible."

"Don't." Laurie's sharp tone surprised everyone. "We just don't talk about her."

The word "her" trembled from her lips. "I need some air." She stood and walked out to the deck so quickly the rest of us looked from face to face for an answer. Debbie started to follow her, but Colleen placed a hand on her arm. "Give her some time. She'll work it out."

"How about a trip out to the lighthouse? I think I dropped my tape measure yesterday," Joan asked and waited for a response.

I had no inclination to return. Hadn't liked the vibes or the vision in that place.

"I'll take a pass. You know, been there, done that. Go ahead, I'll stay here and work on some lunch for us."

Joan, Debbie, and Colleen nodded as one and left soon after, chatting down the steps about the letter's intent. "How could a Gran tell her baby to stay put and tolerate?"

"Different times—no one married for love."

"Oh now, that's cynical."

I lost the rest of their conversation as they walked to the road. It would be a pleasant walk on a crisp morning. I'd walked it with Joan each time I'd stayed at the cottage, but yesterday was the last time I'd go there, at least willingly. I rolled my shoulders to dislodge the palpable weight of that memory.

"What's wrong?" I jumped at the sound of Laurie's voice. "Didn't mean to startle you. I thought everyone left."

"They went to the lighthouse; I've seen it before—yesterday, in fact." I felt like I babbled the entire sentence in a higher pitched voice than normal. Laurie didn't know me; we'd only met once before a few summers ago.

She refilled her teacup before she sat down. Laurie folded her arms across her chest and the steaming mug sat forgotten on the table. "Garry is Amelia's great-great nephew. His family lived speculation and innuendo about their crazy aunt. Doesn't bother Garry's generation, but his parents took the stories to heart."

"Crazy aunt? Does Joan know all this? 'Cause she's going to pump you dry for the historical museum."

She shook her head. A brief smile played at her lips. "I know she's been scrambling after clues, tracking down papers, and searching each nook and cranny for anything about Amelia." She paused, and her smile grew. We grinned, each of us knowing the tenacity of our mutual friend.

"Are you going to tell her? I mean, what are the chances that a relative would be in her circle of friends."

"Actually, quite good. Amelia's brother Joshua had eleven children–not uncommon in those days. Most of his descendents live in Penetanguishene and Lafontaine; a few migrated to other provinces."

"Eleven, yikes. Sounds like an Irish Catholic family to me."

"On this island, in this area, Catholics are plentiful. The shrine is nearby."

I nodded and tried to remember the stories Joan told about the Martyrs of the Shrine.

Boots on wood distracted me. An old man stood at the sliding glass door. His coarse hair stood out in tufts at either side of his head under a Tim Horton cap. He didn't reach for the handle; he seemed to be waiting for permission to enter. I looked at Laurie. "Do you know him?"

She shook her head. "Probably wants to talk to Dave." She raised her voice and over-enunciated, "Dave is down at the water."

He stood looking in for so long I thought he might not understand English.

"At the water," Laurie repeated, this time pointing behind him.

Another moment, then he nodded and turned toward the steps to the bay. His stare seemed to remain, and Laurie and I shivered at the same time.

"Maybe that was him last night," I said more to myself. I caught Laurie looking at me and filled her in. "Dave said it was one of the islanders, and he did kind of stand there looking in just like he did now, but…" I didn't want to think about it, and I certainly wasn't going to tell an almost complete stranger that I'd seen the same man in a fog in the lighthouse.

"But what?"

"Just that the figure I saw looked older–not in years maybe, but in style or something. He had on one of those long, oilskin slickers with the slanted hat. 'Course it was storming last night and difficult to see clearly, but I could have sworn the he had a thick short beard and–"

The mug dropped and shattered, and Laurie stared at the puddle soaking into the plywood floor. Her face glowed white against her dark sweater.

I threw a towel over the liquid. "Are you okay? Sit, I'll get this." I picked up the three large pieces of ceramic and sopped up the tea and smaller pieces with the towel. I used paper towels to pat dry the area and wrapped them and the wet towel in a plastic bag for disposal.

In a stage whisper I pleaded, "Don't tell Joan I threw out the towel instead of washing it." Some color returned to her face. "If you don't tell her I broke the Loon mug," she joked back at me.

"Deal. Which one of us peed on the floor?"

Laurie burst into giggles. Dave, Marty, and Ken came in on the laughter.

"Good joke?" Marty asked. He moved around Laurie's chair and stopped directly on the stain. His boots were damp and sand clumped around the top edges.

Laurie and I looked at each other and burst into renewed laughter. We had our scapegoat.

The guys looked at each other and shrugged with an almost spoken 'it's a girl thing' expression. Garry pulled Laurie's coat off the peg. "How about a walk?"

I wondered if she'd share our conversation with Garry, then wondered if she'd tell me what had upset her. They left, promising to be back in an hour. The group agreed to one last series of Washshoe for the championship of Christian Island. I'd participated once in this cottage game played with two 1-pound size coffee cans and ten 2-inch diameter washers. Horseshoes with washers.

"Dave, did a man come down to the water?"

"Yeah, Joe needed a cable and pulley to move a tree knocked over in the storm. I didn't have what he needed, but I told him we'd help him cut it up into movable pieces this afternoon. Make good firewood in about two years."

"Was he the same man you found out here last night?"

Dave nodded. "Now he knows we're on island, he'll be around."

I couldn't decide how that made me feel.

# Chapter Six

The storm of our first day disappeared, and in its stead came balmy weather for the first week of January. The female half of the equation had decided that if the weather held we'd take the ferry to the mainland on Wednesday.

Laurie and Garry had decided to loan Amelia's letters to the Huronia Heritage Society. One of our stops on the mainland, then, would be to Garry's sister's home to pick up the letters. She'd agreed after the assurance that they would remain in the protective sheets and that they would be returned within two weeks. Joan planned on photographing the lot with a special camera on loan to her from the Society.

I couldn't help but remember my Shakespeare: "Neither a borrower nor a lender be…" Too many chances for damage or loss with other people's stuff.

The ride across proved bumpier than it looked; the stiff wind coming from the top of the bay churned the deep water. Dave had left his vehicle at the landing, and we piled in for the hour's drive.

"Laurie, I really appreciate you and Garry convincing Sandra to loan the letters to the Society. This is such a great find. I know they'll authenticate so much of what we don't know–at least I hope they do."

"They could be whiney and personal with no information about the time or the people. Amelia became known through the ages as a bit of a whiner."

"Can you blame her? Her life sounded awful."

"Once she moved back to the family's home with Joshua, her life was under a different sort of control. She took care of her bachelor brother and, even when he married, she stayed on to run the house and help care for her eleven nieces and nephews."

"Seems she traded one set of bonds for another." Colleen's observation chilled the jovial mood.

Speculation about Amelia's life bounced from front seat to back while we drove from errand to errand and stopped for an early lunch in Midland. We split forces there. Joan and I headed for the library, while Laurie took the car to Barrie to collect the letters. Deb and Colleen volunteered to pick up the 'extras' we had decided we needed. We agreed to meet at the library in time to board the last ferry.

Joan had called from the cottage to set up a brief meeting with Bruce Benningfurth, Director of the Huronia Heritage Society. He hurried from behind the desk piled with books, papers, and artifacts. His quick short steps looked like a stutter in movement.

"Good morning, so nice to meet you." He pumped my hand and squinted at me through half-moon wire-rim glasses. "Please sit down."

Joan lifted a pile of folders from the chair he indicated. "Here, give me those." He scanned the area around his desk for an open spot, and then carefully leaned the folders against one leg of the credenza.

He sat down at his desk and looked expectantly at Joan. She explained about the letters that would soon be in her possession and her plan to photograph them. Benningfurth seemed less enthusiastic than I expected, and I knew from the tilt of her head that Joan felt the same lack of excitement.

"Bruce, you don't seem too interested in these letters. Do you already have a source like this?"

"Ah, no, no. The letters sound interesting. I'm only concerned that unsubstantiated comments could adversely affect the charm and mystique of the Christian Island Lighthouse Museum. I would prefer to review the letters before making photographs of what could be erroneous information. The greater good of the museum and its presence in the community and legacy for the area should be our first priority."

"Mr. Benningfurth," I put in. "Any information from the original source would be valid history even if it proved to be inaccurate. These letters are opinion and comment from one person, not gospel."

He stared at us for a moment and then nodded his head. "Of course, of course. I'll leave it to your good judgment." He stood and we knew the meeting was over. He accompanied us to the door and all but waited to make sure we left.

"Sheesh, what just happened?"

Joan shrugged. "I don't know him that well, but he's never appeared to be that rude at the meetings."

"I wouldn't say rude describes it. More like panicked, or nervous about those letters coming to light." I thought about what I'd said and remembered Depot Days in my small town. I'd been excited about finding some old abandoned trunks, and, as part of a fundraiser for the Lisle Heritage Society I'd planned an auction. I shivered at the secret we'd unlocked. Maybe Benningfurth had good reason to be nervous.

"Yeah, nervous. You'd think he'd be thrilled to unlock some secrets." Joan's comment leaped from my thoughts. That happened to us sometimes. Her grin did nothing to cheer me. I felt a scary sense of *déjà vu* and wished we'd never found the secret drawer.

"Well, I'm thrilled to get the letters, and I'm sure most of the board will be. I can't wait to read them." Joan practically walked on air down the stone steps of the library.

"Be careful what you wish for." It came out grimmer than I wanted. I tried to lighten my tone. "I mean, you may be disappointed with some young woman's whiny description of her life. I mean, didn't Laurie say her letters were whiny?"

Joan put her hand on my arm. "You're babbling. What's wrong?"

People who knew me understood my discourse from my babble.

"We have time to kill. Let's go back to the restaurant and wait. It's so close." We reached the restaurant and Joan opened the door. She nudged me in. We sat at the first booth. "Now, what is it?"

I shook my head. "Joanie, sometimes it's not smart to disturb the past. I know you're excited about the letters and the stuff we found in the lighthouse, but I can't shake this feeling."

Joan's blue eyes stared at me, wanting to understand my trepidation. The waitress moved in with menus. We ordered tea. Joan tried again, "What do you mean?"

"When we were in the lighthouse and I asked you about the fog, I saw fog and, and…" Oh Lord, this might freak her out. I can't tell her. "I got this creepy feeling like someone else was there with us."

There, kind of the truth.

"Cool. I mean, interesting. Maybe it was Amelia. Could you tell if it was a male or female?"

"Geez, Joan I'm not some weirdo psychic."

"Hey, don't get upset. I didn't mean anything; just that maybe you got a sense of the person. You know, like–"

"I don't know and I don't want to know." I stared down at my hands and realized that I'd pulled a length of braided yarn from my pocket. I rolled the soft material between my thumbs and fingers and felt calmer. Our tea arrived and provided a distraction while we drank.

The door pushed open and Laurie, Deb, and Colleen trooped in fussing with scarves and gloves.

"I thought we were meeting at the library. We spotted you through the window. Push in and I'll get a chair for the end." The waitress appeared, hopeful for a larger order but they too ordered only tea.

Laurie tapped a large manila envelope. "A plethora of great-great Aunt Amelia." She passed it to Joan's eager hands but held tight to her end for a moment and fixed her gaze on Joan. "Remember, they must be returned by the end of next week or I'll be forever in more trouble than I usually am with my in-laws."

Joan nodded and pulled the envelope to her side of the table. She kept her excitement in check and glanced at me. I wondered if she might be remembering my warning. More likely she didn't want to set me 'off.' Her friends had seen me braid before. They knew I struggled with OCD, they knew I was a little quirky by some standards, but they'd never seen me unable to leave a table until I organized and stacked dishes or condiments. They'd never seen me struggle to walk ten feet to the door by way of a compulsive pattern of steps. They'd never seen me annoy the hell out of people by snapping or clicking whatever was at hand.

Joan had, and I think she feared I was close to one of those times. The snap on Colleen's purse looked tempting. I kept my hands in my lap and frantically tied and retied knots in a pattern that I'd used for years.

"We'd best get moving if we want to catch the three-thirty. I hate going over in the dark."

The ride to the landing took less time. The weather remained pleasant, and we waited outside. As departure time approached, so did others wanting to return to the island.

Several men stood off to the side. I recognized Joe. He looked at me just as I found him in the group. His eyes bore into me and a sense of urgency quickened my heart rate. He broke eye contact, spoke to the other men, and they looked toward us but I knew they were looking at me. *Geez, Grace, get a grip. They're not looking at you specifically; they're looking at five good-looking women getting ready to board the same ferry to their island.* I felt better until one of them, a smaller version of Joe, caught my eye, waited a half second, then purposely spit on the ground at his feet. So he spit, big deal. Men spit all the time. I would have charged it off to male hygiene issues if not for the next man, who waited to catch my glance and did the same. I couldn't keep my eyes from looking at the third man, and he too targeted the ground with a stream of spittle.

I turned away from them and stared out over the bay. I knew spit, I had four brothers who at some point all spit for points, distance, bragging rights. This was warning spit. Why? What had I done?

The tender unhooked the line and we filed onto the ferry. I wiggled my way into the middle of my group and kept my eyes on my shoes as we moved to the center area to get inside. The crossing would be cold. I peeked up and felt relief that the men stayed outside. *I'm getting ready to panic and no one here can help me. I need Harry. God, I want Harry.* I fumbled with my pockets, jamming my hands inside. I had to keep still and focus on nothing, focus on white space, blank, draining, empty, white space. My mind told my body to breathe. Slowly I felt an ease settle on my shoulders and slip down my arms into my hands and fingers. A sense of warmth like a blanket over my shoulders calmed me, and my breathing resumed a steady pace.

No one spoke to me. I think Joan had signaled them. She'd always been good at distracting people when she sensed I needed space. Her pretty face and cheerful chatter easily turned friends from the bushy-haired, scared-looking brunette…never mind that in those moments of confusion my lavender eyes turned pansy purple, which would have drawn more stares. She never let them get that close.

By the time we walked off the ferry, the men were gone. We piled into the vehicle that Dave had earlier left for us and started back to the cottage as the sky grew darker. The turnoff to their lane and cottage was easy to miss if you didn't know the area. I would have missed it for sure. Total darkness hid the cottage until we pulled into the driveway; no lights welcomed us. Joan left the high beams on until she could unlock the door.

We grumbled up the back steps wondering where the guys were. This was their night to prepare dinner. The cottage leapt to life with lights.

"I'll get a fire going to take the chill off," Debbie offered. "Man, it's really cold in here."

"Where the heck are they? Is there a note?"

"Look at this." Laurie pointed to the sliding door. It stood open about a foot. "Do these guys live in a barn?" she joked.

Joan slid the door closed. She stared down at the catch. "They didn't leave it open. Someone broke the latch." We rushed to the door to see for ourselves. "Should we call the police?"

"Do you think anything was taken?"

"Could they still be in the cottage?" We backed against the sliding door and stared at the interior.

The loud thud caught us by surprise. One scream sounded like another in the cacophony of terror.

# Chapter Seven

"It's in there," Deb screamed, pointing toward the back of the cottage.

"No, up there." Laurie stared at the ceiling above the stove.

In a moment of disconnect my thoughts were, *it's a bird, it's a plane, it's Superman*.

Marty stumbled out of the bedroom rubbing his shoulder. We stood in shocked silence, and then burst into laughter. He looked as dazed as a ten-year-old.

"That wasn't funny," he said. "I could have been hurt."

Colleen and Laurie rushed forward. "Sorry, we didn't mean to laugh at you. We thought someone was in the house…or on it," Colleen amended.

"We were relieved it was you. Nervous laughter, that's all."

Marty shrugged off their explanations. His dazed look seemed to clear. "Are you saying one of you didn't pull me off that bunk?"

"Of course we didn't. We didn't even know you were in the house. Your thud scared us." Colleen looked to all of us for backup.

"Marty, are you saying someone pulled you out of bed?" My voice hit a higher note than normal; my fingers itched to calm the rising panic in my brain.

He stared at me and slowly shook his head. "Must have been dreaming and rolled too far, like the old days, eh, Gracie?" The phony smile reassured the others. I focused on the tips of his ears, the giveaway when he lied. Slowly, the pink appeared. He knew I knew, like I did when we were kids. His gaze broke off abruptly.

"Where are the guys?" He looked beyond us.

"We were wondering the same."

Marty shrugged. "I sacked out for awhile, bad headache. They were down at the water."

I looked at my brother. He'd had several since he backed off the self-medicating routine he'd fallen into; a pitfall of pharmaceutical sales…little blue pill for this, yellow for that. He avoided eye contact.

A scraping sound on the roof startled us. It sounded like tiles sliding off the cottage.

"What the hell is that?" Marty turned toward the noise.

"I told you I thought the noise came from up there." Laurie said.

"Maybe the guys are doing something on the roof. Dave mentioned the home inspector wrote up some missing shingles. Maybe they left some stuff up there when it got dark and it slid off. I'll check." Joan pulled on her jacket.

Marty slipped on his shoes. "I'll go with you."

"Brrrr. It's getting cold." Laurie slid the door closed behind him. "Did he grow up in a barn?"

I shrugged. "I did the best I could."

Colleen filled the electric kettle. "Tea in two minutes."

A second loud scraping sound, and Joan's scream reached our ears in a dead heat with Marty's warning of "look out!"

We rushed out the door and down the stairs to the back of the cottage, nearly colliding with Joan and Marty who stood staring down at the body dressed in leather buckskin pants and nothing else, like a voyageur, one of the old-time French explorers. The corpse lay face down in the scrub grass–one arm caught under his chest, the other stretched out with fingers splayed, both legs straight out.

Laurie screamed and grabbed my arm. "Oh my God, oh my God. Is he dead?"

Only Deb slowly stepped forward.

"Don't touch him." Laurie's fingers tightened around my arm.

"Just feel for a pulse," my brother said. "Don't touch anything else."

Deb nodded, and crouched near the head…she slowly reached two fingers to feel for life. Marty stared at the body and suddenly stopped Deb's outstretched hand.

"Don't bother."

"Is he dead?" I slipped my arm out from under Laurie's vice-like grip before she could clamp down further.

"Try, is he real?" Marty answered.

# Chapter Eight

Marty stood and motioned for Deb to move. He pushed his foot under the corpse's chest and rolled it over. Face up, the charade became immediately apparent. The vacant stare affected by wide-open eyes without pupils chilled me. I remembered the smooth marble eyes of the statues in the museum, and a childhood fear tugged at my brain.

I stood silent amid shouts for explanation.

"If this is somebody's idea of a joke," Marty looked around the circle of women, "would one of your husbands do this as a practical joke? On me? Maybe not thinking you'd be back so soon?" he added.

"No way."

"Absolutely not."

"Never."

We waited for the fourth confident disclaimer. Colleen understood the silence and blushed. She quickly added, "No, of course not." Her eyes moved back to the *corpse* and her shoulders straightened. "No, never." Her voice didn't match the vigor of the others, and her face lacked color.

"Should we leave it out here?" Laurie looked around the circle.

Marty took charge. "Let's get inside; we're not accomplishing anything out here. When Dave gets back we'll decide what to do with our visitor."

No argument from anyone. I think Marty thought it was a crummy practical joke aimed at him because of his 'city boy' status. If one of them had rigged this, they were not aware of my brother's temper. I mentally reviewed the ferry schedule and considered we might be leaving in the morning.

Tea flowed freely from pot to cup. Colleen encouraged everyone to use extra honey to counteract the effect of the burst of adrenaline we'd experienced. I never used a sweetener of any kind in my coffee or tea; I sipped at the hot liquid feeling the warmth slide down my throat and waiting for the heat to permeate my cold body.

Marty added a few drops to his cup from a tiny bottle. It looked like the little plastic bottles in the food coloring box. Liquid sweetener? Liquid elixir? He'd promised me he'd left all his 'little friends' back home, said he'd disposed of them. My brother's challenge, the family euphemism for his addiction, was partially responsible for his accompanying me to Canada. When his wife said she was moving out until he straightened out the whole family bristled at Eve's ultimatum and 1993 started on a sour note in the Morelli family. I'd question him later, alone.

Footsteps and laughter announced the guys' return.

"Can't believe you told the Metro Water Police, 'License, we don't need no stinkin' license.'" Another round of laughter accompanied the sounds of scraping boots on the mat and deck before they came through the sliding door.

"Colleen, you should have seen your husband with the police when they approached and asked to see licenses." Dave grinned and clapped Ken's shoulder. "Professional courtesy, gentlemen. They recognized one of their own." Ken grinned, a short-lived smile when he noticed our somber faces. "What's wrong? Somebody die?" His attempt at humor missed horribly.

Marty explained, his words terse, revealing the anger he felt. "So, if this was some jackass's idea of a joke let's take it outside and I'll show you how funny it was." My brother's hands curled slightly at his side and his eyes swept the male faces staring at him.

Dave stepped in front of the others and looked squarely at Marty. "No one here would do that. You have my word." The men behind him nodded in agreement, but I saw expressions of anger, confusion, and concern, and I mentally prepared a parting speech. How could we stay when our hosts' best friends viewed my brother as dangerous, delusional, or at best annoying?

"We need to call the police. Or did you?" Dave looked at Joan. She shook her head.

"We just came in to gather our wits. It was terrible when we thought he, it…"

Garry turned and motioned to Bob. "Let's take a look and wait for the police."

"Good idea. I'll call."

Marty moved away from the table. I followed him to the couch and sat down next to him. From this vantage point I felt the distinction of *them* and *us*.

"Sorry, Sis. Didn't mean to mess up your vacation." He looked remorseful, or maybe whatever he'd dripped into his tea caused his calm demeanor. I hated not knowing if Marty functioned with or without the benefit of drugs. He'd resigned from his lucrative pharmaceutical sales position. My brother Mike said the resignation stemmed from a deal with the company to not expose questionable arrangements with client doctors…Marty had swapped stock with the doctors he'd befriended outside of work; only my brother had lost on the deal. Maybe losing would be the only way to save himself.

I nodded toward his cup. He understood. "Liquid sweetener, Gracie, I promise."

"More like liquid courage." I lowered my voice. "What if all of them had planted it? Were you going to take them one at a time?" I punched his arm.

"Yeah, well, I hadn't planned it all the way." His grin lit up the boyish face.

Hurried footsteps distracted me. Garry rushed through the door.

"Dave, did you call?"

"Yeah, just hung up. Had a little trouble getting the tone."

"There's nothing out there."

Chairs scraped against the floor and cups jostled against saucers.

"What do you mean?" Laurie's shrill voice sliced into the silence.

"There's nothing out there."

We looked at each other until Colleen spoke. "Then someone came and removed the prop since we've been inside. Maybe this was an island joke on all of us."

"That's not all that's been removed." Dave looked at the countertop. "Joanie, did you move the knife?"

She shook her head.

"Shit. Why didn't I put it away out of sight? What's going on around here?"

"The knife was wrapped in plastic. Only we knew what it was. It looked like a loaf of bread on the counter."

Marty jumped up. "What are you saying, one of us took it?" His defensive tone didn't build his stock with them.

"No. Relax, okay? Maybe someone came in to take food or clothing. Threw it all in a sack. Is anything else missing, food or clothing?"

I tried to remember what had been in the rooms this morning. I'd sat on this couch with my coffee and fiddled with the fringe on the throw. It wasn't there now. "Joan, did you move the throw that was here, the one with the fringe?"

"I noticed you took out a new jar of honey. Where is the one from this morning?" Debbie asked.

Joan's head swiveled from me to Debbie. "I didn't move it and I thought we'd used up the jar. Is it in the trash?"

Laurie lifted the lid on the kitchen trash. "No." She turned and opened the fridge. "Looks like dinner has gone missing, too," she straightened and opened the small freezer, "and tomorrow's salmon dinner."

When the officer arrived thirty minutes later, we greeted him with a different crime.

Danny King worked as the island police force. I'd met him on my last visit when Joan and I attended mass at St. Francis Xavier Church. His aunt and uncle, Arthur and Christina Daly, had celebrated forty years of marriage at that service and a small tea had followed the mass. Danny lived on island and handled routine calls. Honey Harbour and Port Severn had more policemen and cycled one through Christian Island every two weeks. The off-season, when cottagers deplete the population by almost half, never needed extra assignments.

"Let's get right to it, eh." He pushed his cap back on his head revealing thick black hair and a high forehead. His summer tan over his naturally darker complexion gave him the healthy glow of an 'endless summer' Coppertone ad.

Dave pointed to the coat pegs. "Take off your jacket, Danny. Can I get you a cup of coffee?"

"Maybe after you show me the dummy. Around back or on the side?"

"Yeah, well, the situation has changed since I called you."

The officer's eyes widened. "Don't tell me now it's a real body." He fixed his eyes on Dave's face.

"No, hell no. The dummy's gone. I'd already hung up with you."

"You coulda' called back, eh."

None of Joan's friends used the colloquial ending of the Great North. Dave slipped into the "eh" ending on occasion.

"Something else came up. The cottage was broken into and a few things are missing."

Danny nodded and slipped out of his jacket. Joan took it and hung it from a peg.

Dave motioned toward a chair, and for the next fifteen minutes he explained about the dummy sliding off the roof, the food missing, and finally the knife.

"That lighthouse, what was you doing at the lighthouse? Not too many people at that end of the island. You shouldn't be messing around in the place; it looks ready to cave in." His tone sounded condescending, implying off-islanders didn't belong here in the off-season, and his slight singsong cadence reminded me of a Cajun dialect. I'd ask Joan if it were some kind of Canadian-French accent.

"The lighthouse belongs to the Huronia Historical Society. I'm on the board and on the restoration committee."

"Restoration, eh? They should think instead about demolition. Nothing but trouble since it went up." His sour comment surprised everyone. He noticed the raised eyebrows and shrugged. "My family, we been connected many years to that tired lighthouse. My father's great-aunt married the brother of the widow Havilland. Nothing but trouble and tragedy, anyone will say."

I couldn't stop my eyes from seeking out Laurie's face. She paled and turned away from my gaze.

Danny grinned and snugged his cap on his head. "Dave, you're sure about the knife?"

"Absolutely, it was a beauty. Not as old as you'd think given where they found it, but at least fifty, maybe sixty years old. I was going to check it against my catalogs, but I'm pretty sure the red, green, and brown band on the handle pegs it from the forties."

Danny closed his notebook. "I'll take that cup of coffee you was offering." His smile fit his face and seemed genuine enough. "The dummy was probably some kid's idea of a practical joke. Climbed up the tree and dropped it on the roof while his buddies waited in the brush for your reaction. Wouldn't worry. The knife, though…" He left the thought for each of us to finish in our own way.

Joan poured a cup of coffee and handed it to Danny. "I think the thief thought it was bread. He could have grabbed it along with other food. I just noticed a jar of sugar and a jar of peanut butter are missing too."

Danny nodded. "Could be. I'll keep my eyes open for someone with a new knife; if they're foolish enough to use it in plain sight." He sipped the coffee and looked around the room. His eyes sparked recognition when he looked at me. He pointed at me with his cup. "I met you before. You're the friend from the States, eh." He looked around the room.

"My husband's not with me this time," I answered his unasked question.

He nodded. "Brit, weren't he?" He looked at Marty.

"This is my brother, Martin Morelli." Marty stepped forward to shake hands.

Dave swept his arm in an inclusive gesture. "These are some friends from Lafontaine and Penetanguishene."

"How long you planning to stay? Kind of surprised to hear any cottagers were on island."

"Who'd you hear it from?" popped out of my mouth.

Danny King seemed to consider the question. "Old Joe told Bea he'd seen you during the storm. She told Harold, and he told my dad at their checker game." He shrugged. "Christian Island grapevine."

Joan looked at me and Laurie, and spoke. "This may be nothing, Danny, but Old Joe was on the ferry with us this afternoon and he kept looking at us. In a strange way, I mean. I don't know, do you think he could be behind the dummy?"

Danny laughed, then became serious. "Old Joe, he looks scary but he don't mean no harm. He probably couldn't figure why you'd be coming across. We don't see cottagers this time of year. Why are you on island?"

"We sold the cottage, and we wanted to have one more fling with our friends. The weather predictions were for a mild January and we thought to give it a go."

"That so? If that rain woulda' been snow, you'd be looking at six feet right up against your lee." He waved at the side of the cottage facing the bay.

"We don't plan on being here for any snowstorm."

"Hmm. You don't plan, eh." Danny stood and reached for his jacket. "Sometimes, you don't get to plan." He opened the sliding door. "I'll let you know if I hear anything."

A chill settled over the room with his departure. His words replayed in my head. I'd learned this past year how true he spoke, and shivered with the memory.

"Let's get some heat in here; we've got some shivering folk." Garry grinned and put his arms around Laurie.

Was it the cold or, like me, did she shiver from a memory?

# Chapter Nine

I rarely slept through the night anymore. I grabbed my slippers from the foot of the upper bunk and carefully stepped on the freezer lid and down to the floor. I had to shuffle carefully in case my messy brother had left something in my path, perhaps even himself, but I ran into only two obstacles before I cleared the room.

I didn't expect to stumble over anything in the kitchen and lost my balance when I stepped on something uneven. When I tried to unstep, I landed on my left hip and forearm.

"Oww!"

"Yeeh!"

"Who's there?" Bob's voice came from the pullout couch in the pit; the scream had been Debbie's. Lights came on in the bedroom, and I heard the sliding door open.

"What's going on?" Dave's bleary voice preceded Joan's shaky one.

"Is everyone okay?" Light flooded the kitchen.

"Oh, my God." The collective sharp intake of breath and the stares at the floor behind me gave me the motivation to scooch forward across the floor toward Dave. Only when his hand connected to mine did I feel safe in looking behind me.

The voyageur lay on the floor face up, sightless eyes staring at the ceiling.

"Arrgh." Fear and phlegm caught in my throat and my meaningful comment became gibberish.

"Hey there, Grace. You okay? Anything hurt?"

I shook my head slowly and rubbed my forearm. "Startled, more than anything. Glad I landed on my left side." My eyes turned to the floor. "Who's playing this joke on us, and why?"

Marty rolled out of the low bunk and landed on all fours. It was the way he always got out of bed as a kid and I imagined he couldn't resist doing it now…or maybe he wasn't totally awake. Either way, his eyes snapped wider when they focused on what lay ahead of him. Marty scrambled to his feet and backed away.

"What the heck?"

Dave stepped forward and pushed his toe against the dummy. "It would appear your friend from this afternoon is back."

"Not unless he grew a beard since then." Marty's comment brought nods of agreement.

"Is there an entire family of these things?" I meant to sound breezy and flip, but my squeaky voice betrayed me.

"You okay, Sis?"

"Yeah, just thirsty. I got up to get a drink of water. Remind me to take a water bottle to bed with me." I grinned, and the mood lightened a little.

"I'm calling Danny King."

"Dave, it's two o'clock in the morning."

"Exactly. Who's messing with us? I want answers." He reached for the phone.

Marty stepped over the dummy. "How'd he get in?"

Sheepish looks bounced between Joan and Dave. "Uh, we didn't lock the sliding door," she explained, "in case we needed to use the bathroom."

"Maybe a chamber pot," I mumbled. Joan jabbed me with her elbow.

"Hey, he can whiz in the woods. What about me? Besides, we never lock our doors."

Marty shook his head. "Wouldn't matter much. You could open these locks with a hard twist."

Dave hung up the phone. His conversation had been brief. We looked at him for the next step. "Danny wants us to go back to sleep and he'll be here at five o'clock."

"Go back to sleep! Fat chance. The last time we walked away from our buddy here, he disappeared and we looked like idiots. I'm waking this dearly never departed."

Marty's mixed metaphor brought smiles to most faces.

"I'll put the kettle on," Debbie offered.

"Coffee too?" I smiled at her.

"Why couldn't he come now?" Joan questioned her husband amid the increased activity in her kitchen.

"He's busy processing some kids who he thinks might be part of this prank and some others on the island. Someone broke into the shed at the community center and scattered the contents over half the island. The Huronia Days Voyageurs are missing." Dave jerked his thumb at the dummy. "He's one of them."

"So they caught whoever did this?"

"Are they the ones that stole the food?"

"And the knife?"

"Hey there, do I look like the island constable?" Dave's hands were up, palms out. "Danny will stop in when he's figured it out. Then we'll know." He stretched and rolled his neck from side to side. "Meantime, how's about that coffee?"

By the time we sat down to coffee, tea, and sweet rolls, most of us had dressed. Only Debbie stayed in her flannel Dr. Denton's, fleecy robe, and furry slippers. Joan and I moved to the two chairs in the pit near the Franklin stove and puttered with starting a fire. My reason for accepting Joan's invitation seemed pointless now. During the last year I'd discovered a terrible ability within me. Marty called it "cool" and my sister-in-law Hannah thought it was a "gift" to be treasured. My dad wouldn't talk about it, and my husband…well, he couldn't be bothered right now with the supernatural. He was off struggling with the here and now in the form of an eleven-year-old son he'd only met last summer.

Laurie pulled a chair over. "The further away from that thing, the better." She squared off the chair with her back to the kitchen. "What a day."

She didn't expect a response beyond a nod. We settled into our own thoughts and enjoyed the warmth emanating from the potbellied member of our group.

"Gracie, here's your coffee."

Marty stood in front of me with a steaming cup. I sat up, blinked, and reached for the mug. "Hmm. Thanks, I must have dozed off." I sipped the coffee and sat up straighter. It could only have been a few minutes. I noticed Joan and Laurie's chairs were closer together, while Debbie slept curled up at one end of the couch. The guys were playing cards at the table. Maybe I'd been out longer than I thought.

"How you feeling? Your hip, I mean." Marty squatted next to my chair.

"A little tender, but that's all. I'm fine." He squeezed my arm and stood.

"Gotta' get back to my cards before they get cold." His grin transformed his tired face.

"You're not betting or anything, are you?"

"Why would I play poker and not bet?" He leaned toward me and gently tapped my temple with his finger. "I'm kidding. Stop being so serious. We're using elbow macaroni." He grinned and left me wondering.

"Your brother's a hoot," Laurie smiled. "Is he married? My youngest sister Maddie would find him entirely interesting."

"He's married and has a teenaged daughter. Katie is involved in national cheerleading competitions, and she and her mom are in Atlanta, Georgia, this week."

"Why isn't your brother with them?"

Good question, from a stranger. The Morelli family knows why.

I smiled. "Does the phrase 'bull in a china shop' give you a visual? He accompanied them to a few in the beginning, but he couldn't get distraught over the wrong color glitter or recalcitrant curls."

Laurie laughed and nodded. "Oh, he would have been so right for Maddie. She eschews makeup, high heels, and curling irons. We older sisters tried, but she's our natural beauty."

I recognized the pride and love in her blue eyes and soft voice. We were alone and bonding. Now could be the right time. "Laurie, what's your take on the letter and this voyageur."

Her shoulders tensed for a second, then relaxed. "You think they're connected? Why? You heard Danny King; some kids goofing around playing a prank on the cottagers."

"I don't believe in coincidence, and it seems odd that the pranks didn't start until we found the letter and the knife."

Laurie shook her head. "I believe it has everything to do with our being on island off-season. They're bored, and we are excellent targets."

It could be that way. I liked her scenario better, but I couldn't let go of the feeling. "What about the person I saw?"

"Dave explained it was the old man, Joe."

"I mean the person I saw at the lighthouse, the old keeper. I think you've seen him too."

Laurie's face blanched and the mug she held slipped from her fingers. "Damn," she muttered.

Joan called out from the kitchen, "Something wrong?"

"I've gone and spilt my tea. Sorry."

"It's a cottage, no worry." She brought over a kitchen towel and dropped it on the small puddle. "We're all wound up a fair bit."

"Not her." Laurie pointed to Debbie. "She'd sleep through an earthquake."

It could have been my own lack of sleep, but Laurie's tone seemed a tad angry. Maybe she envied her friend's ability to relax through adversity. Maybe they weren't the good friends I thought them to be. If not, why? Their husbands were great pals, curling buddies from their University days. Maybe she'd tried confiding her ideas about Garry's ancestor to her. According to Joan, Deb was the pragmatist of the group—maybe not the best choice to garner sympathy for a long-dead woman.

A rap on the glass drew attention to the sliding door. Danny King wiped his feet on the mat before entering and whipped off his hat crossing the threshold. He held the felt hat by the brim and slid the door closed.

"Evening, or morning. Think we're closer to morning."

Dave stepped forward. "Thanks for coming out. I know it's not the real thing, but I wanted you to see it and I didn't know if we should chuck it out the door or invite it to tea."

Dave's sense of humor lightened the mood; the tension in my neck and shoulders eased. Danny King looked at the table and fixed Dave with a mock look of surprise. "You're not gambling on Band Council property, are you?"

"Not us. It's pasta poker," Marty answered. Everyone grinned at the name.

King nodded toward him. "He's not from around here, eh?" We burst into laughter.

I joined them in the kitchen and put my hand on Marty's shoulder, "I take full responsibility for this one." More laughter at Marty's expense. His ears turned pink.

King nodded his head and walked toward the dummy. "Yeah, that's Benjamin Beauprie. From your description of the one that came off your roof, he'd be Rupert Beauprie, this one's son."

The beautiful French names rolled effortlessly from his lips and reminded me of the strong connection of Canada to the French. I always considered Canada influenced by the English.

"So how many more of the *family* can we expect?" Marty's quip brought smiles. I saw the corner of Danny King's mouth lift, then settle down.

"You won't need to set tea for the Beaupries. The boys I brought in admit to stealing the dummies and dropping one on your roof–a prank on the cottagers." King shrugged. "One thing, though. Who was the last to turn in, and what time?"

We looked at each other, trying to organize a timeline. Dave pointed to me. "Grace and her brother went to their room around the same time as Deb and Bob. Joanie and I turned in about eleven." He looked at Garry to continue the timeline.

Garry rolled his shoulders. "Hmm. We pulled out the beds right after you left. Lights out by midnight, I'd say." The other hide-a-bed occupants nodded.

"Well, this is sticky." Danny King rubbed at his left eye with the back of his hand. "I picked up Bradley and Theo about that time. Got a call from Mrs. Quintane reporting noise in her yard. I was hauling those two to my office at midnight."

"Maybe there was another boy involved."

"Could be. They say it was just them having a bit of fun with you. They were fixing to leave your first visitor in your car."

"That proves they were here."

Danny King shook his head. "They never made it here. I found them out behind Mrs. Pendergast's shed with Rupert in tow. They said weren't them that left Benjamin; they hadn't made it out this far."

"They're covering up for someone, then."

"Yeah, maybe. Makes no sense they come out here to leave one and not the other in the car."

"Maybe–"

"Maybe we stand here all morning and know nothing more than right this minute." Danny King reached down and lifted the dummy to a standing position. "Hmmm, he's gained weight since me and Walter Renfu tied him to Mrs. Pendergast's clothesline and hoisted him to her window." His mouth spread in a wide grin. He felt down the legs, like a one-handed pat down. "I feel rocks in here. Probably added them to keep him from blowing off the roof."

"But this isn't the one on the roof. The other one had–"

"Oh yeah, you had Rupert." He scratched his hairline and repositioned his cap. "I wouldn't dwell on it. Just kids having a prank at your expense. No damage, eh?"

Dave shook his head. Joan shook her finger at the dummy. "That thing shocked the cra…stuffing out of us. I call that a little damage."

Danny King stared at Joan in open disbelief. "Are you thinking of filing a complaint?"

Joan's eyes slid from face to face. From my perspective I didn't see too much eye contact. She took a deep breath and exhaled in a burst. "No, I guess not. We're only here until the end of next week. Impress upon them that if we see them around the cottage we will complain."

Danny King nodded and repositioned Benjamin under his arm.

"Go out this way, it's shorter." Dave pointed toward the back door and hurried to unlock it.

The island officer hitched the dummy closer and sent a quick wave with his free hand. We heard his boots on the wooden stairs, then the opening and closing of car doors, and then the rumble from the strong engine broke the early morning silence.

"Do you get the feeling he thinks we're making a mountain out of a molehill?" Joan looked at me.

"How about a mountain of pancakes?" Bob asked. "Who has

breakfast duty?"

Nods of agreement criss-crossed the room. Food would be a good starting place for any further conversation. Bob looked at the schedule on the fridge. "Grace/Marty."

Several pairs of eyes swung toward me. "Mountain of pancakes, coming up," I smiled and turned to Marty. He wasn't there. We looked around the room. "Where'd he go? Did you see him leave?"

Debbie spoke up from the couch. "He went out the sliding door when the cop left." She waved her hand in an inclusive gesture. "I wasn't asleep the entire time. You guys made enough noise to wake the dead. Marty walked past the window here."

"Dave, can I borrow a flashlight?" I lifted my jacket from its peg and noticed that Marty's was gone.

"It's a package deal, me and my flashlight."

"Thanks, Dave. I was hoping you practiced the buddy system." I waited for him to get his jacket. He slid open the door and clicked on the flashlight. The click sounded comforting.

"Ready?" Dave focused the beam on the deck.

"We'll do breakfast," Laurie offered.

I nodded to both and stepped outside. It would be dawn soon…a pink blush hinted low on the lake, but turning into the woods next to the cottage obliterated any natural light. The cold air settled around my neck and the predawn dew soaked my shoes after a few steps into the brush. Following the bouncing beam of light, we rounded the corner and I realized I'd been holding my breath as we stepped uneasily toward the spot of our first *visitor*. I breathed out slowly and filled my lungs with fresh air, just in time to scream.

# Chapter Ten

The moving beam revealed Marty's boot on the ground, and my mind barely registered when the light played against my brother's form slumped against a tree. That's when I screamed.

Marty's hand reached out to block the light from his face. "Geez Louise, get that outta my face."

"Sorry. Trying to see if you're hurt."

"Mainly my pride as a woodsman." Marty straightened his back against the tree. "Caught my foot in a hole and took a header. Stupid of me, I hadn't laced my boots tight. I crawled over here to pull myself up."

"You looked unconscious. I thought…" My throat tightened. I couldn't finish the sentence without bursting into tears. Marty heard my concern.

"Hey, hey. I may have been resting my eyes when you found me. I'm okay. Could use a hand getting up."

Two beams of light bounced around the corner following the same course…first the empty boot, then the tree. Ken and Garry skidded to a stop.

"Holy crap, what happened?"

Dave swept the beam toward the boot. "Marty tripped. Give me a hand getting him into the house." He handed me his flashlight. "Go get a spot ready for him."

I nodded and picked up his boot on my way. In spite of the heavy cloud cover, the sun tinged the edges of the water and the back of the cottage glowed with an eerie weak light. I clicked off the flashlight. *Oh, not now.* I recognized the OCD demand and resigned myself. On, off. 1, 2, 3. On off. 1, 2, 3. On, off. 1, 2, 3. The metallic click soothed me, and I adjusted my pace to be able to do seven more series before I reached the door. Then I could stop. I held the flashlight down; it was light enough to see and it wasn't about the light, only the click.

I reached for the door as I thought *1, 2, 3.* Perfect, but I had to get rid of it. I handed the flashlight to the first person near the door. "Marty hurt his ankle. The guys are helping him in. Let's put him in the chair by the stove, he's going to need to warm up."

"Why'd he go out there?"

"That's my first question."

Dave and Garry helped Marty across the kitchen to the chair, his leg bent at the knee to keep his foot off the floor. I pulled over the ottoman and Marty lifted his foot to the cushion. Joan put some small pieces of wood in the stove and added water to the pot to produce some humidity. "Your clothes are soaked. You'd better change," Joan said.

Marty shook his head, "I'll dry."

I knew my brother. "Get your boot off, at least. And your socks." I pulled at the remaining boot, then carefully rolled down the sock on his injured foot. "Now for the moment of truth," I intoned in a stage whisper.

Marty glared at me. "You're not taking this seriously."

"*Au contraire*, I'm totally serious about why you felt the need to skulk into the woods." I continued to roll the sodden sock away from his swollen ankle.

He pushed his hands down on the seat and scooted back in the chair. "Easy, easy. No need to yank at it."

"I'm not yanking at it, you big baby. Serves you right, running around in the dark. No light, not prepared. Some Eagle Scout." I had the sock off and tossed it toward the boot.

"I was following a light." His quiet statement silenced me. I stared into his eyes and saw the unease lurking at the edge of the excitement.

"What light?"

"When?"

"Why didn't you say something?"

Dave held up his hand to stop the interrogation. "Let's figure out the extent of his injury. First ferry is eight o'clock if we have to take him to hospital."

Debbie stepped forward. "I've dealt with a few twisties in my time. Let me take a look. Okay with you, Marty?"

I moved away and stepped up against the metal shovel leaning against the stove. It shifted forward, then back against the iron potbelly stove as I caught myself from stepping all the way back, then lurched against the chair and almost toppled onto Marty. I caught my balance and moved around the back of the chair.

"I keep telling him not to leave it there." Joan hoisted a short, squat shovel in the air. "It's an old coal shovel that Dave cut down so we could use it to clear out the ashes. It belongs at the back door," her voice lifted with reprimand.

"Way to go, 'Graceful,' there were almost two of us needing Debbie's care." My brother waved her on. "Have at it." He grinned and gripped the sides of the cushion. Debbie knelt next to the ottoman and deftly ran her hands over the swollen ankle. Marty winced and paled. "Nice hands, but a bit heavy," he quipped while his fingers crushed the fabric.

"Nothing broken that I can tell, so it's not a major bone. Might have a slight fracture, but I'm thinking a bad sprain. Let's get some ice on it and see what we have by lunchtime. If you're the size of a moose-meat sausage then, we'll know it's a bust."

"Thank you, Dr. Debbie." Marty flashed the Morelli smirk that I knew so well.

"Don't dismiss her diagnosis. Deb was athlete trainer for the curling and soccer teams at university. She iced and taped them all." Joan waggled her finger at Marty, who smiled and turned his honey brown eyes on Deb.

"I am in your debt," he glossed.

Debbie took the two packages of frozen peas I handed her and looked Marty level in the eyes. "Yeah, that's what they all said." Without warning she pushed one package on either side of the ankle and secured it with the thin scarf I'd seen her wearing yesterday.

"Oww!" Marty yelped.

"Yeah, they said that too."

Marty grinned. "Okay, I'll behave." His eyes lingered on her face and I hoped I was the only one noticing my little brother flirting with a married woman whose husband was in the room. I couldn't see her face, but her body language didn't scream, "How dare you?" In fact, she seemed to hover longer than medicinally necessary.

"More tea or coffee?" Joan approached with the coffee pot. "Sorry it's not the one you brought. I just grabbed the usual in all the confusion."

"Don't give it a thought. We'll make Cinnamon Nut Swirl in the morning."

We both burst out laughing. "Dinner, I'll make it for dinner."

"We're laughing, but we're going to be walking zombies if we don't get some sleep." Her point made, she picked up her mug. "I'm going back to bed and I hope to sleep."

Seemed like a good idea, and a better one to break up the patient-nurse relationship. "C'mon, little brother. I'll give you a hand to your bunk."

Marty bristled at my tone. I think he knew I disapproved. Debbie stepped forward, I waved her off. "No need. I've got him. Thanks."

Marty mumbled, "She's bossy; takes her big sister role to heart."

Dave handed Marty a walking stick about six feet tall. The top twelve inches of the hardwood had been carved into the face of a wind spirit; a foot below the end of the flowing beard strips of leather provided a handgrip. "Theo Stevens carves these. You pay dearly for them in the States."

Marty gripped the wood and hoisted himself up on his good foot. "Thanks, works great." He shifted the stick to his bum side and made quick progress, even hopping the two steps on his own.

"Careful when you remove your jeans, Marty. Try not to dislodge the ice packs." Debbie's voice sounded casual. Was I the only one who felt uncomfortable about her talking about my brother's jeans? *Don't be ridiculous.*

I accepted my inner chastisement and climbed onto the top bunk. I could hear people preparing to turn in for a long nap. At least two people decided not to sleep and I heard the low murmur of conversation; I actually became drowsy with the hum in my ears.

I dreamt I stood outside the lantern room of the lighthouse, leaning against the railing searching the inky dark night for hope. I didn't understand the despair. It wasn't mine to grasp, but had been thrust upon me like an ill-fitting coat that never brought complete warmth. Whose despair filled my heart?

I felt the eyes. When I turned, she stood inside the room and stared ahead, though me searching the horizon. Her eyes flamed with a steady light unlike the intermittent blink of the white light on its perpetual sweep.

She moved toward me–first across the inside room, then through the brick–disappearing into the solid mass and slowly reassembling to push through the final bit of stone. Her form drifted with the breeze, her eyes more defined in a shapeless face. They locked on mine and I heard a low keening, a sobbing. A muffled voice sounded low and urgent. I leaned back against the railing, ignoring the pressure of the wrought iron against my back.

"Gracie," a low whisper reached my ears. "Gracie, wake up."

I felt the jab through the mattress. "Okay, I'm awake."

Another jab found my lower back. "Oww. I *said* I'm awake."

"Just making sure. Sometimes you sleep talk."

I rolled to the edge of the bunk and leaned over. "Sleep talk? Don't make me come down there."

"Now I know you're awake. You were moaning, then crying. I knew you were dreaming. Didn't want to shout even though if you got any louder the whole cottage would have heard you through the door."

Through the door. I thought about the woman I'd seen...no, dreamt about. Marty said something; I climbed down and sat on the floor next to my brother's bunk as he continued: "The only words I could make out were something about ice or eyes. You were mumbling. Did you have one of your 'eye' dreams?"

I nodded and crossed my arms against my chest. Inanimate eyes had haunted my childhood dreams so much that my mother removed my dolls from my room. In third grade the nun assigned me to a desk that had a birds-eye grain. I couldn't bear to look at the top and waited anxiously for the next grading period when we moved desks again. No one understood the drop in my grades. During high school the dreams began to include human eyes, and those dreams stayed with me.

Marty reached out and patted my shoulder the same comforting way he'd done many times when we were children. With mother and sister both sensitive, the Morelli men were accustomed to bad dreams interrupting countless nights of sleep.

A light tap on the door stopped my thoughts. "Everything okay?" Joan's voice sounded tense. Poor Joanie, I thought...she invites us up for a last fling and the whole thing comes unraveled. Bet she's happy to be selling the cottage after this week.

"We're fine. Thanks." I stood and opened the door to continue the conversation. "I think I'm finished napping. I'll just turn in early."

She nodded. "Most of us decided that. I'm making breakfast again. More like brunch. Want anything?"

"Yeah, to give you a hand." I looked down at Marty. "Need anything, little brother?"

"I'm getting up too. Give me a hand with the veggies." He nodded toward his foot. The towel and plastic bag Deb had wrapped around his ankle made his lower extremity look like the Michelin Man's ankle.

I removed the soggy splint and noticed that his ankle looked pretty good. "I think this worked. The test will be if you can stand on it."

Joan took the bundle. "Might as well mark these 'ice packs' and refreeze them. I'll see you in the kitchen."

I slipped into my shoes and leaned in to Marty. "I'll give you a hand up."

"And pull me up with your back. That's how you get hurt; you gotta lift with your legs. I tell Eve that all the time…" Marty stopped.

I knew he missed his wife and daughter, knew he wondered if he'd be able to convince Eve he'd dealt with his potential addiction to prescription drugs. I wondered if he doubted himself. Inviting him to the Great North seemed like a good idea at the time. We both seemed to have too much house and not enough people.

Marty lurched up and used the walking stick to keep his balance. He grinned. "Feels much better." He looked down at his bare foot. "Sock, please." We both burst into laughter. As children, I would help him dress. The game was to name the item of clothing: "shirt, please," "sock, please," "shoe, please." Took forever, but mom insisted he'd learn words and manners.

"Sounds like someone's on the mend." Deb stood in the doorway.

Marty smiled. "I'm feeling much better, thank you. You know your first aid."

Debbie shook her head and pointed at his foot. "That was simple. You should have seen some of the lads I splinted and wrapped." She smiled in that easy way that said she was happy in her skin. In the daylight she didn't seem to be flirting, just pleasant and competent. I looked at Marty. His neutral expression belied nothing. Had I imagined those longing and lustful looks? *Geez, Grace, cut it out. You sound like a cheap novel.*

Breakfast came and went in a fun fashion; the scare of the night replaced by psyche-centering jokes and delicious blueberry pancakes. By the last crumbs they'd decided to go with the teenage prank story and have a laugh about it.

I seemed to be the only holdout. They hadn't seen what I'd seen; hadn't felt eyes searing through their skin. I silently reserved my opinion. Only Laurie seemed to laugh a few beats later, as though trying to catch up.

The menfolk, as we were calling them, were headed out on the water. Bob had a map of the early treks on the bay and one account took place at this time of year. They were going to follow the route in canoes. Of course they'd be back for dinner, since the menu called for Yankee pot roast, steamed veggies, and roasted potatoes. Marty bowed out of the adventure, opting to enjoy a day around the cottage with the ladies of the lake, their term for us.

"Sorry you can't join us, Marty. We'd postpone, but Danny King mentioned a cold front coming in and that's going to churn up the bay."

Marty waved them off. "No problem. I'm good at entertaining myself." His lopsided grin endeared him to me and at least two other women in the kitchen. Maybe I wasn't off target after all.

I scooped up the silverware from the table and brought it to Laurie at the sink. Fluffy suds peaked in the hot water. Laurie absent-mindedly ran her fingers through the foamy points. "Ready for these?" My voice startled her, and her hand dipped into the hot water.

"Oww. You could boil a lobster in this."

"I think that's tomorrow's dinner," Colleen joked.

"Wear the gloves, silly. Under the sink on the right," Joan directed from the doorway. "I'll be right back."

She slipped out the door and down the steps to her bedroom.

"You're not scheduled for this." Laurie gestured for me to put the silverware in the water.

"The schedule for today seems to be shot; I figured I'd pitch in.

Actually I'm trying to earn brownie points with Joan so she invites me to her next cottage." My conspiratorial tone cracked them up.

The door slid open. "What's so funny?"

"Your friend. She's a hoot." Colleen smiled and continued, "Fits right in with the ladies of the lake."

"Yes, not like the last one," Debbie added. "She didn't at all. Pity." Debbie's remorse seemed exaggerated and I suspected I was becoming the butt of a joke, but I couldn't resist asking: "What happened to her?"

"Oh, she became a 'lady of the lake.'" Debbie drew her finger across her throat and then jerked her thumb toward the water.

My face must have reflected my initial disbelief before I realized full and well that I'd been snookered. Their laughter surrounded me in a friendly manner; only Laurie seemed less jovial.

We turned to our tasks and the kitchen sparkled from our efforts. Joan brought out the box of photos and the oilskin packet with the letters. "I'm going to drink tea 'til I float and photograph these before I have to return them." She spread out the photos and the letters. "Gracie, read the letters and see if there's a mention of season or people…maybe we can match up some pictures."

I sat across from her and gently maneuvered one letter from the packet. Laurie sat next to me, "Maybe we should take them all out and read them in chronological order. Might make more sense."

I knew Laurie had an interest in her husband's ancestor. Something in her manner, a kind of sorrow when she spoke of her, seemed odd. Not even Garry's mother would have known her, yet Laurie grieved over the long-dead woman's situation in a personal way. I wondered how personal. I knew firsthand the touch of someone from beyond the grave: a gentle wave of sensation, an increasing urgency to have their story told, and finally a desperate haunting to find justice. I wondered. Laurie's hand trembled slightly as she unfolded, smoothed, and slid each old missive into special plastic sleeves Joan had signed out from the Historical Society. We could handle the letters with minimal damage from the oils on our hands. Some of the creases had obliterated the words written there and some areas were splotched from water damage, but all in all, we were lucky to find so many intact.

"While you three hunt in the past, we're going to check out the present." Debbie and Colleen stood at the door, coats in hand. "We're going to check out the lighthouse and look for any landmarks." Deb held up her camera.

That left only Marty at odds. I turned in my seat in time to watch him lower himself to a chair near the stove and rest his injured ankle atop the hassock. I saw him glance around and spot his mug on the counter where he'd left it.

"Looking for this?" I stood and picked up the full mug from the countertop. He smiled when I brought it to him.

"Thanks, Sis. So close and yet so far," he joked.

"You look pretty well settled in 'til lunch. What's all this?" I pointed to the sheaf of papers in his lap. "This is supposed to be R & R for you…us."

He ducked his head and stayed quiet. When he did lift his head he stared at me with a mixture of apprehension and excitement. "I'm going back to school to get my MBA. Going to get out of sales, into management."

The news stunned me speechless. This from the brother who had visions of a medical career until he realized how much work that involved. He'd lucked into a profitable career as a pharmaceutical salesman because of his medical training. That luck had turned south when the easy attitudes of several doctors he sold to reciprocated with an occasional script for sleep aids, energy boosters, etc. My brother had taken a leave of absence to get his head straight and save his marriage.

"You going to just stand there?"

"Of course not. I'm going to give you a congratulatory nugee and hug." I ground my knuckles into his short hair and shoulder-hugged him.

"Aughh, let go."

"I'll leave you to it. Call if you get stuck on the big words." I sauntered away and felt the soft thump between my shoulders when the small pillow hit me. Never turn your back on a little brother who'd been an ace pitcher in high school. I laughed and kept walking.

* * *

Laurie had organized the plastic-covered letters in chronological order. She looked up when I sat down. "I don't understand this. I expected these letters to be only the ones Aunt Amelia wrote when she was in Lafontaine. Some of these seem to be as old as the ones in the oilskin. I didn't think anything had survived."

"Survived?"

"There was an earlier fire in the lighthouse; right after her husband died. Some speculated that in their haste to get him to medical attention they left a lantern unattended."

I grinned. "Chicago's worst fire was started by a cow kicking over a lantern. Dangerous things, those unattended lanterns." I nodded at the letters. "They were probably in someone else's possession at the time. Maybe they'd already been mailed home and they've just been mixed in."

"No, I meant the other way around. Letters from much later are in the oilskin. How would they get there if she left them in the hidden drawer after the fire? She'd have to come back to the island to add them."

Joan spoke up from her task. "Does it matter? Maybe she did come back; maybe they were special letters that referred to the earlier ones."

Laurie nodded. "I'll see if there's a connection," and bowed her head to her new task.

We worked in companionable silence for the next forty-five minutes amid the clicking of Joan's camera and the rustling of plastic pages. Joan stopped first. "Done. Each letter and picture photographed and documented."

Laurie lifted her head. "I've still more letters to read, difficult to make out all the words."

"Me too. How about a break? My eyes are blurring."

"Hmm. Sounds good. I'll put on the kettle. Coffee for you, Grace?"

"Tea's fine. How about you, Marty?" I turned for his answer and saw a slack-jawed head tilted back against the chair. He'd put both feet up and slouched down.

I had a feeling it would be an early night for all of us.

Clumping sounds on the back steps preceded excited voices. Colleen and Deb hurried through the door.

"Look at this. I can't believe it. We didn't see it when we looked."

Deb spread a series of pictures across the table. The square Polaroid pictures lined up showing the same photo of the lighthouse. It looked familiar and I pulled out one of the photos from Joan's pile.

"It's the same shot."

"Not the lighthouse, look at the inukshuk."

We leaned closer. Laurie lifted the photo into better light. Joan looked over Laurie's shoulder. "It's not an inukshuk, it's an inunnguaq. When it's shaped like a person, that's what it's called. It's much more difficult to make, and it's not always a trail marker. They attribute those to Europeans in the early nineteenth century who used them for memorials."

"I thought you majored in Education at NIU. Are you the resident local lore expert?"

"By default only. When I joined this restoration project, I ended up with boxes of material from the last attempt to get landmark designation for the lighthouse. Show me the other photos." The excitement in her voice caused all of us to look at her. I slid the other photos out. "The cut-up ones, those are the ones."

She quickly spread them out across the table. "I think these are different angles or pictures of a series of inuksuit cut up so the direction or location of something wouldn't be easily determined."

"Why make the marker and then make it difficult to follow? Isn't the idea of an inukshuk to show the way?"

"Maybe the creator of this group hid something and wanted only one person to find it. Maybe they couldn't talk to the person or they feared writing it in a letter."

"You're thinking Amelia took these photos?"

"No, someone much later than she. Amelia wouldn't have had the technology or resources. Only the wealthy could afford a photographer. We do have some family photos of Amelia and Joshua and his wife Lissette and, of course, their eleven children."

"Eleven kids, holy crap." Marty's voice startled us. He stood and made his way over to us. "Eleven kids? How do you raise eleven kids?"

The rhetorical question brought amused looks and some laughter. Colleen said it best, "What woman would want to be pregnant and give birth eleven times?"

"Oh yeah, that too, I guess," Marty mumbled. He had reached the table and looked at the cut-up pieces. "I'm pretty good at puzzles; let me have a crack at it."

"I'm keen on these types too. Let's collaborate." Debbie pulled a chair out for Marty and within moments their heads were bent close over the square pieces, mumbling directions to each other and bumping fingers when they reached for the same piece.

I watched them from my seat across the table. "Grace, you look upset. Wouldn't want you looking that way at me," Colleen said when she placed my mug of sweet tea on the table.

I looked at her and tried a smile. "Mmm. Just tired. Thanks for the tea, this should pick me up." *I know Marty's hurting. Why is he flying so close to the flame? Because he's a guy trying to feel better about himself by flirting with a pretty lady, who happens to be flirting back.* I hate it when I answer myself. I turned off my internal Q&A and stared into my mug.

"I need some fresh air; these letters are making my eyes cross." Joan stood and stretched. "Anyone for a walk?"

Laurie shook her head. "I want to keep at these letters. Thanks all the same."

"Colleen?"

"Oh, I've had my share of fresh air and it's highly overrated." She grinned and saluted us with her mug. "Have at it."

"Which way?"

We stood at the road behind the cottage. To the left the path to the lighthouse, to the right the road to the ferry and Band Council buildings.

"How about that way?" I pointed straight ahead. "I've never walked to the middle of the island. What's there?"

"I don't know. It's too overgrown in the summer and the bugs aren't inviting. Besides, we're up in the summer to do water things."

"Then exploring it is. This way." I pulled gloves from my pocket and tugged my hat down closer on my head. In a childish manner we linked arms, did a bundled and booted version of we're off to see the Wizard, and followed our yellow brick road. Fifty yards into the woods, our road melted into a tangle of brush and saplings that brought us up short. We burst into laughter that felt so good I didn't care if our expedition was a bust.

"Leave it to us—great fanfare and mediocre results." Joan shook with laughter and pointed to her left. A perfectly proper trail ran parallel to our sorry attempt to trail blaze.

"Well, where's the fun in following the crowd?" I mumbled as we retraced our steps. We found the single-file footpath from the main road. "Talk about the road least traveled. I'd never have thought this went anywhere if we hadn't seen it from inside. Wait till we tell Dave. I bet he doesn't know this is here."

"I bet Danny King knows. They probably all know. It is their island."

"I think they tolerate outsiders in the summer because we bring dollars to their community, but I'm getting the feeling that we're intruding at this off time of year."

"Yeah, and they're not happy about it. Those kids were trying to scare us off the island." We'd walked to the point where the trail widened and I moved up next to Joan. The sudden quiet, like our voices had been swallowed up, made me shiver. I took comfort in the presence of my friend and knew I'd never go into these woods alone. The memory of recent events in the woods back home bought me a moment of unreasonable panic. I pulled a length of cord from my pocket and twisted the beaded end between my fingers, back and forth, back and forth. No cults here, no danger. Did I know that for sure? Would I bet my life?

# Chapter Eleven

We continued in silence–not by design, but more by demand from the environs. It seemed inappropriate to yak away. We walked slowly and became aware of the resident birds and animals– spotting a redwing blackbird preening on a low bare branch. We stopped and waited when three deer spotted us about the same time we saw them. The standoff lasted only a minute, but to stare into huge liquid brown eyes across mere yards heightened the feeling of wilderness. I rolled the beaded cord in my hand. From statue stillness to startled sprint, they were gone.

"Sorry," I whispered.

"It's okay. I didn't even know there were deer on the island. Wait till I tell Dave."

"What's over there?" I pointed toward where the deer had disappeared. "It looks like a clearing," I said softly.

"Why are you whispering? You're giving me the creeps." Joan's voice boomed in the quiet. She shook her head. Her voice lowered to an inside voice, but not a whisper. "I don't know. Maybe a firepit or bonfire area. I think I heard that the islanders still have seasonal celebrations. Two summers past I stumbled onto an old sweat lodge that looked abandoned. Let's have a look."

I grabbed Joan's arm. "Wait. Maybe we shouldn't. I mean, if those kids were trying to scare us, imagine what a good job they could do if they found us here." My jovial tone came out strained.

"What's wrong? You're the brave one, remember?" Joan's eyes searched my face. I tried on a smile, but it felt lopsided. Seasonal celebrations. Mother Earth? Father Sky? Crazy guy in a hood? The memory of the hooded marauders in Robinson Woods paralyzed me and Joan gained fifteen yards on me. Her teal parka flashed through the branches, her movements sure and smooth. The silence rolled toward me like fog over a hollow. The loss of my companion spurred me to action and I covered the ground between us quickly. She stopped moving, in fact she stepped backward, and that cautious motion kick-started the hairs on the back of my neck. I slowed and moved up behind her to look beyond her shoulder.

The island cemetery lay before us in a clearing created for this purpose. The underbrush and saplings circled the hallowed plot, keeping a respectful distance from the interred. Joan stood firm to the spot as I brushed past her toward the graveyard. I turned when I realized she hadn't moved.

"Aren't you coming?"

"Like I said, you're the brave one. I never liked cemeteries, not even Mt. Carmel, where you knew most everyone."

The old joke eased her tension and she smiled. The high school we attended, Proviso West, sits across the street from Mt. Carmel Catholic Cemetery, home to the Morelli deceased, Al Capone, and the Italian Bride. Most Sundays in my early youth were spent visiting the dead, praying, cleaning graves, and planting flowers. Rather than gruesome it actually grounded me in a sense of continuity. It also removed the usual fear of cemeteries. My dad always told us, "It's the live ones that can hurt you."

I walked carefully into the circle of tombstones and made my way to the center. I'd never seen a cemetery plotted in the round and knew I'd come back to photograph the island graveyard. Each stone faced in toward the center, like wagons circled against an enemy or Emperor Penguins circled against the frigid cold.

"Some of these graves date back to the sixteen hundreds. Are these Indian graves or French settlers or Jesuits? The carvings have all but smoothed out; can't make out names. Do you know if they still use it today?"

"I don't see why not. I've never thought about it. I suppose they could take the coffin across to a mainland cemetery, but I thought they had a cemetery near the church."

The pattern appealed to me much as the straight lines and rows of clean white stones at Arlington National Cemetery bespoke a dignity and respect for those buried there. The symmetry mesmerized me and I found myself turning slowly, making tiny arcs sighting up each row from the center point, which was not a grave but rather a stone altar about four feet high. The stone arms pointed east to west.

"Wow, this is the real thing." Joan gently patted the smooth stone. "This piece started the whole shebang. I read about it during my research. These were mystic markers, designating holy ground. If we could see this from above, I bet the arms point a straight line from the Barr Sand Point to the original village, maybe even exactly dead center."

"Interesting choice of words." I smiled.

"The lighthouse wouldn't have been built yet, but maybe the lighthouse keeper is buried here."

"If the center is…let's say 1600 and he died in 1882, he should be out a few circles, no?" I walked out a few rows trying to read a date. "Look how close the graves are here, and then the distance spreads out toward the back of the circle. Wonder why."

"Yeah, the graves are shorter closer to the altar stone. Maybe they were conserving space; maybe the holy area doesn't extend beyond a certain point."

"Maybe they buried them upright. I think I read something like that about an Indian tribe in South America. They do it so the recently deceased can walk easily to his reward in the afterlife."

Joan shrugged her shoulders. "If we knew which year the Jesuits arrived and started evangelizing and converting, it might coincide with people being buried horizontally and that could explain the change in length of grave. The Jesuits and a few thousand Huron took refuge on this island, but most of them died of starvation. It marked the end of the Huron Nation. Maybe the survivors weren't strong enough to dig deep so they dug shallow graves. Or not."

We burst into laughter at her final assessment. I'd found a stone in the fifth circle that looked promising. "Fortinier, 1843," I called out. "Sounds French."

Joan nodded from a row further out. "Maurice Gereaux, 1867. Definitely French." I marveled at the exactness of each stone…not only the shape and carving, but down to the phrasing on the stone face. They seemed so sturdy, so oblivious to the elements through all the time they've stood. Being within a forest in a hollow rather than on a high windy hill probably accounted for the excellent condition of the stones.

"I found him," Joan's shout pulled me to her side. "'Burton Havilland, 1882.' Boy, they didn't wax poetic about him." She'd noticed the difference. The other stones carried the name and date of death, but also a brief line of identification like 'honored island storyteller.'

"Why wouldn't he have 'Lighthouse Keeper' on his stone? How odd." Joan's voice held the same puzzled tone I heard in my head.

Odd indeed. I fished a small notebook and pen out of my pocket and jotted down the meager information, then copied the epitaphs from the stones on either side of Mr. Havilland. The person to his left had died three days later; another English name, Thornsberry. They must have known each other.

"Leave it to you to have a notebook handy; still Harriet the Spy, eh?" Joan grinned. She stood at a grave one ring over. I shrugged and smiled. I hadn't been referred to as Harriet for years. Spending time with a childhood friend filled a need that nothing else could. Joan moved to the next stone and stopped abruptly. Her body stiffened, and when she turned, her pale face framed shock-filled eyes. I hurried to her side and read the inscription, "Lissette Banelieu, Back Where She Belongs."

A shiver moved up my spine and tingled at the base of my neck. I scribbled the notation and dates. "Do you think Garry knows his great, great-grandmother is buried here?"

Joan shook her head. "This can't be the same woman; must be some fluke." She drew her hood up. "It's getting colder. Might be a storm coming in. We should head back."

"I saw that name already, over here." I walked back to the grave on the other side of the lighthouse keeper and read aloud, "Laurent Banelieu, Trésor d'Ile. I took German in high school…what does that mean?"

"It means literally 'treasure of the island;' colloquially probably something like 'worth his weight in gold.' You know, a good person."

"Do you think this Banelieu knew that one?"

"They must have been maybe brother and sister or cousins. He died young, whereas she lived into her seventies."

"The graves in this row look like an animal has been at them. Look at the clumps of disturbed dirt. Must be digging for grubs and other goodies."

"The temp is really dropping. Let's go." Joan tugged at my sleeve.

The light in the circle grew dim as though clouds were dipping closer to the ground; the tips of the stones closest to the center looked covered in a glistening mist, appearing to glow in the low light. The phenomena moved toward us.

I slowly backed out of the circle–not wanting to stop watching the metamorphosis as the stone appeared to change to crystal, yet not wanting to risk being touched by the mist. I realized that Joan hadn't moved. She stood stock still twenty-five feet in front of me and only three rings away from the fog. I rushed up behind her and shook her shoulder. "Let's go."

Her face appeared lit from within, and my first fear was that somehow this mist had already touched her. She smiled and shook off my hand. "Gracie, this is fabulous. Can you believe we're experiencing a 'hunter's fog?'" Her whispered delight did nothing to reassure me.

"Let's experience it from behind the circle." She didn't budge. Two circles away from the fog I felt a rising panic, and worse than that a building compulsion to pattern-step around the stones. I hadn't felt this compulsion so strongly since I was a kid. I whispered quickly, "It would be more respectful from beyond the circle." I tugged at her sleeve and she moved…one step, two steps… Oh no, not now. I'd lost my focus and now abandoned myself to the demon that twisted words and thoughts into action. One step, two steps, circle round, stop. One step, two steps, circle round, stop.

I felt Joan staring at me and I saw the mist light on the row before me, but I moved to my own strict pattern. I could control my forward movement by taking baby steps, not giant steps, but I couldn't stop the pattern until I'd done it ten times. My fear, that no matter how tiny my steps I would meet the mist head on, paralyzed my brain until only the count in my head made perfect sense. One step, two steps, circle round, stop. One step, two steps, circle round, stop. I saw Joan reaching for me and I shook my head, "No! Can't stop." She backed away; in my last circle step, her face filled with fear and I felt the thin tendrils of ice-cold air reach for my body. I collapsed to the ground and flattened myself between two graves, hoping this was a meteorological event and not a supernatural one. I felt the unnatural cold move over me, finding ingress through my loose, tumbled clothing. The maelstrom I feared never occurred. Frigid air moved over and around me in a silent swirl. In a moment of near hysteria I thought I heard soft tones like mumbled voices moving along the current. Snatches of words rolled over me, but were they in my mind or on the air? The winter-bent grass smothered my nose and I turned my face to breathe easier. Icy points of air stabbed at my nostrils when I inhaled. The light within this cloud left the stone surfaces coated with shimmer. My eyes stung from the air, and I opened them wider to catch the ambient light. From my low perch I'd spotted an etching on the smooth stone. An inukshuk, intricate by most standards, indicating multiple directions. All paths lead to Heaven.

The heavy cold lifted and disappeared. The temperature changed and I slumped into the ground from the relief. "Gracie, are you okay?" I felt her hands on my shoulders and twisted to look up.

"What the heck was that?" My voice trembled and cracked with released tension. She helped me up.

"That was the scariest thing I've ever seen. The fog rolled all the way to the end of the circle, seemed to hover and pulsate, and then it shot up, I mean straight up like a cloud or…or like a space saucer."

My pal's eyes were as wide as saucers. "Let's get back, you're soaked."

I wanted to tell her about the inukshuk, wanted to go back and look at it, but my teeth tapped against each other no matter how hard I tried to keep them clenched. I nodded and we headed back through the brush. Only now the dusky sky played havoc with our recollection of the quasi-path we'd blazed. We needed an inukshuk assist.

"I think we came through here. Remember the clearing popped up on our left?" Popped up? Like Brigadoon? Is it there now or did we stumble across it on the one day it appears? Had the villagers been there earlier to honor their dead? Was the vapor cloud a closing ceremony of sorts?

"Grace, where are you going?"

I heard the panic in Joan's voice and realized I'd turned back to the clearing.

She grabbed me by the arm and pulled me toward her. "C'mon, you don't look so good."

The concern on her face touched me. I stepped toward her and play punched her in the arm. "Yeah, well you're no raving beauty either."

Her face creased into a grin and we stepped quickly down what we hoped was the right trail. I noticed she held tight to my arm until we reached a point where we could continue only single file. Joan slowed to let me lead. I felt giddy with the adventure and started dipping into 'spy stances' and humming the tune from 'The Man from U.N.C.L.E.'; I the dark haired Napoleon Solo, she the blonde Illyia Kurirakin. Her giggles assuaged my guilt for scaring her with my behavior. I pushed a branch out of my way and announced, "Incoming" before I let go. In that nanosecond I wondered if Joan had ever hiked in the woods with her brother and if she would understand "incoming," and if she would duck. All that in the millisecond before I heard the thwap of wood on skin.

"Oww!"

"Oh my God. I'm sorry. Joanie, are you okay?" She stood still, holding her hand to her forehead. "God, that was stupid. I'm so sorry." Her eyes didn't focus on me, but rather behind me. I didn't like that one bit. Her mouth opened but no words issued…only a short groan, and then she collapsed. I turned to see what she'd seen—either to defend us against it or to ask for help—but nothing loomed on the path.

I'd knocked her silly was my first thought. My second was that she shouldn't be unconscious. "Joanie, Joanie, wake up." I tapped her cheeks gently and cringed at the sight of the goose egg developing on her forehead; it seemed to grow as I watched. I pushed up her jacket sleeve and rubbed her wrist between my hands like trying to start a fire the old-fashioned way. I was trying to light a fire in her. "C'mon, Joanie. Wake up." A low moan rewarded my efforts. "That's it, c'mon Joan, open your eyes." Her blue eyes blinked once, then the lids shut down again. I chaffed her wrist with renewed vigor. "Joan, Joan." This time she blinked and blinked again. Her eyes were focused on mine and they looked clear.

She struggled to sit up and I helped her stand, ready in case she wobbled. Joan reached up and gently touched her forehead. The grimace confirmed that it hurt; I felt lower than a crumb. Joan's body tensed. She whirled and stared down the path, then looked to me for an answer. "Where'd it go?"

I remembered the look in her eyes before she collapsed, but my blank expression answered her.

"You didn't see it? On the path in front of us?"

I shook my head. "When you hit the ground I looked back, but there was no one there. Was it another voyageur?"

Joan shook her head in little quick shakes and wrapped her arms around her chest. I thought she might be in shock. "Let's get back before it's too dark to see our way, whichever way that might be." Our original problem presented itself. We were likely lost. I put my arm around Joan's shoulders and started walking. "I think this is the right path because it did narrow down and then open up right before the clearing. It should open up to a wider path in a bit." I spoke with more confidence than I felt and concentrated on maneuvering through the trees, using my left arm and shoulder to hold back branches. This wasn't the path; it should have opened up by now.

Joan stopped and stared ahead into the failing light. Her mouth compressed to a thin line, and her eyes grew so wide she looked like a caricature of her normally beautiful features.

Great, now what? I stared into the gloom. Was there something off the path? Nothing moved, including us. I couldn't budge her.

"Joanie, let's keep moving. There's nothing there, just the light and the trees playing tricks on your mind. Please, Joan, we have to keep moving. I think you're in shock."

Her shoulders convulsed under my arm. I quickly took off my jacket and snugged it over her. The cool air felt refreshing against my sweaty clothes, but I knew I'd be cold soon…my bright pink down vest worked best under a jacket. Her shoulders slumped and I urged her forward. "Just a little further and it should open up." I didn't know if it would, but I knew this was the general direction–at least I hoped the years of camping with my brothers at family scout events had honed some sense of orienteering.

I stared down the path trying to see anything that could have frightened Joan. A stealthy movement off the path caught my eye. Too far away to see clearly, the object looked grey like stone but it definitely moved a little. Maybe we moved and a curve in the path made it look like it moved. That's it…probably a rock formation near the path, although I didn't recall a rock formation off the path on the way in. For sure we were on the wrong trail, but I'd rather that be true than what I was thinking; that we were on a path with a big, scary, furry native creature called Bigfoot or Yeti! My breathing slowed and I chided myself for my runaway imagination. The path widened abruptly and the rock formation moved.

# Chapter Twelve

Two screams split the air. Joan's hit higher on the scale, but mine was no less intense.

"Holy crap, oh my God, what is it?" Joan's voice shook with the fear I felt. The object of our panic moved a bit closer, prompting us to step back onto the narrower path.

"It looks like an inunnguaq. Is that what you see?" I asked in a whisper without taking my eyes off it.

"Yes, yes," she whispered back.

"That's all I wanted to know." I bent down and picked up an orange-sized rock, took three quick steps to position myself, and threw one of my better fastballs at its head. *Thunk*. Direct hit!

"Oww."

It was human. The fear for my mental wellbeing flooded my psyche and focused on this incredible mean-spirited person inside that costume. I ran toward it, "You sick bastard. You son of a bitch," and hurled my body at the 'stone man' to punctuate my rant. We went down in a heap. I heard the telltale whoosh and knew I had the upper hand, at least until the person under my knees caught his breath. Not if I could help it. If I'd learned anything at the hands of two older brothers who'd rejoiced in a pink 'punching bag' for a little sister, it was how to fight like a boy. Pummeling and pirouetting vied for equal time in my childhood. I pounded the person beneath me, hearing rewarding *omphs* and *owws*.

Strong arms grabbed me from behind and, for a sickening moment, I thought another attacker must have hurt Joan. Dave's voice finally penetrated the fog I raged in and I relaxed and let him pull me up. Dave slowly released my arms and I realized Garry and Bob stared across the clearing at me. I couldn't tell in the low light if they were shocked or amused. Dave lifted my arm above my head. "The winner and still champion, Graaaceee Marsden." His announcer voice filled the clearing, and the laughter followed.

Only Joan seemed concerned. "You shouldn't have done that.

You could have been hurt." She put her arm around my shoulder and squeezed.

"Are you kidding? She had him down for the count. Speaking of which," Dave spoke to the huddle on the ground, "you can get up now and you'd better have some answers or I'll let her have a go at you again."

The figure on the ground slowly sat up and removed the costume mask and covering. The gesture was one of total compliance. I heard a young voice speak before the mask had cleared his head. "I told them I didn't want to do it. Stupid joke." The teen stood, trailing the mask from one hand while he rubbed his chest. "Geez, lady, you hurt me. You flew at me like some kind of crazy person."

The adrenaline rush that chose fight rather than flight had long since ebbed. I felt foolish amid the proud comments and laughter from the guys and the chilling observation from the teen I'd attacked. *Some kind of crazy person.*

Dave questioned the boy and sent him on his way. He made him take off the costume and walk home in his shorts and undershirt. The boy whined about the cold, but left quickly. Garry bundled up the costume and led the way out of the woods. We had been on the right trail.

"We only spotted you because of your neon pink vest. You practically glowed. Don't know why we didn't see it sooner."

"Because she gave me her jacket." Joan shrugged inside the extra layer of my forest green jacket. She pushed the hood off her head and pulled the coat from around her shoulders. "Thanks. I'm warmer." It was then that Dave spotted the goose egg.

"Joanie, what happened?" Dave whirled in the direction the teen had taken. "Did he do that? I don't care if he is a kid, I'll…"

"I did it. Not on purpose. I yelled 'incoming,' but I, I mean she, I mean…" Any attempt at an explanation seemed lame. Dave's glare crumbled my last shred of hope that he'd understand and I felt my eyes fill with tears. I looked away and bit my lower lip to keep in the sob I felt building.

"Let's get you home. I want Debbie to take a look at that lump." He pulled Joan close within his arm and started down the trail.

Home. That's where I should be. Or with Harry. I could have met him as he asked after he picked up Will in London. I'd be with him and his parents at their home. Instead, I dug in my heels and insisted I would go to Canada and that if he and Will wanted to visit they could come down next week and then we'd go home together. Home.

I realized that Garry and Bob waited on the path ahead for me to sandwich myself between them. I stepped forward. "Sorry."

Bob put his hand on my shoulder. "He'll be all right. Just shook him up seeing that goose egg on her forehead." I merely nodded, not sure I could speak without crying. I'd really messed up. All the way back to the cottage I thought about leaving the island. It would be best. Marty would be more comfortable at home than hobbling around a crowded cottage. I'd all but made up my mind when a singular thought struck me. I'd run to Canada to escape the bones and spirits that seemed to search me out. Even here, where I know no one, something, or someone tries to reach out to me, and I can't seem to escape the contact. Running wouldn't solve the problem, not here and not back home.

None of us spoke, the silence broken only by the natural noises of the night. The lights of the cottage gleamed ahead and I realized that darkness had overtaken us. I was grateful Joan and I weren't out in this alone. I asked God to send a little courage my way to face the hostility within.

Joan flung open the back door. "What did you guys do, stop to take pictures? We've been back for ten minutes." Her smile filled my heart, but I remembered it wasn't Joan who glared at me. She stepped aside and we trouped past her. I saw the frozen veggie bag in her hand and cursed myself again for my stupid, rash behavior.

"Joanie, I'm so sorry."

She grinned at me. "Get over it." The lump did seem smaller; the telltale redness from the ice application circled the spot.

I walked toward the bedroom mumbling about changing my shoes. I wanted to hide away for a moment to collect my thoughts, maybe just sit on the bunk for a few minutes, and try to organize events. My head couldn't stand it if I didn't put my thoughts in order, give it time to pigeonhole the day. Okay. Twenty slip knots, easy tie, easy pull. That will help. Here we go.

While untying my boot I'd pulled the lace through and sat happily tying and untying the same knot until the chaos in my brain began to lessen. Ten more? Yes, ten more will do nicely. Easy tie, easy pull. Easy tie, easy pull.

The gentle knock came at number seven. Marty's low voice asked, "Almost ready?" My brother knew. They probably all did. I'd walk out and see the curiosity on their faces. Ten more? No, I have to go out there. Ten more. I'll stay.

"Gracie?"

"In a minute," I answered quickly, not wanting to disrupt the flow. Marty knew I had to finish. He'd stall for me. I pulled out the last knot and tossed the lace at my boot. My fingers hurried to untie the other lace; the roughness of the cord tickled my skin and tempted my mind. No, I'm finished. I put on my slippers and leaped up without leaning forward.

"Oww. Dammit!"

"Grace. Are you okay?" Marty must have waited by the door.

"Yes, yes," I said. I opened the door. "I stood up and hit the bunk. Geez, that hurts."

"Ouch, I've done that. I think you need this more than she does." Dave took the frozen veggie bag from his wife's hand and offered it to me. "Sorry about…earlier." His eyes asked forgiveness. I nodded and accepted the bag. The mood lightened and we relaxed.

"No more injuries or we're out of side dishes." Debbie's pronouncement melted the vestiges of tension. Amid the laughter, I learned two things: I'd acquired a nickname, 'Rocky,' and Laurie wanted to leave the island tonight. Apparently, she'd paled and nearly fainted at Joan's description of the contained fog.

Debbie rapped a wooden spoon on the counter. Her husband rolled his eyes and grinned, "She's such a drama queen." Deb grinned back and raised the spoon in his direction. "This has been a horrible twenty-four hours, agreed?" Of course we nodded.

"We can't fold and slink away…not that any of us slink," she said, glancing quickly at Laurie. "What I mean is, Laurie and Colleen prepared a fabulous dinner; I pieced together that damn picture puzzle, although it makes no sense; and 'Dudley Do Right' stopped by earlier to assure us that all the wandering voyageurs are accounted for. Now," she nodded at the bundle on the floor, "so is the island inunnguaq. We have weathered the storm and deserve to relax. The fellas caught a most excellent fish and we have added that to the fare."

I looked at Laurie and felt as she did that leaving the island was a good idea. I saw her face reflect her resignation to the fact that the group seemed buoyed by Debbie's take on the situation. She forced a hearty smile; I knew it was forced because her eyes still flared with tiny pinpoints of fear. I saw it because I felt it. I too knew how to slap on a smile that could light up a room.

Debbie looked from one toothpaste ad smile to another and rapped the counter twice. "Sold! We stay."

"Can we eat now?" Bob's pretend whiney voice brought laughter from everyone. Dinner actually went well. The baked fish and beef kabobs, our island 'surf and turf,' tasted as good as any prepared on the mainland. The conversation covered meteorological explanations for the fog to island superstition about walking inunnguaq, possibly an island version of Yeti. We continued the conversation in the pit with tea and brandy.

"My Aunt Josie, one of Joshua's granddaughters, used to tell stories about the inunnguaq and how lost travelers in the North provinces would swear they owed their lives to the rock creature that would appear on the path to point the direction to safety." Garry spoke with the low, clear tones of a good storyteller.

"Nothing odd there," interrupted Marty. "The travelers stumbled upon someone else's guidepost."

Garry shook his head and continued, "You'd think so, but the stories all report the same thing happening next." Garry leaned in, and that shift brought us all forward in our seats. "When they turned to check and mark the position, the inunnguaq had disappeared. The only sign of its existence was a depression where it had stood and a trail of scraped ground as wide as its base, like a rook moving solidly across the chessboard." He waited a beat and continued, "The legend says it is death to see them move. Some foolhardy traveler tried following the trail and their party reported that he never returned."

"Good thing Joan and Grace didn't know that story, eh? Would have given me pause to see one of them moving about," Garry smiled and leaned back, signaling his story's end.

"Now that makes me wonder why the young fellow today wanted to scare you," Marty mused. "Is this part of a teen prank like Danny King claims?"

"Why'd they want to scare me and Joan? We've been coming here for years, never had trouble, not even much contact with the Band."

"Exactly," Ken said. "So what's different about this time?"

Joan looked around. "Well, we've a houseful of people."

"We've had them up before, even more." Dave shook his head.

"Never in winter. Maybe that's it. Some unwritten rule that cottagers don't belong here in the winter."

Several of us nodded with her logic.

"I can't imagine someone would go to all this trouble over cottagers on the island for a week or so." Marty spoke slowly as though working out the reason in his head before speaking. "But what if they didn't like the attention to the lighthouse keeper and his family; the letters we found, the questions you've been asking. What if someone doesn't want that information put out there?"

"Put out where, Marty?" Joan asked. "It's not like we're bringing in camera crews to document the restoration, we're just restoring a landmark for the people of Christian Island."

"Did you have to get someone's permission, like from here?"

"Of course we did. The Band Council approved the proposal from the Huronia Society. The Council will reap the benefits of the tourist dollars spent at the lighthouse, taking the tour, buying the souvenirs. The society is footing the bill and the Council is pocketing the money."

"Sweet deal." Marty's admiring comment brought laughter. "So the Council's all for this restoration."

"They'd be crazy not to want it."

"Maybe not everyone is as civic minded." Marty grinned. "Were there any council members who voted nay?"

Dave shook his head. "Don't know. You hear anything about that from Benningfurth?" he asked Joan.

"He didn't mention it, but as long as the vote carried he may not have known. I'll call him tomorrow."

Colleen stood and stretched. "Hmm, tomorrow, as in after a night's sleep. Sounds good to me." She pointed to the three people on the couch. "Off my bed, please."

Dave arranged the cushions on the floor and brought extra blankets and pillows from the bedroom. He dumped the lot and stood with his hands on his hips surveying the results. "No chance for any visitors tonight." He nodded to Joan, who'd followed him from the outside bedroom. She locked the sliding door and dropped a pole into the track. Chuckles surrounded the quick 'goodnights' tossed back and forth across the room. I smiled and thought of the signature sign-off from the old TV show, 'The Waltons.' "Good night John Boy," I said softly to my brother. He smiled. "That would make you that bratty, Elizabeth." I stuck out my tongue at him and climbed into the top bunk.

I lay sleepless for the longest time trying to empty my brain, longing for the release of dreamless sleep. I systematically sorted the events, sights, and sounds of my day. My brain demanded order and usually pigeonholed my experiences. During this sorting of reality, sometimes impressions came through. I used to think they were dreams, but I'd learned over the years that I lay wide awake when these premonitions rolled over me like chaff blowing off harvested grain. Why try so hard to scare us away? What do we know? What do we have? We know Amelia was miserable until her husband died. We know she moved back to the mainland and lived happily ever after, never succumbing to marriage again. We have her letters and some photos. We knew nothing, we had nothing. As for the knife being stolen, that was dumb luck on the intruder's part to find a good hunting knife calling his name.

"His name!" I jerked up in bed and gave a quick moment of thanks I wasn't in the lower bunk. I heard Marty mumble, "Are you okay?"

"Fine, fine, but why didn't we see this sooner?" I leaned over and explained. "What if the hunting knife belongs to someone local? Dave said it wasn't an old piece. What if that person had to get it back before the connection was made?"

I felt the dull thud of blood building in my head and sat up, continuing my thread as a disembodied voice rather than an upside-down talking head. "People on the island would know who the knife belonged to. What if all this was an elaborate ruse to steal the knife and make it look like the motive was to scare us and not the theft?"

Marty's voice floated up around the thin mattress. "But the knife had been there for years, maybe not all those years, but years."

"Are we sure? How long does it take for blood to turn brown?

How new is that knife?"

His silence prompted me further. "Maybe the knife was used in a current crime and hidden there recently."

"If someone knew about the hidden drawer, why leave everything else behind?"

He had me there. I certainly wouldn't have left the other bundles. Of course I wasn't trying to hide a possible murder weapon. He might have not cared what else was in there.

I felt a poke in my back from Marty's fist. "Hey, Nancy Drew, how about that?"

"Yeah, I'm working on it. Gloating doesn't suit you, little brother."

"That's the 'G' in my middle name." I could hear the Morelli smirk in his voice.

Marty's face loomed over the edge of my bunk. "I won't be able to get back to sleep. Let's make some coffee."

"No, we'll wake up the house. We have to stay in here until daybreak."

He bent down and I saw the brief glow from his luminous watch. "Gracie, it's only two o'clock. I can't stay in here for three or four more hours." The strain in his voice wasn't a pretense. Marty disliked closed spaces and I had to admit that being awake in this tiny room did seem a tad claustrophobic. I swung my legs over the edge and hopped down. "C'mon. Sit. I have a deck of cards in my bag." I unzipped an inside pocket and tossed him the deck, then rolled my dirty jeans into a draft stopper, or in this case, a light blocker and pushed them against the bottom of the door. I flipped on the light. "Okay, we're good to go."

Marty had the cards out and shuffled. "What'll it be?" his hand poised to deal as he waited for my choice. "War, of course." He grinned and dealt the cards.

"You know what would be perfect?" He didn't wait for an answer. "Coffee or hot chocolate. Wouldn't coffee be perfect? Hot, steamy cinnamon swirl…"

"Stop already and play." I pulled his pillow up behind me and leaned against the wall. The childhood game soon occupied us and I felt relaxed. I hoped my subconscious would take this down time to slot events so I wouldn't suffer the jitters that overwhelm me when too much hits me at once. I shifted my shoulders forward and scooped up a row of cards I'd just captured. Marty's comment about a hot cup of coffee stuck in my head. It would be perfect. I sniffed the air.

"You smell that?" I sniffed again like our childhood Beagle searching the air for scent of rabbit.

Marty grinned. "You look like Sadie Jane in the back yard. Are you going to start baying too?" His grin lessened and he inhaled. "Hey, that is coffee." Marty pushed my jeans away and opened the door. Colleen looked up from the living room. She held up her mug. "Coffee, tea?"

I popped up behind Marty and quickly found my slippers. "C'mon, you're the one who wanted coffee." Most everyone was up and dressed, with only one lumpy sleeping bag curled up on the re-made couch. Sunlight streamed though the sliding glass door. I looked at Marty's wrist and pulled it toward me. Twenty to eight! He yanked his arm away and reddened around the ears. "I must have looked at it upside down." He ducked his head, shuffled past me to the stove, and poured two mugs full from the coffee pot.

Dave walked in from the deck. "Hey, sleepyheads. Thought you'd be up and about earlier." I shook my head and smiled.

"We're up now. What's the plan for today?"

"No plan, just relax and enjoy now that this foolishness is over."

"I'd like to find that cemetery again and take some pictures. Do you think we could find it?"

Joan's head popped out of the sleeping bag. "I knew you'd want to go back." She sat up and pushed the bag off her shoulders.

"Good morning. How's the forehead?" I flipped a teabag into a mug and covered it with hot water. "Does it still hurt?" I handed her the tea and sat next to her on the couch.

"Pretty good." She touched her forehead. "Seems down. Bet I'll be a deep shade of purple." She sipped her tea. "How about you?"

"Fine."

"Yeah, that's Gracie's least vulnerable spot." Marty grinned. "She has the Morelli hard head, *capotosto*." He rapped his knuckles against his head.

"In more ways than one," Joan muttered.

"If you don't want to go back, that's fine. I'm curious about the markings, that's all." That wasn't all, but why tangle them in my personal web of the bizarre? I wanted to see the graveyard early in the day and without any meteorological interference.

"What markings?" Laurie asked.

I described the fog and the cold and explained that I had spotted the etchings on the side of the grave marker almost obscured by the ground. "I meant to ask last night about the religion on the island. I know St. John's is Catholic; is there another denomination on the island? Those markings and some of the carvings on the interior stones didn't look Catholic."

Garry spoke from the kitchen. "They're not. The interior graves, the ones closer placed, are from the original burial ground. The early inhabitants followed the cycle of Mother Earth, Brother Sun, etc."

From the startled glances around the room, I gathered that Garry had never shared his knowledge of island lore with anyone. Even Laurie looked surprised. Garry smiled sheepishly.

"Lissette was my great, great-grandmother and she did grow up on this island. My great-uncle inherited the entire kit and caboodle."

"What about Amelia?"

"Never had any children, remember? As a woman she couldn't inherit so the entire estate stayed with Joshua and Lissette's heirs. When Joshua died, the normal course would have been for all monies and properties to pass to the eldest son. Since then the law has changed and the family fortune has been diluted by having to share with everyone, even the girls." He laughed. "Progress, they call it."

"All of his heirs, or just the ones from the firstborn son?" Bob asked. "I thought I read in one of my journals that estate laws at that time were still bound to the firstborn."

"Right you are. My father kept our line going. He was the eldest son in a family of four daughters and then two sons. The law changed with my siblings. My brothers and sisters share the trust. Thank goodness for the change, I'm not the oldest son. It's not the Mother Lode we'd get if our line had had the first male heir." He slung his arm around Laurie's shoulders and pulled her close. "It lets me lavish her with a few baubles and beads."

We all laughed and nodded. Laurie was probably the least material person in the group. She seemed unconcerned with current trends and stuck to her tried and true brands.

Colleen nudged Ken. "You couldn't come from a line with a big payday?"

More laughter. The light mood felt good. We refilled cups and chatted about the plans for the day. Only Laurie seemed quiet and preoccupied. I approached her when no one else stood near. "You seem upset, or at least not thrilled with some of our plans. Is anything wrong?" Laurie stepped away and waited for me to move closer.

"What you and Joan described, what you said you felt and heard, she described over ninety years ago." Her lackluster voice matched her pale face and the feeling of talking with a ghost tingled at my neck and disappeared as quickly as it came. She must have read my face and rushed to explain. "In her letters; she describes the fog and more. I thought she must have been insane by that time."

"Amelia's letters?"

"No, Lissette's. They're not all letters, really—only a few letters back home and odd-looking ones smeared in spots like she didn't blot. Mostly she wrote in a diary of sorts; a popular pastime in that era. I am surprised she could write; it was not necessary in those days. I knew Amelia had been schooled, but Lissette's letters show basic knowledge, certainly not as smooth and articulate as Amelia's except for one small journal. That one talks about the cemetery and other items of island life. The sentiments seem beyond what a minimally educated person could write."

"Will you come to the graveyard with us?"

Laurie shook her head. "Not for me. I've been there in her words and I don't need to see it."

"May I read those letters and the journal?"

"I'll get them. You might want to take a look at the photo Colleen and Deb reconstructed yesterday." Her casual invitation sounded a shade nervous.

I'd forgotten all about that. "Deb, where's the puzzle photo? I heard you and Colleen pieced it up."

"Pieced is right. I still don't pretend to understand why someone would photograph and then cut up the same picture of the same rocks."

"Any idea when the pictures were taken?"

"Can't imagine. I mean there aren't any words like Kodak on the backs. I know they're black and white and faded. The size is odd...squarer than our rectangular photos, but I can't believe a professional photographer with a Hasselblad and tripod took these. Maybe one of those Brownie box things from the thirties." Deb pointed to the part of the counter being used as a staging area for the lighthouse artifacts, as we called them. They hadn't wanted to glue or tape the pieces in case the preservation people found fault with that method, so they laid the pieces on thick cardboard and used the glass and frame from a picture in the cottage to hold it in place. I picked up the puzzle picture and nearly dropped it in the next moment.

The photo showed a series of inusuit, each just like the one on the gravestone. Laurie must have suspected as much, her voice had been strained, her expression guarded. What in Heaven's name does she know? Maybe I've got the location wrong and Heaven's not involved.

"Strange, isn't it? Grace?"

Deb waited for an answer to a question I'd barely heard. Strange is an understatement. I focused on her. "Yes, strange. Good job on the pieces." My head wanted to take this new wrinkle and go process it somewhere, preferably in front of the grave. Deb continued. "It was tricky."

"Fair bit, I'd say," Colleen said. "What you're holding is five small photos taken of overlaying sections. Most picture puzzles are triptychs and you can line them up from left to right or the other way. A more complicated version is a quadrant puzzle where you need to line them up top left, top right, bottom left and bottom right. You have to find the right combination. This one was a penta-"

"More like pentagram," Deb sniffed. "We had the devil's own time figuring out the points."

I'd had enough exposure to pentagrams and those who used them for evil to last me a lifetime. I thought again how rushing up to Canada to escape my problems hadn't put much distance between me and them. At least I didn't expect to find a satanic cult in the woods on Christian Island. The name alone should ward off some evil, I hoped.

Joan joined us at the counter. "What do you mean, points?"

Colleen held the photo. "Until we oriented the inusuit this way with one of them being the top, one on either side of middle, and two at the bottom, we couldn't get the rocks to line up. See, follow the points…head, arms, legs, the entire picture becomes an inunnguaq."

"That's brilliant. Wait till the Huronia people see this. I wonder if the same person who took the photos is the one who created this elaborate puzzle. But why? I don't see anything incriminating or suspicious. There's a woman in the background too out of focus to identify. You can see bits of the lighthouse in the background. I don't get it."

"Is the inunnguaq pointing a certain way?"

"Hard to tell since it has two arms."

"Look at the bottom. Sometimes they'd put additional directional stones on the ground," Laurie suggested. She handed me a packet of letters. "They're quite interesting, poignant even."

"Thanks. I'll be careful with them."

"Laurie's right. Good call. Look at the bottom. Definitely extra stones pointing toward…nothing. I could see if they pointed toward the lighthouse or even the person, but this goes nowhere."

"Let me see." Joan leaned in closer. "Yep, dead end. Darn, I thought we were on to something."

Colleen tapped the glass. "There is that tree at the edge. It's pointing right at it."

"Why point to a tree?"

"We'll never know until we hike out there and have a look see, eh." Dave's matter-of-fact tone and the sparkle in his blue eyes indicated an adventure. "We've a bluebird day. Let's take advantage of it. Someone slap some sandwiches together, I'll make up coffee and tea thermoses. Bring your cameras. We'll find the exact spot that person stood to take those photos. Bring the frame too."

The idea of adventure appealed to most of the group. We scrambled to clean up, dress up, and get ready. I tucked the unopened packet into my backpack. We divided the food, beverages, and extras like candy bars, fruit, and cups into three backpacks for the guys to carry. Each of us carried our own camera and water bottle. Within fifteen minutes of Dave's suggestion we were champing at the bit, ready to explore. We headed toward the southern tip of the island. The weather indeed was bluebird: mid-thirties, sunny, calm air. The pine scent that tickled my nose vied for a few moments with a less natural, more acrid smell, like someone had struck a match. The crisp smell of outdoors won the struggle and I inhaled deeply. It was a perfect day for hiking and a picnic. We'd decided to walk to the lighthouse, start there, and find the graveyard on our way back. That took no time at all. The well-worn path on which we could stride two abreast made walking easy, and the rubble of the keeper's house came into view before we knew it.

Dave moved a few feet ahead in his mode of tour director. "Okay, let's pair up, cameraman and watcher. Make sure your partner doesn't step in a hole or off the edge while they're trying to line up a shot." We laughed and chose up teams. I wanted to be with Laurie, but she immediately took Garry's arm. They were the one couple who seemed less enthusiastic about this outing. Garry had been quiet on the walk over, missing a question from Marty about the connection between Garry's ancestors and the Beausoleil Band. He hadn't answered even when Marty repeated the question.

Colleen and Deb had paired up, but neither one of them had a camera so Marty joined them. They had the photo, however, so they immediately huddled and then took off for an area behind us. The leftover husbands established "base camp" in the open-air house. They pulled a ground cloth and space blanket from one of the backpacks and busied themselves setting up a picnic area, after which I was confidant they'd pop a LeBlatt from the fanny pack Bob carried.

Joan and I each had a camera, so Dave agreed to be our watcher. "If I topple over the edge while he's telling me, 'a little to the left, dear,' you'll be my witness." I shook my head. "Not if he makes it worth my while."

"Ah, the cruelest cut of all." Joan pushed the back of her hand to her forehead in a Sarah Bernhardt gesture. "Oww." I felt a tinge of guilt at her pain.

We decided to orient ourselves from the lighthouse and look for the spot on which our mystery photographer must have stood. I walked back a few paces and scanned the scenery, keeping in mind that the photo had been taken when the forest had been younger, with shorter trees. Joan moved further toward the trees, then turned her back to the forest and stared at me. I shrugged my shoulders and walked toward her; detoured around a gulley, and stopped to digest what I was seeing. The hairs on the back of my neck stirred and the feeling of *déjà vu* slapped me upside my head. "Joan, come here." I'd kept my voice low, but the panicky squeak came through. Joan walked toward me quickly. Dave looked up and I waved him over.

Joan's coat flapped open as she covered the last few feet in a controlled jog. "What's up?"

"Down would be more like it." I pointed to the inukshuk and the bones.

"Oh my God. Are they, I mean, animal bones, right, Dave?" Dave squatted for a closer look. "I can't tell for sure, but I don't like the looks of that one." He looked up at his wife. "I feel foolish calling in the police if this is nothing more than a cupboard for some animal."

Ken and Bob peered over Dave's shoulder. "Wondered what you'd found. Those short ones there and some of those look like small game." Ken stopped and leaned closer. "That one is police business."

Amid the comments and speculation swirling around my head, I head a low chuckle. Who would laugh at this? I looked at each animated face in the circle around me. No one had.

"Look at the inukshuk," Joan said. "It looks like it's pointing exactly at that bone. Isn't that bizarre?"

"Joanie, it's just pointing in that direction, actually toward," Dave swiveled on the balls of his feet, "that small copse."

My mind heard "corpse" and the cruel chuckle sounded again. I whirled toward the lighthouse behind me and saw his face in the window for an instant. The chuckle had been his, but how was that possible? Everyone had joined us by now; no chance one of them had stood at that window.

"This way, Gracie." My brother tapped my shoulder and pointed toward the small band of trees. Everyone else's focus followed the inukshuk's bidding, only I stood looking back. Marty's eyes asked.

I shrugged. "You know me, different drummer thing."

"Whole damn orchestra," he muttered and put his arm around my shoulder. I wanted to peek around his shoulder like a little kid wanting to be scared but knowing she was safe within trusted strong arms. The only problem was that no amount of strong arms could protect my mind. I didn't look.

"It does look like that, doesn't it?" Joan's face split into a smile. "I bet I know what's in there. Gracie, remember how we walked down into like a bowl? The graveyard is in those woods, I'm sure of it. We couldn't see the lighthouse because we were so low and the trees formed a dense block. If we had walked out in this direction, we would have known our way immediately." Joan shook her head. "I can't believe how turned around we were. I've walked here a hundred times."

"Never through the woods. Why go the long way around when the trail is so direct and easy?"

"I've never seen this inukshuk in all those hundred times. It's not that far away from the lighthouse–I can't believe we overlooked it."

"Maybe it wasn't here, at least not easily visible," Bob hurried to explain. "It's in a gulley, which suggests this area has been washed away over time."

"So all this could have been buried for some time."

"Not for eighty years. This is newer, much newer," Ken spoke. "Had this been uncovered by erosion and rain, the inukshuk wouldn't be in such good shape. And there's evidence of recent animal activity. See those misshaped strips near the center?" As though identifying the remains made it meaningful to my senses, I smelled the cloying scent of decay and put my gloved hand up against my nose. Only Laurie stood with her hand blocking the smell. Didn't the rest of them smell it? The stench rose from the gulley streaming into the chilled air. I stared at Laurie; her eyes reflected my confusion…and then it clicked. We both realized in that instant that only the two of us smelled death. We dropped our hands from our faces and each tried to mask our sensitivity with bland faces. I looked at Laurie and hoped my face looked more relaxed than her pinched expression.

"Laurie, what's wrong? You look ill." Deb asked from my side of the group. All eyes shifted to Laurie. She did look ill. Two bright spots on her cheeks stood out against a pale face. She shook her head and stepped back. "I'm okay, just a little cold." Garry put his arm around her and rubbed her shoulders.

"The wind's picked up a bit. Let's eat in the lighthouse. I don't think the house will block enough wind."

Food was the last thing I wanted, but at least we moved away from the pit. Dave and Marty took photos of the inukshuk and the bones, especially the one they suspected was human.

"You guys stay here and finish the outing. Now that we know how close we are to the cemetery, you can check it out after lunch. I'm heading back to the cottage to call Danny King. He should know about this, eh?" Dave looked at Bob and Ken. "Keep an eye on that one." He jerked his thumb at Joan and grinned. "I'll catch up with you at the cemetery; should be back in about thirty minutes."

We relocated the picnic to the lighthouse floor and Joan retold the story of the lightning strike. I loved the symmetry of the stones and the conical shape, and found myself drifting in thought to what it must have been like to live here and tend the light. Did Amelia long for companions her own age, for children, for a husband who treated her gently and kindly? Everyone seemed content to munch in silence. I pulled the letters from my pack and read the top one.

*Mrs. Havilland,*

*There's no call for those threats, wife. You are ungrateful and spoiled. Your kin visit too often. No natural brother cares to see his sister on so regular a basis. He wants only to drain my hospitality and stores to avoid using his own. The answer is still no. He will not be welcome here. Your duty is at my side and you had best return quickly. No amount of your tears will change my mind. I have said it, it is so. Do not disobey me, wife.*

*Your husband,*

*Burton Havilland*

The words sounded in my head as though spoken at my shoulder. I whirled and my plate tipped. Olives and carrot sticks careened across the blanket. I managed to right the plate before the potato salad slid over my lap.

"Whoa, slow down. What's wrong?"

"Hmm, thought I heard something. It's nothing." I waved my hand in dismissal and scooped up my errant food. So Amelia didn't want to come home to her *duty*. I didn't blame her one bit. The fact that her brother seemed to be a freeloader interested me. I thought he had land and a big house in Lafontaine. Havilland's meager stores wouldn't have meant much to him. As much as the *duty* part irritated me, there seemed to be a sadness in the tone of the letter. Could he have cared for her in his own gruff way, or was she part and parcel of the lighthouse?

"Beer?" Ken offered, sliding open the cooler.

"Not me, but I'll take some coffee." Marty held out his cup to Joan, who had unscrewed the top of the thermos.

"Me too." I lifted my cup from the blanket and passed it to her.

Joan looked up from her task. "One lump or two?" She grinned and picked an olive out of my mug. "Finders, keepers," and popped it in her mouth. "Mocha madness and olive juice, yum." She passed the mug to me and filled Marty's. Colleen's thermos of tea had more takers. The hot flavored coffee soothed my nerves; it calmed my jitters rather than caused them.

I opened the second letter, another 'how to' from Amelia's grandmother.

> *Dearest Child,*
>
> *I am pleased to read that your circumstances have changed in the regard of Mr. Havilland's demands. Perhaps he has realized his crudeness only pushed you further from his affections. How fortunate for you to have a respite from his proclivities. Should he renew his demands, however, remember you are his wife and must comply.*
>
> *On the subject of your island servant, be ever so careful with her. I have found that servants only smile to your face and do as little as possible behind your back. Keep your jewelry and important papers under lock and key. If you do not have a reticule with a key, I will send one with Joshua.*
>
> *Be certain to supervise any putting up of preserves and stores. Mustn't allow the simple creature to mistake poke for blackberries. Keep a close hand with your contact with her but do not fear using an open hand across her face if necessary. I have found that combination most successful.*
>
> *Fondly,*
>
> *Mrs. Arthur Pantier*

Yuck! What a toad this grandmother must have been. I replaced the letter in the group and packed it away. I'd read more when I could spread them out and get a sense of the timeline. According to those two dates, Amelia came back and had a housekeeper of sorts. I wondered if she negotiated that as part of her return package.

Laurie sighed and stretched. "This is nice. Let's just sit here, relax and tell stories, and snooze. It'll be like Scout camp," Laurie's voice pleaded, or maybe only I heard the slight panic in her tone.

"Were you a Girl Scout?" Marty asked.

"In Canada it's just Scouts. Both girls and boys participate. I stayed in until I left for University."

"That's about right for us too. You always think you'll stay involved, but school takes up more time."

I nudged Marty. "Would that be party time, ditch time, beer time, or girl time you're referring to?"

"I said 'time.' You don't have to get so specific." He grinned.

"Oh no, that never happens at University." We burst into laughter at Deb's deadpan statement.

Joan looked at her watch. "We'd better get going. Dave will be in the cemetery before we get there."

We gathered containers and papers and filled the backpacks, carried the trash out, and made sure to secure the door.

"Okay, bellies full, heads empty, we begin." We laughed at Bob's assessment. Laurie and Garry stood at the edge of the explorer circle.

"I think we'll head back. I've had enough outdoors for today." He pulled Laurie closer to him and smiled. "We won't wait up for you kids."

"Yeah, yeah, how you could choose afternoon delight over adventure is beyond me," Ken said.

"But not beyond Colleen, eh?" He grinned and pretended to cover his head from possible retaliation.

"Funny, very funny. Hey Laurie, meet us when it's over…what, maybe five, six minutes?" Good-natured laughter followed Laurie and Garry down the trail.

"Okay, now we have the serious explorers. Joanie, lead on."

"I can't be sure from this direction, but I think if we went into the copse from here we'll find it."

There was that word again. I could only hear "corpse." Was that because of the old lighthouse keeper or was it because of something yet to come? I chilled at the thought and shivered.

"I saw that giant shiver. Are you warm enough to stay out here?" Colleen looked at me.

"I'll be fine. Anyway, looks like the cottage will be occupied."

She laughed and slipped her arm through mine. "Come on, we'll be the rear guard." She chuckled and we hurried to catch up. I felt a chill, but tensed against the shiver.

Guarding against what?

# Chapter Thirteen

"I felt that. What's wrong?" Colleen kept walking, but turned her head toward me and spoke softly. "I've been watching you all morning...it's like something spooked you–and Laurie too, come to think of it."

Pragmatic, sensible Colleen had tuned in on my feelings. Funny, Joan described them as "creative, sensitive Laurie," "excitable, gutsy Deb," and "in-charge, logical Colleen." It's difficult to judge people by one dimension of acquaintance. Most people who knew me only as an ex-librarian from Regina or a children's author with severe writer's block may have glimpsed, but never guessed, at the inner machinations of my OCD brain.

"I can't explain this feeling that we're not alone when we come to this area." I spread my arm out. "If we keep choosing to come here, things will happen."

Colleen tensed and looked behind us. "What things? You're spooking me now." She dropped her arm from around my shoulder and walked a few steps in silence. I could sense that her logical mind hurried to process my words and their meaning.

"You mean the Band Council members who were playing jokes on us." She said it like a statement with only a hint of uplift at the end.

I shook my head. "No, not them. I told you I can't explain it. I wish Joan and I had never found the cemetery. In all the years they've been on the island they never stumbled across it, and now in three days I lead her to an island burial ground."

"Oh, you think this is about you somehow." Colleen's tone brought me up short. I stopped walking and stared at her.

"What do you mean? What are you saying?"

Colleen turned to face me. "Joan's mentioned your, uh, discovery, the skeleton in the wall? She said you've somehow become sensitive to those kinds of places, with bones I mean."

I stared at her, searching for assuring words to ease her discomfort in perhaps seeing her friend's wacky childhood chum in action. Bits and pieces of nonsense popped into my head, but I kept quiet.

"Honestly, Grace, it would make sense that you're feeling uncomfortable. I mean, for God's sake you found an entire cemetery full of bones." Her pinched expression begged for agreement.

I didn't mean to be uncooperative or to upset people. I tried to smile and agree; instead, I shrugged and walked past her on the path, hurrying to catch up to the others; hurrying to reach the field of bones she'd mentioned.

A flash of bright movement on the path ahead caught my attention. Joan's turquoise scarf contrasted against the bare trees and evergreens. I hurried to reach her, leaving Colleen to wonder at my silence. The trail narrowed and tree branches brushed against me. Joan must have heard me crashing through the brush. She stopped and greeted me.

"C'mon, slowpoke. What were you two doing back there?"

"Talking, walking. Guess we slowed down."

Joan looked behind me. "Where's Colleen? Thought you said you were together."

I turned and stared back the way I'd come. "We were. I mean, I picked up the pace a little to catch up, but she was right behind me." I thought of when I spotted Joan's scarf and how I veered around some bushes. Maybe by the time Colleen reached that spot she stayed straight. "She may have missed the turn." I waved at the trail. "I saw you up ahead and sort of headed to the right. Maybe you were out of sight by that time and she missed me. The evergreens are denser on this path."

"Ken turned this way, thought it would be more like bushwhacking." She grinned and shook her head. "Men. The easier path goes straight, that's probably what Colleen followed."

"Lucky me, spotting your flash of blue. I certainly didn't want to miss bushwhacking." We both laughed at my deadpan expression and Joan playfully punched my arm.

"It's great having you up here. Glad you came even if Harry couldn't make it. It's fun seeing Marty too, only don't tell him that. He's full of himself enough." Joan lowered her voice, aware of how sound carries. She walked ahead of me, apparently not willing to let me lead. I lost some of what she said when she turned forward for a few steps to negotiate some branches. "Incoming," she called and giggled as she let a branch go.

She was no match for the sister of four Eagles. I learned to watch the trees' proximity to the path after the first few whacks in the head on the trail with my older brothers. I parried with my forearm and ducked around the limb. The trail widened and I scooted up next to her. "You're out of your league, girlie. I'm glad I came up, too." I slipped my arm through hers. "You started to ask me something right before you got cute with the tree branch. What was it?"

"I wondered about Marty. I think he's a great guy. From the little you told me, it sounds like he's struggling with a lot. You know he's my favorite brother. Don't tell the others, especially Glenn." She grinned and her blue eyes sparkled with complicity.

I solemnly crossed my heart. "My lips are sealed." We burst into giggles and realized how loud that sounded in the still air. I stopped and pulled on Joan's arm. "Shhh. Listen." The crisp air settled around us and the treetops pushed back against the wind, creating a low whistle.

"It's the pines."

"Not that."

"What? I don't hear anything."

"I don't know. Sorry, thought I heard barking. Thought maybe there were dogs around."

"As far as I know Christian Island has no feral dogs…a few overexcited mongrel pups now and then, but no killer packs." Joan grinned. "Now, howling I've heard."

As if on cue, the sound of a mournful single note pierced the air. The hair on my neck stiffened against my collar; Ken and Debbie rushed down the trail.

"Did you hear that? Holy cripes, what was that?" Debbie's eyes widened with fear.

"We came back when we realized you'd stopped. Is anything wrong?"

The grieving sound came again, tinged with pain and loss. It wasn't human, but the message so clear I lost my thought in its anguish. If I could throw back my head and howl, would I heal? I moved my head back and felt the breeze more cleanly across my exposed neck. I tucked my chin to my chest and struggled to keep still. Am I absolutely bonkers?

"I wonder if that helps," Debbie asked as the third howl lifted to the skies. "I mean, do they howl from instinct to mark an event or do they howl from sadness to let go of their grief?"

"Whatever the reason, it sounds like it's coming from where we're headed."

"So maybe we shouldn't be headed there."

"Dave's meeting us there. We can't leave him." Joan's concern made the decision.

"Let's go." Ken led the way. "The others should be there since they took the better trail."

Joan stepped in behind Ken, leaving Deb and me to follow. We walked in silence; I think each waiting for the next expression of grief. The scream that rent the air had no sorrow, only raw fear.

# Chapter Fourteen

"Holy cripes, what was that?" Debbie grabbed my arm.

"You mean who. Colleen's the only other woman out here." Ken's voice shook when he realized the scream had to have come from Colleen. "Oh, God."

We ran the rest of the way down the trail and burst upon the clearing ringing the cemetery, out of breath and out of control. I'd seen Ken's eyes and I knew gut-wrenching fear propelled him across the ground to the centerpiece of the graveyard. That damn fog hovered directly above them, adding to the surreal quality of the tableau at first glance. Marty, crouched next to the large stone, held a wolf by the collar. Colleen stood across from him staring at the ground, her mouth open, nostrils flaring, her eyes almost rolled back in her head. There should have been sound, but it was as though someone had pressed mute. Bob's pose struck me as almost humorous, frozen half down or was it half up…and when they were halfway up they were neither up nor down. The childhood rhyme ran through my head.

"Colleen!" Ken's shout broke the mood and a second scream stalled in her throat. He'd reached her side and pulled her into his arms, pressing her head into his chest. The flame of fear in his eyes died, replaced by surprise, then horror.

Rightfully so. The body of a voyageur lay sprawled head and shoulders against the center stone, only this body bore no resemblance to the cloth and plastic dolls we'd been tricked with before. This body, dressed in the bizarre clothing, was Old Joe.

Marty stood and slipped his arm around my shoulder. The dog, which looked like a wolf only in my imagination, whined and stretched his head to lick his dead master's hand. The fingers held tight a strip of cloth covered with beading that looked familiar, but I couldn't place it in the confusion. The dog's whining and Colleen's sobbing seemed synchronized; the cadence calmed me in a weird way.

"Where's Dave?" Joan's voice rose from behind, almost like a wail itself.

"He ran out to the lighthouse to catch Danny King and bring him here." Marty opened his other arm to Joan and tucked her close. "Bob and I arrived first, but we started reading the markers on the outside circle. When Colleen breezed in, she started for the center and that's when we heard the dog. We couldn't see him from where we stood. The sound in here is weird, and the second howl sounded like it came from the trail you were on. We spotted the dog when we moved toward that end, but we still couldn't see the body. The dog broke off howling when he saw us and let Marty move closer to him.

"I was focused on watching the dog in case he changed his mind and wanted to shake hands with his mouth; I didn't see the body until I heard Colleen scream. I was about to tell her we'd been tricked again when I saw the blood, still wet. He must have bled to death while we were looking at the graves. I held the dog's collar so Bob could check for a pulse."

"The body was still warm. For the briefest moment I thought I felt a pulse, but nothing. He was dying behind this stone, alone." Bob rubbed his hand over his eyes.

"My God, how could this happen? Who would do this?" Joan looked around the circle like she expected an answer. "Why is he dressed like that?"

Marty dropped his arms from around our shoulders and stepped closer to the body. "All good questions. But there's one more. Isn't that the knife we found in the lighthouse?"

The hilt of the hunting knife stuck out from Joe's chest. The thought of that long, wide blade piercing skin and slicing through muscle, even cracking through bone, turned my stomach. I looked away. With my back to the scene, I saw Dave and Danny King rushing toward us. Dave's face showed enormous relief when he spotted Joan.

Everyone backed away without being told and King knelt quickly to check the body. He pushed the dog's muzzle away from the corpse and lifted the limp wrist, then touched two fingers to the man's throat. All procedure, by the book. He stood and moved out to our circle. "Who found him?"

Bob pointed to Colleen and Marty. "We all did. Walked in from there and found him."

"Where was the rest of your crowd?"

Debbie answered quickly. "We came up the other path, over there."

Danny looked around the circle of friends. "Why the two paths? There used to be ten."

Ten paths, I thought to myself, and then realized he meant ten of us. I smiled and regretted the lapse a moment later.

"Was that funny? All this makes you smile?"

"Of course not. I thought, I mean…" I felt the rush of heat to my face.

Dave stepped closer to King, who moved back at the advance. "Hey, Danny, lighten up. Grace didn't mean any disrespect." Dave had moved in half a step ahead of Marty, who stood tensed, his brows tightened…not to mention his fists.

*Geez, Grace. Think what you want, but keep a damn poker face.* I ducked my chin and stared at my boot tops. My gaze traveled to others' boots and beyond the circle to the dog still nuzzling his master's hand, coaxing him to rise and come home. The strip of cloth was gone. I kept my head down and raked the area with my eyes searching for the colorful bit and beads. If it had been pulled loose by the dog's ministrations, it would be on the ground near the hand. It wouldn't have blown away. One of us took it. I raised my eyes and began to casually look at people's hands and pockets. My own hands found distraction with a length of yarn from my pocket. Since most eyes were focused on Danny and Dave, I glanced toward hands then looked back at shoes or knees. Hands, knees, feet, knot; hands, knees, feet, knot. I worked that pattern until I'd completed my scan.

"What's she doing?" King's question brought my head up sharply and his eyes caught mine. I felt the blush on my neck. His dark eyes squinted at me; I didn't care for the expression.

"Tying knots, she's tying knots, okay? Leave her out of this."

Marty's voice rose. "She wasn't even here when we found the body. Haven't you lost precious time yammering at us instead of calling this in...or whatever you do out here?" He needn't have added the last bit. King's posture bristled and I saw Dave roll his eyes up.

"I'm doing just that. Where are those other two?"

Marty punched the air with his fists. "Who cares? Back at the cottage having a much better time than we are." He turned away from us and moved toward the dog.

"Don't go near the body," King warned.

Marty's shoulders hunched and he turned slowly. "I just want to get the dog. Thought I'd take him back with us; take care of him."

"No need. Joe's family will do that." He patted the side of his leg and whistled. The dog raised his head, whined, and lowered his muzzle to the cold, empty hand. With everyone's attention on the hand I tried to catch a guilty glance. No one seemed fazed by it. Maybe they hadn't spotted the cloth. I did seem to always find the odd piece; always won at *Where's Waldo*.

He whistled again and the dog reluctantly obeyed. King's fingers scratched the dog's head. "Good boy." The dog whined and looked back, but stayed put. "Joe was my uncle."

"Oh, shit. Hey man, look I'm sorry about what I said before."

My brother could be a pain in the ass and a touch arrogant, but he understood and valued family.

The crackle from the radio on King's hip covered an awkward moment. We all heard the transmission. He held the radio to his mouth and responded. "You can go. Use that path back to your cottage. I'll be by later, so don't go anywhere this afternoon."

An officer from the mainland had ferried across and was being driven to the path head by King's deputy. They'd have to hike in with their equipment.

I remembered why I wanted to revisit this place and looked longingly at the area where I thought I'd seen the carvings. The fog that had seemed menacing yesterday had rolled in, covered the same circular area, and lifted during our 'interrogation' by King. Nothing sinister, in fact the air smelled fresher and the quartz bits in the stones sparkled. I dared not meander around the tombstones; King had told us to leave. I didn't think I could convince anyone to come back with me, so it was now or never.

"Officer King, when I was here yesterday I believe I dropped my reading glasses. We came here to look at the cemetery, but also to look for my glasses."

Marty and Joan, from years of familiarity, caught the line and went with it. "She kept putting them on to read, then taking them off to walk. She's probably at the age where she should have bifocals." Her sweet smile layered over the smirking grin I knew lurked in her soul. *At that age, my butt! We're the same age. I'll get you for that one, my pretty.* I grinned at her and shook my head. Competitive Marty chimed in with, "I've told her to wear one of those chains around her neck to hold the glasses. I've seen them with pearls, very stylish. She prefers to stumble around having her friends–"

"Fine." Danny King held up his hand to stop Marty's chatter. "Fine. Take a few minutes as long as you don't go near the center. Understood?"

Heads bobbed up and down in agreement. King nodded and walked toward the path head to wait for the crime team. Debbie looked at me. "Eyeglasses? Since when?"

I smiled and checked my watch. "Since about five minutes ago. I don't want to come back here, but I really want to check out those etchings I saw. They look so much like the inunnguaq in the photo." I moved toward an outer ring. "I think I was over here."

"Those inusuit all look alike to me." Bob posed with his arms out and his feet set at shoulder width. He scrunched his shoulders up and stared wide-eyed straight ahead, statue-like in his stillness.

We burst into laughter and drew a glare from King, who stepped toward us but stopped as his deputy hailed him from the woods. We had a few minutes at best. The stones were so similar I racked my brain to think of any name or marking that would stand out. Lissette. Of course, Lissette. I wondered at her grave here rather than on the mainland with her husband. I meant to ask Laurie and Garry.

"Look for the name Lissette. That's the last name I remember before the fog rolled over me. I think it's the last row or maybe one in."

Colleen called out. "Here, it's here. I've been leaning against the damn thing…uh, darn thing."

"Too late, you blasphemed. The Fog will seek you out now and…"

"Knock it off, Deb, this place gives me the creeps." Colleen stepped away from the stone and bumped into Marty. Off guard and shaken, she shouted her surprise. "Oh cripes, you scared me. Don't sneak around."

"*I* was standing still, *you* moved." Marty waved his camera at me. "Never mind, let's get this done and get out of here. If this is the one, get down there and take a picture. We'll stand around you so they," he jerked his thumb over his shoulder, "don't wonder what the hell it is you're doing."

"Good idea. Move around here and look at the stones in this row. Okay, good. Grace, have at it; you're covered." Dave's jovial tone sounded like he drew some enjoyment from this dismal day.

I crouched at the base of the stone and moved the grass away. The markings almost blended with the stone, weathered over time. I hoped the photo would show something besides blank granite. I snapped several frames to make sure I captured something. "Got it." I stood and brushed the soil from my knees.

"Got what?" King's voice paralyzed me and apparently some of the others. Ken pressed something into my hand. Sunglasses? I'm a goner now. "What are you doing there?" He pushed through between Deb and Bob and stared at the grave in question. His squint deepened until his eyes looked like slits across a stony mask. "What's your interest in Lissette?" His tone as mean as the set of his face, he pinned me with his glare when I turned.

"What interest? Geez Louise, Danny, back off here, eh." Dave smiled and nodded toward my hand clenched around as much of the lenses as I could cover. "She found her glasses, just happened to be here."

I pasted a weak smile on my lips and slipped the glasses into my pocket. "Thanks for your help, everybody."

"Why'd she say 'got it' instead of 'got them'?"

My opinion of King shot up the scale. Why indeed? *Okay, team, who has this one? You know if I start explaining I'll be in cuffs by the end of a minute.* The silence seemed to indicate that we all underestimated Danny King because of his casual speech.

"Son of a bitch! Somebody get this dog outta' here." The explosive language and frantic barking distracted King. Joe's dog stood guard over the body, protecting it from any examination.

Dave motioned us to move. "We'll be leaving now." Our little troupe hurried around the stones toward the interior path.

"Not the island though, eh?"

"Absolutely."

We all seemed lost in our own thoughts on the trek to the cottage. I moved next to Ken and offered him the glasses. "Thanks, fast thinking on your part." He smiled. "Sorry I couldn't come up with something better."

"Good enough."

Marty came up behind us. "Boy, King looked pissed when he saw that grave. Why does he care about her?"

"Don't know, but he cares. Maybe Dave knows."

"I'm thinking Laurie and Garry know more about their ancestors than they say. I think that's why they went back; Laurie didn't want to go to the cemetery." I shrugged. "Just a feeling."

"Joanie's told us about your feelings. I'd bet on you."

Oh, great. What stories has Joan shared about her freak friend from back home?

Ken moved on to catch up with Colleen who, for someone who'd found a dead body, looked remarkably chipper. Marty slipped into Ken's spot.

"Exactly what you thought you left behind, eh?"

"What's with the 'eh'? You were born at Elmhurst Memorial and raised in the shadow of Chicago."

Marty grinned and quick-shrugged like a hiccup. "Dunno. I like it up here. It's fresh and honest. I feel like I did when we'd camp for a week. By the third or fourth day I'd always think about living somewhere like that." He play-punched my arm. "I blame you and those 'House on the Prairie' books you made me read when we played library."

"You loved those books."

"Yeah, I know. Something about fending for yourself, real community, the pioneer spirit…"

"Incoming!" Marty shouted and sprinted up the path.

My subconscious 'brother mode' and his pause had given me a nanosecond to react. The branch whooshed past my head close enough to brush the edge of my shoulder. *Close but no cigar, little brother. And payback is a bi…*

"Gracie, over here." Joan's voice added speed to my steps. She didn't sound scared, more excited, her voice pitched low and urgent. I hadn't realized I'd fallen behind. Without Ken and Marty to pace me I'd slowed down while thinking of the lighthouse, the letters, and the bone pit. We'd taken pictures, but would have to go to the mainland to get them developed. That could take two days longer if we really couldn't leave the island. I patted my pocket checking for the camera.

Joan stood off the path a bit staring into the woods, her hand held up behind her to warn me to slow. Ken, Colleen, and Marty stood statue-still a few yards beyond Joan; Dave and Deb weren't with them. Nine deer stood stock-still staring at them, the only movement their twitching noses scenting the air for predators.

"Take a picture," Joan spoke between clenched teeth to minimize movement.

How was I supposed to get close enough without startling them? I moved Indian slow and steady, willing my foot to 'feel' the ground before I stepped, keeping my eyes on the deer. I carefully pulled the camera from my pocket and moved it ever so slowly to my eye level. I saw them in the viewfinder and twisted the dial slightly to sharpen the focus. A split second before I pressed the button I saw the alert, then panic in their eyes and I saw the lighthouse keeper walk into their midst. Click. I heard the click and saw the herd scatter, so panicked that one ran directly at Ken and Colleen, forcing them to leap aside to avoid collision. I lowered the camera from my eyes and stared at the empty scene–no deer, no keeper. I raised the camera and viewed the area. A column of mist hovered over the spot where I'd seen him. Click.

"They're long gone, Gracie. Your first click must have scared them. It sounded like a shot." Joan smiled at me unaware of what I'd seen. "Did you get it?"

I nodded and walked past her toward the deer stand.

"Hey, the path is back this way. Grace?" I kept walking and heard her follow me. I scanned the ground trying to gauge the distance from where I'd seen the mist. "What are you looking for?"

"This." I pointed to an inunnguaq dead center in where the deer had stood and exactly where he had stopped. I tweaked the lens and took several shots. "This one is just like the one in the pit."

"How can you tell, they all look the same to me." I smiled at Joan's comment. "I mean, you see one inukshuk you've seen them all, especially during tourist season."

"I'd bet these have the same number of stones and the ones giving the direction have the same blue cast to them, like the builder used it as his signature."

"You're right. Do you think it's important?"

I shrugged. "Who knows? Probably means nothing, it's just interesting to me." I wasn't ready to tell Joan how I knew to look for it. I'd wait until the pictures were developed to see if I had proof or only more questions about what I'd seen.

"Wondered what you two were up to." Marty looked at the inunnguaq. "Geez, these things are everywhere." He looked behind us toward the path. "How the hell did you spot it from back there?"

I held up the camera.

"Oh yeah, right." He stared at me a little longer than necessary, as if he wanted to ask more.

"Where'd Ken and Colleen go?"

"To the cottage, where we should be headed. It'll be dark soon. They couldn't wait to tell the others about their close encounter."

Joan laughed. "Imagine the deer recounting his day, 'then this crazy human jumps off the path right in front of me.'"

I nodded and thought about what else the deer might tell, 'then this dead guy just walks up to us…'

# Chapter Fifteen

'Babel' could only describe the scene at the cottage. As many people present totaled the number of conversations bouncing around the room when Marty, Joan, and I entered.

My interest centered on Laurie who, up to this point, seemed reticent to talk about the past. She stood near Colleen, who sat in one of the wingback chairs. Laurie leaned down and took Colleen's mug. I moved closer to the counter, assuming she would be looking for hot water.

"Do you need a fresh bag?" I offered, removing the lid from the tea box.

"No, more water is all." She held out the mug; her hand trembled and I waited for a steady target.

"Colleen surely must be shaken; I guess maybe all of us," I smiled and nodded at her hand.

Laurie put the mug on the counter. I filled it and another for myself. "Are you having tea?"

She shook her head. "Been drinking it all afternoon. I'm ready for something a little stronger."

"I second that." Deb carried her empty cup. "I think Colleen is too."

"That settles it. Ladies, fill your mugs but leave room for a little something the Morellis add to their tea." I smiled and reached under the counter for the bottle of anisette liqueur Marty and I brought. I slit the paper seal with a practiced slide of my thumbnail, twisted open the cap, and waved the bottle under eager noses.

"Hmm, anise?"

"You bet. It's lovely in tea or coffee."

"Even better straight up." Marty pulled some small juice glasses from the cabinet and set them on the counter. He took the bottle from my hand and poured two fingers into each glass. "Cleans the palate, helps with digestion, produces beneficial enzymes, and if you drink enough you're a drunk with sweet breath. How do you want it–straight or sneaky?"

Marty's humor brought us into the kitchen to choose our poison. He happily poured and mixed. Joan tapped her cup against mine. "It's not *mano rosa*, but it hits the spot."

Caught off guard by her comment I nearly spewed tea through my nose.

"*Mano* what?" Deb asked. "There's a story here."

Joan laughed and nodded. "Oh, yeah. We were in high school and at Grace's house. Her parents kept their liquor in the linen closet in the hallway. Gracie decided we should create a drink–"

"*Who* decided?" I interrupted her. She had the decency to blush.

"Okay, *we* decided to mix a new drink. We used all the bottles."

Deb groaned, and Ken and Bob laughed.

"But we only used a little," I held my thumb and forefinger to indicate the amount.

"Yeah, but there were at least ten bottles up there," Marty grinned. "If you're going to tell the story, tell it right. Remember, I was there."

"Oh, yeah, we were babysitting." Joan and I dissolved into giggles.

The laughter felt good…each of us releasing the tension and fear of the day. The anisette helped too.

I watched Laurie drink her tea and accept a laced refill. She left the kitchen and sat on one end of the couch. Her face looked calm as she stared out the window.

Should I destroy her peace? Just 'cause I see weird things doesn't mean she does, but I think she does. Okay, okay, I'll ask; if she really panics, I'll stop. Having moved and seconded my plan, I sat down near her and followed her line of vision.

"The island is so different in the winter. I'm glad I got the chance to see it this way; just not everything that's happened." I waited. She didn't blink. "I mean from day one strange, unaccountable events…" I stopped, not certain of what more I should say. Our glances slid toward each other like magnet and metal.

Her eyes gleamed with anxiety and relief, perhaps a reflection of my own. "Let's go on the deck."

We grabbed our jackets and I refilled our mugs, adding more tongue-loosening, mind-releasing anisette to our hot tea. Marty touched my arm. "Don't drive anything with more horsepower than a lawn chair." He nodded at the mug and slid open the patio door.

Laurie and I pulled two cushions from the bin and settled our chairs facing the bay. Light from the cottage spilled over our shoulders. The deepening sky dipped into the water, coloring the evening inky blue, and leaving only stubborn streaks of pale gray above the horizon. A crisp breeze slipped across my face.

I waited for her to set the pace. Laurie held up her mug for a toast. "To freaks."

My hand stopped and my jaw fell in shock. I stared at her, looking for the hint of a smile around her mouth or eyes. Nothing. *Get over it, Gracie. It's not like no one's ever used that word before. Better than 'crazy.'* I tapped her mug, "To freaks of nature."

Surprise touched her eyes and the smile came. "Drama queen, eh?" She settled back in her chair and gazed at the water. "There's something odd going on, but it started years ago when I married into this family. The letters we picked up from Garry's sister were originally in our possession. When I read them or handled them, I would have the most bizarre dreams about Amelia and her husband. It bothered me to the point where I didn't want them in the house." She pulled her gaze away and locked eyes with me. "Do you think that makes me a freak?"

Her abrupt question startled me. I turned the tables on her. "Since the first day at the lighthouse I've seen Burton Havilland three times. Do you think that makes me crazy?" There. The 'c' word was on the table.

A genuine smile spread across her lips and she shook her head. "No, I think it makes us allies." We chinked mugs again and enjoyed a companionable silence.

Allies. I like that. But against whom or what?

# Chapter Sixteen

Laurie and I spent an hour sharing what we'd felt, heard, and seen since arriving on the island. With our heads bent close and our voices kept low, we must have looked like conspirators. We agreed that our conversation should be kept private.

"My husband Harry understands. I don't know if he *understands*, but he doesn't scoff. He's English and his parents were academic types. He grew up more tolerant, and I think the stories about the Druids helped." I wanted to keep some semblance of lightness between us.

Laurie smiled, then shook her head. "Must be nice. Garry doesn't know what to make of it. He gets this panicky look on his face and then stares at me like I'll crack and shatter at any moment." She rubbed her hands together. "Maybe I will someday." Her soft comment was made more to herself, and I wondered if she realized she'd spoken out loud. She straightened her shoulders and rolled her neck. Her poignant tone disappeared, replaced by a brisk 'outline' voice that must be her trademark at her job. Staring out at the bay, she held up her gloved fist and started enumerating…lifting a finger for each point.

"One. The letters talk about her lack of control over her life, her sadness at having no children, his infidelity, and finally a hint at his cruelness.

"Two. The standard law of the time left her no recourse. The matriarch of the family tells her that to keep her man at home, she needs to offer sex more often.

"Three. Her brother seems to be her only friend and ally."

I longed for paper and pen. I had a photographic memory, but lousy auditory recall.

Laurie broke off her list and turned to me. "Which is odd. They hadn't really been close as children since they weren't raised together."

"They weren't? Why not?"

"Gold. Amelia's father left home to make his fortune in a gold strike. He took her two older brothers and a cousin to help him. He never returned. They'd staked and worked a small claim that gave up a good vein. The father succumbed to 'gold fever' and wouldn't leave when Joshua and the cousin came home. The other brother chose to stay in the gold fields. By the time Joshua returned with enough money to establish a nice living for his mother and sister, Amelia had been married off to Havilland."

"How sad for them. I can't imagine." My thoughts turned to my own brothers.

"According to several letters, Joshua spent more time with his sister in her home or at least on island than he did on mainland in the beautiful home he purchased. That's how he came to know Lissette, his wife. He must have met her during his time on island. Actually, no one saw it coming according to Great, Great-Aunt Beatrice's account. After Amelia's husband died, Joshua brought her home. It wasn't until a month or so later that he rushed back to Christian Island and married Lissette."

"Couldn't stand to be away from her?"

"I hate to puncture the fairy tale, but more likely she found out she was pregnant and he had to make it right."

"Ah, the old bow-and-arrow wedding," I giggled. "But he lived on the mainland. I mean, island girl versus townie."

"Joshua was in mid-negotiations with the Band Council to build a hotel on island for rich people who wanted to get away and play on the bay."

"Sounds like something the Office of Tourism would promote– get away to the bay and play, play, play. We should mention that to Joanie; it might help her restoration project. Joshua needed to keep the Band Council happy, and marriage to the island girl he impregnated was on the table."

"Absolutely. I will say in Joshua's behalf he must have cared for Lissette; I mean they had eleven children, for heavens sake."

I shook my head. "Don't blame that on divine intervention. Joshua and Lissette had rabbit genes."

"I suppose it was those cold dark nights up North. What's a couple to do?" Laurie grinned and shrugged.

"Do about what?"

We both jumped a bit. Garry had walked up behind us. I hadn't heard the door slide open. He placed his hands on Laurie's shoulders. "What are you two buzzing about out here?"

His tone, his timing…something bothered me. I hoped Laurie would be vague.

"Just chatting about your side of the family…you know, your rabbit ancestors, Lissette and Joshua."

"Does that make you related to anyone on this island?" I hadn't thought to ask that before.

Laurie waved her hand in a loose figure eight. "Probably third cousins twice removed or something. I've suggested he–oww, that hurts."

"Sorry, getting the kinks out. Your shoulders are tight." Garry loosened his grip and I saw the fabric of her jacket slump. "Came out to tell you two it's supper time."

I stood quickly. "Thanks. Didn't realize the time. We'll talk again, Laurie. I'm fascinated by the history of this area." My ploy to disguise our real topic may or may not have worked; in the deepening night, faces were hard to read. I hurried inside.

"Picking up the slack for my…" Marty's stage whisper dripped with drama. "Oh, there you are, sister dear. No, no don't give it a second thought." He swiped his brow with his hand. "I've fulfilled the Morelli obligation to prepare dinner for these lovely people."

The table practically bowed under a huge antipasto tray and two bowls of mostaccioli and meatballs. "Somebody circle the day in red," I teased and picked a carrot stick from the tray. "This is a first. Must be the island air. Can we bottle it?"

Marty selected a small stuffed mushroom cap and pushed it toward my mouth. I chose to eat it rather than wear it. "Mmm. Delicious. What did you do?"

"Oh, a little of this, a little of that. Joanie and I created it." He beamed at Joan and she grinned.

"I helped," Dave insisted.

"That's true. We couldn't find the cayenne pepper until Dave remembered he'd put it in his tackle box."

A few raised eyebrows solicited further comment.

Joan waved her hand. "Don't ask. Some weird island trick for fishing."

"Does it work?" Bob asked.

"What broke?" Colleen asked coming out of the bedroom.

"Nothing broke, we're talking about fishing."

She wrinkled her nose, inhaling deeply. "Smells delicious; kudos to the chefs. Doesn't smell like fish, what kind is it?"

We burst into laughter. Colleen looked at the table and realized her error. She grinned. "You sure can lose something joining a conversation in midstream."

"Midstream? Is that a fishing joke?" Ken asked his wife.

"Fun-nee." She pushed at his chest. "Out of my way, I'm swimming upstream here." Groans and grins followed her to the table.

Amid the good-natured teasing and talking and somewhere between the salad and the meatballs, my mind caught hold of a thought and began to chew on the idea of 'midstream.' What if we are reading the letters *'in media res'* and not from the beginning? Would earlier letters make more sense or change our perception? Would that explain the picture puzzle and the need for it? What had someone tried to hide and from whom?

"Christian Island to Gracie. Come in, please." Dave sat to my left and held a basket of bread in one hand and the plate of fried zucchini in the other. "Got a fair bit of a backup here."

"Sorry, must have slipped away for a moment." I took some from both and passed them on. Dave passed the grated cheese and giardiniera.

"You did seem to be somewhere else. Peaceful spot you skedaddled to?" Dave's question brought unwanted attention.

"Mmm," Joan swallowed quickly. "She used to do that all the time. We'd be in the strangest places…I mean people, noise, you name it, and Gracie would 'slip away,' as she calls it."

From the corner of my eye I noticed Garry look sidelong at Laurie. I stared across the table at Marty, willing him to not, for once, take center stage with a Gracie story. No use. His lips were twitching to talk, waiting for Joan to finish. The knock at the door stopped him cold.

It would have been better to let him talk.

# Chapter Seventeen

Officer King stood in the doorway. He removed his hat when he crossed the threshold and turned slightly to motion two men waiting on the stairs to enter.

A posse. This can't be good.

"Evening, Danny," Dave called from the table. We had all stopped talking and eating.

"Sorry to interrupt your supper. Got to have some conversations with you and one of your guests."

Oh, God, not me. Pleeease, not me. Not Marty either.

My quick prayer worked, he didn't want either of us.

Dave stood and moved around the table, pausing behind Joan to squeeze her shoulder. "Doesn't look like you're going to let it wait, so let's talk. Or have you something else in mind? They don't look like they're here to take notes."

Danny King, to his credit, allowed the ghost of a smile to touch his lips before the line tightened to almost straight. He shook his head. "I'm here to ask you to come down to the Council office. And him too." He pointed to Garry. "You was the other fella not accounted for when Joe was killed."

The reason for the extra manpower became apparent. Danny asked, but we understood there was no declining the invite. I noticed the holstered gun under his open jacket and wondered if the other two men were armed, or just strong.

Garry pushed back from the table, knocking his chair over. Both men jumped forward. "Wait," King cautioned.

Garry must have realized his error in exciting those two. His voice sounded clear and calm. "Officer, I am accounted for. I was here with my wife the entire time."

I expected Laurie's head to bob up and down. She sat motionless staring at Garry. Her eyes registered confusion, then fear. At that point she slowly turned in her chair to face King. "That's right, all afternoon." Her normally soft, smooth voice cracked with hoarseness.

Garry looked smug. "There, see."

"You'll pardon my saying, but she's your wife. What else would she say? Anyway, we wouldn't take her statement as gospel." King dipped his head at Laurie. "Nothing personal, ma'am." He looked around the table. "The sooner we can get these questions answered the sooner you can be back. We've got supper waitin' too. Don't want to drag this out."

The distinct 'oout' pronunciation reminded me I wasn't in the United States and that I should keep my mouth and my mind shut. The mouth I thought I could accomplish; the mind, well, all bets were off. I watched as Dave and Garry pulled their jackets from the kitchen pegs.

"We'll be back shortly. Just a formality," Dave assured Joan and Laurie. They left quickly with one deputy leading the way for Dave and Garry, followed by King, and ending with the other deputy guarding the rear as he gave a last glance to make sure we hadn't moved.

Colleen and Deb converged on Laurie, coaxing her to sit and have something hot to drink. She did look a little shocky. Joan seemed in better shape; perhaps she was convinced that Dave played no part in the murder. I remembered Laurie's eyes when Garry named her as his alibi, and I'd bet she didn't have that same strong sense of innocence about her husband.

Geez! What am I saying, that Garry killed Joe? No, not that, but something. They weren't together all afternoon. So where'd he go?

I knew I'd feel like a crumb for asking, but I asked anyway. "Laurie. When we were out on the deck and Garry came up to us, he didn't come from inside the house." I paused to give her a chance to talk. Her eyes questioned me. "I didn't hear the door open." Some of the confusion in her glance cleared. She spoke slowly.

"He knew it was time for supper," she offered.

Bob cleared his throat. "That's because I went out to the car and saw him near the road. I asked him what he was doing and where he'd been. He looked at me kind of strange and said he'd just come out for a smoke. "Filthy things, but I love 'em," is what he said." Bob hesitated. No one else spoke. He shrugged and exhaled the deep breath he'd taken. "Bothersome thing, I didn't see any cigarettes and I've never seen Garry smoke."

"That's because he quit when I did three years ago next month, before you started curling with us. We quit cold turkey on a bet from Dave," Laurie explained.

Joan nodded. "Cost Dave two bottles of Wild Turkey Whiskey to commemorate their one-month nonsmoking status." She turned to me. "Remember, you brought them up last time you and Harry visited?"

"Yeah, along with black olives, pepperoni, giardiniera, and Italian beef–all the luxuries of civilization," I joked.

Bob's face stayed stern. "Has anyone seen him smoking this week, or smelled cigarette smoke for that matter?"

"More importantly," my brother spoke softly, "did anyone see him when we returned?" The question hung in the air.

"We rushed in with the news and started telling Laurie. Colleen got a little pale, and Bob suggested she lie down for a bit." Deb looked around the room like she was trying to recapture the immediate past. "Dave made a phone call–"

"To whom?"

"I don't know." She looked at Joan, who shrugged and shook her head. Deb continued, nodding toward me. "Then you arrived, we poured drinks, you two went out, and Marty and Joan started puttering in the kitchen." Deb paused and looked around the room, her clear green eyes recapturing the immediate past. "I didn't see Garry, I'm sure of it." She turned to Laurie. "Was he here all afternoon?" Her gentle tone held no accusation. I think Laurie knew her friends only wanted to help.

She leaned heavily against the chair and slumped to the seat. Her sad eyes brimmed with tears when she lifted her face. "When we got back, he made a phone call." She held up her hand to stop the question. "I don't know who he called. When I asked, he said he was just checking on something, nothing important. Then he said I should rest. I haven't been sleeping well. We made tea and both curled up with blankets on the couch. I must have slept soundly because I didn't wake up until you all came bursting through the door with that awful news." Laurie wrapped her arms around her chest. She stared at the table. "I don't know when Garry left. Or why." The last part was spoken so softly it barely carried to my ears. She lifted a tearful face. "I begged Garry to stop tracking Lissette. I thought he'd stopped. I was thrilled when you said you'd sold the cottage—one less excuse for him to be on this blasted island. When Dave called to invite us, I didn't want to come. Then you three found those letters and photos and he went on the alert again."

The astonished faces around the room would have looked comical if it weren't for Laurie's sobs. She buried her head in her arms crossed on the table as Colleen and Joan attempted to console her.

I wanted to ask more questions about Garry's interest in his ancestors. I felt my fingers itching to act if my mind couldn't, and pulled a short length of blue cording from my pocket. The cord felt comforting in my hands and I tied and untied a figure eight while I watched Laurie's bunched shoulders slow their jerky motion and finally relax. I still couldn't jump right in with the questions bursting in my mind. I continued tying and untying, searching for my own calming mechanism. I stared at my hands and envisioned the blue cord as a wave rising and falling, rising and falling. Most people can tell when someone is staring at them. When you're OCD you can sense it immediately, but you can't always respond until you finish the task at hand. I knew when I raised my eyes they'd all be looking at me or my hands which fumbled to complete two more sets.

The part of my mind locked to this function held me fast, but the sliver that resisted wondered why Marty didn't run interference for me, cause a diversion, distract the crowd. I hadn't heard him speak for a while. He was behind me…what if he left? Where would he go? I don't know, but what if he did? *Turn around, Gracie. Keep an eye on your little brother.* My mother's voice sounded in my head as it had twenty years ago. I was in third grade learning cursive writing. I'd practiced the letter 'I' across Marty's back using a magic marker. My mom found me gently forming the letter on my sleeping baby brother's bare skin, crooning "keep an 'I' on your brother, keep an 'I' on your brother." She took me to the doctor the next day.

I jerked my last knot free and looked up, searching faces but not finding one. "Where's Marty?"

Joan swiveled her head scanning the room and shrugged. "Don't know. He was here a minute ago."

I hurried to the room we shared. Empty.

"His jacket is here," Joan called after me. "He wouldn't have gone out without it."

I spotted the edge of his duffle bag under the bed and shamelessly searched it for the thick hooded sweatshirt I knew he'd packed. Nothing. At least I knew he wouldn't be cold doing whatever he decided to do out there.

"Where's he going in the dark? He doesn't know the island." Joan's concern touched me. "I mean, even we don't run around out here in the dark."

"At least it's not totally dark. The moon's rising and it will be a bright one." Bob's comment drew our attention to the windows, and sure enough, the moonshine scattered the shadows, leaving only deep corners in darkness.

"Marty knows his way around in the woods. He's been on many treks." I heard the pride in my voice.

"Oh, yes that Eagle thing. I suppose Lord Baden-Powell would be proud."

"Not just that, Bob. He's always been a hiker and camper, long after he left scouts. He's done some climbing with his buddies and several backpacking trips, one or two around Lake Superior. Didn't you see all the gadgets on his belt this afternoon?"

"I'd suspect he'd be some sort of geologist or forestry person. Seems a waste to be a pharmaceutical panhandler." He smiled. "No disrespect."

"He started out in premed, washed out of that early on. By then he had a wife and baby to support and grabbed the first high-paying offer that came down the pike. Phaeten Pharmaceuticals recruited him through an executive headhunter. Six figures and perks was hard to turn down."

"Lordy, he'd be a pauper here. In fact, I think I read you Americans are starting to buy your drugs from us."

I nodded my head. "That reminds me, I've five orders for those 222 capsules. Joanie brought some back years ago and now we're all hooked. I'm the mule this trip."

The laughter eased some of the concern for the three men. Laurie moved away from the harbor of Colleen and Deb and shot me a glance. I couldn't tell her intent and decided to wait for another signal. It came sooner rather than later.

"After the day I've had, I think I'm ready for some of Grace's coffee. What's in the pot?"

I knew she wanted to talk. "Oh, that's old. I'll make fresh. C'mon, I'll show you the proportions. I brought extra coffee from Joyful's Café for all of you to take home." She joined me at the stove and beneath my normal strain of coffee instructions Laurie whispered, "I'm so confused by all of this. There are more letters. I need to work this out; should have done it sooner; maybe Garry wouldn't be in trouble if I had."

"Laurie, Garry wasn't here this afternoon, was he?" I figured she wouldn't give him up that easily. "No one thinks Garry had anything to do with Joe's death, at least no one here." I remembered the look on King's face and the fact that he'd brought backup. Maybe she should be calling an attorney. Speaking of calls, who did Dave call? And where the hell is Marty?

I noticed Laurie staring at me, seemingly trying to decide something. "He wasn't here." Her shoulders slumped and she looked on the verge of fainting. She leaned against the counter and lowered her head momentarily. I ran cold water in a glass and pushed it into her hand. She sipped, then downed the entire amount. "Thank you." Her color heightened and her eyes cleared.

I filled two mugs and stepped into the pit to claim the chairs near the Franklin stove. Colleen, Ken, Debbie, and Bob had cleared the table and started a lively game of Yahtzee to pass the time. That left Joan curled up on the couch trying to read. Her eyes kept darting from page to door. Laurie followed my glance. She touched my hand and nodded. At that moment I caught Joan looking up and crooked my finger, motioning her to join us.

"Thanks, I'm all sixes and eights over this." Harry used that expression all the time. I'm not sure of its origin, but I got the gist of it. Harry. Is he at sixes and eights spending his holiday with Will in England, or is Lily there to smooth the edges of his new fatherhood? *You could be there, Gracie. He invited you; you turned him down, told him to join you later on his way home. And Lily won't be there to pick up Will until the end of this week. She is his mother after all. 'Mother' sounds lovely, doesn't it? Not for you, Gracie. Not for you.*

"…we were waiting until Garry could do more research."

Laurie and Joan had started a conversation. I shook off the melancholy and tried to catch up. "What kind of research?" I asked, hoping she hadn't said.

"Property laws, inheritance laws, things like that. Garry has several colleagues at University who teach that type of law and he'd been meeting with them lately. When Dave called to invite us, Garry immediately cancelled two other appointments."

"I have a feeling it wasn't our stellar hospitality that encouraged him to come."

Joan's dry humor eased the building tension. Laurie leaned forward and squeezed Joan's shoulder. "You know we love coming here, but this time Garry seemed driven to come. I think he would have found a reason to come on his own if Dave hadn't called."

"Why, what's here that he needs to see?"

"Maybe someone he needed to talk to who wouldn't come to him."

"Or couldn't," Joan explained, "Some older Indians live in housing for the elders. I've heard that some of the residents are over ninety years old; they would have been youngsters when Amelia lived here. Maybe Garry wanted to talk to them and knew they couldn't come to him."

Laurie stared at Joan. "I think that's it. He kept trying to track Lissette after she left the mainland."

"But she's dead. We saw her grave. Her family brought her body back to the island where they felt she always belonged. If it weren't for the fact that Joshua got her pregnant, they never would have allowed the marriage to a white man."

Laurie ran her hands through her hair, pushing it behind her ears. "Laurie, doesn't Garry believe Lissette is dead?"

Laurie's eyes filled with tears. She shook her head slowly. "No." Her emotion-choked voice tugged at my heart, and I felt like a heel for pushing her. Somehow we'd all become involved in Garry's investigation, and someone had died maybe because of it.

Joan had refilled Laurie's mug. She handed it to her and slipped her a tissue. Her comment echoed my thoughts. "We're sort of all in this together. Anything else you can think of?"

Excellent. Coming from a friend, the question seemed easier to answer.

Laurie began slowly, "It began with those damn letters." Her anger seemed to give her the gumption to continue. "Some of them were similar to the one we read about Amelia's naïveté, but later ones were filled with demands and decisions made by the lady of the house: notes to the tradesmen in town, elaborate menus, even notations about a ledger she kept."

"She was the mistress of the house when she returned with her brother. Why is that behavior so unusual?"

"By then, she wasn't the mistress of the house. Joshua had brought home his pregnant bride and those duties would have been Lissette's."

"Look, no disrespect intended to Garry's great, great-grandmother, but I didn't get the sense that she was educated in the ways of the society of the time or even for that matter in academic areas. Am I wrong in that assumption?"

"One would think that, but one would be wrong. We have Lissette's letters home filled with stories of parties and events. She was educated to the level of the time for her position. Garry's sister has Lissette's ledger of household expenses. We laughed over it once…there really did exist a category entitled egg money in those days."

"How did you get her things? I mean, I can see how the ledger stayed with the house, but what about her letters home?"

"That is an odd story. They came to us from the Georgian Bay Native Friendship Centre. Garry's sister Lissanne was in Midland and visited the centre. She signed the book, and an alert docent spotted the family name and called the curator. He offered Lissanne a special tour and ended up showing her the letters. She told him about the Amelia letters, and somehow they decided to offer each to the other for copying. The curator thought that would round out his information since so many of the original letters referred to the natives and Christian Island. Lissanne was thrilled to find out her great, great-grandmother had been educated. Win-win."

"And that's what prompted Garry's interest?"

"Yes, he found some mention of property rights, but also some dates that didn't match up between the two women's letters."

"But why does he think Lissette is still alive?"

"One letter written in her hand is dated seven days after her death."

# Chapter Eighteen

"That would do it." Further comment stopped with a heavy knock at the door.

"They're back!" Laurie jumped up from her seat.

"Why would they knock?" I wondered out loud. Bob stepped in front of Laurie and pulled open the door; a blast of cold air swirled through the opening. Marty stood on the stoop holding a cardboard box.

"Geez, about time." He hurried into the room and down the steps to carefully place the box on the floor. His actions were so gentle I was afraid he'd brought home a stray. It wouldn't be the first time. "Whew, that's heavier than I thought."

He pushed the hood off his head and his forehead glistened with sweat. It, whatever *it* was, must be heavy. Marty knelt next to the box, pulled his knife from his pocket, and easily cut away the sides of the box to reveal an inukshuk.

"You went out in the woods in the dark to get a souvenir? Are you crazy? There's a killer out there and you're collecting rocks?" My voice shook with anger and relief.

Ken put a hand on my shoulder. "She's right, Marty, that was damn silly of you to take a risk to get a souvenir. You could have waited until tomorrow…you can't hardly move about without tripping over one."

"Not this one. It's from the gravel pit we found today. I took some measurements, walked off some yardage, and lifted it intact. By tomorrow I'm afraid this one would be gone, and this one has something to do with current happenings–maybe even Joe's murder."

"Then it's evidence that should be turned over to solve the murder."

"Maybe, or maybe it's evidence pointing to another murder."

"Now that's nuts. Don't go around stirring up something you know nothing about. I think it's time we leave and get back to a normal life." Deb's firm voice prompted nods from most of the group;

the dissenting voice surprised me.

"Let him explain. Why do you think so, Marty?" Laurie asked.

"I didn't suspect anything when I first saw it, but the more I thought about it–where it was placed and what it pointed to–I remembered the stain on the arm that indicated direction." The brown stain stood out on the edges. "I think that's blood."

Surprised voices filled the room.

Marty waved his hand for quiet, and continued. "I also think this could be the murder weapon."

"Whose murder?"

"That I don't know yet. This rock has been protected by the soil and shale on that part of the island for years and years. Someone left it out in the open to guide someone else to a grave, or to hide the murder weapon in plain sight until help could arrive, or maybe both."

"Why not keep the rock in a safe place and turn it over to the police?"

"Maybe the person didn't have a private place to hide it, but wanted someone to know."

Marty stood and shook his head quickly. "That's all conjecture. Can we determine instead when some kind of severe land change could have occurred to bury this?"

"What do you mean, like an earthquake?"

"Actually, more like a mudslide if there is such a thing on a flat island."

"One actually begot the other, so to speak." Ken cleared his throat and continued. "When the Huron constructed the fort, they built up the land for strategic venue by scraping the surrounding soil into a huge mound. When a small quake hit this area in the early 1900s, the abandoned fort's foundation cracked because of the loose soil beneath it. That caused the stone to crumble, which in turn caused a bit of a mudslide from the ensuing rains. You've seen how quickly and heavily it rains on the island. It's totally possible that your inukshuk has been buried since the beginning of the century and only revealed after that last storm."

"That's another reason I wanted to get it tonight. There is another storm brewing; the temp has dropped drastically. It might even snow."

"That's not good. The ferry tender doesn't like to run in that weather."

"What, a little snow? It's a big boat. Anyway, don't they have a contract or something to keep running?" I looked at Joan.

"It's not the snow, it's the temperature. The bay freezes up quickly from the shallow edges out. As for a contract, they work for the Band Council. I doubt they'd care about a bunch of cottagers stranded until the thaw." She noticed my worried expression.

"It's been warm all week; it's not going to deep freeze now." She patted my arm. "Hey, didn't mean to worry you."

The back door pushed open and Dave, his eyes flaring with anger, hurried through. Garry wasn't with him. Laurie rushed to his side, asking the question on our minds.

"Where's Garry? What's wrong?"

"That bunch of horses' asses. They're keeping him overnight—some crap about his being a flight risk."

"Why?" Laurie's question seemed rhetorical. We all knew why. They suspected Garry of stabbing Joe.

"He's got no alibi for when the murder occurred. He's been asking questions about Lissette. He met with Old Joe last night. He filed some kind of deed that Joe was protesting...would have protested to the Band Council meeting tomorrow night."

"What deed?"

"I don't know; something about the parcel of land where the fort and the lighthouse stand. I didn't know Garry had dealings with the Council."

"He doesn't," Laurie said.

"He does now. Danny King said his uncle had confided that a descendant was trying to claim land under his right as quarter Indian blood."

"Why would Garry want land here? Everyone leases their land for the cottages from the Band Council."

"Everyone who is white," Joan put in. "Remember, Lissette's descendants could be entitled to some rights. I don't know all the particulars, but I think it's not enough to be a quarter Indian, you also have to establish residency...something like that."

"How do you know that?"

Joan shrugged. "I read it in some of the research I did. The Band Council voted in some tough bylaws to keep quarter-bloods from trying to force the Council into selling or building on the island. Even owning a cottage or living on the island in the summer months doesn't count toward residency."

Laurie kept shaking her head. "I don't know what he wanted to do. He's had several meetings with a friend, John Larchmore, who specializes in real estate trusts and deeds; his specialty is land dispute. He's been in court with cases dating back to the 1600s."

"Could he have been questioning the land trust for the Beausoleil First Nation, or his right to own land?"

"I don't know, and I don't care. What are we going to do? Does Garry have to stay there; shouldn't we get a lawyer?"

"It wouldn't hurt, Laurie. Can you call this Larchmore and get someone from his firm that handles, uh, well, handles things other than business law?" Dave's awkward phrasing made me aware of the seriousness of Garry's case.

"I don't know anyone's home number, even if I knew who to call. How can this be happening?" Laurie twisted the tissue between her fingers. "What can we do? We can't leave…" Her voice caught in her throat and the rest of the sentence came out in a sob.

The men shot glances across the room at each other while the 'fairer' sex whipped out tissue; refilled her mug with hot, sweet tea; and offered our shoulders. Laurie calmed down enough to be induced to try to sleep. Marty had squatted near where she sat at one point and spoken to her quietly. He placed a small tablet in her hand, brought her a glass of water, and waited judiciously until she'd swallowed. I stopped him on his way to the sink.

"Marty, you told me…no, you promised me that you hadn't brought any drugs with you. You broke your promise and now you're prescribing for Laurie, putting her at risk." He casually rinsed out the glass and placed it upside down in the drainer. I wanted to grab him by the ear like our nonna would have. Instead, I continued my tirade in a low whisper. "What do you know about her health history? What–"

"I know she's not allergic to aspirin or codeine. That's what I gave her–a 222 tablet." Marty stared at me, his glare part anger, part disappointment.

"Oh, aspirin. I…Marty, I'm sorry. I thought…aspirin." My stammered apology sounded lame.

"Oh, Yes, aspirin." His harsh mimicry told me how I'd hurt him.

"I'm sorry." I reached for his arm, but he pulled free and walked away.

Wonderful. Couldn't I have kept my mouth shut? Did I really think my brother would hand out drugs willy-nilly? Guess I didn't think, period.

I could beat myself up better than anyone I knew. As a child I'd overheard my aunts talking about me at a family party.

"Did you see her at the table, eating the food in order, one bite of this, one bite of that, all around the plate, always the same pattern? And what about when we made the sign of the cross? She signed herself with her left hand too. Mike should do something." My Aunt Minnie didn't like quirks and didn't like me. She was my dad's brother's wife. Aunt Mary came to my defense, she always did.

"So the child likes patterns. I admit it's awkward at times, but she's a good girl, doesn't cause any problems.

"You think so, Mary? I think Minnie is right, Mike spoils her." Aunt Edna always sided with Aunt Minnie.

Within the hour we'd all taken to our beds knowing tomorrow would be busy and stressful, depending on what happened to Garry. Marty had pretended sleep when I finally came in and carefully climbed to the top bunk. Years of familiarity gave him away. I knew his 'pretend' tone from the real sonorous one. I'd have to work on him in the morning. It bothered me to have him angry with me; it killed me to have him disappointed in me. I finally found sleep and hoped my brother would follow.

"Holy Cripes!" Marty's voice shouted from somewhere outside our room. I jumped from the bunk fearing another voyageur dummy or worse.

It was worse.

# Chapter Nineteen

A wall of white lay beyond the sliding door. I rubbed my eyes to make sure they hadn't filmed over with sleep. Blink as I may, the white remained and the eerie effect unsettled me. I wasn't alone. Ken and Colleen rushed from the bedroom, nearly tripping on Dave who had moved his sleeping bag and cushion to the kitchen floor.

"Can we get out?" were the first words Colleen spoke and the panic in her voice set the tone. Ken put his arm around her shoulders.

"Of course we can. This is bay-effect snow blown across and up against the high points around the water." He sounded confident, but not positive. "Right, Dave?"

Dave shrugged. "Seems right, but I don't know for sure. We've never been island side during winter."

Bob and Debbie had hurriedly yanked at all the cords to pull the blinds on other windows aside. Each time, a wall of impenetrable snow lay beyond. The density of the drifts kept natural light out and the thought of being in a cave or in an avalanche popped into my head. I knew neither to be true and a giggle escaped my lips. Heads turned to stare at me, and suddenly Joan laughed from her position at the back door. She lifted the curtain and bright sunlight streamed through the small window.

"There's absolutely no snow on this side. Not a flake."

We rushed to crowd around the window until Joan, flattened against the door, squeaked a protest. She elbowed a space and pulled open the door, sending cascading light into the gloomy den the interior had become.

"This must be what a bear feels like waking up from hibernation," Ken joked. It had been only minutes, but the sunlight was a welcome sight. None of us would make it as spelunkers.

We rushed into jackets and boots and out of doors. I'd never seen anything like it. The bay side of the cottage had disappeared under a wave of snow, yet a few feet on either side were only wet spots indicating there'd been moisture at all. And then several feet more, and the next cottage succumbed to the white wave. This effect went on for several cottages on either side. Camera shutters clicked like a staccato beat until we'd shot all we could without risking life and limb to get down to the water, or rather ice.

The mandatory first-snow-of-the-season snowball fight started when Joan lobbed one at Marty. He retaliated and pursued her relentlessly and accurately. Joanie must have forgotten that Marty had been a pitcher in high school. I tried to help, but my aim was crap, especially since recently recovering from a broken wrist. I inadvertently hit Debbie and my "oops, sorry" was lost in her retaliatory volley. Colleen drilled two at Bob and Ken, and effectively drew them into the target zone. Whoops and hollers filled the air along with snowy missiles, some on target, some hopelessly off. Marty, Colleen, and Ken launched their snowballs from strong arms and even stronger wrists, sending the orbs errorlessly and forcefully at us. It was like watching the hatchet toss competition at Jamboree. Dave's lobs had too much hang-time, Bob's weak shoulder prevented him from throwing any distance, and Joan, Deb, and I were crummy shots. My wrist ached after a few minutes, so I began throwing less and ducking more.

The 'aces' joined forces and pinned us down near the car–strategic for them since they stood between us and the snow. Our icy ammo ran low, then out. With surrender imminent, we hatched a hurried, crazy offense–we outnumbered them and decided to rush them, chanting "melt, melt, melt," and making silly faces as we charged. Joan and I switched to warrior princess Xena's "*e-ya, ya, ya, e*" as we charged our target, Marty. He was laughing so hard he couldn't get much zip in his defense and, with our momentum we pushed him backwards into the snow. Bob had swept Colleen off her feet and ran the distance to a bigger drift, where he dropped her while Dave and Deb brought down Ken.

Marty staggered to his feet, wiping the snow from his eyes and spitting out a bit of pine that mixed in with the face wash. "No fair. What kind of defensive tactic was that, especially you, Joan? How'd you run straight with your eyes crossed like that?"

We burst into laughter and almost missed Laurie's frantic call from the back porch.

"Hey, everybody, hey." We turned and ran toward her, reacting to the tone of her voice.

"What is it? What's wrong?"

"Nothing. King called, they're bringing Garry back. Isn't that great?" Her smile split her face from ear to ear. We rushed up the steps and piled into the cottage, pulling off wet boots and jackets as we went through the short hallway.

Laurie continued to grin and explained further. "I'd just set the kettle on thinking you'd all soon want something hot to drink when the phone rang. I never expected that news."

Joan and Deb pulled mugs out of the drainer. "Hot chocolate or tea?" Marty quickly moved the inukshuk to our bedroom. Dave's eyes scanned the room looking for anything suspicious. We spotted the batch of letters on the coffee table at the same time; I scooped them up. "Best we put these away from prying eyes too." I carried them into the small bedroom and pondered where to hide them. My glance fell on the freezer I'd been using as a step up to the top bunk. I shuffled the letters carefully into the heavy plastic bag they'd been in and tucked them between cod fillets and frozen hash browns, then walked into the main room a moment before the back door burst open. Garry rushed through and made a beeline for Laurie, who threw her arms around his neck gripping him like a hungry boa constrictor. Danny King stood quietly at the doorway; no backup with him. Dave motioned him in, but the officer shook his head.

"We're not finished investigating, but there's nowhere for him to run–ferry's not running. No sense our feeding him. The winds blew across the bay all night; there's a fair bit of ice on our side. Won't be running two days at least, and there's another front coming in. Did you mean to experience winter on the island?" The hint of a smirk played at the corners of his mouth. He tapped the bill of his cap and left.

We hurried to Garry's side, asking questions about his detention. "Did they say anything about the knife?" Dave asked.

"They can't be too concerned or they wouldn't have let him go." My brother's comment brought a smile to most lips.

"He was serious about not incurring the expense or inconvenience of housing a suspect if they didn't need to. Very frugal, the Band members." Bob swept his arm at the wall of snow smothering the bay side of the cottage. "There's no way off the island."

"Boats, snowmobile, something?" Marty suggested.

"Nope. Too much ice for boats; not enough ice for snowmobiles. We are in the part of winter the Indians call, loosely translated, 'when the gods look away'."

Marty wouldn't give up. "What about in case of an emergency?"

"You mean like a murder investigation?"

Bob's attempt at humor fell short; no one even smiled.

"No, like an illness or breech birth or heart attack, like that kind of emergency."

Joan answered. "There's a Band clinic on the island with trained personnel. The doctor comes out every two weeks to monitor the care being given. If someone knows they need surgery, they go mainland for that. Some first-time moms go mainland the last couple of weeks of their pregnancy, but most stay here and use midwives or doulas."

"Doula? What is that, like a witch doctor?"

I poked Marty in the ribs, but the laughter his remark caused eased the tension in the room. I leaned over and stage whispered, "I'll tell you when you're older." More laughter and the subject was dropped.

Laurie and Garry moved off to sit alone. Marty engaged Bob and Ken in a conversation about the weird weather patterns on the island. I heard him saying, "Wish I'd studied meteorology." Colleen and Deb stayed close to the kettle, refilling mugs and discussing food for the day. They'd volunteered to cook today's meals. I gravitated toward Dave and Joan.

"I don't understand the Band Council thing. Do they have total autonomy from the Metro Police? Are they their own little district or province?"

"More like country," Dave smiled. "The treaty of sometime in the 1800s gave the islands of Georgian Bay to the different tribes who had settled and populated the area. Each tribe has their own governing body and police. Of course they still are under the auspice of Ontario Province, sort of."

I laughed at his grin. "It sounds complicated. How did the Huronia Historical Society get permission to do anything with the lighthouse?"

"Ah, well, that's different. The land under and around the

lighthouse does not belong to the First Nation. It's government land, and since the lighthouse has never been decommissioned it still shows on the books as government property. The Band Council has tried repeatedly to get it decommissioned so the land would revert to them."

"What difference would it make?"

"Big difference." Dave warmed to the subject. "If the historical people get it as a landmark and use it for tourism, by treaty part of the revenue goes to the Band Council and any jobs created must go to Band members. If, however the land stays on government rolls, at some point a developer might pick it up at auction or even negotiate to purchase it outright."

"They wouldn't have to give the Band any money?"

Dave shook his head. "Not a sou. Now, some members might profit if they could swing the band vote toward development if a deal were in place to pay the Band money up front. A savvy developer would want to sweeten the pot and keep the Band Council on his side by offering money for votes, high-paying construction jobs, permanent jobs in the facility, etc."

"So they would give them money?"

Dave shrugged. "It depends. That might be a safe, savvy way to minimize trouble or problems with the site, but some developers might not see it that way, preferring to bring in their own crews, set up makeshift housing, and pay premium for their own staffs once completed. Could depend on who's backing the project: conservative English, moderate Canadian, rabid French."

I laughed at his assessment. "Seems easiest to leave it be altogether. What did Old Joe want? Could he have run up against someone who wanted something else more?"

"I've been wondering the same myself. Joanie, what say we take a little trip in to the grocery store? Maybe we can hear some talk."

"Can I go with you?"

"Grace, these people are standoffish enough to us, let alone American strangers."

"Oh, yeah, ugly American, eh?"

"Although, when you say it that way you sound more Canadian than Joan."

A loud knock at the door stopped all conversation, but before anyone could open it Danny King pushed in, slamming the door against the wall. He stood feet apart, arms tensed at his side as though ready to fight, his usual ruddy complexion blotched from the cold and, I suspect, anger.

"I don't care to be made a fool. Not by anyone, least alone cottagers." He spat out the word like a bitter rind. "The Council's had a call from Benningfurth at the Huronia Society, meddling old fart, asking if the Council knows of any letters concerning Lissette Banelieu. They'd like to display them with the ones Mrs. Hamilton found concerning Amelia Havilland. Those letters are Band property." He held out his hand, expecting what he wanted to drop into his palm.

Joan's face paled. She glanced at me, then quickly looked at King. Too late, he'd seen her mark me. He moved toward me. "Maybe it wasn't Mrs. Hamilton who found them. You're the American," he consulted a notebook he pulled from his pocket. "Grace Marsden. What do you know about these letters?"

I thought quickly about what I could say. I didn't want to mention Garry at all; he seemed to be in enough trouble. A lie could be verified by phone to Benningfurth. I decided to go with half truth and half lie. "I found the letters in the lighthouse, and since they were on government land, we brought them to the Huronia's attention. Left them for photocopying, I think was the plan?" I looked to Joan for a quick assist.

She nodded. "Handed them off to the secretary."

"There was nothing in that lighthouse. We checked…" King seemed to think better of continuing. He switched gears. "What about the Banelieu letters? Can't say *they* were in the lighthouse." His nasty tone sounded more personal than professional. I wondered if he had a vested interest in the land.

"And another thing," he swung round on the others, "which one of you tourists took the inukshuk we uncovered the other day?" His voice grew nastier and nastier.

Marty's voice sounded angelic by comparison. "Officer King, I think it was we who discovered it and called you. Wasn't it moved yesterday?" I knew from years of listening and watching Marty weasel out of trouble that he played the part of wrongly accused well.

King fumbled with the leather strap on his field radio. He

worried it between his fingers. It looked comforting and I began to itch to feel that sensation. *Sure, Gracie, just walk up and grab his radio.*

"We were involved with a murder, if you remember." He glared at Marty.

"Of course," Marty murmured. "Maybe the snow covered it or the wind may have knocked it apart. Were there any rocks strewn around?"

"The wind ain't gonna knock 'em over and the snow's melted, just water in the pit." King paused. "Some rocks lying about." He seemed to hesitate, then made up his mind. "But not enough to have been that inukshuk. Don't play me for a fool," he shouted, "I want it back. Don't make me tear this place apart."

My brother just couldn't leave it be. "Don't you require a warrant or something up here?"

Dave rolled his eyes and started to speak, but King moved faster. He backhanded Marty across the face and snarled, "Stupid American. Too much of your television."

We stood frozen at his action. I moved first and stood next to my brother. "Are you okay?" He held his jaw and moved it gingerly side to side like a puppeteer working on a doll. He nodded. I didn't know what ultimate authority King had over American citizens, and I didn't want to find out.

Dave moved between them. "Little harsh, eh?" He smiled affably, with his hands palm up at his side.

King bristled at Dave's insinuation. "If I find out any of you are involved in my uncle's death or that you've taken anything that belongs to Band, 'harsh' ain't gonna be close. I've got you for the next two days, at least." He backed away from Dave, then turned and stomped out the door.

I realized I'd been holding my breath and released it in a short huff. Similar sounds told me I hadn't been the only one. Dave went to the back door and peered out before closing the door. "Don't see his vehicle; don't think he would have walked. He's gone. Let's get the story, as we know it, nailed down. If we're trapped on the island, so is he. King can't get any more help from the mainland so he's basically a one-man show with a one-man posse."

"That means we can't get any help either." Laurie's small voice tugged at my heart. I knew the terror of watching helplessly while your husband is accused of an ugly crime. I wanted to tell her it would be all right, but I'd known beyond doubt that Harry was innocent of murder. I didn't know that about Garry, and I felt terrible not to be able to believe in him.

"No, but it means we have time to figure this out for ourselves before Dudley Do--" Marty stopped. "Sorry, didn't mean anything."

Bob smiled and clapped him on the back. "Hey, we call the ones that are a pain in the arse Dudleys too. Don't we?" Dave, Ken, and Garry nodded and grinned, each one in turn clapped him on the back, each *pat* increasing in force until Marty winced at Garry's heavy hand. Marty rolled his shoulders and grinned.

"Okay, I get it. I still think we can put this puzzle together and get an idea of who might want the old gent dead. Joan, do you have any paperwork on the deeds or laws concerning first right of refusal or anything like that? Any plats of survey?"

"If what I had to carry in is any indication, she has half the Huronia records in those boxes," Dave said. "Don't know what you were thinking, we're supposed to be on holiday."

Joan blushed and took a long sip at her tea. I knew exactly what she'd been thinking–it was classic Joan.

"You weren't thinking that you might engage your friends in a 'seek and sort' mission? Perhaps something to while away the hours on a winter's night, on an island, where we couldn't get away from you, were you?" My exaggerated tone caused smiles and some raised eyebrows.

Joan's beet red face answered for her.

Marty impulsively put his arm around her shoulders. "That's great, we can begin immediately. Do you have as much as when you made me and Glenn sort all your papers from K through grade eight?"

Astonished faces turned to Joan. She squirmed under Marty's question and arm. "I didn't *make* you. I said you might as well help me before we watched the movie."

"You wouldn't let us watch TV until we finished," Marty explained, "Everyone was somewhere that night and Gracie and Joan offered to 'sit' for us, even though we didn't need a sitter. She came over with two big boxes. All smiles she was until we were alone, then," Marty paused for dramatic effect, "the real Joan took over. No

TV, no popcorn until we did the 'seek and sort.' It took hours, we missed Star Trek."

We were all laughing, even Joan. My brother's description lightened the mood and set the stage for our own version of 'seek and sort,' this one infinitely more important. "C'mon, I'll help you carry them." He squeezed her shoulders and let go. "Lead on."

"Okay, okay. But I want to set the record straight. Those two boxes were only K through grade four. Only a *loser* would have only two boxes for eight years." Joan flounced toward the sliding door, then stopped. The snow lay against the glass.

"I'll tunnel in from the side. Temp is too low for any melting." Dave grabbed his jacket and gloves. Bob followed him. "I'll help you."

Joan and I cleared the table and countertop, offering last refills on hot water. We heard the two trailblazers laughing as they dismantled the wall by pushing and shoving through the snow. No one thought to bring a garden spade in January.

Within thirty minutes we saw movement at the sliding door. Bob's grinning face appeared, plastered against the glass about three feet above the deck. He crouched against the door, cleared the snow from around his head, and pushed it back behind him. He appeared to be shoveling the snow out the way he came in to create a space for his body. Eventually he stood and repeated the process until we could tell by the increase in light that the tunnel was complete. Bob motioned for someone to unlatch the catch; Garry slid open the door. A line of disturbed snow fell into the opening, but the hood of snow descending from the roof stayed intact. Bob handed boxes to Garry until five boxes sat on the kitchen table. He pulled the door closed and waved. We heard them on the back porch a minute later, stomping and laughing.

A rousing cheer went up when they entered the kitchen. "Impressive, it's like a snow fort." Marty's tone seemed caught between wanting to sort the papers and wanting to play in the fort.

"Yeah, well, I wouldn't recommend using it. There are about fifteen feet of snow above and about four feet behind that unstable tunnel. Hate to see you caught up in a mini-avalanche."

"Just in case," I poked Marty in the ribs, "remember to spit before you dig."

We left three boxes at the kitchen table, put one on the countertop, and one on the coffee table, then divvied up to investigate each box. The counter box turned out to hold a headdress, the type we'd seen on the voyageur dummy.

"Why'd you need to bring this?"

Joan shrugged. "I took everything marked Christian Island; didn't have time to check each box. That's what we're doing now."

Her impeccable logic brought groans from Dave and Bob. "We risked our lives to bring in Indian headgear?" Their good-natured joking kept the mood light.

We gave the countertop people a box from the kitchen table and began again. The coffee table people had the chaps and footgear that completed the ensemble from the countertop box. Two boxes 'sorted,' only three to go. The remaining boxes contained files, papers, photographs, and currency from that period.

"Let's organize this by eras: pre-1850, 1850-1900, and 1900-1950. Separate everything by those dates, even the currency. Let's see where the preponderance of material is and work from the least to the most, eliminating or reassigning as we go." I hadn't meant to take over but we…I… needed to organize.

"Is that library talk?" Deb teased.

Marty looked up from his box. "That's OCD talk, loud and clear. And a tip I'll share–don't let her find you've put them in the wrong pile." He slid his forefinger across his neck.

"Sounds a bit like Joan." Deb looked at us.

Joan patted my shoulder. "I learned from the best."

"Except she," Marty nodded at me, "has a photographic memory, so don't think you can change those piles." The laughter at my expense started the project on a fun note.

We separated in silence, only occasionally commenting on an item. Within one hour the papers were laid out in three piles on each surface. We combined the two 'remote' locations with headquarters and marveled at the size of the middle pile, 1850–1900.

"Okay, let's take the most current era over to the counter. We're looking for any mention of development, island politics, land sales, anything." Marty carried the substantial pile to the counter. Already he wasn't following the plan…the smallest pile was the pre-1850. I stood near the small stack of parchments and noticed one with a wax seal. Cool. Like Nancy Drew in *The Clue in the Old Album*. My fingertips itched to follow the design of the wax.

"No, no, no." Garry wagged his finger at me. "We sort one pile at a time. I believe that was your suggestion." His forced smile flashed, then faded when he spotted the seal. He swooped up the documents and moved them to the other end of the table. "Out of sight…"

*Who the hell does he think he is? What an ass. Look at him, fist leaning on the papers like a hairy paperweight. He'd best not damage them.*

Dave's low whistle attracted everyone's attention. He held up a sheaf of papers fastened across the top by a thin band of paper. "This could explain some of the tension. New World Builders brought suit against the First Nation for breach of contact. First they said 'yes,' then they fell back on treaty status and pulled the plug."

"Too bad we don't know more about this New World group. Does it say what happened?"

"No, this was the first volley." Dave kept scanning through the pages. He stopped and looked up, a confused expression covering his face. "Maybe Bob can explain New World Builders," Dave held out the papers to him, "since his name is listed as a principal."

Bob's hand stayed rock steady when he reached for the extended sheaf. His cursory glance told us he already knew the sum and contents of the document he held. He lowered it to the counter and made no comment.

"No wonder you knew so much about deeds, developers, what they'd offer, what they wouldn't. You'd been through it with your company," Garry said.

"Not my company, for God's sake. You know I'm in real estate–"

"Yes, houses of course, you've sold all of ours, and the occasional condo home or flat. But developing an island? Bit of a grandstand by our standards."

"Dammit, Garry. Don't look up your arse for the answer. I was an investor, bought in when the plans were still on the drawing board. New World moved along slick as could be, getting every variance, meeting every paper deadline. I invested more. The last bit of money gave me principal status. Worst investment I ever made. Company is still tied up in court battling with the Band; some hotshot Indian rights attorney took their case pro bono. They've thrown everything except a tomahawk at the company. New World, last I was informed, was making one last-ditch effort, then walking away and looking into a development on Hope Island."

"Why didn't you tell us? You're always going on about real estate being the best investment. Didn't think your curling buddies might want a bit of that luscious pie?" Garry's tone changed from sincerity to sarcasm, lashing out at Bob with that last comment.

Bob looked at each friend in turn. "At first I thought about suggesting we all invest as a mini-company, then I thought I'd just mention it after curling one night. In the end, I became greedy and wanted to succeed really big without you. At its peak I did decide I'd been a scum to not get you all in and planned to bring a prospectus to curling. The Monday before is when everything started falling apart." Bob ran his hand through his hair. He looked deflated and embarrassed. "Be happy I was such a greedy bastard, or you may have lost your garters." He walked around the table and grabbed his jacket. No one made a move to interfere. Debbie glanced from face to face, took her coat, and followed her husband. If she hadn't known before, there'd be a whole lot of talking going on out there.

I pulled a length of cord from my pocket and leaned against the counter, out of the fray of the chatter around me. I slipped the rough cord through my fingers and my thoughts turned to Debbie. What if she had known? Was she out there consoling him or chastising him? What did this reversal in fortune mean to them? Did they lose a bit, one third, one half, most of their money?

Loop, lose a bit, one third, one half, most. Loop, lose a bit... He had said negotiations still raged. *Would Joe's death mean anything in the scheme of things? Would he consider killing as an option? Why not? You don't know him and it's not like people haven't killed for less. Not people I know. Really? I seem to recall...Okay, okay, just quit it. I can't think with your incessant comments.*

"You don't know him, really. And people have killed for less."

My head snapped up. Had I spoken out loud? It happened

sometimes.

Garry stood facing Dave and Ken. He hurried to defend his comment. "It's true. How well do we know each other?"

Dave snapped a terse reply. "We could have thought that about you." He stared across the table until Garry looked away. "Let's remember that we are friends and have been for years before we throw someone to the dogs."

Garry hunched and rolled his shoulders and leaned his head back. He lifted both hands, palms up outstretched. "Look, I'm not thinking straight. I don't believe Bob's guilty any more than I am. It was stupid of me to say those things. Please, don't tell Bob. I know how much money gives you principal status. If he lost that, he could be in severe financial trouble."

I moved to a chair in the pit and listened while they discussed what, if anything, they could do for Bob and Debbie. Seemed to me that pending financial ruin was a great motive for murder. Garry's comments, given sincerely, I guess, made Bob appear desperate.

Desperate people do desperate things. My dad always said that. He had a saying for everything; sometimes in Italian…those were from Nonna Santa, my grandmother.

Marty plopped down on the floor next to my chair. "Fine time we're having. Did you not come here to leave murder and mayhem behind?" He smiled and reached for my hand holding the cord, deftly wiggled it from my grasp, studied the pattern, and continued the loops. "You always did do these better than I did, actually better than most of the guys in the troop. Except for…" Marty held the word and waited.

"Knotty Pine," I answered, a grin shifting my mouth. Burke Pine had been an older scout in the troop when Marty bridged. He was one of those needy and nerdy kids–a difficult combination in a boy's life. He always carried a length of rope with him, always demonstrating new knots he'd learned–knots beyond the scope of the requirements. The adult leaders pointed to Burke as an example to emulate. Sometimes boys pick up another boy's true colors before adults do. You want to see the good in all kids when you're an adult. Burke fooled even my dad until the campout when Burke gagged and lashed a younger scout to a tree and left him there for two hours. Afterward, he'd told the story that he and the younger scout had a bet that the kid could free himself, and if he couldn't he would give Burke his scout dollars from popcorn sales. The younger scout, although frightened by the experience, corroborated Burke's story.

What if something like that was in play here? Maybe the Band Council had opposing sides, maybe one side wanted to scare us off the island. King mentioned there would be a Council vote later in the week. Maybe Bob was here for that reason. I'd have to ask Joan if Bob asked for this specific week. Or Garry…he could have a vested interest if his bloodline benefits from a certain vote. What if a few Band members dared or bet each other to find ways to scare off the cottagers or garner more votes for their particular side of the issue? What if Joe got caught in a shift in tactics? Maybe he didn't want to continue with the plan. Could it have involved hurting one of us?

Bob and Debbie returned and I caught a few murmured apologies on both sides. After taking a moment for everyone to settle, Marty suggested we continue our review of the papers.

"Might as well, we're not going anywhere. It's snowing again." Deb waved toward the windows.

I moved to the side of the table where I'd seen Garry put the document with the seal. It wasn't there; the other papers he'd scooped up lay there face up. He glanced across the table at me and his eyes screamed a warning. Did he want me to remain silent for his sake, or was someone else involved?

Marty lifted two small stacks bound with pink ribbon. "Joan, why don't you and Gracie take these two small packets?"

"Sounds like a plan." Joan turned to me. "I think there's another small box with more letters wrapped in this ribbon in our room. I didn't see it come in with the rest. We'll get that later."

I whipped the soft, silky ribbon over and between my fingers, soothing my skin, and shaping the material into soft granny bows. The time to confront Garry had passed for now…I'd find a way later. I glanced up and caught him staring at me. Did he think I'd lost my nerve or my mind?

Joan and I took the next hour and delved into Lissette's unhappy life. She'd been thrilled when Joshua returned to Christian Island to ask for her hand. He'd brought wedding gifts, bribes by my standards. Lissette didn't know it, but she'd been sold. The tone of her letters changed slowly, mentioning the strict supervision put upon her by Amelia, her sister-in-law. Duties that fell to other wives were handled by Amelia: market lists, household budgets, menus, clothing allowances, etc. Lissette had to ask permission to visit the dressmaker, although based on how many children she had, she needed only maternity clothes. Two were so close in age she must have become pregnant the night after she gave birth! No saying 'no' in those days.

Joan moved her head closer, "This Joshua is starting to sound like an ass. He must have known it was too soon to have sex."

"A different era. No acknowledgement of birth stress, no inkling of postpartum depression. It's a wonder moms didn't snap."

"Yeah. I know they always talk about strong pioneer women, but listen to this."

*I fear for Joshua; he acts so listless and lonely. The other one taunts him and bullies him even though they are so close in age. An evil spawn, the Shaman would say. I do all that I can to protect him, but soon I'll be confined with his little brother or sister. I hope this child brings us joy.*

"Holy cow, evil spawn? What an awful thing to say about your own child. She must have been in full blown prepartum, postpartum, something."

"She never had a chance to stay un-pregnant long enough to clear her mind. How awful to feel that way about your own child."

I nodded slowly, remembering how my father had taken me aside the day after they came home from the hospital with Marty. My dad had tried to explain that Mom would be very tired and maybe say and do things that didn't seem like her. He asked me to be helpful and not argue with her during the day. He told me if Mom got upset, to go upstairs and get Nonna Santa right away. I learned years later that my mother suffered from manic depression and had become increasingly distant and disturbed with each pregnancy.

The tone of Lissette's letters became listless. She wrote of outings and events with no enthusiasm. She seemed drained of joy. The last one in the bunch had a different tone…incredulous bordering on angry.

They think I'm stupid. Think I haven't watched. That I don't understand. I am First Nation from ancestors of honor.

"Honor?" I spoke the word out loud and regretted it.

"What about honor? Whose honor?" Debbie asked.

Joan shrugged her shoulders. "Lissette mentions she comes from honorable ancestors. Not sure where she's going with this. The next letter might give us a clue." Joan patted the table. "They must be in that box, out there." She jerked her thumb at the wall of snow.

Suddenly, I didn't want anyone else going through those letters. I stretched and rolled my neck from side to side. "Why don't we break for the night? I don't know about the rest of you, but I'm hungry and tired of squinting at this loopy writing."

Laurie spoke up. "Grace is right. Let's put this aside for now and get a fresh start in the morning."

Was there something Laurie didn't want us to find? My paranoia touched everyone except Marty, Dave, Joan, and me, and I wondered about me. I smiled at the joke at my expense.

"What's so funny?"

I glanced around the table. Faces, that before this morning I'd viewed as open, honest, and friendly. I shrugged and started sidestepping toward the counter. "Just thinking about how I'm going to eat the last of that yummy pastrami." I bolted for the refrigerator, shouting, "Dibs on the pastrami!" and stood with my back against the appliance with my arms stretched out blocking the crowd.

Laughter rang out as others called 'dibs' on favorite leftovers. Only Garry stood off to the side, quiet and staring. I knew he wondered about me, about what Laurie must have told me about him. I wondered about him too.

# Chapter Twenty

The glow from my travel clock showed me it was only fifteen minutes since the last time I looked–three o'clock. Three hours before I could decently stir and run the risk of waking everyone. Marty's soft snores should have lulled me to sleep, but Lissette's letters filled my mind and left no room to relax.

I can lie here for three hours and count barely discernible ceiling tiles, or inuksuit, or inunnguaq, or gravestones…

I shook my head to dispel the thoughts. Marty stirred at the creak any movement brought to the old bunks. I knew I had to get up, or I'd spend the remaining two and a half hours in a *noir* funk that would only serve to increase my paranoia. Better to get up, make a bathroom visit, and stay up, maybe read. I'd taken the precaution of bringing a small book light to bed with me since the night I'd tripped over the mannequin. If I sat in the corner under the coat rack, my light wouldn't disturb anyone. I quickly shined my tiny beam at the coats, searching for mine and Marty's to make a sort of nest. I thought about the other corner away from the glass door, but that was directly in line with the pullout bed. I put on my coat and stuffed Marty's under me, pulling the sides over my knees. I wore my shoes instead of slippers.

Three pages later a thought began to invade my mind. The words in front of my eyes swam like noodle-type cells in a Petri dish under a high school microscope. I leaned my head against the wall and let the thoughts move unfettered into my conscious mind. My brain couldn't abide clutter and worked endlessly to seek and sort in its own way. With my eyes closed a series of images floated into view–no great detail, more gossamer than substance. Lissette standing with several children surrounding her, Amelia and Joshua in a posed family portrait, him seated, her with her hand on his shoulder, Lissette in a rocker holding an infant and smiling at three boys seated on the floor at her feet, Amelia with a small boy clinging to her skirts while another peeked from behind her slender body. Were these her two nephews so close in age? No, too much difference in size, more like

Glenn and Marty sizes, and they're two years apart. The other letters might have the answers.

My head snapped forward. I could get the other letters and be reading them instead. I pulled the book light off the page and tucked the paperback inside my coat pocket. By the weak light I could see that the tunnel was intact, at least right outside the door. I knew Joan and Dave had a proper flashlight somewhere, but I'd wake the whole house rummaging through drawers to find it. Not like ours at home. Harry insisted on mounting "torches" at strategic points in our house. I could use one of those now. I could use Harry now.

The thought stopped me cold. He wouldn't approve of my crawling through a snow tunnel. He would tell me it was a foolish idea and an unnecessary risk…again

*It's just you, Gracie. Do it or don't, but get on with something.* My mantra–do something, even if it's wrong. I slid the door open a few inches, then further to allow me to scrunch through and squat on the deck. *I hope this isn't 'even if it's wrong.'* I slid the door closed and felt the immediate silence. The normal sounds comprising the fabric of the night–ticking clock, appliance motor, steady snoring–stopped. The silence felt like cotton batting…I'd never realized how noisy the quiet inside had been. The other surprise was the darkness. My tiny light penetrated only inches into the overwhelming dark. Any ambient light from the cottage was lost in the dark hole I'd crawled into. I don't know why I thought snow would somehow be brighter than the dark. My outstretched, bare hand found the top of the first step. Just a few stairs and a few feet to the bedroom door. I placed the book light between my teeth to free my hands. I'd never before crawled downstairs facing forward, and I feared I'd end up on my nose. The wet wood was coated with thin ice. I stretched out my neck and pushed my chin forward trying to force the inadequate beam further into the dark. If I had a tail, like a hunting dog, it would have whipped straight out in the position of 'on set.' My focus blurred and scattered when I realized I could see farther because of another light source.

A powerful beam moved inside the bedroom, spilling ancillary light onto the deck. Someone else had the same idea. Who? Marty was the only person I could account for–I didn't check sleeping bags when I sneaked through the kitchen.

*Criminee, now what? Do something. Stay put. Whoever is in*

*there will see me on their way back. Go back. What if it's not one of us? Definitely go back! What if it is one of us? Cripes, Gracie, do something.*

Suddenly I realized two things: the light in the bedroom was off, and mine wasn't. I snatched the book light from my mouth and smothered the light against my coat. Had they seen a pinpoint of light when they turned theirs off? I knew I couldn't remain where I sat, directly at the bottom of the stairs. Whoever was in there would have to crawl over me.

Am I the only Curious George in the bunch? It's only one of the cottagers wanting to read the letters Joan mentioned, that's all. Make a noise, say hello, don't scare the crap out of them when they come out the door on all fours.

The hairs on the back of my neck lifted in a primeval warning. The light blinked on, again pointing full force out into the tunnel. I moved purposefully to my right…pushing into the snow, scooping it away from my face, sculpting a hidey-hole into the side of the wall. I kept shoveling snow behind me, pushing further in turning slightly to conceal myself better until I felt my cocoon was impenetrable, at least from a cursory glance.

I heard the scrape of a sliding door moving across the metal runner. That would be the bedroom door. A faint glow hovered beyond my hiding place, which meant I'd left some holes. The insanity of sitting under a pile of snow because I didn't want to be seen struck me with the giggles and I clamped my hand over my mouth.

My light! Must have dropped it when I was tunneling. The loss of that tiny bit of illumination caused me to panic. *For heaven's sake just push out. You know which way you came in, just go back.*

On the verge of heeding my own advice, I heard another scrape, louder and longer in time. I identified the source and realized my danger in the split second before my cocoon plunged into darkness. Someone shoveled snow against my escape hole. They knew I was in here. The scrape of metal across the icy planks sounded harsh and threatening. I'd always loved the sound of my dad's double-wide Ace Hardware shovel against the sidewalk…always felt the sound signaled accomplishment. I enjoyed the brisk air, the sun-sparkled snow, and the mist of snow that blew off the shovel into my face when I heaved the load over the bushes. Memories of standing upright, master of the snow, faded until only scary thoughts remained. Another noise penetrated the soundproofed den I'd created. Smack, smack. He was patting down the area, sealing me in. I had to take my chances with a shovel-wielding psycho and get out fast, to at least have a chance.

"Help, help," I shouted and began pushing out the way I'd dug in. The packed snow didn't fall away before my hands like it had earlier. I heard a crack, then a *sweesh*, and felt the snow shift above me. All this digging and movement must have caused the snow to collapse. Did my attacker make it inside, or was he lying under the collapsed tunnel?

The silence terrified me and all I could imagine was being buried alive and slowly suffocating. The image galvanized my movement. I pulled my coat sleeves over my numb hands and started punching at the snow, shifting and punching out more snow, always creating a pocket of space and air in front of my face. I worked feverishly, feeling the snow melt around me from my body heat. I vaguely wondered if that meant I was losing body heat and would soon succumb. My hands continued pummeling the snow–finding easy egress in some areas and shifting, but always keeping my course.

All at once I stopped. Frenzied by my fear, I had plunged ahead pushing and pummeling, not realizing how disorienting complete silence and total darkness could be. *Why do I need to push snow away from my face if I'm headed out the way I came in? It didn't take me this long to crawl in. He couldn't have shoveled two feet of snow, could he? Or maybe the cave-in had piled the snow behind me? Or maybe I've been tunneling in the wrong direction?*

I stopped scrambling and sat still, hoping to get a sense of direction. I was paralyzed with fear and held my breath, eliminating the distraction of my shaky breathing, and listening for a clue. Light penetrated the snow cave–a beam to my right, then it was gone. *Am I hallucinating? Going to the right would plunge me off the deck into deeper snow, wouldn't it?* Again the right side of the cave lit up. I stared at the spot, blinking at the brightness, confused that my sense of direction could be so wrong. The dark swallowed the light again. Maybe someone is out there with a flashlight. *Do something, Gracie. I know, I know, even if it's wrong. That's how I got into this mess.*

I hadn't been still for long, but I feared the danger of freezing to the deck. My body felt leaden and my feet seemed useless like they'd rooted to the deck. The light shone again, and this time it was so glaring I shut my eyes against the brightness on my eyelids. It was as if an occult hand had flipped a switch on a celestial beacon. The sudden darkness felt cool against my face. My eyes flew open and I lunged to my right, pushing at the snow and gasping for the air pockets formed by my movements. My sluggish movements frustrated me and I began to think I might not make it. Isn't that how people froze to death, they got tired and stopped moving and went to sleep?

*Where's my beacon? It's been long enough, it should shine again. What if I'm off course? I'd moved directly at the light...punching and pummeling the hard-packed snow, and parting and pushing the fluffier stuff. I didn't stray this time, or did I? C'mon, c'mon, light up one more time. What is this, three strikes you're out? No, no...third time's the charm.*

With that encouragement, I kept going, noticed that the dark was lighter, and smelled the opening before I pushed into it. The stale odor of recycled air inches from my mouth slipstreamed behind me as crisp air rushed to fill the new cavity, and then my right arm moved freely into air. I wasn't out of danger yet, but at least I was in the tunnel that would take me there. Compared to where I'd been, this snow had ambient light that I hadn't noticed before. I crawled toward where I was confident the stairs would be; within two crawls I hit the bottom stair and could discern weak light spilling from the bottom of the door. The lights were on in the cottage. I'd made it to safety thanks to whoever had turned on the outside light, obviously not the person who shoveled snow over me.

My hands were too numb to work the catch. I thumped my head against the glass. One, one thousand, two, one thousand, three, one thousand, stop. My brain worked in compulsive mode and calmed me with familiar repetition. One, one thousand, two, one thousand...

# Chapter Twenty-one

The scrape of the metal runner gave me a millisecond of warning, but I still tumbled sidelong into the kitchen when the door opened.

"Holy Halifax!" Dave shouted for help. "Marty, Joan, get over here." He lifted my hips and legs over the threshold and slid the door closed. Warm air slammed against every bit of bare skin and valiantly attempted to penetrate my chilled clothing. I could feel the rush of comfort to my lungs as I inhaled the cottage air.

Joan helped her husband pull me to standing position. "Gracie, what happened?" She eased me out of my jacket. "You're soaked, even your sweater." She looked me up and down and shook her head. I glanced at my feet. Water from the hem of my ice-crusted jeans dripped and pooled around my boots. All I could think of was my childhood puppy Bobo when he'd pee on himself in his excitement. I sniffed the warm air alarmed that maybe I'd done just that!

"Let's get your shoes off and get you some dry clothes." I shivered once and then again, and then I couldn't stop. Marty walked toward me, his eyes searching my face then quickly assessing the rest of me. "Hurry, she may be going into shock." He held me up while Joan pulled off my sodden shoes. Oddly, I felt no great release when my right foot popped out…I didn't feel anything. That can't be good. Marty lifted me and the second shoe came off. "Make some tea. I'll put her in my bunk."

"Put her in my bag first." Debbie stood at the far end of the kitchen near the bedrooms. Marty carried me into the bunkroom and nodded, "Right. Get her clothes off." Joan and Debbie quickly undressed me and slipped me into Deb's bag. The violent shivering continued, and I felt my clenched teeth grind top to bottom. Joan plugged in a small hairdryer and worked the hot air through my thick hair to my scalp. I wiggled under the heat and tucked my chin forward to feel the air on my neck. Joan held my head in that position through another wave of body shivers. "She's gonna' shake apart, for crying out loud." The concern in her voice caused me to wonder at my condition.

"Shivering is good; shows her body's system is working to balance her internal temp. Bad would be if she stops shivering too soon, indicating her body doesn't have anything left or if she began convulsing, indicating a serious shut-down." Debbie's calm diagnosis startled me. I didn't think either would happen and then I realized I hadn't moved; I lay still in the bag. Oh boy. Is this the bad? When Joan starting drying my hair, I closed my eyes and enjoyed the warm sensation. My eyelids felt heavy. I made an attempt to open them, but I think it must have looked like I lifted my eyebrows; my eyes stayed shut. And their voices sounded far away. This can't be good.

"Get her up, hurry." I heard the panic in Marty's voice and felt myself being lifted and pushed forward at the waist. Deb pulled down the zipper and I felt cold air rush at my back. Icy hands began chafing and massaging my back below the blades. The rather dreamy sensation that had taken hold of my body started to recede with each hurried thump on my back and the once cold hands felt warmer as the friction created by their continued movement spread heat across my back. My senses sharpened and the last thirty minutes of my life replayed with great clarity. Someone shoveled me into a snowdrift. Someone wanted to kill me.

"Okay, okay. You can stop. Really, I'm okay." The massaging stopped and I heard a sigh of relief.

Marty leaned around and looked carefully at me. His smile faded when I shivered.

"I'm fine. It's freezing in here with this thing unzipped." He grinned and straightened up.

"She's good. I'll go get that tea."

"I'll help you." Debbie left the room with Marty. Joan re-zipped the bag and I butt-scooted 'til I could sit up against the headboard with the bag snug around my neck. Joan sat down on the edge of the bunk. Her blue eyes showed concern and relief. I realized I couldn't talk if I didn't have at least one hand free, so I unzipped my warm cocoon and slipped out my left arm. She smiled and laid a towel over my bare shoulder.

"Thanks. I'd be speechless stuck in here." We both laughed, but her eyes never lost their concern.

"What happened? Why were you out there? What were you thinking?" The rapidfire questions were deserved, but I wanted to ask a few of my own. I held up my hand and motioned her closer. The door was open and I didn't know who was nearby.

She leaned in.

"Who was up when Dave found me? Did you see anyone moving around?"

Joan's eyes widened.

She leaned even closer. "What are you saying?"

"Someone shoveled snow over me. On purpose," I added for effect. It hadn't been necessary; I watched my friend's eyes grow even larger. She leaned away and stared at me with a dawning fear on her face.

"You think one of us tried to kill you?" Her voice rose on the 'kill you' and I waited a heartbeat to see if anyone heard.

"Ssssh. Not you or Dave or Marty. But I don't know these other people. One of them was out there; in your bedroom searching for something."

To her credit she didn't melt or rant. She nodded her head slowly. "Why couldn't it be someone from the Band?"

Good question. At least she's considering the unpleasant possibility. I hadn't framed the event in my mind yet, I was too much 'in the moment'; I knew my brain would sort and filter each minute for me when it had the chance to sit quietly without my constant flurry of thoughts and impressions.

She nodded again, seemingly accepting the possibility. I quickly explained what had happened. Joan sat quietly…I could watch her thought processes cross her face. We'd always done that with each, even finishing each other's sentences. I saw her face lighten. She reached for my hand. "What if your pushing the snow out behind you caused that person to shovel it out of the way, not to trap you but to clear the tunnel? Your snow movement might have caused some collapse. They didn't try to kill you; they didn't know you were there." Her smile implored me to give her scenario a chance.

Could it have happened that way? Who carries a shovel with them? Someone smart enough to think ahead in case of a cave-in. I had to give her something, she looked so hopeful. I shrugged. "Then why wouldn't someone come forward when Dave dragged me in?

Because they didn't want us to know they'd been in your room," I answered my own question. "What the heck is so important?"

"What were you looking for?"

"The other letters. Could that be what they were after? Let's find out. Hand me my duffle bag, please." I indicated the top bunk. "Can't ask questions in the buff."

"You shouldn't be asking questions at all. Lie down and get some rest."

I didn't move.

"You're not going to lie down and let this go, are you?" She knew me, she knew the answer.

Joan stood and pulled the duffle down to the floor. I put on a set of dry everything and was in the process of choosing socks when Marty walked in with two mugs of tea. He looked at Joan. She put her hands out palms up. "Hey, you know your sister." She held out her hand. "Is one of those for me?"

Marty stammered, "No, uh, I actually wanted to talk to Grace. Ah…here." He pushed the mug toward her. "Sorry."

Joan didn't take the mug. "No problem. You two talk, I'll get my own." She looked at me. I couldn't get a sense of her mood. Marty stood rooted to the spot staring at me. "Is one of those for me?" He shook his head as though to rid himself of some fugue. "Yes, yeah, of course." He offered me the mug in his right hand.

I scooted over to make room on the bed. "I have to tell you what happened, but first, I want to see whose gloves are wet. Everyone puts them on the sill by the back door to dry. I just thought of that. Someone's gloves are soaked."

"Gracie, wait. I have to know…"

"I know, I know, I'll fill you in. Just let me check this out." I stood up and started to move past him. Marty put his arm out and blocked my way. I stared at his arm like it was an alien appendage.

"Sis," he squirmed and years fell away from this grown man. I remembered the awkward shift from leg to leg where the upper body movement ran opposite his lower extremities. He didn't sway, rather squirmed like an 'S' curve.

A frantic shout snapped the time warp and we rushed to the source. Laurie stood with her hands clutching a jacket. "He's not here. Where's Garry?" Her voice cracked and her next words were spoken so softly I strained to hear her. "Why did he…" She stopped and sat down abruptly like a spring unwound.

Why did he what? Steal the letters, hide the deed? Try to kill me? We stood frozen, each of us with our own thoughts; mine were so damning. Dave banged in from the back porch out of breath. "The car is here. It's snowing harder; I couldn't see any footprints."

Joan leaned toward Laurie and gently pulled the jacket from her hands. "It's wet," she announced to no one in particular. Of course it's wet. I didn't need to find out about the gloves, I had my proof. She passed the jacket behind her to Colleen. I reached for the jacket. "I'll hang it up." I wanted to check the pockets for my book light; proof positive that he tried to kill me. Marty followed me to the kitchen. He leaned close to me whispering, "What are you doing?" I guess my casual patdown wasn't as transparent as I hoped. Deep pockets weren't easily searched with a cursory feel.

I whispered back, "I'm trying to find my book light. That'll prove he was out there." Marty groaned and rubbed his face with his hand. "Grace, stop."

One more pocket. "What are you doing?" Colleen's voice came from right behind me. She'd kept her tone low, but I heard the accusation. Caught with one hand thrust deeply into an inside pocket, it had to look bad–slowly removing my hand, I turned to face her. My brain grasped for anything plausible. "Just checking for gloves, to dry out, on the sill." *Geez, girl, shut up!* I prayed that Joan wouldn't walk in on us. She knew about my 'lie detector' eyes; a peculiar point of my physiology that deepened the lavender hue of my eyes when I was in high adrenaline output.

"I hardly think someone would put wet gloves in their inside pocket. Why are you searching his jacket?" Her voice attracted Debbie's attention. "What's going on?" Her question caused heads to turn toward us.

"That's what I want to know. She was searching Garry's jacket."

Well, that just brought everyone running. "Did she take anything?" She. Spoken with the same tone you'd use to describe gum stuck on the bottom of your shoe, I felt as though I'd become invisible as the comments continued. "She wouldn't take anything."

"Then what was she doing?"

I forced myself to stay calm and not clamp my hands over my

ears chanting, "La, la, la, la," like a kid handling confrontation.

"She wasn't doing anything wrong."

"I don't care what she was doing," Laurie spoke. "I just want to know where Garry is." Laurie walked over to me. "Do you know where Garry is, Grace?" It was nice to hear my name again. Laurie's expression appeared on the brink of more tears. Her look implored me for an answer. I shook my head. The accusation on my lips to explain my behavior stayed put.

The heavy-handed knock at the door startled everyone. Dave moved first. "Who'd be out here this early?" His tone sounded worried. Danny King walked confidently into the room, striding toward the group of us, radiating cold air from the surface of his black down jacket. He pulled off his gloves and unzipped his jacket, looking like he intended to stay a bit. "One of your group went off island tonight. Forced the ferry tender to take him across. I want to know who and why."

"How do you know it was someone from this cottage? Why couldn't it be another cottager or even an islander?" Bob shrugged his shoulders. "Could be a number of people."

"He was a cottager, no doubt. He had on an expensive jacket and he wore one of those face masks...ski masks," he corrected quickly. "Islanders don't wear those kinds of clothes."

I stared pointedly at King's nice-looking down jacket and wondered if the scrap of material stuffed in his pocket might be a ski mask. He caught my look and shifted away from me.

"The ferry tender didn't even see his face? That's crazy you came here."

"We know it was a cottager because he paid triple to get across off schedule. He said he had to get across before the storm hit...had to get to his company."

Those in the group who played poker stayed still, unblinking. Then there was Joan, Colleen, and me, who all swiveled our necks to face Laurie who, burst into tears of confusion and concern.

King touched his fingers to his forehead in mock salute. "Thank you, ladies." He stepped toward Laurie, and seven people scrambled like jet fighters.

"What does it matter if he left? He obviously had business on the mainland first thing. Doesn't sound like he forced anyone; he paid him extra to do his job. That's his job last time I looked." Dave's calm tone barely concealed his growing anger.

King glared at the interruption. "His job is not to make special runs or to run against company safety regulations. The ferry isn't equipped to run in high seas."

"Seems to me your concern should be with the ferryman who couldn't resist pocketing the extra money. Why do you care if someone left?"

"Pete Andrews was found dead a few hours back. Somebody said he'd been arguing with one of the cottagers earlier in the day. They couldn't hear what about, but they could see Pete and the guy going at it."

Laurie gasped and swallowed hard. Her tear-swollen eyes sharpened and focused on King. "You think my husband killed this man and then calmly came back to the cottage, chatted, ate dinner, sneaked out in the middle of the night, and caught the ferry to Midland? You honestly think that?"

Put that way, it sounded silly. Unfortunately, it didn't look like King was taking it that way. He rolled his neck inside his loosened collar and his dark eyes gleamed. I hadn't noticed how haggard he'd become since our first meeting a few days ago.

"Pete was Joe's son, he was my first cousin. I'm not paid to think fancy ideas, I'm paid to follow solid leads, and that brings me here." He faced Laurie. "Why did your husband leave the island?"

It was a question I was interested in too, but not at her expense. The brief moment of confidence and anger flared and sputtered. She stood slack-jawed, tears slipping down her cheeks. Joan reached her first, slipped her arm around her shoulders, and led her to the couch.

King stood awkwardly. He rolled his neck again and I wondered if the gesture was habit or pain relief. "Someone needs to give me answers." His tone held no bravado or threat. He sounded a tad panicked. Two murders on his watch and the cavalry had left for Midland on the evening ferry. With seas too dangerous to navigate, King was on his own. In his mind, the killer made it off the island.

In my mind, I didn't know what to think. It was obvious now that Garry couldn't have been the person on the deck–he'd already left the cottage and possibly the island. So who had tried to turn me into an Eskimo Pie?

"King, we don't know why Garry left. We didn't know he'd left the cottage until, well, until right before you barged in with your accusations." Dave's words summed it up–we had as many questions as he did.

He seemed satisfied with that answer. "At least I don't have to tell you not to leave island, because you can't." His barked laughter sounded harsh in the small room. "No one in, no one out. We'll catch your friend; I called it in to the mainland." He rolled his neck, adding a backward dip to the rotation before he zipped up his parka and left.

The door barely closed on his figure before Dave and Bob both swung round to face Laurie. Dave's voice sounded comforting after the threatening words from King. "What is he up to? Laurie, if you know what he's doing you've got to tell us. King thinks he's killed two men. The police will be after him with only King's mistaken ideas. Worse, King's not looking for the killer on the island–he thinks the island is safe. We could all be in danger from this nutcase. We need to sort this out. Laurie, can you try reaching him? Where would he go, home? His office?"

"I don't know where he'd go; I don't know why he left. Ever since…" Laurie stopped and looked down at her hands. They lay folded one into the other.

I spoke a thought my mind snapped to me on the run. "Ever since we found those letters and started trying to piece together this bit of history?" I hardly expected her response. She brought her hands up to her mouth, pressing them against her lips.

"I told him, begged him, not to pursue it. He wouldn't listen. He was obsessed with knowing."

"Knowing what?"

She looked at each of us, took a deep breath, and shared her burden. "If his bloodline owned Christian Island." Just the saying of the words lifted the weight. Laurie stood and reached her hands out to Bob and Debbie. "I know you're our good friends." She motioned to the others. "All of you. Please understand that Garry's been consumed by having to know, even if the answer destroys his family."

"Laurie, you're not making any sense. Try calling Garry. We have to talk with him, get this straightened out before he's arrested." Dave pulled Laurie gently along to the kitchen phone. He lifted the receiver and handed it to her. "Try to find him." Laurie nodded and accepted the phone almost in slow motion. She lifted her other hand to dial, then stopped. She moved the phone away from her ear and stared at it. "There's no dial tone."

Dave took the receiver and checked, pushing and releasing the prongs in the cradle. He hung up the phone, rushed into the short hallway to the back door, and flung it open. Back inside in a flash, he slammed the door. "Bastard messed with the phone wires."

I wasn't sure who he referred to: King, the killer, or possibly Garry. Several voices raised in protest, confusion, and fear. I couldn't separate them all, mine included. I thought I heard me shouting for calm, but maybe that was my inside voice telling me to chill. Guess not, since everyone stopped talking and turned to me. "Let's go at this from the beginning. If we can figure out who or what is involved and might win or lose, maybe we can point the finger away from Garry and protect ourselves from the real killer."

Ken backed me immediately. "Dave, bring in the boxes on your bed and we'll spread out everything in here. Grace, you bring out the letters you have from the lighthouse. Joan, how about we whip up some breakfast for everyone before we start?" Everyone listened, and probably because no one offered a different plan, we agreed to try.

On my way to retrieve my stash, my mind replayed the last scene and my steps slowed as I reached the doorway. *Dave, bring in the boxes on your bed*…not *bring in the boxes* or *bring in the boxes on the floor*. I looked over my shoulder. How would he know the boxes were on the bed unless…

"You're blocking the door, kiddo," Marty said. "Move it or lose it, Gracie."

I had almost lost it, hadn't I? A chill gripped me and I shivered.

"Wait, before you go." Marty's voice labored with concern and something else. "Gracie, I have to talk to you."

I swung around and whispered. "I know it wasn't Garry. It was Ken. He knew about the boxes being on the bed; he wouldn't say that unless he saw them. Where'd he put his wet jacket? We never checked for gloves, did we?" I moved to step around my brother. He groaned and rubbed the side of his face. "Marty, what's wrong? Are you okay? Is it, you know, not taking anything?"

Marty straightened and shook his head. "I'm not going through withdrawal if that's what you're trying to ask." His tone made me ashamed of what I'd been thinking.

Dave motioned to Marty. "Give me a hand, eh? I want to bring in the wood stored under the porch. I'm not waiting to drag in fuel in the middle of the night."

"But your generator…"

"Only works off the battery for ten hours. Like I said, I want to be prepared."

Colleen nodded toward the bedroom. "You've the last of it," reminding me of what I had started to do. The chairs had been handed down into the family room and the table turned diagonally. A small folding table filled the space up to the cabinet opposite the sliding door. Notes, files, folders, and letters covered the top of the grey Formica with nary a space for a paper clip. The artifacts were displayed on the smaller table. Joan even included a slip of paper with the words 'hunting knife' to replace the missing item.

I wanted to start with the boxes, the contents of which added considerable bulk, and I watched carefully as Colleen lifted papers out and sorted them according to type. I watched Ken's face to look for a particular interest he might show as she called out what she'd pulled from the box. "This packet says, 'trusts and deeds,' the top one is dated 1907."

The deed I'd seen last night predated those, but I didn't see that one on the table. It had a distinctive seal, rather fancy, and though faded by time, still a bright shade of blue, easy to spot. Did Garry take it with him to prove something to someone? Or did he destroy it on his way off the island?

"Biscuits up," Joan announced. I knew she had another batch baking and stayed near the table. Ken and I looked at each other across the pile of history and possibly clues to two murders. He tipped his head toward the table. "Amazing how all this stuff's been gathered from the nooks and crannies of people's homes and businesses." He fingered a tag tied with white butcher string round a mailing tube. "Supposedly this contains navigational charts found in the storage room of Midland Shipbuilding Company, which used to be the Midland Navigational Company. The tag indicates they might have been used by the Jesuits and Huron when they fled from Ste. Marie to Christian Island. I don't buy that. Can't imagine the Huron checking French charts."

"Would that be before or after they buried their treasure on Beausoleil?" Joan asked.

"For a transplant, you know your Georgian Bay history," Ken teased.

"I always wondered why they stopped there to bury treasure. Supposedly the pot of French and Spanish coins is concealed under a slab of stone with a Latin inscription explaining the treasure. It's never been found–how easily can you hide a slab of stone, and why there? They were running for their lives; why stop to bury treasure? Why not bring the treasure to Christian Island and bury it here?"

"Beausoleil is a lot bigger. Maybe the 'Black Robes' thought it would be safer. I'm sure they planned to return."

"There's no record they did. When most of the three thousand Huron starved that first winter, the remaining few hundred begged the Jesuits to leave the island. They left for New France, never setting foot on Beausoleil Island. I think they buried the treasure here, and when they left they took it with them. Fifteen years ago some people snorkeling off the lighthouse point found three French coins. Might have been from their cache."

"More biscuits," Dave announced. "My American wife grew up reading Nancy Drew with her 'chum' over there." He nodded toward me. "A conspiracy behind every tree..." His smile slipped. "Seems we have stumbled onto something."

The mood which had lifted ever so slightly settled back. I hurried to grab a biscuit before the tray emptied, slathering butter and marmalade on both halves, Marty motioned to a spot next to him and held up a cup of coffee as further enticement.

"Sis, I have to talk to you. Dave and I are going into town, or whatever they call it, to use the phone. Laurie's coming with us. We have to find Garry. I think I should call Harry and let him know what's going on."

I'd thought of Harry a million times, wishing he were here a week early instead of happily vacationing with his newly discovered son. My heart still ached at the thought that another woman had been able to give him the child I couldn't. We hadn't learned of the boy's existence until eight months ago, and Harry had been trying to make up for all the lost years.

"Did you hear me? I said I think we should–"

"I heard. He's with Will. They'll be here next week. Don't bother him."

"Bother him? Gracie, there have been two murders on this island and we're stranded on it. Bother him?" My brother's voice rose in urgency. He shook his head as though to restart a thought. "Anyway, before I go I have to tell you–"

"Ready, Marty?" The interruption came from Dave. "Ken went out to start the car. Let's go." Dave held his jacket and helped Laurie slip into hers. She tied her scarf around her neck and pulled small gloves from her pocket.

"I know, I know. You want to tell me to be careful. I will. I promise. Now go, you're holding up the parade."

Ken stomped into the room, banging the door behind him. "Somebody's taken out the rotor arm."

His statement chilled me as no amount of cold air could. One by one our escape routes were being blocked. Why? Who?

"Then we'll do it on foot. I have snowshoes in the trunk–thought we'd have races if we caught some snow. It's not too deep on the inland side, but we'll move faster and stay drier." Dave turned to Laurie. "Write down those numbers for me. I'll call around. I don't want you out there; there are only two pairs anyway."

Laurie didn't argue.

"I'm already dressed, Marty. I'll go with Dave," Ken offered.

"Good idea. Until we know what's going on, I think two guys here is good. I'll get the snowshoes."

"No." Ken backed up a step. "I mean I'm ready to go. I'll get them out, you get the numbers."

"Grab the duct tape on your way out; one of the shoes needs a bit of a wrap," Dave called over his shoulder. He pulled on his jacket and grinned at Joan. "C'mon now, I've the easy part, taking a stroll with a pal on a winter's day. You've all got to make your way through that stuff and make sense of it."

Marty laughed. "Why do you think I wanted to go with you?"

I would have felt better if Marty had gone with them. I didn't trust Ken, but how could I tell Dave I suspected his friend of attempted murder now that, in my mind, his other friend had been cleared of the same suspicion?

Joan and Colleen walked with Dave to the back door and stood there watching them go. Colleen returned first. "If it weren't so serious, they would look like two friends taking a walk around."

"Let's hold up our end of the task and see what we get." Bob stood behind the table in the small triangle of space made by the wall and the sliding door. "I've continued to separate everything based on dates as we started to last night."

Last night seemed ages ago, not hours. What is Garry's secret? What is Ken's plan? Is Dave safe?

A light tapping noise interrupted my thoughts and I realized I was the source. I'd unconsciously picked up one of the bones from the artifact table and had been tapping it against the carved stick. Marty moved his hands over mine and removed the noisemaker, then traded places with me.

Bob cleared his throat and continued with the plan. I waited until he finished. "A deed is missing from last night. I saw it, then it disappeared." I looked at Laurie, hoping the events of the night would prompt her to explain. She stared back and I thought I'd lost the tug-of-war I'd spotted in her eyes.

"I told him it didn't matter, to leave it alone." Everyone stood quietly waiting. Laurie searched each face before she continued. "He's obsessed with knowing he and his siblings have any voting rights."

Joan spoke first. "Laurie, you said that before. It's not possible. The island is part of a National Trust. I know Garry's family is descended from Lissette, but only the firstborn and his descendants had any inheriting rights."

"The firstborn of Joshua and Lissette," agreed Laurie.

"Yes, the firstborn of Joshua…" Joan stared at Laurie. "What are you saying?"

Laurie shook her head. "It's Garry's theory; he's been researching for two years. He thought he had proof from some medical records he found that his grandfather was the firstborn of Joshua and Lissette."

"That's crazy. We know from records that they had two children before that, a girl and a boy. The girl had no inheritance rights, but the boy did. From the birth dates we can tell that Garry's grandfather was born seven months after the first boy. Talk about poor family planning. In those days, a preemie was lucky to make it at all."

"I know it sounds crazy, but Garry insisted that he found proof through the blood types that his great uncle could not have been Lissette's biological son."

"Did they even have blood types then? I mean record them as a matter of course?"

"Lissette had surgery when she was well into her seventies. Those were the records that noted her blood type. Garry's great uncle served in World War I, and his blood type was on his records and on his identification medal." Laurie's voice sounded tired rather than triumphant. "I wanted him to drop the whole thing, but he kept on about birth rights."

"A bigger chunk of change every year wouldn't be bad either," Bob smiled when he spoke and Laurie merely nodded.

My brain reeled with possibilities that I had to explore. "Does anyone else in the group have a connection to the land development?" I hoped Ken's attack on me might make sense in a larger context. Silence filled the room and the hairs rose on the back of my neck. What in God's name is going on with me? Only it wasn't with me. I looked at Marty and unconsciously shifted toward him.

Bob spoke slowly. "My gain would be considerable if the deal could be salvaged. If it did turn gold I'd want to include all of you. You see, there would be something in it for all of us. I'm sorry I didn't bring you in sooner, but I told you how it happened; I wasn't hiding anything. It started out that we'd come on island one last time before the new owners took possession. When I found out that this was the week the meetings to decide the fate of the development would take place, I thought the timing would be perfect. Be right here when the die was cast, so to speak."

"You're all connected to this?"

Joan shook her head.

Bob cleared his throat as though preparing for a presentation—only the flip chart was missing. "There was nothing definite. Part of the long-range plan, to make it more appealing to the Band, is to have set-asides for a huge recreational area. I thought of Dave immediately to head that program." Bob paused. "I'm slated to be their controller, and Ken looks good for the biggest plum, director of guest services."

"So you'd all move here and what, live in the big house like *Dynasty* or something?" I looked at Joan. "Did you know about this? Why'd you invite me? This was business."

Joan blanched and looked stunned. "No, I had no idea. I don't know what..." she straightened her shoulders.

"He never approached Dave." Her voice grew stronger. "He knew better."

Her voice dropped. "I really wanted to enjoy the cottage with my friends one last time. I wish we'd never come." She glanced around the table. "It's wrong."

"What's wrong?" Marty asked. "Sounds like everyone will make out." He waved his hand at them. "You all get great jobs with high salaries, the Band Council gets more jobs and a share of the profits for their lifetime. Sounds sweet to me."

Bob shook his head slowly. "Not everyone gets a share. Only those directly descended from Joshua and Lissette."

"Oh, so if there are enough descendants they can swing the vote in favor and live happily ever after." Marty's sarcasm put a few backs up. I didn't want this to turn ugly since Marty and I were stuck here for the duration. I tried to change tack, or at least use some tact.

"Garry is convinced that his grandfather was the firstborn, and so the inheritance line is his bloodline. Who is the current bloodline?" My question brought a pained response from Laurie.

Her tiny voice quivered. "Danny King is a direct descendant. His family inherits."

Joan added, "The King family is well known, and large."

"Not as large as a week ago."

# Chapter Twenty-two

Marty's voice dropped between us like a book pushed off a library table. He ticked off names, "Joe and Pete, both in the King line, right?"

Laurie's eyes widened. "I didn't think of it that way." She pinned Bob with an angry glance. "Did you?"

Bob shrugged. "Not really, but…uh…if you think about it, it's too much of a coincidence to be one. Don't you think?" He looked at me, of all people, for affirmation.

"What I think is that we need to get off this island."

"Not without knowing where Garry is." Laurie's chin lifted.

"He's on the mainland, Laurie. I don't know why he didn't tell us his plans, but he's safer than we are." Debbie whispered the last part.

Marty shook his head and moved his neck from side to side. He ran the palm of his hand over his face and took a deep breath. "Let me follow this, because honestly, this whole set-up has the makings of a B movie. Garry thinks he is the rightful inheritor because he's the oldest male in the line. King's family has for years held that distinction, with Joe being the oldest male. Now he is deceased, so it passes to Peter, who is now also dead, so it passes to King? However, if King's line has been the wrong one and Garry can prove it, then it passes to Garry and someone has killed two people for nothing."

"That's probably why Garry went off island, to get help. He must have figured out he could be a target and didn't want anyone else caught up in it." Debbie's words brought Laurie comfort. She smiled.

"Yes, Garry would do that. Do you think help can get across to us? You heard what King said about the high waves."

Joan tried to assure her, maybe all of us. "Those Metro Water boats can really haul. If anything can make it, one of those can."

My spirits lifted with her words. The only thing that would make this situation better would be to know that Harry would be on one of those boats. The entire year in review slid past my brain, and at each junction where light met dark, Harry had been there to pull me back.

Could Marty replace Harry as my rock during a crisis? My little brother whom I always protected? I looked at him in profile: strong chin, straight, slightly oversize nose, over six feet, lean muscled body, shock of Morelli dark hair. I'd watched him play sports; he had the strength, did he have the spirit?

Marty spoke. "We can't do much till they return. Let's get back to sorting through all this. Focus this time on any letters or other info that would support Garry's theory. I don't know why he took the deed." He looked at Laurie.

She shrugged. "Maybe to buy time if that was the deed leaving the island to Joshua and Lissette's descendants?"

"Could be. And let's look at that crazy photograph again from a different viewpoint."

"Which viewpoint?"

Marty slowly looked at each of us, his eyes gleaming with a secret. "Buried treasure."

There was silence first, then a cacophony of voices discordant with theories and opinions.

"I knew it!" Joan clapped in glee. "The Jesuit treasure, right?"

"Seems like a fairy tale to me," Bob's dry tone indicated disbelief. "There's never been any mention of that possibility."

"Doesn't mean it isn't so," defended his wife. "It could have happened."

"I'm just saying it's a waste of time."

Marty waved his hands to quell the storm of argument brewing. "Listen, the photo seems to point to the graveyard. Whoever left this clue couldn't very well take a photo of a grave. Instead they did this series to confuse people. Maybe one of the letters mentioned the photo telling the reader to 'look closely and see beyond.' Maybe the reader never put it together and the letter and photo got separated."

"Who left the clue? Was the graveyard even there when the Huron and Jesuits came here?"

"We know the inner circle and the stone altar were here around that time. The lighthouse didn't get built till two hundred years later."

"So the lighthouse keeper found the treasure but didn't do anything with it?"

Bob held up a hand, almost asking permission to interrupt. "Depending on when deeds were signed, it could have been that he wouldn't have been allowed to keep it. He'd have had to wait until he could get it off island in secret. I think Marty's idea is close. Let's look at everything again, looking for any talk about 'plenty,' 'bounty,' 'harvest'…any word that might indicate treasure on the mainland. If the treasure had been here, it would have been discovered by now."

Bob's words validated part of Marty's theory, and the energy in the room peaked. Joan and I began a systematic search of the contents. Anything not written by Lissette or Amelia we put aside. Anything not referring to property also went into that pile. Our efforts separated the papers into two very uneven stacks. After almost an hour, we'd only discounted two letters from our 'possible pile.'

"These people wrote like they were writing for the Bible," Joanie complained at one point. "Listen to this," she waved a thin sheet of paper with cramped writing all over it. I recognized the writing as Amelia's. "It's to her brother, Joshua."

*Dearest brother,*

*Your visit left me renewed and invigorated to my task of making this year the year of our bounty on the island. I missed your encouragement and presence the moment* The Midland *pulled away from the dock.*

"What the heck does that mean? She's planting a bigger vegetable garden, she's trading trinkets with the Indians?"

We burst into laughter. Several heads turned at our outburst and we dissolved into giggles.

"This could take a while. Want a refill?" Joan stood.

"Actually, I think I'll switch to tea, thanks. Whatever you're having." I handed up my mug. A lavender envelope caught my eye– lovely color for stationery, I thought. It was from the grandmother…pity, not in the search range. Wonder what old grandmamma had to say this time? *Submit, my dear, it's our lot.* Yuck. I glanced at Joan, occupied brewing tea; I could take a peek.

*Dearest child,*

*Your letter to your brother arrived the afternoon he left to visit you and Mr. Havilland. I am pleased that the relationship between you and Joshua is more heartening than when you were children. He has truly become the watchful, caring, older brother we hoped he would.*

*He of course has missed your instructions of what to*

*bring to you, but I see no need for those frivolous items for a woman in your position. In my opinion, my dear, even a brother should not be asked to bring clothing. I am certain you can redo last year's dresses to make do. After all, for whom would you wear new dresses?*

*The photograph you enclosed is odd indeed. It would appear to be the same image imprinted several times. I do not know of these things. I shall leave it for your brother.*

*Remember your position in life, my child. It does no one good to strive for what one cannot or should not have. Know your place and you shall know contentment.*

*Your grandmother,*

*Mrs. Pantier*

"What a loser."

Joan stood above me, offering a mug. "What did you say?"

I hadn't realized I'd spoken out loud. That happened a lot lately. My brain seemed to forget to stop the thought at my mouth.

"I cheated and took a peek at 'grandmamma's sage advice'."

"Anything good?"

"Same old story about her station, position, place, etc. in life."

We both rolled our eyes.

"She does mention Amelia wanting new clothes and that she didn't need them because who would she impress? That does make me wonder who she would *want* to impress. I mean, it's apparent from the other letters that she'd prefer to avoid the attention of her husband."

"Maybe Amelia had a sweetheart on the island."

"An Indian?"

"There were other families on the island by that time. There was a school. In fact, the light keeper from Hope Island wanted to trade posts with the keeper before Havilland so his children could attend school on Christian Island."

"Amelia may have been attracted to someone. She was pretty, probably a change from most women on the island. Maybe it was an Indian. Have you seen some of the photos of the voyageurs? A couple of them could keep their shoes next to my bed."

I poked her in the arm and grinned. "I think they were barefoot."

Joan squinched her nose at me. "You know what I mean."

"Yeah, and that's scary." Our laughter brought a mild reprimand. "Is that how you two work?"

"Hey, some very successful little people whistled while they worked. We choose to giggle."

"Anyway," Joan sputtered, "we think Amelia had an affair."

Marty rolled his eyes. "If anyone could ferret out that bit of info, it would be those two. Keep working, girls."

I leaned close to Joan. "I don't think they're taking us seriously."

Laurie waved a letter in the air. "Look at this. I wouldn't have given it a second thought until you guys mentioned your theory. Doesn't this 'e' in 'Dearest Sister' look like it started as an 'a' then was written over?"

Marty looked over her shoulder at the letter. "So he had sloppy writing or couldn't spell. Gee, even then men lagged behind in those social graces." Debbie grinned and shook her head.

"Laurie's right."

Joan and I popped up like corks on a wave and rushed to look.

"Oh my, this could change everything."

Marty and Bob looked lost. I took pity and turned my sweetest smile on them. "Might be he started to write, 'dar' as in 'darling'."

Marty reacted first. "Oh, that's just wrong. He was her brother." His tone left no doubt as to his feelings on that subject.

Debbie patted Marty's arm. "One of the letters mentioned that they weren't raised together; that he didn't meet her until he was older. Attraction doesn't always stay within the lines."

"Especially if the lines were blurred," I added. "In this letter, the grandmother says she's happy to see Joshua stepping up to be an attentive brother to Amelia."

"Maybe too attentive." Joan's comment left us silent to accept or reject the tenuous theory that Amelia and Joshua may have committed incest.

"I'd rather look for treasure," Marty mumbled and bent his head to his stack.

# Chapter Twenty-three

The back door burst open and Dave struggled to shut it against the blowing wind. Snow swirled around his body until he slammed the door against it.

"Holy Halifax! It's howling out there, closest thing to a 'whiteout' I've seen in years." Dave brushed the snow from his jacket and rubbed his hands together. "Kicked up right after we split up." He looked around the room. "Where is he, using up all the hot water?" He glanced at the open door of the bathroom.

Colleen's soft brown eyes flared to a dark shade. "Where is he? He was with you."

Dave nodded. "Up until an hour ago. No luck with reaching Garry at those numbers. I had to wait for one more phone call from the mainland and I wanted to talk to King again. He was a jerk when he was here, but he was also reacting to two dead family members in less than two days. Ken wanted to come back, said he had thought of something that might help…something he needed to do."

"This is nuts!" Colleen tossed down the sheaf of papers she'd been reading and pushed around her end of the table. "First Garry, now Ken. This is crazy." She looked fiercely at Dave, who stared back in amazement. He tried to grab one of her flailing hands.

"What, you think Ken left the island? Hey, take it easy. He said he had something to do; probably took him longer with the weather. It really came up fast."

Colleen calmed momentarily until another thought must have hit her. "What if he's hurt out there? Maybe he fell or got lost; he doesn't know the island like you do."

I heard the panic in her voice and realized I felt the same tightness. Whiteout conditions would turn even the familiar into the unknown.

"We have to go look for him," her voice rose in pitch, then

cracked. "Please."

Everyone looked at Dave. I didn't envy the words I knew he had to say.

"We're not prepared to search, Colleen. We're not prepared for this weather, it wasn't supposed to happen. I heard a report at the store that the storm's closed down air traffic and roads on the mainland. It's blowing right down the gullet." Dave shook his head. "I'm sorry, but we can't risk stumbling around in that."

The storm's path was hurtling down from the northern shores, drawing strength from the open water until it acted like a combination hurricane-blizzard. This weather anomaly had wreaked havoc on the islands throughout Georgian Bay's recorded history. I'd given Joanie *Ghosts of the Bay* when I found out she and Dave were buying this cottage. It was one of the books she kept on the coffee table.

Stumbling around. I wondered if anyone else thought of Ken out there doing just that. I glanced at their faces–they had.

Colleen's wild-eyed stare tugged at my heart. What would I feel if it were Harry out there? Or Marty? He'd been ready to go with them. Dave's heart wasn't made of stone; he had to be devastated by his inability to help his friend.

I found myself grasping at straws and speaking before I thought it through. "Can we erect some kind of light to guide him? Maybe lanterns in the tree? He could be looking right at us and not see the cottage."

Colleen's face cleared with hope and I felt crummy for speaking out loud in case the idea couldn't work.

"They'd blow right out of the trees." I saw her shoulders slump and wanted to kick myself. "It's blowing hardest closest to shore; maybe we can set up some lights on the interior pointing him this way."

The rise in determination and excitement catapulted everyone into action. Everyone except Laurie, who stood quietly against the wall at her position around the table. I read the resignation on her face–no help for her husband. She caught me looking and dropped her gaze to the papers in her hands. I sidestepped the scurry of activity and stood next to her.

"He wouldn't have left me, Grace. I know he's still on the island. Something's happened to him." Her voice couldn't compete against the flurry of ideas slamming around the room, and I leaned in closer.

"Maybe he thought he had more evidence on the mainland."

Laurie's eyes mocked me. "Would your husband leave without a word?" She pushed past me and walked into the bedroom, closing the door against the hopefulness of another man's rescue.

"This will be like Havilland's Hope," Joan said. She referred to the plan that Marty had suggested–lashing three lanterns to three prominent trees just the other side of the road. One lantern would be lashed between two branches in a manner that would allow it to swing but not smash against the trunk. The other two would be lashed against each tree. The swaying light would catch attention and the two constant lights would point the way across the road.

"Havilland's Hope? What's that?"

Joan blushed. "It's an urban legend, or in this case rural legend, about the light. The Indians say that the spirit of Havilland still watches the point and the island. When people have been lost or in imminent danger, it's lore that he turns on the beacon and illuminates the way. Two island kids swear that's what kept them from tumbling into an abandoned well. They'd missed the inukshuk guiding them back to town and strayed from the path. Suddenly a powerful light lit the path from behind and they spotted the gaping hole in the dark earth. When they turned to thank the person with the light, there was no one there. The light swung around one more time and they were able to get their bearings to safety."

I thought about the powerful light that had turned me from the wrong 'path.' Had Havilland's Hope saved me? The beam had been stronger than any porch light. My face must have reflected my confusion.

"It's just a ghost story, Gracie. Sorry I brought it up." My friend's cheeks flamed. "Not the right time for stories."

"Not the right time for lights, either," Bob offered. "It's too light for any contrast. We'll have to wait until dark for that to be effective."

Colleen gasped. "Please, we have to do something."

"We will." Marty's confidence brought some color to her pale face. "We are going to set up a calling line. We can do that until dark, then use the lanterns and drop the call line to this side of the road."

I knew what he meant. He was referring to a scouting technique to help find a lost scout.

"Each of us will tie on to a rope and walk out as far as we can, with the pivot person standing on the interior side of the road holding the lines. Every five minutes the pivot person will walk in ten feet and everyone on a line moves forward. I don't think our voices will carry in that howl. Does anyone have a whistle or any type of loud noisemaker?"

Dave and Joan grinned; Joan rushed to the cabinet under the counter and pulled out a box with a variety of New Year's Eve-type noisemakers. She held one up and blew. The shrill whistle sound filled the small room. Laurie ran out from her room.

"Sorry, Laurie. I, uh, we, well..."

Marty jumped in. "We're setting up a call line in case Ken is within hearing distance. We could use your help if you're up to it."

Laurie's eyes leaped with hope and she nodded. I knew she felt this could help Garry too. She alone believed he was still on island.

"Thanks. Dave, how much rope or line do you have?"

"Several coils in the boathouse, but we can't reach it."

"I have two new clotheslines and we can take down the double one on the line outside."

"Good, good. Anything else?"

"I always keep a couple of coils in the trunk, usually ones that are too worn for mooring." He stopped. "Cripes! Ken's got the keys."

The hopeful mood burst like a child's balloon, all at once and unexpectedly.

Colleen sagged against Bob, and I worried she was about to faint. He helped her to a chair and Joan filled a glass with water. I personally thought something a little stronger might help more.

"I'll break the lock, I don't care. Give me something I can use."

"Wait, wait. The back seat. One side folds down, remember?"

"Cripes I forgot, never use it. Too small for my stuff, but the ropes are probably right up against the back." He grinned and the room filled with purpose again. "I'll get them." Dave pulled on his still wet jacket and braced the door so it wouldn't fly open against him as he turned the knob. Even that opening, just enough for him squeeze through, allowed the wind to scream into the room pushing icy air ahead of its protest.

"Geez Louise," Marty rubbed his arms against the cold air. "I hope it's calmer on the interior." He looked around. "Everyone get ready. I'll be the pivot man and hold your lines. Walk out as far as you can until the line is taut. When you feel the slack, walk out further until the line is taut again. Try to make your signal sound like a signal–I mean, be consistent so he'll hear a pattern and know it's help and not storm noise. Any questions?"

Heads nodded in understanding as Marty looked around the room. My brother had always excelled at the outdoor survival aspects of scouting. We'd all assumed he'd be a forest ranger or professional scouter or outfitter. I watched him now making small talk with Deb and Laurie, checking that they had gloves and hats in preparation for the rescue mission.

The door banged open and Dave yelled from the porch. "Help me. Hurry. Garry's in the trunk."

Marty sprinted for the door, pushing his arms into his jacket on the run. Laurie screamed and rushed forward. Colleen and Debbie blocked her, coaxing her to slow down. "The stairs are narrow; give them room. Help us get blankets and hot water."

Debbie spoke as though he were alive. Of course she would–Dave's urgency suggested that. I don't know that I could have waited. Colleen took her into the kitchen while Debbie opened the sofa bed and pulled blankets from all the other beds. My fingers sought the comfort of the length of yarn tied to my belt loop.

How ineffective I am. Everyone is doing something; I'm standing here stroking yarn. I suppose not adding to the fray is some help.

I absentmindedly tied and untied five slipknots and the tingling in my fingers abated. The first time I told my parents my fingertips tingled and my arms felt like strands of spaghetti would pop out of my skin, they rushed me to a neurologist. Too many tests later someone figured it out.

I wanted to do something. My glance fell on the Franklin stove. Perfect. Several pieces of kindling lay in the box. I knelt next to it and pulled open the metal door.

I spotted a bit of bright color and my stomach lurched with the certainty that someone had burned the original deed I'd seen last night. Garry had taken it; seems logical that he burned it. But if Garry hadn't been the one to shovel me into an igloo, he wouldn't have my book light. I slipped my hand into the ashes and picked out the bit of parchment. A quick brush through turned up nothing else.

"Do you need more wood?" Debbie spoke from over my shoulder and I jerked in surprise, dragging ashes onto the floor. "Sorry, Grace, didn't mean to startle you."

"Uh, no, I mean yes, I need a couple of pieces. Sorry, lost in thought–"

A blast of cold announced their arrival and the next few minutes played like a slow-motion tableau with *noir* special effects. The icy air swirled around our heads and stung our eyes as we watched the slow procession. Dave and Marty carried Garry between them, holding him under his arms and legs. Bob supported the unconscious man's head and shoulders–at least I hoped he was unconscious and not dead. The swirling stopped when Joan heaved her slight frame against the door. The secure slam of the door snapped the slow-motion sensation. They rushed Garry to the bed.

"Garry, oh my God. Garry!" Laurie swept into the space left when Dave straightened. She stared down at the white face and blue lips and shrieked, collapsing next to her husband. Dave knelt next to her, shaking her shoulders and lifting her in one movement. "He's alive, Laurie. We have to work fast to keep him that way."

Debbie pulled Laurie back a little. Marty and Dave slipped out of their jackets and started calling the shots and handling Garry. "Get his boots off. His clothes are damp; get them off too. Pull those blankets over him, roll him into a dry one, there, good." Marty and Dave's hands flew over the unconscious man until they had him tucked into a cocoon of woolen blankets. They left room to reach his hands and each took one and chaffed the wrist between their palms.

"Joan, get all the empty water bottles and fill them with hot water. We'll pack them around his body." Dave looked at Marty with a new appreciation. I went to help Joan. I heard my brother asking someone to get the stove going. I'd become distracted before I could start the fire. Big help I turned out to be.

"I was going to do that," I mumbled to no one; Joan heard me.

She nodded toward my grimy hand. "Looks like you tried, sort of." She led me around the corner. We found ten bottles and filled them. Laurie had recovered from her initial shock and helped us. Her eyes brimmed with tears. She struggled to keep herself together.

Dave and Marty continued chafing, lifted him to a sitting position and rubbing his back. They packed the bottles around his body between the layers, but not next to his skin. We would need to refill them soon. Joan heated more water.

Laurie sat on the floor close to Garry's head and gently stroked his cheek. His breathing remained shallow but steady. We'd done what we could and now we'd wait.

Colleen seemed to sense the timing and spoke quietly. "Can we search for Ken now?" Her usual boisterous tone diminished by her fear, she sounded like Laurie looked and I wondered how this holiday could have gone so wrong.

"Of course we can. Two people need to stay here with Garry. Laurie and…"

"I'll stay," Deb offered quickly. Marty nodded. "I noticed rope on the back seat when we pulled Garry out. I'll get it and meet you outside." He looked at his search party–from eight to six. The classic Christie thriller, *Ten Little Indians*, popped into my head, quickly followed by the end of the nursery rhyme…'and then there were none.'

# Chapter Twenty-four

Marty's instructions were clear: move forward when the line slackened until it became taut, make a patterned noise, then wait for the slack and move forward again. Marty cautioned us to be aware of wrapping our line around brush and getting snared. We'd moved twice now, pushing further into the interior. The destination was toward the cemetery and then shift toward the lighthouse, then shift again toward the cottage. If we returned to the cottage without Ken, then we'd try a circle toward the other direction, toward town. Bob and Dave were on the outside ropes, Joan and I in the middle.

The cold air seemed more manageable with the biting wind blocked by the trees. I tried to imagine what it must have been like that first and only winter for the Huron and Jesuits who fled to this island. The few hundred who survived left the island to be populated later by Indians from Beausoliel Island, who came in small groups that could be sustained by the land. Did those first Indians come because they, too, thought the Jesuits had hidden their gold on Christian Island?

The tug against my waist pulled me out of my thoughts. I'd walked out the length and needed to signal. My noisemaker filled the air with a harsh *clackity clackity clackity*. This part of the rescue was right up my alley. If I spun it twice then sort of snapped it, the pattern was *clackity, clackity, clack*. I designed a pattern with two sets of the usual and then one set of the odd hoping the structured sound would find Ken. *Or will we stumble upon his body, or will we never find him or will we...geez, Gracie, stop already*. I shook my head to clear the morbid thoughts and moved against my rope to see if I should continue. I began walking.

The visibility wasn't good. It began to snow again, but rather than flakes it created a fog that made watching your step critical. I remembered the story of the couple who swore the ghost of the lighthouse keeper had saved their lives when they wandered off the path. The fog thickened around me, and in the instant when your brain makes that 'blink of an eye' connection, I knew the fog was only around me. I stopped walking and waited, knowing I was throwing off the pattern, but scared to move blindly ahead. If I signal off pattern, will they understand I need help? It feels like I'm under the snow again. *Don't move. Who thinks I'm moving? You can't just stand there. Who says? Do something, Gracie, even if it's wrong. That's exactly how I get into trouble. I'm not budging.* My mind embroiled in controversy, my feet rooted to the spot, the scream burst from my throat fueled from frustration and fear. The cathartic effect calmed me and allowed me to focus a little better on my problem. If this fog only surrounded me, then it was here for a reason. "What reason, dammit?" I tilted my head back and yelled at 'up' since I couldn't see the sky through the velvety cover. "Is this a warning? Is there a sinkhole in front of me? What?" I hardly expected an answer, so when the rope around my waist slipped down to my feet I jumped and whirled around, only to tangle my feet and lose my balance. No cosmic hand at work here, just OCD rearing its pesky head. I'd more than likely untied my rope during my mental ruminations. I reached out to regain my rope and it slithered away from my fingertips. Marty must have pivoted, and without me anchoring the rope it pulled away. I scrambled to my feet, but realized too late that I couldn't see the ground clearly. *How stupid of me. Why didn't I just crawl forward when I was still connected?* I dropped to all fours and looked for the end of the rope. No use, I couldn't find it. *What's happening to me? Is this fog real? Are they going to find me clearly visible cowering on the ground? This fog has to be real or I'm going crazy.*

I shook my head and pounded the ground to shake the 'C' word from my head. My mother's struggles with manic depression kept the fear of my predisposition close at my elbow—always crowding me when I reached for clarity. *I'm not going crazy, so it is real, so I need to stay low and move backwards until I find the damn rope.*

It felt good to have a plan. I crawled along the way I'd walked praying I'd find the end. My mind synched with my knees and hands. One, two, three, four, crawl along the forest floor…One, two, three, four, crawl along the forest floor...

I giggled and the sound outside my head brought me up abruptly on the 'normal side' of my brain. *This is serious, I shouldn't giggle. It means I'm stressed. Okay, so I'm stressed. Who wouldn't be? It's inappropriate. It's not; anyway I'm stopping, I only agreed to ten.*

I stopped and peered into the white gloom. Another round of noise reached my ears. Since I'd doubled back it sounded weak, but discernible as a signal. If I were lost I'd realize help was near. My hand brushed across the rope. I gripped it with a sense of accomplishment. "Yes!" I shouted at the sky I believed to still be up there and scrambled to my feet. I tied the slack rope around my waist and double knotted it. I'd have to hike back the trail quite a distance to catch up to everyone else.

I moved slowly shuffling my feet through the path my hands and knees had already marked. I heard the signaling again and stopped to add my *clackity, clackity, clack. At least I could make noise even if I wasn't in the right spot. I've surely been walking faster than I crawled; I must be close to where I lost the rope, where I thought the fog might be hiding a gaping hole.* And with that memory the fear of a nagging premonition returned. My heart raced, my feet stopped and fear owned me.

*Cripes, Gracie. You'll be here all day.*

*If you're in such a damn hurry, go ahead.*

The child psychologist my parents had sent me to taught me how to focus outside of my head whenever my internal monologue turned to dialog. A simple thing that a child could do in a classroom, in a group of children on the playground, in church, and not draw attention to herself.

I bit down on the inside of my cheek, hard enough to introduce pain and break up the conversation. If I wasn't so bundled up, I would have pinched myself. I spoke out loud to shore up my confidence. "If it's real fog, it's not a warning. If it's real fog, it could be obscuring a hole. If it's 'woo woo' fog, there's definitely a hole." During the millisecond between deciding and moving, the hairs on the back of my neck stiffened against my scarf. Something moved toward me.

# Chapter Twenty-five

Flight or fight? I had the adrenaline, felt the energy rush to my extremities. Fight who or what? Flee where? I strained, trying to see shape, size…something to give me a clue as to what was coming.

A figure materialized a scant five feet in front of me. We gasped and jumped in chorus. Danny King rushed at me. I stepped back quickly and tripped over the rope, landing hard on my rear. "Omph! Oww!" I tried to 'butt-scoot' backwards. King dropped to his knees next to me and grabbed my shoulder. He must have sensed the scream about to erupt and clamped his hand over my mouth. In my disadvantaged position I couldn't struggle against his strength.

"You're the American. I'm not going to hurt you; stop wiggling." He had to lean close to be heard above the wind, which suddenly increased. "We've got big wind coming; we can't stay here." He removed his hand from my mouth and pulled me to my feet. I don't think my scream would have carried in the storm careening down on us. The temperature must have dropped or the wind made it seem that way. He gestured to the rope. "What's this?" He didn't wait for an answer; his bare fingers fumbled with the double knot. "Come on, too late to get to the cottage. We need cover." He pulled me along with him, breaking the path and holding branches as we passed.

Grim thoughts raced through my head. Had the killer found me? Was I next? Would he bother to drag me behind him if he wanted to kill me? The wind howled around us, whipping the branches and urging us to run the gauntlet. Only we couldn't run. King walked steadily, keeping me behind him and safer from the painful slashes. Would he try to protect me this way, only to kill me later? He could use both hands to protect himself if he wasn't holding on to me. Protecting or abducting? My face felt numb and the icy cold was penetrating my gloves and boots. If I'd fallen into that hole, if there was a hole, at least I'd be out of the wind.

The wind lessened and I realized we were next to a large stone…no, a wall. He'd brought us to the crumbled house. We scrambled the dozen feet to the lighthouse. The immediate cessation of the wind was bliss. King's back stiffened a split second before I saw the other occupant.

"Found your way out of the storm, eh? Or were you looking maybe for something else and just got caught up in our big wind?"

Ken stepped out of the shadows. "Damn thing came up on me, got me all turned around." He looked at me, his expression hesitant– not what I'd expect from someone who should be happy to see friends. Maybe he didn't consider us friends, especially King.

"What are you doing this end of the island? Nothin' down here 'cept old ruins and ghosts."

Ken stared at him and then glanced at me. He knew I knew where he'd started out with Dave. Would he lie about that?

"Dave and I went to the post to use the phones. The cottage phone is out. Dave wanted to find you, but I wanted to get back to my wife. I thought I knew my way back. In the summer I'd turn at the house with the purple birdfeeder on the high pole and then turn again when I could see the yellow canoe stuck upright in the sand." He looked embarrassed. "There's nothing out there now but snow."

King laughed and the creases around his eyes deepened. "Bethanne, she will be tickled to hear her birdhouse is a cottager's inukshuk." He turned serious as quickly as he'd laughed. "Wind coulda' messed with that line. Maybe old line?"

Ken shook his head. "Wind couldn't get at it, someone did."

His tone left no room for inference. King pulled off his furry hat and thick gloves. He focused his attention on me. "What were you doing wandering in the woods?"

Anger flared inside me. I was tired, scared, worried, and this island yahoo questioned me like I was a truculent child. "I was not wandering; I was part of a search party out looking for him."

"Part of a…Holy Jezzies, are there more of you out there?" His body snapped to action. He looked ready to rush out the door.

I nodded. Ken's voice cracked. "Colleen? Is she out there?"

I nodded again. Now Ken looked ready to jump into action. King stepped toward him. "She's safer with them then you'd be on your own out there." It looked like he was prepared to stop him.

Ken pointed to the walkie-talkie on King's hip. "Can't you call for help on that?"

"Storm's too centered right now–nothing gets through."

Ken swung back to me. "Who's out there with her?" His expression looked pained, but something else, cagey like he was treading around wanting to ask me something, but not wanting to.

Both men waited for me to announce the roster. Should I tell them about Garry? Did Ken already know? He's the one who'd taken out the snowshoes. He'd jumped to the task, protecting his secret a little longer. "Everybody's looking for you. Except Garry, who's on the mainland, I guess. Dave tried to call him from the post." They seemed to accept my explanation. "Marty gave us long ropes and he wrangled us…letting us walk forward till the rope tightened, letting us signal, then walking forward to give us slack to move again."

Ken shook his head. "I didn't hear anything. Colleen is out there now?"

"They may not be looking for you by now." King shrugged. "I know that search method. The pivot person tugs each line to make sure the tension is there. When he tugged on your line and it slackened, he may have signaled the others to come back." He shook his head and pushed his hair off his forehead. "Amateurs."

"Well, you weren't helping us. We told you Garry was missing, not running away. You knew about the break-ins and the pranks."

He threw his hands up and paced off some agitation before he whirled and fixed me with an icy stare. Even the fading light couldn't hide the anger that sparked from his eyes. I stepped back and realized I was already against the wall.

"Missing, not running; pranks," he mimicked. "My uncle and cousin are dead. You people are the only strangers."

"Not true." Ken's low voice stopped King. The cop turned.

"What's that supposed to mean?"

"The developer's been on the island since Tuesday. Along with the gaming commissioner and the president of Maple Bank. This is the week the Council votes and everyone wanted to be on hand."

"Gaming commissioner?"

Ken smiled. "There's a rumor that once the development goes through, the next vote is for a casino with a substantial percentage of gross receipts divvied up between the bona fide Band residents."

"That's crap!" King swung round to face Ken. "No one wants a casino. You're saying a world-renowned developer, a highly placed public servant, and the president of one of Canada's largest banks are conspiring to kill off 'no' votes?"

It did sound bizarre when you heard it out loud. I looked at Ken. He seemed to lose some wind, but hurried to counter. "Maybe not them, but they can hire it to be done, or maybe an overzealous underling hoping to swing the vote to the 'aye' aisle."

"Junior henchmen?" I asked. "That doesn't make sense."

"What doesn't make sense is that my uncle and cousin were split. Unless there are two hit squads, only my cousin would have qualified."

"Your cousin? I would have thought…"

"Yeah, me too. Old Joe wanted to live the soft life for whatever time he had left. He loved to gamble. It was my cousin who opposed the development. He and about two dozen young Band members formed a tight group that wanted to return the island to its early days and use. Home school their kids, grow their own food, no electricity. Personally, I think it's a cult."

"What kind of cult?"

"They wanted to go back to Indian ways and the culture on the island before the French and Jesuits interfered."

Ken voiced my thought. "Maybe one of your own people killed your cousin to break the group." He stared at King and shrugged. "Why kill the old man first, or at all, if he was voting yes?"

King spoke slowly. "Because if they'd killed my cousin first, there'd be no place on this island or off they could hide from Joe. He'd hunt them down and kill them hard."

I didn't want to know what that meant and cleared my throat to stifle the queasy feeling. Both men looked at me. A thought popped into my head and out my mouth. "Sounds like the killer is someone who knew enough about his victim to kill the father first, which sounds like a Band member, not a stranger."

King's posture shifted and I knew he'd probably thought of that already, but hadn't wanted to believe that the killer was one of his people—perhaps a friend or associate. I'd felt that sinking sensation. Were there two killers on this small island—one killing Band members for a vote and one attempting to kill cottagers for…what?

# Chapter Twenty-six

Questions galloped through my head jockeying for pole position in my mind. I couldn't keep any order to the thoughts; the jumble of 'what ifs' and 'whys' began to fade to a blurred twirling, like a merry-go-round out of control. I heard the two of them arguing over whose side seemed more capable of murder. I ignored them and focused on nothing, hoping the roiling condition of my mind would subside. The Velcro strips on the wrists of my gloves had long since been pressed into service. I smoothed scratchy ends together and pulled them apart. Together…apart…short staccato bursts…slow, staccato, slow…

About the time the annoying noise must have penetrated their conversation, a clear line of questions formed in my head.

"What are you doing?" King nodded at my hands. "It's annoying as hell."

I shrugged. "I needed to calm down to think straight. Sometimes ideas get turned around in my head and I have to–"

"Stand at the straight part of the river," King finished. I looked at him in surprise.

"My grandmother always told us we couldn't see what was coming if we made plans standing at the bend in the river." He smiled slightly. "My cousin, he looked from the bend."

His analogy struck a chord in me and I felt better about him as a person. My decision must have been as transparent as a thought crossing behind a glass forehead. Ken stared at me and exploded. "What? So his grandmother said some stupid crap and now he's a good guy? He's the only person who said Garry left the island. How do we know he didn't do something to Garry?"

"Because you stuffed Garry in the trunk of the car and left him to die. Because you tried to kill me last night when you packed snow around me." The outburst left me panting from my anger and regretting what I'd blurted.

Reaction from both men came fast and opposite. King stood quietly, seemingly processing this information against his own thoughts. Ken jumped toward me. "Are you crazy? I didn't try to kill you, or kill anyone. Garry's dead? I thought..." His voice trailed off.

I'd slid toward King when Ken reacted. Was I feeling safer with him because he was a cop, or did some instinct lead me to that conclusion? Ken looked homicidal, he was so angry. Is that what happened with Garry, he just snapped? Maybe Ken saw him burn the deed. Why would he care? Why do they care–jobs, inheritance, buried treasure, land? *Take your pick, Gracie girl.* I hate when I ask tough questions. Too many questions, too many angles.

Ken backed away and tried a different tack. He spoke calmly, "I didn't try to hurt you and I didn't hurt Garry. I'm going to leave to go look for Colleen. I don't expect anyone," he stared at King, "to try and stop me. My wife is out there and I'm going to her."

As if on cue the wind howled louder, pounding against the thick walls.

"It's a blow. You won't get to her. You can't find your way in this. They're in a group and where I found this one was close to the cemetery. There's shelter there, Dave knows that." He stopped.

"What shelter? There's nothing there except tombstones." Ken stepped toward him. "You're saying that to keep me here."

"He didn't mean to say that, Ken." The interior was too dark now to read the look in King's eyes. "Did you?"

"The altar stone, there's a room under it. If you shift the top the short end rotates open. It takes two men to do it, the ancient mechanism doesn't move easily."

My curiosity outstripped the bit of fear gnawing at me. "Who built it? Why do you think Dave knows about it?"

"He grew up close by. Spent lots of time on the island with scouts and then on his own. I've known him since those days; days when he thought the best life would be to live on island and fish and swim, and I thought the best life would be mainland wearing shoes and having people call me 'mister.'"

King sighed. I couldn't tell if he thought wistfully about those younger days, or if he'd said more than he could afford for us to know and regretted his next step. "Davy knows," he finished softly.

I didn't like the way he spoke. I wanted to keep him talking and not thinking. "Who built it?"

He looked from Ken to me and apparently decided he could tell us. He switched into 'Chamber of Commerce' mode. "The altar stone was constructed, near as folks can tell, by the Plano Indians, descendents of the Palaeo Indians, long before Huron and Iroquois First Nations were here. The upright stones came much later. Archeologists suspect the cave-room might have been where an offering was kept before sacrifice. Both animal and human bones were found inside."

I shivered from the thought. Ken mistook it for cold, and pointed toward the charred cabinet. "Let's get a fire going with that. I brought in a few pieces of wood. Anything else left in here we can burn?"

"No, when we went through here this was the only piece left. I'm okay. Don't start a fire yet, we may need it later."

"Good advice," King nodded. "I think the storm's pitchin' high."

I didn't recognize the colloquialism, but I understood its meaning…the storm was peaking. Hopefully it would blow out soon. I sat down on the cold stone floor and leaned against the wall.

"You be best served by sitting back on your heels. The cold will hurt you bad."

I silently grumbled, but realized he was right and shifted onto my feet and into a squat with my lower back against the wall and my arms resting on my thighs. King and Ken followed suit. We looked like three squat statues holding up the wall.

The wind screamed and thundered through the open windows and the lantern room. The sound reminded me of unquenchable anger and inconsolable sorrow and I tried to concentrate on something else. A sense of sorrow plucked at my heart and I felt my fingers begin to itch inside my gloves. Part of me knew what was coming next. The cold that brought strange thoughts and sights always brightened the room to crystal clarity. I was seeing the faces of King and Ken more clearly than a moment before. The temperature dropped and ice crystals hung in the air, brightly lit by a source other than nature. They circled downward, swirling and gliding toward a three-foot-square area landing and coating only that spot.

The light dimmed and I felt the warmth rush back to my body. I stood, using the wall to guide my unsteady rise. "What's under there?"

King and Ken glanced where I pointed.

"I see dirt," King said.

Ken leaned forward. "Can't believe we didn't see it sooner." He picked up a piece of wood and scraped at the outline in the dirt.

"Good eyes," he said.

Apparently, only I'd seen the markers. "Is the ground wet?"

"No, why?"

"No reason." I leaned against the wall and wondered again why bizarre always happened to me.

"Give me a hand. This old dirt sticks like glue on the edges."

Ken's face strained with the effort. I heard the sound of wood releasing from wood like old windows painted shut, and I knew they'd broken the seal. The three-foot-square lifted back against a hinge and hit the floor with a low thud. Dust jumped up from its edges rushing to fill King's and Ken's eyes. "Cripes, what is this?"

"The area around the point has caves and tunnels reaching hundreds of yards into the island." He pulled a mini-maglite from his inside pocket and trained the beam on the ladder against the edge. "Looks like no one's been down this end for years."

"What is it, a storm cellar?"

King grinned over his shoulder. I saw the gleam of white in the low light. "Escape route, more likely." King climbed down and by the depth of the beam the drop looked like about eight feet. He shined the light up. "Uncle Joe always swore you could get out to the stone from here." The beam and his voice were moving away from us.

Ken moved to follow him. He stopped on the third step down, his head just above the opening. "Staying or coming?"

I froze with indecision. Did I want to climb down into a dark hole with two men, one of whom might be a killer? Absolutely not!

"I'll wait here. You know, keep a light on in the window." My quip sounded stupid, but I had skidded into nervous mode.

"Suit yourself, but I'm dying to know where this goes." Ken's head disappeared. I heard him call, "King, where are you? Shine that light back here." I barely heard a response and didn't see any light.

Did I choose wisely for a change? I think so. I pulled some of the wood over to the edge and sat on that rather than the icy floor. I heard distant shouts, but couldn't make out the words. That sounded serious. *Should I go? Absolutely not! Maybe they're hurt and need my help. Yeah, like you'd be a big help.*

I bit the inside of my cheek to stop the dialog. Dammit, I hated that I couldn't think straight in times of stress.

I edged closer to the ladder. If everyone was down there, I certainly didn't want to be the only one up here. With that thought in mind I slowly climbed down, looking up at the opening pulling further away from me, or so it seemed to my mind. I stood still and the square light moved up, up, and away.' *...in my beautiful balloon...* bits of an old sixties song ran through my head. "Not now," I pleaded. The sound of my voice snapped the fugue feeling and I moved quickly down the remaining rungs, not looking up.

The darkness surrounded me, and I fought the urge to rush up the ladder. Instead, I waited until my eyes grew accustomed to the minimal light provided by the open trap door. I was about to call out when I heard sounds of a scuffle further down the chamber. I moved away from the ladder until I felt my back against the wall. It was cold but not icy, and I wondered idly if the temperature would be a constant fifty-five degrees like Eagle Cave, where the scouts went every year. At least it wasn't dripping in here.

I heard a slight noise against the far wall and my focus returned. I wanted to call out, but found my voice unwilling. Should I reveal myself? I stayed quiet and strained to see. Movement at the bottom of the ladder caught my eye. Just enough light to faintly outline a man. Was it Ken? Dark jacket, dark pants. A noise from the other end startled me, and I turned to stare in that direction. Maybe they were walking toward the ladder and the scuffle sound was people tripping. They should be making more noise if they are a 'they' and not a 'he.'

A scraping noise, the ladder being pulled up, stunned me, then spurred me to action. I'd taken two steps toward the dim square of light and then it was obliterated with the crashing sound of wood against wood. In my panicked brain I visualized the torn edges sealing quickly and securely against each other.

*Oh, God. Oh, God. Please, I can't stay here. Please, help me. Please!* The keening in my head finally escaped through my stiff lips.

"Grace? Grace! Are you down here?"

I turned toward the voice and pressed the palms of my hands into my eyes to absorb the tears. I strained to see Ken; I could sense he was moving toward me. I swallowed hard and called out in a croaky voice. "Over here, against the wall."

A tiny light appeared and preceded him to my side. I stared at my book light in his hand.

# Chapter Twenty-seven

"Thought you were staying up top. Why'd you come down?"

I stared at the tiny light and could only focus on the thought that I was trapped with the man who'd tried to kill me.

"Grace, are you okay?" He moved the light up to my face.

I squinted and he lowered the light. "I'm confused. I'm scared. I thought I heard someone say Dave and I thought everyone was down here. Why did King leave us here?" I really was confused on that point. If Ken was responsible for the attempts and deaths, why would King leave us to die? If King was responsible, why does Ken have my book light?

"Bastard tricked me too. He was ahead of me, bouncing his beam enough that I could follow. He called out like he saw Dave, and shouted some crap that he always thought the rooms connected. Then his light went out. Next thing I know he's trying to sneak past me in the dark, only he didn't know I had this and it was just enough light for me to spot his movement. I admit I was slow to understand, and he knocked the wind out of me and shoved me against the wall. I wish you had stayed up there."

"You and me both." I decided to deal with one crisis at a time and made an effort to speak calmly. I hoped any nervousness I showed would be expected given our circumstances. "Maybe we can push the door up if I stand on your shoulders."

Ken looked up, taking some time to answer. "I don't know, I suppose it's worth a try. Trap door looks ten feet high or more."

"I thought it was only about eight feet. You're six feet and I'm five four. That's enough." I thought I made perfect sense. I'd seen this in the movies and it worked beautifully. Why is he hesitating? Doesn't he want to get out of here? Maybe he only wants to get himself out of here. Or maybe he doesn't trust me to go for help once he boosts me out. Ridiculous. He's probably worried he can't lift me.

I thought about that. Standing next to him, he didn't appear as tall as Harry's six-foot frame and he wasn't nearly as muscular. I had put on a few pounds this past year…only seven, but at my height it accounted for snugger jeans and a shadow of a love handle.

"Suppose we have no other choice." Ken widened his stance and squatted, bracing himself like a tripod. He folded his hands palms up and interlaced his fingers. "Step here, hold my shoulders and step onto them. When I feel your foot steady I'll grab hold of your ankle with one hand and push your other foot up. Use the ceiling for balance if you can reach it."

I removed my hat and gloves and stuffed them into roomy pockets, then nodded, took a deep breath, and placed my foot in his hands and my hands on his shoulders. I lurched up a few inches off the ground and settled back, slipping out of his handhold.

"What's wrong?"

"I lost my balance. I'm ready now."

Ken repositioned himself. "Okay. One, two, three."

I stepped into his hand 'stirrup' and launched myself onto his frame. I felt him wobble under my weight and hurried to swing my free foot to his shoulder. At this point I realized it only looked easy in the movies or if we'd both had ballet training. My momentum was slowing and I felt like I was shifting backwards. Ken must have sensed my shift and lifted up with hands to keep me steady. I managed to get my foot on his shoulder, but when he grabbed my ankle he couldn't get a firm grip because of the hiking boot. He still tried to push my other foot up, but I overbalanced and started to slide.

"Wait, wait. Let me down." I slid down assisted by his arm. I had a cramp in my calf. "This is harder than it looks."

Ken stood straight and stretched. "Why don't I get down and you climb on my shoulders? You'll be more stable that way."

"Great idea." I could do this. Ken assumed the position and I eagerly clambered onto his shoulders. "Okay, I'm set." I resisted the urge to cue him with 'giddy-up.'

Ken slowly stood. I watched the ambient light seeping through the disturbed edges of the trap door. Ken had given me the book light to find the latch side of the door. I clicked on the tiny beam. A little more and I would touch the door. I reached out my hand. It was inches from the panel. Ken was upright.

"I can't reach it."

"Okay, I'm bringing you down. You'll have to kneel on my shoulders." He lowered me until I could hop off his back. Ken stood and rolled his neck and shoulders. I couldn't imagine how much this effort hurt him. I could sense rather than see his movements. "Let's try it again." I groped for his shoulders and managed to get on. I heard his sharp intake of breath and knew my knees must feel like bony rocks burrowing into his shoulders. He held onto my thighs and stood swaying momentarily till he firmed his stance.

The ceiling rushed toward me and I ducked my head fearing a collision. My upward motion stopped in time. "I can reach it. I got it."

"Great. Push it open." His short terse reply told me how much effort he was making to hold me up here. I shifted a bit to get a better position. I felt him wince.

"Sorry."

"Just hurry."

My full palms lay flat on the panel with my elbows bent slightly. I would have liked to have been closer so I could use the full flex of my elbows to leverage the door up. I wished I could be upside down since my leg strength was many times stronger than my upper body strength. I pushed and extended my elbows. The panel didn't budge. I pushed harder…still no movement. Tears rushed to my eyes and I dug in my knees and prepared to launch myself against the door if necessary. Suddenly I dropped two feet and realized Ken had dropped to his knees. I jumped, half fell off his shoulders, and heard his gasp.

"Sorry, I couldn't hold you. My shoulders feel like they're on fire. Let me rest a little, and we'll try again."

I knew that wouldn't work. I wasn't strong enough to push it open from that distance and together we weren't tall enough to get me a better shot. If I could push up with my back and shoulders… No matter, it wasn't going to happen. Ken's breath whistled through his teeth. We had to find another way.

"The tunnel you mentioned. Do you think they do connect?"

"Problem is, it's not just one tunnel. I could tell King had turned down at least two by how his light moved. He knows these tunnels."

"I don't know. He seemed surprised to find the door and the ladder did have a lot of cobwebs like it hadn't been used for a while." I surprised myself that I'd noticed. My brain stored odds and ends for processing. Did I have the luxury of taking the time to let it sort?

I could sense Ken shaking his head. "No, he knew where to turn. I'm sure of that; he moved too fast. He'd swing the light high to check the openings and then turn into one."

"He was following the inusuit. You couldn't see them with your tiny light. He knows how to read them. If we can find them we can get out of here. C'mon." I stood and lurched against him on the uneven ground. Would he take his chance now to finish the job he'd started? Did he feel confident he could follow the trail without me?

Ken steadied me with his arm. "Okay, it's worth a try. Anything is better than waiting. You think you can figure these out? To me they look like they're pointing in all directions."

"They set them that way to confuse the people. Joan said each group would have a common element to look for that was known only to them. Like a visual password. If they topped the inukshuk with a reddish stone or round stone, that could mean turn right. Otherwise, the wrong people might find them."

"If that's true, then only people in their clan, tribe, whatever could help them or find them. We don't have a password."

His statement flattened my enthusiastic explanation. "Maybe we don't need one; maybe the same clan built this tunnel and the markers are straightforward. Let's find one and see."

Ken shrugged. "Like I said, it's better than waiting here. Give me the light." He crossed in front of me and our shoulders brushed in the narrow tunnel. He could turn on me any time. He thought he needed me to get out. He still does. I stepped back. If he noticed my abrupt move, he didn't comment. Ken moved slowly, holding the tiny light at the level of his eyes and searching the wall for crude drawings. I couldn't stand the silence. "Do you think this started out to be a connecting tunnel? It doesn't seem logical that two such diverse groups in two different eras would want to connect to each other."

"I think I found one." Ken's voice shook with excitement. "Look.

Can you make it out?"

I'd have to stand close to him to see the drawing in the low light. Was the light weaker than before? How long could a book light last? The urgency of the moment forced me next to him. I strained to remember the pictures I'd seen in Joan's library books. "This looks straightforward enough. It's pointing us to the left."

"That's wrong. There's no tunnel on the left and if there were it would be turning us back toward the lighthouse."

"How can you tell? I'm already turned around."

"I don't know, just feels that way." I couldn't see his expression.

"I'm pretty sure this means go to the left, or maybe it doesn't mean turn but just stay left."

"Until when, the light?" His tone held more panic than sarcasm. "Can we try?"

He mumbled and crossed the few feet to the other wall. He kept walking with the light pointing down at his feet. He moved quickly and I could barely see the weak beam on the ground. I kept my hand on the wall as I hurried to follow. The light blinked out of my sight and my hand hit thin air. I stumbled and shouted. "Here, back here."

Ken's footsteps smacked loudly against the dirt floor. He pushed his light forward into the thin air I'd found, illuminating another more narrow and lower tunnel. "Never would have seen this. Good job."

The 'atta girl' sounded genuine, even friendly. Was I wrong about Ken? This tunnel path spanned less than two feet. Were we walking down a tunnel to nowhere?

"Ken, wait. Let's try and mark this entrance in case we get turned around or if someone comes looking for us or…" I didn't want to follow the thought any further.

"Good idea, and I've got just the thing." He pulled a roll of duct tape from his inside pocket and ripped off a piece, using his teeth. "We'll tape it eye-level."

"Fold the edges and make a point like an arrow." He handed me the light while he worked the tape. "Won't stick with the ends folded." He quickly ripped three more strips, one as long as the first and two shorter ones. He made a double wide arrow and then added the two short pieces at angles to make the point.

"Perfect. Let's find another inukshuk before this goes out."

I handed the light to him, preferring to follow rather than have my back to him. We could only move single file, so we decided to each keep a hand on our side of the tunnel in case we missed the sign but found a tunnel. I had the left side. The beam waned and we decided to conserve the light and move slowly until we found a side tunnel and then back up and look for the drawing. The one we'd found was about twenty feet from the opening. Ken stayed in front and our progress was slow but safe. No room for twisted ankles or broken bones. I'd put on my glove to protect my hand and found the sound of my Gore-Tex glove against the rough wall soothing. *Swish, swish, swish.* Sounded like the rustling of taffeta. *Swish, swish, swish.* I felt my mind relaxing, and with that calmness came the natural process of sorting the data: the bits of conversation, the scraps of papers, the 'flotsam and jetsam' of my life. An idea…no, more of an explanation began to form and work its way to my consciousness. I slowed trying to rush the answer.

"Oww! Dammit." Ken's voice boomed from ahead of me. "Mind your head, the ceiling dips."

At my shorter height I didn't run the same risk, yet. Ken hunched over and continued more slowly. Soon I had to crouch and Ken found it easier to move ahead on all fours. He kept his elbow bowed out to catch any opening in the wall. My legs were unaccustomed to this stride and unused muscles began to ache.

Ken stopped moving, causing me to lumber into him. I reached out to stop my fall and instinctively stood up, hitting the crown of my head smack against the ceiling. "Ouch. Why'd you stop?" I snapped. The top of my head felt warm and the iron smell of blood filled my nostrils. I pulled my hat from an inside pocket and jammed it on my head–meager protection from dirt and further scrapes.

"Sorry, didn't think. We must have missed another tunnel. It's getting lower. Let's go back."

"Back to where? We know we can't get out that way."

"This is going nowhere."

"Maybe they built them economically. I mean, why build high when you're only moving through them to get to the other end? It had to be high to get out from under the lighthouse. Maybe the ceiling isn't getting lower, but the ground higher."

"What?"

Sometimes my logic was apparent only to me. I hurried to explain. "If the cemetery is on higher ground, then when they started to connect the rooms and the lighthouse room had been dug out for a cellar, the tunnel would slant down coming toward us because otherwise there'd be a huge drop." I thought I made sense.

"So if we keep going we'll get to a larger room at the other end?"

"Exactly."

"Why didn't you just say so?" he mumbled.

I assumed that was rhetorical and waited in silence until he began to move again. We'd moved a few feet when Ken called out, "I feel an opening."

I moved closer. We cast the light slowly over the rocky wall.

"There! Stop!" The inukshuk pointed straight.

"That's not possible," I mumbled.

"What is it? What's wrong?"

"This says to go straight. Why would they have a tunnel here if we're to go straight?"

"You read it wrong, is all. It's not like you're an expert."

He started to move away. "Ken, wait. It's pointing down this tunnel. We need to keep going."

"I'm going down this tunnel. You can go straight if you want to."

He knew I wouldn't be able to read any more signs without the light. Then again, he didn't follow the signs when we found them.

"Okay, but I'll take my light." I froze after I spoke.

"Your light?"

Praise the Lord that he can't see my eyes turning purple. What's the rest of that saying–and pass the ammunition. Wish I had something besides gloves and a noisemaker in my pockets.

"Yes," I said softly. "It's my book light. I lost it somewhere."

Would he admit he found it on the deck right before he tried to bury me?

"I found it wedged in the bumper of Dave's car when I got out the snowshoes. Guess I just put it in my pocket. Here. I don't think these drawings mean anything anyway." He handed me the light. "Let's put up some duct tape in case one of us has to backtrack."

My head raced with the new information. If he found the light on the bumper, who dropped it there? Have I been wrong in my suspicions? The sound of duct tape ripping broke into my thoughts.

"Ken, without the light you won't be able to see the tape."

"I won't need to. This is the right tunnel, I can feel it. Decide, Grace. Come with me or don't, but we have to keep moving. Whoever finds help first brings the cavalry."

My lack of movement made his decision. Ken started away from me. I heard him shuffle off, still on all fours. Did I want to do this alone? Why did I believe a crude drawing on the wall over a live person? Because I thought that live person had tried to kill me?

My personal mantra kicked in. *Geez, Gracie, do something even if it's wrong.* I turned back to the original tunnel and started forward. I moved along with both my arms stretched out skimming the walls for new tunnels. Thank goodness the tunnel was narrow enough to do this, otherwise I'd have to bounce from side to side like an errant silver ball running amok through the pins. That visual made me chuckle, and the noise startled me. I started to hear other noises that perhaps the sound of Ken's breathing and our low conversations had covered. Or maybe I was imagining a boogeyman. As a child I'd make deals with the boogeyman in the basement when my mother sent me there to fetch a can of tomato paste or a box of pasta. My brain made a deal; I would take ten steps, then stop, go back two steps, then go forward again for ten steps. This was the only way my mind would let me keep moving. It might take a little longer, but I'd have safe passage.

My pattern established, I moved on letting my mind follow at its own pace. I felt calmness descend over me. I'd chosen correctly. I'd find help for Ken.

A bit of air drifted across my face and I realized that I'd passed an opening on my left without making note of it. Thank God for the air movement or I'd have daydreamed right past it. The air had to mean there was an opening down this way, but I had to check the wall for the inukshuk. I backed up and scanned the wall. Nothing. Maybe this didn't lead to the outside. Could be just movement caused the air current. Whose movement? Now I didn't know if I should turn in there. I realized that the other signs had been on the right hand side and I shifted to scan the other wall. There it was, and it indicated a turn. This had to be the right way. The air came from outside and that's where I was headed.

I found the opening and moved carefully into the new tunnel. It seemed as low as the one I'd left, but it smelled less dank and dusty. I stopped abruptly. Should I try to signal Ken, call out to him? I'd have to go back to the other tunnel. Could I find it in the dark, even with my light? I could back up to the main tunnel and call him from there and tell him to look for the light. Even a tiny light would shine like a beacon in the pitch-black tunnel, if it could penetrate far enough into the gloom. Now why'd I have to think that? I turned half circle to go back. Within a few moments I crouched in the opening and clicked on my light to guide him to me. Darkness continued. I shook it and tapped it lightly against my hand, but it stayed dark.

I shoved it into my pocket. My fingers touched the noisemaker. Why not, I thought. I could attract his attention and he could follow the sound of my voice or the *clackity clackity clack*.

I squatted on my heels, back against the wall, and began twirling the party favor. The noise reverberated through the tunnels until I thought the inusuit themselves would leave to regain some peace.

I stopped, fully expecting I'd attracted his attention. "Ken, come back. I found the way out. Come to the opening on your side and follow the tunnel to me. Ken, I found the way out." I waited for a response. I did another set of noise and shouts, and again waited in vain. He was out of earshot or he couldn't respond; I couldn't look for him, not without a light. He couldn't or wouldn't come to me. I had to leave. If he were injured he'd need help. I stuffed the noisemaker in my pocket. Lot of good it did.

A light bobbed toward me. Someone had heard me, but whom?

# Chapter Twenty-eight

The bright beam moved steadily down the tunnel. I'd expected to be thrilled to have rescue, but now I suspected the motives of whoever held the flashlight. Instead of calling out and revealing my position, I backed up into the side tunnel and waited.

My heart hammered against my chest and I breathed in shallow breaths. The air in this tunnel seemed fresher. *This must be the way out. I should follow it to the altar stone and my friends. You don't know that they're there. The storm may have let up and they're gone. Can you find your way from the cemetery at night? Without a light?*

Okay, I get it. The shrink had assured me that most everyone uses a form of internal dialog to assist in decision making. My issue was the length of dialog and multiple participants. Two people in my head for under a minute played perfectly sane. A troop of people, some of them deceased, chatting for minutes at a time, not so sane.

"Mrs. Marsden, can you hear me?"

King's voice sounded like he was only feet away.

"Mrs. Marsden, are you there? Mrs. Marsden, stay where you are, don't move. The side tunnels are dangerous."

He must have stopped moving to listen.

Dangerous? What does he mean? Is he saying that to get me to reveal myself? If he's so concerned, why'd he shut me down here in the first place? I can't think straight.

"Stop, stop, stop!" I'd meant to use my 'inside' voice, but had shouted out loud. I bit down on my lip in frustration.

"Mrs. Marsden, are you all right? You sound close by."

I could hear him making his way toward me and the imminent encounter spurred me to movement; I turned my back on the main tunnel. I heard him call again, but his voice sounded muffled and I knew he'd passed the opening to this tunnel. The quiet overtook me again and my mind wandered to what else might be down here. I hadn't heard any scurrying sounds, but that didn't mean there weren't creatures down here capable of scurrying.

*Don't start thinking about that.*

*I know, I know.*

A new sound reached my ears–water lapping against rock. *That can't be right.*

*Why not? You're in a cave; there could be an underground river. This is an island, right?*

The air felt cooler and heavier against my face. There must be a large area of water nearby. The water movement sounded like splashing now, not as gentle as before. I stopped walking and sat back on my heels, leaning against the wall. It felt good to straighten my spine. The wall felt damp; the humidity a direct result of the water I could hear.

How do I get into these situations? How am I going to get out?

I knew I had to make a decision. It seemed like this was the way out, but how big was the water source? The thought of tumbling into a pool of icy cold water paralyzed my mind. I could only envision me struggling within my heavy coat, slowly sinking to the bottom and being flushed out into Georgian Bay with the next tide. Was there a tide on the bay?

*This isn't the time for Trivial Pursuit questions.*

I know. I'm thinking.

I moved forward, hugging the wall and assuming that any water would be in the middle of the tunnel and not at the edges.

*Why do you think the water is only in the middle? This isn't a built-in pool, Gracie. The water could fill the tunnel at the next bend.*

*Do you have a better idea?*

I stayed close to the wall as it veered to the right. The air chilled immediately, and the sound of surf filled my head…only there was no surf. This was the white noise that signaled I'd overloaded and needed to stop. I sat down, ignoring the cold ground, and pulled my knees up to my chest. If I stayed still, the harsh static in my head would dissipate. I lowered my face to my knees and wrapped my arms around my legs–my breathing slowed and I felt a lessening of the tension across my shoulders. Muscles ached from activity and fear.

The temperature plummeted, no doubt the effect of the frigid water in an enclosed area. I must be close to the water.

*Don't think, just breathe.* I forced myself to empty my mind of 'what ifs' and concentrated on breathing. The cold thwarted my attempts to relax, but I didn't want to lift my head or move my arms to reposition myself on my heels. I tried harder to calm myself and let my mind settle down, but it was no use. Unbidden thoughts clamored for attention. I had to move or I'd root to the spot; some action had to be better than sitting here for eternity. With that resolve I loosened my arms and lurched up into a crouch, then stepped in place to regain the circulation in my legs. The smell of water and dank vegetation wafted toward me. I reached out for the wall and stepped forward.

# Chapter Twenty-nine

The light from behind me shone so brightly into the tunnel that my eyes squinted and closed in protest–I had to squinch them to a slit to acclimate to the brightness. They watered badly, and I blinked several times to clear them. Slowly, keeping my back to the light source, I opened my eyes.

My heart lurched and I leaned heavily against the wall. The water I'd heard and smelled lay ten feet ahead of me, stretched across the tunnel floor. No safe passage along the wall. As my knees weakened, I let myself slide to the ground, closed my eyes, and breathed a prayer of thanks. Thank God for Danny King and his persistence. I opened my eyes slowly to prepare for the brightness, but the light had dimmed. My eyes must be used to it, didn't seem nearly as strong. The beam bobbed toward me; I could make out his form behind the light. Something moved near him, a shadow in the light. I blinked, but now the beam filled my vision.

"Mrs. Marsden, are you in here?"

It was King. How did he miss seeing me? The tunnel had been lit up like birthday cake for an octogenarian.

"I'm here, to your right."

He swept the beam toward me, it bobbed and dipped with his crouched stride, finally reaching me. He hurried forward and knelt next to me. He kept the light pointed down between us. "Are you hurt?" I relished being able to see him in the low light.

"I'm fine, thanks to you and your timely illumination."

. His face showed confusion.

"Your light. I was headed for that." I guided his hand holding the flashlight toward the water. The light barely reached the edge, but I knew it was there because I'd seen the black water. "I don't understand. It was like high noon in here five minutes ago. Did your other light go out?" A thought pushed at the back of my mind, but I didn't want that explanation.

King stared at me. "I wasn't here five minutes ago. This is the only torch I have."

His words chilled me and, while I watched, he moved forward playing his light out before him. A low whistle escaped his lips. "Whatever lit up this water saved your life, Mrs. Marsden, but it wasn't me." He backtracked to my side. "Follow me out. We're closer to the cemetery than the lighthouse." He stopped, looked at me, and raised the light a little. "Can you do that? Are you all right?"

I could only nod. I looked in the direction of what surely would have been my death and, in that instant, remembered seeing something in the bright light on the far side of the pool. A vision of something shiny played in my head. I wouldn't be back to investigate, but I'd tell someone. Someone I trusted.

We retraced our steps to the main tunnel, backtracked to the tunnel Ken had taken, and followed that for maybe twenty yards before it opened up a little. Soon I could stand and King had only to hunch his shoulders. He stopped briefly to illuminate an inukshuk that pointed out a new tunnel. King ignored the direction and continued straight. Had I not seen it clearly? He missed the turn.

We veered to the left and dead-ended into a cavern. The area glowed in spots from small smudge pots set on the ground. The room's dimensions appeared to match the one under the lighthouse; no doubt made by the same hand.

"Why didn't you follow the inukshuk? We've missed the turn."

"I did follow them. I found you, didn't I?"

I sighed and closed my eyes for an instant remembering how close I'd come to death.

"Why aren't we in the other room? Who put out these pots?"

"You ask too many questions." His low tone made me uneasy.

"My brothers always said that. I've gotten better."

His eyebrow lifted. "Not good enough," he said softly.

The hairs on my neck set up and instinct screamed at me to get away. The low light covered the surprise and decision on my face. I grabbed the flashlight in his hand and thrust up at his chin, hitting the bony jaw dead center and then pulling the metal toward me. The crack from the blow sounded loud in my ears; his shout of pain and surprise louder. I had the light and took at least a few steps before the pain took a backseat to his anger.

Hopefully, he didn't have another flashlight. I hurried to the point where the tunnel peeled off from the main. I'd be safe if I could get to the others. Having the stronger light made my steps surer and faster. I thought I head steps behind me.

*Stupid, stupid. He's following my light.*

*Turn off the light.*

*Are you crazy? It'll be pitch black in here.*

*What did we agree about using the 'C' word?*

*Not now! I won't be able to see.*

*Neither will he.*

Sometimes you make me want to scream.

*Good idea.*

The pitch and duration of my scream shook the walls. In the eerie silence after the last reverberation, before voices lifted in concern, I heard steps moving away from me.

"Over here. Can you hear me?"

A man's voice sounded close, but I knew how sound played tricks down here.

"Answer us." Another clear voice rose in panic.

I didn't recognize the voices, maybe Bob's and Colleen's. The tunnel distorted the sound.

I inhaled to shout and froze a split second before a rough hand clamped over my mouth and pulled me back off my feet. The flashlight bounced out of my hand and rolled…settling against the far wall, its beam illuminating ten feet along the ground.

I fought the hand covering my mouth and tried to dig in my heels, but the angle eliminated that option and he dragged me away from rescue. I tasted blood in my mouth from the inside of my cheek.

"Can you hear me?" The first voice boomed. I knew I was being pulled away faster than he could follow. His voice would fade soon.

It dawned on me that I hadn't heard my brother's voice. Why? Surely he'd be shouting for me. Unless he wasn't there. Where would he be? Fear for his safety rose in my throat. He'd be rushing down the tunnel after me if he could. Oh my God, was he hurt? The thought of Marty injured or worse tore at my heart. I felt my knees crumble, and that movement caused my captor to stumble and loosen his grip to recover his balance. I pushed my elbow back hard hoping to topple him; his foot kicked at me and connected with the back of my knee. The pain jolted up through my thigh and to my back, but the kick had pushed me forward. I scrambled to a crouch and moved toward the glow from the flashlight. If I could reach it I'd have a weapon again.

He caught the back of my boot and I sprawled forward, hitting my chin so hard a stream of blood erupted from the gash. The coppery smell filled my nose and threatened to gag me. King's hand reached around my ankle and he lurched up to grab more of me. In his fervor he forgot the ceiling. I heard the *thunk* of his head hitting the rock and his shout of pain. I wiggled free and scooted back to a running crouch. I scooped up the light and rounded on my pursuer to blind him. I hunched, panting, playing the light across the tunnel scanning for King. No sign of him.

Fine by me. I turned and passed the point where he grabbed me before glancing uneasily behind me, frightened that history would repeat itself.

"Over here. Can you hear me?"

I could hear them again. Thank God. Their voices sounded close, closer than before.

I shouted back. "I'm here. I'm close."

I waited for more shouts to zero in on them. Silence.

"Hello, hello. Where are you?"

I leaned against the wall, lowering the light to my side. A bright circle of light on the dark ground offered little comfort in this labyrinth. I heard the shuffle of boots and turned toward the sound.

"Over here. Can you hear me?" The voice came from behind me but I didn't want to turn my back on King.

"Yes, yes. I'm nearby."

My spirits lifted with renewed hope for rescue. I pointed the flashlight at King and began to back away.

"Mrs. Marsden, stop. Stop moving."

*Yeah, stop moving, my butt. So you can jump me again.*

"Please."

The urgency and concern in his voice slowed my steps. *This is some kind of trick–no way, buddy.*

"Back up," my voice croaked after all the shouting.

"I will if that makes you stop moving." He shuffled backwards.

"Over here. Can you hear me?"

I turned to look over my shoulder toward the sound and heard him moving. I snapped my head back and shouted for him to stop. He stared down at his feet, not at me, and then he backed up and stepped forward quickly.

"Over here. Can you hear me?"

My head swiveled between the sound and King. He took another step, and again I heard the query.

"Over here. Can you hear me?"

King couldn't see my face, but in the low light he could read my body language. I waved the flashlight at him. He moved a few steps toward me, I leveled the light at his boots and inched the beam across the ground until I spotted the small receptacle.

"It's some sort of motion detector that sets off the recordings. There's probably another one farther down the tunnel. After that, in the dark it would be too late."

"What do you mean, too late?"

"I'll show you. Give me the light."

*Does he think I just fell off the cannoli truck, for God's sake?*

"So you can crack me over the head and leave me down here?"

"Mrs. Marsden, if I wanted to leave you down here, I wouldn't have come back for you."

"Come back?"

"Yes, come back. I pulled the ladder up to keep that cottager down here a bit till I could sort out who was guilty. I thought you were up top. When I realized you weren't there, I thought you'd left on your own. The storm's worst had passed and I made it to the cemetery in time to see Dave and Joan coming out from under the altar stone. They told me that they'd taken cover there, but had lost sight of Bob and Colleen."

"What about my brother?" I interrupted.

"They didn't say anything about him. I told them about you leaving the lighthouse and they said they'd look for you between the cemetery and the cottage. I realized then that you might have climbed down here. I came back in through the altar stone and worked my way back to the lighthouse. I'd told that fellow to stay put and I'd be back, but I did throw a bit of a scare at him. Told him if he didn't want to wait for me, he could try finding his way out on his own. Told him to always choose right."

"Choose right? Like make a good choice?"

"No, choose right. Not left, but right."

"He never said a word. When the inukshuk pointed left, he insisted that he was going to the right because he had a feeling. That little weasel." I realized that he'd stepped closer to me. I raised the light to his eyes and he turned his head sharply. "Don't."

He nodded, and I lowered the beam.

"You have to know how to read them, and then you have to know if the inukshuk tells the truth."

"The clan password. I didn't think it mattered down here. I thought it was just to mark the tunnel."

"To mark the tunnel for the clan and send intruders to their deaths. The inusuit only told truth to their own."

"Your clan dug these tunnels hundreds of years ago, before there was a lighthouse."

"The people before my people dug these tunnels. My people only marked the way, probably after several of them died mapping the treachery in the tunnels."

"And the treasure," I mumbled.

"The what?" King's voice rose.

I couldn't believe he didn't know. These were his tunnels, for heaven's sake. Probably better for my health if he didn't know I knew. "Hard to measure," I amended. "How to navigate these tunnels." I waved my hand toward the darkness. A thought sailed into my head cleaving the thoughts roiling in my brain. What if the topography of the island had been different? They found those coins off the lighthouse point. What if, in those days, a small boat could maneuver in and out of what looked like a simple cave? Great hiding place for your treasure. My mind shifted to stress mode and I conjured up man-size inusuit with their rocky arms folded like giant x's across their chests guarding the entrance. X marks the spot.

"Mrs. Marsden?"

King stood next to me, his hand lightly on my shoulder. I'd zoned out and missed his movement. Part of me knew I hadn't been on high guard because I'd decided somewhere in my head that he wasn't a threat.

"Mrs. Marsden, give me the light. I want to show you what lies ahead, if only so you believe me." I handed him the flashlight and hoped to hell that the decision making part of my head was on target.

He shuffled ahead of me, careful to keep me behind him; I heard the water and knew what to expect. He stopped and pointed the beam across the expanse of water–another pool or perhaps an extension of the one I'd seen earlier. The water level lay two feet below the tunnel at the end of a gentle grade and lapped against the far wall.

I shivered at the thought of where the voices had almost led me.

King turned and illuminated the tunnel. "Let's get out of here. I'll take you back to the cottage. Did you recognize those voices?" He'd shifted into police mode. The subtle voice change, a slight tightening in his tone, gave him away. "I know Dave's voice well enough, and Joan's is a giveaway…still sounds American to me."

"I've seen the others around here all summer, some more than others, but I couldn't tell their voices."

"Neither can I. What do you mean 'some more than others'? Don't they come up as a group for weekends?"

"Mostly, but two of the fellows came up regularly during the week. The one I left in the tunnel and the one that went missing."

"Ken and Garry? Why would they come on island without the Hamiltons?"

"Maybe with them."

"No. If there's anything hinky going on, Dave and Joan aren't part of it. I've known Joan since third grade. She'd never do anything illegal, certainly never hurt anyone."

"Hinky? Is that an American term of endearment?"

I heard the teasing in his voice and relaxed. We turned into the large chamber with the smoke pots. Dark smoke lifted from each round canister and drifted across the line of pots until it disappeared through the rock…well, not through the rock, but behind it. I rushed to follow the faint trail and felt the air before I found the passage.

A natural cleft in the rock, enlarged by earlier inhabitants, allowed easy egress to another smaller chamber, like a foyer. There were no smoke pots in this area and I had to wait for King to light the steps that must lead up and out. I turned back to let him go first. He wasn't there…it was as if he'd turned to smoke and sifted through rock, leaving me behind.

# Chapter Thirty

"King, King, where are you?" It sounded like I was calling a dog. "Danny," his Christian name rolled off my tongue, "Danny, please, where are you?"

A muffled noise drew my attention; I waited to hear it again. The low hiss from the burning smudge pots filled my ears, but a dull crack sounded outside the chamber; the crack of a human head hitting a hard surface. My stomach lurched with the fear that someone else stalked the tunnels for intruders. The oily smell from the smudge pots added to my nausea. *If I hide in the tiny room under the altar stone, I'll be trapped. Maybe he doesn't know I'm here...I was hidden when he found King. I can stay here with the light.*

*Or maybe he is disposing of King and coming back for me. If I stay way back in the shadows, I can see who comes in and sneak out if they go to look for me around the rock. If they have a powerful flashlight, they'll spot me–if I take a pot with me, he'll see me moving wherever I go. I have to leave and use the dark to my advantage. I can hide until he leaves.*

In the next instant a splash broke the silence and I knew where they were. Whoever had fallen or been pushed into the underground pool, it meant certain death. *If they're that-a-way, then I'm heading this-a-way.* I needed to lift my butt off the ground and leave before whoever was out there came back this way. And they'd have to–there wasn't any other way out except the altar stone and the lighthouse. The lighthouse! Thoughts and plans collided in my head. *He had to have come down the ladder. Get back to the ladder, hurry! Left, left...always go left. Danny told Ken to always choose right, so reverse it. Hurry!*

My head screamed at me to move and I realized I'd already turned left outside of the room. I didn't need to move in a deep crouch, but I kept one hand up at the level of my forehead prepared to stop if my fingers brushed the ceiling. My other hand brushed the tunnel wall searching for the next left. I moved quietly my ears straining to hear any type of pursuit.

About the time I thought I'd missed the tunnel, my hand moved into open space and I swung in…hurrying to get out of the line of light if someone was following me. The texture of the darkness behind me changed and I realized that there was light coming down the tunnel–faint light for now. I rushed forward, keeping my hands in position to find the next left and to keep my head from being torn off.

Light spilled from the tunnel entrance on my left. I stopped and tried to think in spite of the pounding in my head. *Who's behind me? Who's in front of me? I don't care. I'm not spending another minute down here.*

I heard voices, hopefully ones not luring me to a trap. There was no way to sneak into the room under the lighthouse and I couldn't go back, so forward seemed my best option.

"I don't give a damn who you want to wait for. I'm going now."

A grin split my face. Marty's recalcitrant voice never sounded sweeter. I couldn't resist the dramatic entrance.

"No need for that, little brother."

The light from Coleman lanterns blinded me, momentarily abetted by the tears filling my eyes; clear vision was impossible. Marty reached me in two strides and grabbed me, lifting me in a crushing bear hug.

People stood at the base of the ladder. I heard shouts from up top. Joan's voice assured those above. "We've got her. She found us." A squeak above her normal range revealed her relief. Laughter circled the trapdoor and drifted to my ears.

"Marty, stop. Put me down." The panic in my voice stopped his enthusiasm.

"What's wrong?"

"I think someone's been hurt, or…well, I think someone's been killed. Back there." I jerked my thumb over my shoulder.

"Who?" A tall man with a shock of black hair and deep wrinkles creasing his cheeks asked. He stood ramrod straight. I knew without an introduction that he was Danny King's father.

My throat dried up and I didn't want to tell him his son had been pushed to his death by my friend's guest.

"Grace, what is it?"

There was no avoiding this. Someone else was climbing down to check on the situation. His muddy boots stepped slowly on each rung. I knew the jacket from seeing it on a peg at the cottage, and I knew the owner when I saw the muddy boot prints on his shoulders. He slipped on a lower rung and hop-jumped to catch his balance.

Ken turned and smiled at me. "Boy am I glad to see you."

# Chapter Thirty-one

My jaw slackened and I blinked several times. Ken's grin gave no clue to what he'd done. His face flushed as I stared at him, and the outline of a bruise on his forehead heightened. The words crowded in my mouth, but stalled there like a slalom skier stuck in the gate.

"Yeah, did we give him crap for losing you down here." Dave's smile belied the concern for me apparent in his eyes. "Can't imagine scrambling around in these tunnels."

*'Losing' me? That should be 'leaving' me. What did he tell them? Where has he been all this time? If he wasn't down here, who struggled with King?*

"King." I hadn't meant to speak. Everyone looked at me. Mr. King stepped forward.

I shook my head. "No, I mean your son. I mean," tears rushed to my eyes and my throat ached with the news I had. My demeanor silenced the hurried whispers. Marty kept one arm around me.

"What is it, Sis?"

I swallowed hard and cleared my throat. "Mr. King, I'm so sorry. I think your son might be dead." The outburst around me, Marty's increased grip, the smell of cold, crisp air, faded away until only the old man's eyes locked on mine mattered. I couldn't look away.

He spoke so softly that I strained to hear him.

"Show me where my boy is."

Marty spoke first. "She's been through too much–"

"No, wait. There's more." With Marty's arm around me and everyone else listening I continued. "I wasn't down here alone with Danny King. He was here too." I nodded toward Ken.

He looked around and nodded. "Of course I was until I could find my way out and get help…for you."

"No, you left me, you didn't lose me." I stared at Ken's eyes; his glance swiveled to the others and then toward a spot on the ground.

"We got separated in the dark."

"Liar!"

Colleen gasped. "You're mistaken. Ken told us how he moved ahead too quickly at one point and thought you were following. When he stopped, you weren't behind him. He went back but couldn't find you in the tunnel…he thought you must have found another tunnel and turned in." She'd moved next to her husband and tucked her arm through his.

"I'm not mistaken. We did come to a split. I read the inukshuk to go left. Ken insisted he'd go to the right–said he had a hunch. Some hunch," my voice rose in anger. "You knew to 'choose right' because that's what King told you when he pulled up the ladder."

Dave interrupted. "King left you down here?"

"My son–"

I waved them quiet. "Your son didn't know I came down. I was supposed to stay up top." I heard Marty take a breath and I snapped my head up to stop the rebuke. "Not now." He exhaled slowly.

"King found me; only at first I thought he was trying to kill me. He saved me from stumbling into the underground pool. You were there," I pointed to Ken, "in the shadows. I thought I saw something move. You followed him in and must have seen the treasure. Is that when you decided to kill us?" My angry voice coursed through my throat, leaving a taste of bile at the villainy I spoke.

The room burst into questions, accusations, and denials. Only Mr. King stayed quiet and waited for me to speak to him. "Your son struggled with someone, and I heard a loud splash. I'm sorry. I was afraid to try and find him in the dark. I wanted to help. He saved my life." I touched his arm. Tears rolled down my cheeks.

"You were right not to follow. The tunnel is no place for a stranger. I know the place you say, I will look for my son." His face filled with a determination that replaced some of the sadness.

"That won't be necessary." A dripping Danny King filled the opening, moving down the rungs with remarkable grace for someone I'd reported dead.

He turned and grabbed Ken's arms, pulling them behind so quickly that the click of handcuffs sounded simultaneous with his action. Ken's attempt at a struggle stalled. Marty stepped forward and King glared at him. "Problem?" he asked.

"Only that I wanted to punch him out before you cuffed him."

"Sorry, he's mine. Maybe you'll have your chance later." He looked around. Colleen leaned heavily against Joan, whose face showed her deep distress. Dave stepped forward.

"We need to work this out. Ken is not a Band member–"

"Don't tell me about jurisdiction. He's on my island, he tried to kill me and her, and he's in my handcuffs. Go sort out what you want, but he goes with me."

King moved his prisoner toward the ladder as Marty moved to cover his back, which I didn't think was necessary.

Dave and Bob glared at my brother. We'd really have to consider leaving the island after tonight. Danny King had Ken up top before anyone moved. My brother motioned for me to go next. I turned to allow Mr. King to climb out, but he was gone. The lantern he'd held sat on the ground where he had stood a few minutes earlier. He knew the tunnels, the secrets. We knew at least one secret, the one about treasure that I'd blurted out, although I wasn't sure at the time. Had my brain registered what I saw in the strong beam and stored it for later? I had a feeling this night would last forever.

# Chapter Thirty-two

The weather calmed enough for the ferry to run. Colleen had left for the mainland to get an attorney for Ken. She wouldn't look at me when she left; she would stand by her husband, but did she believe him? Was she the other voice on the 'lure' tape? Should King be notified that she was leaving? Too many questions, no answers. I accepted a mug of tea from Joan and moved away a bit, trying to let my brain sort the sights, sounds, and impressions of my odyssey.

Garry sat up listening to the adventure with a mixture of excitement and relief etched on his face. I think he hated missing the party, but had his own demons of near death to deal with for the moment. While we'd been out searching for Ken, he'd told his wife and Debbie the entire harrowing story of being locked in the trunk.

He repeated it for his new audience. "I admit I took the deed out of the pile of documents. I thought if I could slow down any legal process, it would help. I wanted to hide it until I could read who it benefited, and I sneaked into their bedroom to see what other papers might be important."

"I don't understand," Joan said. "We've heard you think you might be the lawful heir to Christian Island. That's crazy. Beausoleil First Nation owns the island. Everyone knows that."

Garry lowered his head for a moment and rubbed the back of his neck. "It's not about owning the island; it's having a vote in the Band Council. Only direct male descendents of the original signing families have a vote in island matters. I am the rightful heir to that privilege."

Dave held up his hand. "Can we get back to what happened?"

"Someone tried to kill him." Laurie's voice broke with remembered fear.

"Someone tried to kill me out there. I thought it was you." I looked at Garry. "Your jacket was soaked. You were missing."

My brother cleared his throat, drawing our attention. His ears flamed red and his face looked lopsided because of the crooked grimace. His voiced croaked through tight lips. "I've been trying to tell you since it happened." He paused and I saw the truth in his eyes. "I didn't know you were out there. I wanted to look at those records too, but I never made it." He swallowed. "I didn't realize how closed in the snow tunnel was and I…well, I couldn't go any further."

I knew Marty's fear of small places; lived through it with him when he and Glenn got stuck in the old coal bin at Uncle Pete's house. Even the coal dust hadn't hidden the stark terror on his alabaster white face by the time the firemen freed them.

"I'd brought the coal shovel with me in case some snow had collapsed. When I couldn't go on, I started backing up. I thought I heard someone behind me and then I heard a scraping, sliding sound and the snow fell in around me." Marty's face paled and even his ears lessened in color. "I just started shoveling and pushing it away from me as fast as I could. I pushed it away from me and the house," his voice faltered, "right onto you." His eyes filled with tears and his Adams apple bobbed with effort to regain control.

I threw my arms around him and hugged him hard. "It's okay. Shhh. It's okay." We were kids again and I comforted the little brother who'd always tugged at my heart in the way my other brothers never could. I felt him relax and compose himself; I let go and looked into his teary eyes. "Wait 'til I tell Dad. Boy, are you gonna' get it!" The childhood threat did the trick. Everyone burst into laughter.

"Okay, that's one mystery solved. But who put you in the trunk?" I asked Garry. He shook his head slowly.

"Must have been Ken. He had to already be out there, maybe in the room looking for his own proof. I'd foolishly mentioned my theory to some people. Ken and I knew we had a distant relative in common; it's difficult not to be related to someone from the original Pantier family. I'd figured out our connection was closer than most from the letters my sister had and the research I started."

"How close? Ken must have a big stake in this to try to kill you."

"Thinking back, I don't think he wanted to kill me, just get me out of the way…maybe blame the Band."

I shook my head. "How would a Band member get the keys?"

Garry's face reflected the realization. "I'd found out we were third cousins, him from the inheriting line. With more research I began to see that his line wasn't valid. I shouldn't have told him."

"Ken spotted you coming and did what?" Marty tried to get us back on track.

"He must have seen my light first and turned his off. I remember sliding the door open enough to crawl in, and then nothing until I woke up in here."

"He might have meant to leave you outside to freeze, but he must have seen my light or heard me on the deck."

"Holy cripes! We don't get that many of you on the deck in the summer," Dave shouted. "How many of you were out there?"

"I think that's it." I counted off on my fingers, "Marty, me, Garry and Ken, in reverse order actually. Ken went out, saw Garry coming. Knocked him out, saw me coming. Pulled Garry around the side away from the deck. Came in to get the keys–"

"The door was locked," Dave interrupted. "I locked it myself."

"I think he went out that door. It's shorter to come around from that way and if he had to admit being out, he could say he'd stepped out on the back porch because he couldn't sleep. He sneaked in to get the keys off the peg."

Dave nodded in agreement. "So he had to move Garry or you'd have tripped over him. After he moves him he comes in the back door, undresses, and gets back in bed."

"First he stokes the fire," Joan said. "I half woke up and saw him. I figured he'd gotten cold and wanted to warm up the room."

"That's when he burned the deed I'd seen Garry take out of the pile. He must have seen you do it and marked the pile to return for it later. He knew if you were interested he should look at it. Would that deed have mattered?"

Garry shrugged, "I never had the chance to read it. I don't know anything anymore. This has gone beyond common sense and human decency, and I'm sorry I ever started. They can have their island." He seemed to wind down and shrink within himself.

Laurie held his hand. "You need to rest now. Please, lie down again." His grateful smile brightened Laurie's face.

"Forgive me for putting you through this," he whispered.

We moved away from the reconciling couple and took our mugs into the kitchen.

"I can't believe I slept through all that. You were opening and closing the door, shoveling, thumping…I can't believe it," Dave said.

"I think our last brew was doctored," Marty announced. "I know Colleen used sleeping aids and I know she had a prescription with her because she offered it to me. It would have been easy for Ken to slip some into the tea and coffee. Think back to how much you drank."

"I didn't finish my coffee because we were switching bunks. You had a cup of tea." I looked at my brother.

"I've taken so much crap over the years, that little bit wouldn't make a dent." He looked at the others.

Joan spoke first. "I had at least two cups of tea."

"Cripes, I had two cups of coffee. No wonder I didn't hear a thing," Dave said.

Debbie nodded. "I had a full mug of tea, you did too, didn't you?" she looked at Bob. He nodded.

Joan looked thoughtful and started to speak, but then shrugged. She looked at me with our 'across the classroom' signal.

"Another mystery checked off the too-long list," Dave joked, but the tension in his voice belied his attempt at humor.

A full hour passed and I was still explaining my adventure. I could have cut the time in half if not for the interruptions, questions, and exclamations. I'd found out from the other searchers that their lines had all gone slack and stayed that way. Dave had corralled the women at the altar stone and gone back to look for Marty. He found him slumped against a tree regaining consciousness. Marty told him something hit him from behind and he came to with Dave gently shaking his shoulder. When Dave returned to the others with Marty, he'd found out that Bob had found his way to them; Bob thought he'd heard someone shout out and went to help. When he didn't find anyone, he managed to find his way to the cemetery.

I hated telling them how Ken had left me, knowing I was headed in the wrong direction, how he didn't answer me when I called. I told them about the underground pool, how the bright light saved me from stumbling into it. I told them what I'd glimpsed across the other side.

"I think it was the Jesuit's treasure. Joanie's been right all along." My voice caught in my throat. Did she know more than a hunch? Had she and Dave found the treasure? King said Dave roamed this island as a child. Had he heard the stories and put it together? I shook my head to stop those thoughts.

"Sis, what is it?"

I cleared my throat excessively. "Got dry all of a sudden."

"No wonder, we've kept you talking an hour. Maybe you should stop." Joan spoke from the kitchen while she poured me a glass of water. Did she want me to stop talking about the treasure?

"Here, drink this. Relax. We don't have to hear it right this minute."

"Yes, we do. Ken is being held somewhere and even though it sounds like he snapped and went around the bend, we have to know the whole story before we pass judgment." Bob spoke on his friend's behalf. I'd forgotten that Joan told me Bob and Ken had been friends for years before they curled with Dave and Garry.

"He's right. When King found me in that cavern, I had no choice but to let him lead me out. I had an uneasy feeling, but he had the light. In the room with the smudge pots," I stopped and looked at Dave, "any idea why they're there or who put them there?"

Dave shrugged. "I can only guess that there was to be a ritual performed tonight. It's a full moon and I've heard the believers, the natives who believe they should take the culture back to pre-Huron days, meet in the cave as their ancestors did."

For me the room chilled at the mention of ritual. I swallowed hard to keep the bile from rising in my throat. Barely three months had passed since I'd experienced the danger of a warped mind devoted to ritual. I spoke quickly to change the subject.

"I caught King by surprise, hit him with the flashlight, and took off trying to get back to the lighthouse."

"Even with his light, wasn't that risky?" Debbie asked.

"I thought I could reverse the route if I stayed left at every turn. King told me he'd told Ken to choose right if he wanted to find his way out on his own. Ken left me when I insisted on going left; he knew I was choosing wrong, but he let me go."

"I know you're upset, but Ken's not a literal guy. He honestly may not have heard the distinction in 'choose right' and 'choose correctly.'" Debbie shrugged. "We've played charades and Pictionary with him and no one chooses him."

Smiles flickered across a few faces. *If Ken wasn't the bad guy, who put Garry in the trunk?* I thought while I sipped at my water.

"Can you finish telling us?"

I nodded and handed my empty glass to Joan. "King caught up to me and we struggled. The flashlight rolled away and he pulled me back the way I'd come." I stopped and rubbed my hands up and down my arms. The nerves in my arms felt like they would ooze out my pores like spaghetti through a pasta machine. The sensation signaled an imminent shutdown if I wasn't careful.

"I pushed away. When he followed he cracked his head on the uneven ceiling and knocked himself silly. Then I heard the voices calling out to guide me." No one moved a muscle. They thought I was nuts. "One voice said, 'over here, can you hear me?' and then a female voice called, 'answer me'–"

"Who was it?" Laurie and Joan asked. Debbie glanced at Bob and Dave, then down at her feet. Marty must have noticed her anxiety. He stared at the top of her head, waiting to catch her eye.

"What did the voices say? I mean exactly." Dave's tone sounded more than inquisitive.

I closed my eyes and intoned, "Over here. Can you hear me?" I opened my eyes and locked on Debbie staring at me. Her face flushed and her mouth dropped open. Bob closed his arm around her shoulder.

"Easy, easy. It's been a shock." He tightened his grip until her shoulders curved in. "Let's take this up later. We're all exhausted."

"What's your problem? My sister's the one who went through it, not your wife. She looks pretty upset for an innocent bystander…or maybe she isn't. She's been a sick shade of green ever since Gracie mentioned the voices." Marty stepped toward Debbie. "Any reason that affected you?"

Dave moved between them. "You've got a short fuse, Marty. Let's stay calm."

"Not until she tells me why she's so upset. Look at her."

Debbie's pale face burned with feverish eyes. Bob stepped back, pulling her with him. "I tell you she's exhausted. Leave her alone."

Marty moved again. Dave reached out to stop him, but Marty pushed his hands away when Dave gripped him by the forearms. "Calm down. We won't get anywhere tearing each other apart."

Logic didn't apply once Marty's fuse was lit. He brought his arms up between Dave's, broke the hold, and tried to push past him. Dave's solid stance didn't budge. They pushed at each other. I knew my brother; he'd step back, plant his feet, and deliver a powerful shot to Dave's chest, then follow up with a short jab to his head. His style was in close, short bursts. I'd seen him box at Boy Scout Jamboree.

I could think of only one way to stop him. My scream grew from the fear and frustration and leapt from my mouth. In the small room, it had the effect of surround sound and even I jumped.

The back door slammed open and Danny King moved in quickly, scanning the room and keeping his back to the wall. My scream seemed a meager deterrent compared to the gun in his hand.

# Chapter Thirty-three

"Everybody settle down and stand still," King said and I jumped again. He held his gun steady and used his free hand to motion us out of the kitchen area, backing up a bit as we filed past him. He moved into the kitchen and stood with his back against the sink. The left side of his jaw protruded and the band of bruises extended up across his cheekbone and into his hairline. He'd taken a real wallop. I stared at them and tried to let the idea tap dancing at the edge of my mind move forward. No use; my head hummed with too much activity.

"King, you've no call to come in here, waving your gun around and scaring us," Dave spoke from the center of the group.

"First of all, I heard a scream that would shake stones; didn't know what I'd find. And I don't 'wave' my gun around."

"Second, after questioning your friend I realized there's at least one more co-conspirator in this cottage."

We looked around at each other like inept actors in a B-rated movie. Debbie's glance touched a few faces, then settled on staring at the back of her husband's head. He must have felt her stare or turned to look for her. His stern expression softened momentarily while he communicated something to his wife. The brief moment over, his mask of anger reset his features.

"King, King, do you read?" The radio on his belt crackled; the speaker's voice low and urgent. King pulled it off his hip. "Go ahead."

"Danny, it's your father. He's missing."

"I'm on my way." King's face hardened. The vein on the side of his neck stood out across his skin. His eyes flared with fury. "If anything happens to my father, I won't bother with formalities." He backed away and out the door, but he needn't have worried we'd rush him–we stood rooted to the floor. The roar of the gunned engine released us. We scattered, each with our own agenda and destination.

"We're leaving. Should have left when Colleen did," Bob said more to Debbie than to us. "Forget about packing up." He turned to Dave. "Your new tenants can have our stuff for all it's worth."

Debbie stared, not moving a muscle. "We should all go," Bob kept talking as he moved through the room picking up his jacket and matching his actions to his words. "Drive us to the ferry and we'll–"

"You think King doesn't have someone at the ferry?" Marty asked. "Do you think he's too small-town to figure out the perp might rabbit first chance he gets?"

I didn't know if Canadians were up on American cop show talk, but they apparently understood Marty's slang.

Debbie whirled and pointed at me. "She said King attacked her in the tunnels. He's unstable, shouldn't be carrying a gun. We have to do something." Her voice broke and she flung herself into her husband's arms; his stiff acceptance of her sobbing body made me wonder where his thoughts were…certainly not on comforting her.

In a flash the thought that had tap danced in the shadows rushed forward with a 'ta-da' finale. The bruise on Ken's forehead could only have been made by smacking into a low ceiling. King's bruise was the result of being beaned by an object. Ken had grabbed me from behind, not King.

"It wasn't King," I blurted. "The bruise is wrong."

"What are you talking about?"

"The bruise on King's face," I touched the side of my face, "was made by someone hitting him. The bruise on Ken's face was made by hitting the ceiling in the tunnel. I did the same thing." I lifted the hair from my forehead and felt the tenderness extend through the hairline up to the top of my head.

"Man, what a knot. Why didn't you say something?" Marty asked. He pulled a package of frozen peas from the freezer. "It's probably too late, but it might help the swelling."

I'd lost my train of thought and felt silly holding the veggies on my head. My mind raced to pull the threads of my imminent accusation back into a logical line of thought. Nothing clicked.

"If Ken went berserk in the dark, in the tunnels, who are we to blame him? We have to watch out for ourselves. It's regretful if he tried to hurt you, but we have to believe that Colleen will be back with an attorney. There's nothing we can do." Bob disengaged Debbie and held her at arm's length. "We have to take care of ourselves." He spoke the last sentence to his wife.

"I'm not leaving until I find out why he stuffed me in the trunk."

"Maybe it wasn't Ken who knocked you out. Look how Grace thought it was first you, and then Ken, who shoveled snow over her. Mistaken identity." Dave stopped to let his idea sink in.

Marty and I exchanged embarrassed glances. He questioned Dave. "What are you saying, that there's another player we don't know about?" We exchanged nervous glances and spoke at once.

Dave put up his hand to stop all the denials. "Wait, wait. We know the Band members are split over the development issue. Maybe one of them is involved with Ken."

"Why target any of us? We were only going to be here for two weeks. Why bother?"

"The only thing I can think of is that someone got the impression that one or all of us could make a difference."

"We can't even vote."

"I can, and if not me, Ken."

Garry had our rapt attention. He shifted in his chair and pulled the blanket around his shoulders. "The records I kept searching for had nothing to do with land trusts. I was looking for medical records, childhood illnesses, school records, timelines for my grandfather. I found the proof I needed in the letters between Amelia and her grandmother, Amelia and her brother Joshua, and Lissette and her family. It took hundreds of hours of piecing together innocuous comments about school uniforms, whooping cough, and grocery bills until I found the pieces I needed to confirm my suspicion."

Garry pulled the blanket closer and straightened in his chair. "I have proof positive that my grandfather was the rightful heir."

I didn't know Garry that well and really didn't care about his 'line,' but the others clamored for explanations. Even my brother leaned forward to catch the rest of the story. Why wasn't I engaged in his tale of deception? Something nagged at me, telling me that this wasn't as important as something else connected to his legacy, but not connected. I hated when my brain gave me those 'but not' clues; like holding out candy to a chubby toddler, then pulling it out of reach.

"It's not a pretty story, kind of sick when you grasp the whole situation." Garry spoke slowly, making his way through his ancestral labyrinth with caution. *Labyrinth, that's it.* I moved abruptly and turned heads. Garry stopped talking.

"Grace, where are you–"

I didn't answer, but hurried into the bathroom and rummaged through the reading material. It was still there. "This is what I remembered." I waved the glossy magazine in the air.

"All that for a magazine?" Even Marty looked at me with raised eyebrows. He cocked his head to the side to read the title. "Architectural International?"

"Yes. I remembered reading about," my voice slowed while I thumbed the pages to find the article, "this, right here." I cleared my throat, "The addition of a formal maze completes the whimsy of the estate. The unveiling of the maze included a contest based on teams besting the maze in the fastest time. Adding to the mischief was one select group armed with microphones calling out inaccurate directions to lure the participants to dead ends."

I stopped reading and stared at Debbie. Her downward glance affixed her guilt. "Robert Hastings and his wife Debra, along with architect Van Hoousten and owners Mr. and Mrs. Oliver Comptom were the 'teambusters.'" I waved the magazine at Bob. "You set up that trap."

Debbie burst into tears and shrugged off Bob's attempt to console her. "What have you done?" Her words barely distinguishable through the choking tears, she asked, "Why was this different?"

Bob glared at me. "You are a meddling busybody with no sense. You're distorting events and confusing everyone. I didn't set any trap, I didn't lock Garry in the trunk, I didn't pull out the phone wires, I didn't cause the storm, or are you laying that at my feet as well?" His vehemence startled me; it sounded like righteous indignation. Could I have it all wrong?

"How did you know the wires had been pulled out?" Dave asked.

Bob looked at him sharply. "You must have told us. Pulled out, cut, what difference does it make?" His voice held a note of bravado.

"Makes a big difference because I never said. I believe I said someone 'messed with the wires.' You knew because you did it." Dave and Marty stepped closer to Bob. "What's going on? There's nowhere for you to go; we won't let you leave."

Debbie cried out and ran into the bedroom. Laurie followed; Joan seemed torn between offering consolation and being in on the explanation. Bob didn't speak, didn't move.

"Some of this is my fault," Garry said. "I confided in the wrong friends," he nodded toward Bob.

"Confided what?"

"What I was about to tell you before. Laurie knows and only a few others. My grandfather was the rightful line because he was Joshua and Lissette's son. The son accorded the inheritance line was the illegitimate son of Amelia and Joshua."

"Oh, my God. That's crazy." Joan spoke our thoughts.

Garry shook his head. "I don't say it lightly or without proof. I've spent the last two years checking records, and I have the proof. When you brought out all those records I had to be sure there wasn't some document I'd missed, but I didn't want to tell you why."

"So what changes for you? Do you get money or land?" Marty asked.

"What changes is that I have a right to land on this island, actually, the entire island. I know the Band Council would tie me up in court for years and I don't want the island. I want recognition for my grandfather, and voting rights for the future of the island."

"You're a fool. You and Ken, both of you arguing over a stupid legacy. I was trying to bring progress and prosperity to these people."

"Not to mention lining your pockets with a chunk of change."

Bob reacted to Dave's comment with anger. "You wouldn't have held back if I'd offered you a nice cushy job. Endless summers supervising the hotel's outdoor activities, then your winters off on mainland. You wouldn't have drawn a line then!" His face raged, heightening the red splotches on his cheeks.

"You don't know me like you think you do. I draw the line at cheating people," Dave's voice slowed, "and worse."

I stepped toward Bob. "If you know about Mr. King's disappearance, you have to tell. Don't make matters worse with another death."

Bob's harsh laugh took me by surprise. "Make matters worse? How much worse can it get?" He sat down and held his head in his hands. No one else moved. I didn't know what to say. He lifted his head slowly and stared at a point above our heads.

"Everything I have, everything I could borrow has gone into this development. I'd be ruined if it didn't go through. The Band Council agreed and the papers were drawn, and then a faction called for a clan vote above and beyond the board vote. We started polling people and realized the vote might not go our way."

"You discovered something else, didn't you? Another reason why some Band members didn't want the island excavated." Another piece of the puzzle my mind kept handing me fell into place.

He nodded. "Pete, the leader of the faction, had another reason for keeping the island pristine. He'd found the Jesuit treasure buried under certain tombstones in the cemetery. He'd always known about the entrance to the tunnel from the altar stone, and hid what they'd found down there. He was trying to research how much treasure had been buried, making sure he had every last coin and medallion. Greedy bastard screwed up everything."

I found it interesting that someone else's greed was blamed. I guess it was a matter of 'whose ox is being gored.' My dad always said that, and it surely fit this situation. Was Bob a criminal or crazy, or both? I hoped Marty and Dave knew what to do. One of us should go get King, only who? Garry was too weak. The guys had to stay to keep tabs on Bob. Laurie and Debbie were a mess. That left Joan. She knew the way, but I couldn't let her go alone. I looked at my childhood friend and saw understanding dawn in her eyes. It happened to us that way sometimes.

"I think Joan and I should go get King. There's no other way to reach him. We can't stand here staring at each other all day."

A protest died on Marty's lips when he looked around the room and came to the same conclusion. "Be careful."

Joan and I gathered our jackets. I pulled on my gloves and

turned to face Bob. "Before I leave, I want to know why you set that trap. If King hadn't shown up, I would have tumbled into the water."

"We didn't set it up to drown anyone."

I looked toward the bedroom.

"Not Deb, she had nothing to do with any of this. Pete agreed to give me a part of the treasure for my help to get him a 'no' vote by leaking detrimental information about habitat impact so the tree huggers would get involved."

"Why would you do that if you needed the development to save your sorry financial ass?"

My brother's assessment appealed to me.

"I wasn't going to do anything but let him get his treasure moved. I suggested the recording as a way to keep it safe. If Indian teens came into the tunnels and they heard other people they'd leave. The kids use the tunnels to drink and fool around. No one goes into the tunnels without a flashlight or lantern. They'd see the water." His voice rang with authority.

"Okay, so maybe you weren't trying to kill anyone," I paused and added, "that way."

Bob shook his fist. "I never meant to kill anyone. Pete found out I wasn't planning to vote his way and he went ballistic on me, pushing me, slapping me. I thought he was going to kill me. It was self-defense. I swear."

"If it was self-defense, why didn't you go to the police? Especially when the constable from mainland was here investigating Old Joe's death." Dave's eyes narrowed. "What did you have to do with that killing? As I recall, you came around the long way, just you and Deb."

Bob's face blanched. "I swear I didn't kill him." His eyes bugged out in his face. "I think Pete killed his own father." He closed his eyes and took a deep breath. "That's why I thought he would kill me. He was ranting about betrayal and how his own father turned against him and wanted him to return the treasure to the Jesuits. He let slip that he'd taken care of that. After he said that, I knew he couldn't let me live. I swear I didn't kill Joe."

He dropped his head to his hands and didn't appear to be

dangerous to us. Dave must have thought the same. "I'll go get King. You two stay put."

Marty nodded his approval. "He's done."

Bob never looked up. Debbie appeared in the doorway and walked toward her husband. She had dried her eyes and composed herself, even looked like she'd combed her hair. Debbie touched Bob's shoulder and he shifted to let her sit next to him. Now it was the wife who consoled her husband while he sobbed in her arms.

Dave left and Joan, Marty, Laurie, Garry, and I moved to the kitchen and sat around the table. It seemed the decent thing to do. There was nowhere for Bob to go. After a few awkward minutes, Debbie and Bob escaped to the solitude of the bedroom. Their departure opened the floodgates for our conversation. We spoke in quiet tones, but felt free to speculate.

"If Ken and Bob didn't put me in the trunk, who did?"

"Maybe Pete. If he was suspicious about Bob, maybe he was watching the cottage."

"I think he was already dead, wasn't he?"

"I don't know when he died. When he died and when he was found are two different things. I don't know if there's been an autopsy; if not, they couldn't pinpoint the time of death."

Marty stood abruptly. "Too many questions that involve Bob. Let's get him out here. We should have insisted he stay with us."

Joan's whisper added to the sudden unease. "There's a window."

# Chapter Thirty-four

Marty rushed to the bedroom with the rest of us close behind. Only Debbie sat alone on the bed. She looked drained and stunned. Marty shook her by the shoulders and stared at her eyes. "I think she took something, her pupils are dilated. I don't like the way she looks."

"Bob's gone. What if he's after Dave to stop him from getting the police?" Joan spoke at a panic pitch. "I've got to go after him."

"No," Garry said. "You stay and help us with Debbie. Marty, I can tell you how to get–"

"I know the way, I've taken note of landmarks; I can find it."

"See if you can find out what she took and call me on the radio," he yelled over his shoulder while he grabbed his jacket and one of the walkie-talkies.

"I'm coming with you."

"No, Gracie. Stay here."

"Don't waste time. I'm going."

He knew that tone and shrugged. "Let's go, but do exactly as I say when I say it."

I kept pace with my brother even though he had me by six inches in height. I'd learned as the shortest Morelli to keep up if I wanted to be included. Marty's arms swung easily at his side as he glanced up to keep his trail marker in sight. We'd been walking in silence for several minutes.

"Gracie, in case we get separated take your bearing on that giant spruce with the bent top. See how the snow has bent it? That's your marker. Keep it on your right to get back. Dave's cutoff has that dead spindly tree at the 'Y' in the road. I tied a rag to it yesterday."

I stopped and Marty turned. "Gracie, did you hear me?"

I glanced up and back at him. He stepped toward me. "Did you hear me about the bent spruce?"

I nodded and pointed to another bent spruce and another.

"Shit. The damn snow's bent practically all of them. Crap!" Marty's cheeks turned red with embarrassment. "Okay, okay, we're all right. I know this is the way. Don't worry. In about two hundred yards there'll be one of those low electrical boxes that service the houses in the interior. When we find that, it's a piece of cake to the community house and the police station." Marty spoke with confidence and only an older sister who'd heard his bluffs for years could tell he was unsure. We'd made several turns based on his lofty landmark.

We walked slowly, hesitant to log any more time in the wrong direction. The events of the last two days whirled in my brain, but tugged at my legs. I was bone tired, and each step came harder. We'd been up all night talking and watching each other, strategizing who, what, where, and why. "Do you believe what Garry said?" Marty referred to the earlier conversation.

"If Amelia and Joshua had children together, why didn't they move away and pretend they were husband and wife? Why trick Lissette into marrying him?"

"He, they, Amelia and him, needed a cover for their relationship. They must have both been insane." Marty's voice dripped with disgust. He and I had fought like cats and dogs at times, but he'd been raised to respect and protect me.

"My point exactly, why not move?"

"Their wealth was their land and their home. According to some of the ledgers, they did well for themselves. They would have had the respect and admiration of the community; probably on the school board, church board, city council, all that civic stuff."

"Joanie said there is a Pantier Elementary School named for them. They had to stay and apparently weren't going to stop *playing house*, so they needed Lissette to keep up appearances. Wonder when Lissette tumbled to her groom's true nature? Couldn't have been too long after he brought her across. If Garry is right, Lissette had to know immediately when Amelia's pregnancy became obvious. Unless they told Lissette the baby was Mr. Havilland's. That would mean Amelia and Joshua had been messing around during his last visit to the island, during the time Havilland died." I mostly talked to myself at that point, trying to give my brain space to lay out the jumble in my head. I knew I'd seen enough and heard enough, the trick was to piece it together so it made sense.

"There's the box," Marty said. I didn't realize how lost he thought we might be until I heard the excitement in his voice. "Look, I can see lights."

Pale lights glowed in the distance. The community center would be the first building. There must be a gathering of some sort. We hurried toward the light, assuming that we'd find Dave inside.

Hostile eyes stared at us when we pushed through the double doors. At least thirty Indians stood around in several groups sipping at mercifully hot coffee, judging from the steam. I coveted their coffee.

Danny King walked toward us, shook Marty's hand, and nodded at me. "What's wrong? Why are you here?"

I scanned the room for Dave. He wasn't here. Could he have been here and left already? We would have passed him on the road. I heard Marty explaining.

"When we realized Bob left, we thought he might come after Dave to stop him from reaching you. It would buy him time to get off the island or to hide out at a co-conspirator's house."

King nodded a few times and now he turned to the group of men who had inched closer during the conversation. The only woman in the room stood at the table off in the corner where the coffee pot; the signature doughnuts from Tim Horton's, Tim-bits; and the butter tarts were set up. She motioned for me to join her. Probably women weren't allowed at the meeting except to set up and serve, but I wasn't going to miss anything. She motioned to me again, this time holding out a mug. Steam rose from the ceramic circle. I'd just nip over there, get my coffee, and come right back.

No one noticed I left. I reached for the mug. "Thank you."

"Women don't meet with men during Council." She nodded toward a large table at the other end of the room. "Only twelve of them are Council, but the pre-meeting is time for anyone to state his views and concerns. I came early to set up."

I nodded and wondered why she felt the need to explain their procedure, unless it had something to do with Dave.

"Was my friend here to talk to them?"

"They only arrived a few minutes before you came. This is still the pre-meeting time."

"You were here early, to set up, right?"

She nodded.

"Did you see Dave?"

She nodded again.

Her stoicism was annoying. "Did you talk to him? He came to find King. Did he talk to him?"

She shook her head.

Was I supposed to guess? What the hell was her problem? She called me over. That was it; she'd already put herself out and that's all I was going to get unless I asked the right question. Then it popped into my head.

"Was my friend alone?"

She shook her head.

My mouth felt like cotton. "Was he with another cottager?"

She nodded.

"Marty, Bob caught up to Dave."

"They didn't pass us." Marty turned to King. "Where could they go from here?"

King looked at the woman I'd been talking to. She motioned a direction with her head.

"What's in that direction?"

"The cemetery and the burial grounds."

I noticed the distinction he made, the first I'd heard. "When does it become hallowed ground?"

He stared at me. "It is all sacred," he paused. "If you mean which part is Christian influence, that would be the four outer circles."

I knew there'd been something special about that row, almost like a line of demarcation. "I think they're going into the tunnels from the altar stone. That's where Bob and Pete hid the treasure. You saw it when you found me in the cavern," I said to King.

He shook his head. "You said that before, but I didn't see anything, barely spotted you."

"You must have seen it on the far side. Your light lit up the entire room like a beacon…" I stopped abruptly. A chill inched across my shoulders.

The word 'beacon' caused excitement in the room. One man stepped forward. I hadn't noticed him before; it was Mr. King. I looked at his son.

"A miscommunication. He'd gone off to investigate on his own. My father was the police chief until he retired five years ago. But he doesn't stay retired," he raised his voice on the last sentence.

The senior King approached me. "Havilland keeps you safe. You are a good person. He knows."

The chill turned to dread and filled my chest. I didn't know how to respond, or if I should.

"Dad, stop with the ghost talk. Who knows what she saw across the water? She'd been in the dark; my light probably looked like a beacon to her eyes."

Mr. King shook his head and continued to address me. "He won't believe that the keeper stays, helping those who deserve to be safe."

Was that it? I deserved to be safe? On the deck in the snow, in the tunnel; were those examples of the lighthouse keeper's handiwork? I believed in angels, I believed in God. He does work in mysterious ways. But a lighthouse keeper?

I'd missed a question. "Don't be ridiculous. My sister is not someone reincarnated," Marty's voice exclaimed loudly.

Reincarnated? Oh, cripes, what had I missed?

Mr. King produced a small folder the size of a passport which he opened toward me. Two photos…on the left, a bride dressed in an embroidered cotton dress holding a bouquet of wildflowers, on the right, the same woman with two small boys. I knew that I looked at Lissette, and now I understood King's bizarre statement. If the sepia photo could be colorized and Lissette's eyes shaded lavender, then she could be my sister or more likely my grandmother.

I looked at Mr. King and smiled. "There is a resemblance, but I assure you no relation."

"I know you are not of her flesh. You are of her soul."

I felt the blood drain from my face and my mouth dropped open. I didn't want to go where he was leading. My soul had only one destination, and it wasn't detouring through Christian Island's past.

"King, tell your father to stop or I swear I'll shut him up." Marty closed his hands into fists. "I don't care how many of you are here."

My brother often spoke, then thought. King's face broke into a grin. "Take it easy, no one is disrespecting your sister, least of all my father. He is an honorable man whose generation feels the pull of both cultures on the island."

Mr. King spoke to Marty. "I never meant to alarm your sister. You are a good man. Perhaps too bold for your own good, but I respect your motive if not your manner."

I think that ranked as the kindest putdown Marty had ever received. It was his turn to stand slack-jawed.

I nudged him in the ribs. "Not now. Dave's in trouble."

King looked at me with a peculiar expression. "Maybe Dave is part of his own trouble." He raised his hand to stop my answer. "Think about it. Who knows the island better than anyone in your group? He spent summers on the island as a kid beating the bushes with me flushing small game for our arrows."

Marty shifted from foot to foot. He interrupted. "Joan told me she'd found an old abandoned sweat lodge last summer when she was picking blueberries. She'd wandered further into the bush following the berries."

"Who says it was abandoned? Maybe only not in use at that time," Mr. King said.

I stared at him, wondering if that was a cryptic message or some Indian lore baloney. My brother continued. "Joan's also the one who brought up her theory of the Jesuit treasure."

"What are you saying, that my best friend since third grade is part of a plot to stop some stupid vote?" My voice rose to a shout.

"No, of course not. Joan couldn't, wouldn't do any of that. But we don't know Dave, not really. I mean he knows this island; if he found the treasure, he'd stand to gain. You told me Joan invited you and Harry for this last fling before she checked with Dave. Maybe it was supposed to be a working vacation for the guys with the perfect cover of a decommissioning party for the cottage. Joan's interest and investigation of the lighthouse for the historical society would fit right in with a reason for snooping around."

I had to admit his explanation sounded plausible, but I couldn't believe Dave would be a part of murder. Maybe he wasn't. I mean, what if he was only in it for the gold and things got out of hand? Like his partners went berserk and committed the murders–something like that? That still makes him culpable. He should have come forward.

I bit down on the inside of my cheek and winced. My head quieted down. So did the room. King, his father, and my brother stared at me.

"You okay, Gracie? You were mumbling."

I nodded at Marty. "Yeah, fine. Just thinking out loud."

The old man smiled at me. "Or thinking too loud," he said softly.

He knew. I don't know how, but he knew or guessed about the voices in my head. Did he know because his grandmother, Lissette, had done the same? I dug my nails into my palms, a less obvious method of mind control, and refused to think of any connection between me and a long-dead woman.

"If they are all involved, I need to send someone to the cottage to sit on the one left there." King searched the room for someone and motioned him over.

"As long as you have the landing blocked, why bother? I mean, where can they go?"

"I don't want them loose on the island getting desperate and maybe hurting more people. They could hide on this island even in this weather if they had help; it looks like they may have more than one islander on their team. I don't have enough manpower to check all the places they could hide. I'd rather round them up while I can. Did either of you see any indication of guns?"

We shook our heads.

He spoke quickly to the young man who'd walked over to us. "Get George out there. When he brings him in, lock him in the supply room. I don't want him talking to the other one. Tell George not to take chances; assume he's going to fight about coming in."

He nodded and left, his respect for King apparent in his face. King grinned after the departing young man. "Little brother; finishing his degree in Criminal Justice at University this year. He can't wait to take my job." He wore his affection for his sibling as openly on his face as his brother had for him.

Several of the men moved to the table at the other end of the room. King's father joined them. Danny King motioned us toward the refreshment end. "The elders are convening the Council meeting. Most of the men will stay, and more will be joining them. These are the early birds looking for coffee, Tim-bits, and good-natured arguing. I'll grab a couple of men when they come in to get a search party up. Yes, for sure we'll find them."

Every now and then King used an island colloquialism and it threw off the cadence of his mainland speech. Like when Dave said 'eh?' My thoughts turned to him. Was it possible that he could be a guilty party in this conspiracy? They stood to gain from the development and from buried treasure. Did each of them know about the treasure or was that a secret between certain thieves?

A blast of cold air signaled another few men entering the hall, but King didn't approach them. He stood waiting. Probably had his favorites picked out. I refilled my mug, looked at a gooey bear claw, and tried to assess the number of sit-ups necessary to negate the calories. More cold air and three more attendees. King stood quietly, sipping his coffee and watching the door.

I heard the scrape of chairs and realized everyone had stood up and stretched their arms out tilting their heads heavenward. Mr. King stood in front of a large mural of the island and chanted a series of words; the men repeated them. He led them in recitation of a creed. I lowered my head in deference to the solemn words and listened while they asked for guidance and courage. I felt the cold air at my back; King shifted slightly to include the door in his peripheral vision. Whoever entered waited respectfully for the creed to end.

My neck tingled with a familiar sensation and an overwhelming sense of calmness flooded my body. On the final word I whirled to face the newcomers.

"Harry!"

# Chapter Thirty-five

Three quick strides placed me in his waiting arms. The dread, the fear, the uneasiness of deceit and suspicion fell away from my shoulders and I reveled in the feel of my husband. The scent of Colours tickled my nose and I couldn't hug him any tighter. Within his embrace I lost track of time, or maybe time slowed to allow me the rest I needed.

"We thought you were coming next week. Not that I'm not thrilled you're here now. You won't believe what's been happening." My brother's voice expressed the relief I felt.

"I've had tidbits of information. Thought we'd pop over sooner."

'Pop over' would mean from England. The plan to have Harry and Will join us for the last three days had changed dramatically. Instead of Will, Walter accompanied Harry. Walter and Gertrude had traveled with my husband and his son to visit my in-laws in Arundel, England. I suspected that Gertrude was somewhere in Midland with Will waiting for their return or for the all-clear for them to join us.

I felt Harry's arms loosen around me. He kissed the top of my head. "How has she been behaving?" His light tone didn't fool me. I heard the concern.

Marty whooped in relief at being able to pass the burden of 'Gracie watch' to someone else. "She discovered a secret compartment, found her way out of a tunnel under the lighthouse, has accused two different people of trying to smother her in the snow, but that was me...I mean, not on purpose..." My brother's voice lapsed as he realized he had accused himself of almost killing me.

Harry's arm tightened around me. He stared at Marty for a moment while my brother rocked from foot to foot. "Wait till I tell your father," Harry intoned with mock seriousness. Marty grinned and shook his head.

"Hi, Walter." I turned to acknowledge Harry's long-time friend. Theirs was an unusual relationship that had started in England with Harry's father. "I'm sorry you had to cut your visit short."

"No matter, Missus. Vas gut to see mine old friends. Time vas enough to enjoy and not so much we talk out everyting."

His smile lifted my spirits. Through the years I'd learned he'd move heaven and earth to keep Harry safe. In this past year I realized that his mantle of protection included me, and not only because I was Harry's wife.

Danny King had waited and now stepped forward; Harry stretched out his hand to meet him more than halfway. "Thank you for letting me on board. This is Walter Stahl." Walter stepped forward and offered King his thick, muscled hand.

I watched them interact. Harry's blue eyes moved from King's face to Marty's as they explained what they knew, and what they surmised. His eyebrows lifted once or twice, and he glanced at me with an expression I knew I had to deal with later. I didn't know who had called Harry and why King didn't seem to mind his involvement.

"Metro men will get here as fast as they can. This storm has touched off accidents and burglaries," Harry said.

King nodded. "That's what they said when I radioed about the situation here. Who do you know who greased the rails to get you here? They told me you'd been cooling your heels waiting the storm out, trying to hire anyone crazy enough to try a crossing."

Harry smiled. "Almost had a chap ready to take me. When I found out the 'Too Short' nickname didn't refer to height, I reconsidered." His droll delivery made King smile.

"And the person you know?" King wasn't going to be deterred.

"The superintendent and I met in Toronto a few years ago. We recognized similar qualities and goals in each other and have remained in contact."

Harry's long-ago involvement with British Intelligence reared its head every now and then. I'd bet dollars to Tim-bits that at some time they'd worked together, or their governments had. The explanation seemed to suit King. He nodded.

"I agree with your wife that they've gone to the tunnel to retrieve the Jesuit gold. Your friend is either there willingly, or is being forced to help Hastings."

"Dave's the bloke who called me; I don't think he'd ask me to the dance if he were up to no good."

"When did he call you? The phone is out at the cottage."

Harry grinned at Marty. "I never doubted you for a moment, but when I knew you two would be up here for awhile before I arrived, I called Dave and gave him my parents' phone number. Told him to call me at the first sign of anything unusual. Would have been here sooner but for the bloody storm. It's making life miserable on both sides of the bay."

"Doesn't mean he isn't involved now. Maybe he wasn't aware of the gold until after he called. He may have discovered his friend's sideline and insisted on being cut in. Large amounts of money can destroy a man's resolve," King said.

I wasn't convinced, but Marty nodded and Harry agreed. "We'll have to work under the assumption that he's helping Bob until we know for a fact." He looked at the backs of the men seated at the meeting. "Anyone there you're waiting for?"

King considered the question. "Two on the end, third row. They're good men, good trackers. If the tunnel isn't where they've gone, those two," he tapped his nose, "can smell them in the bush." He pulled a radio from his pocket and talked quietly to the woman manning the refreshments table. "Dawn will make sure they get the radio and stay put until I call them."

"Have you another of those?" Harry asked.

"In my car, why?"

"I'd very much like to drop off these two at the cottage and leave them with a means of communication."

Marty snapped to attention. "Hey, what do you mean 'drop me off'? I'm going with you."

I knew better than to protest. No way would Harry, or King for that matter, let me come with them. I didn't want to go underground again. I knew Marty wouldn't be able to stand the smaller tunnels, but he didn't want to be left out of the chase. I tugged at his sleeve and whispered, "Some of the tunnels are really tight. Honest." I looked into his eyes and saw the resignation. He shrugged.

"Take Gracie to the cottage. I'll stay here and wait for you."

He wanted to be part of the mission, but not the part stuck in a cottage with the girls. My heart ached a little for him, but mostly I felt relief that he'd be safe. I couldn't take worrying about him *and* Harry. I knew Harry and Walter were better prepared for chasing down criminals, and with King added to the mix I felt confident that they'd be successful. My fear was that someone would get hurt or worse.

Marty sauntered over to refill his cup, but now whirled so quickly the liquid swirled over the lip onto his hand. He put the cup down and wiped his hand on his sleeve while he approached King. "I thought of another place they might be. Before the snowstorm all four of them went canoeing. Bob said he knew an old route that the Huron and Jesuits may have taken and he wanted to try it. If they can reach the boats through the snow, they might try to leave that way. Can you canoe across the bay in this weather?"

"Anything's possible if you're willing to risk it. If they're all in this together, who's to say they didn't stash the canoes somewhere else for a getaway?"

"Maybe closer to the gold. Whatever I saw was on the far side of that pool like it was being staged to be moved." Thinking back on that reminded me of a question I'd had for King. "After Ken knocked you into the water, how did you get past us to the lighthouse?"

King suddenly looked agitated. "Same way they could get the gold out. It's an underground cave. In the summer you have to hold your breath and swim in to the pool. We found it when we were kids. The water is lower this time of year, low enough for a man crouched over in a canoe to get in and out." He started zipping his jacket. "Thank you, Mrs. Marsden. Let's get you back to the cottage."

Riding to the cottage beat walking. Marty stayed behind, insisting he could be useful. I think he didn't want to be the only male besides a recuperating Garry not involved somehow. We were at the cottage in no time. I hated letting go of Harry's warm hand. His kiss lingered on my lips when we separated. "Don't worry, we'll be back soon. Tell them not to worry, maybe best not to tell them anything about what we're doing."

I climbed out of the car. Harry popped out behind me.

"We don't have time for more good-byes," King said.

"I'm not letting her walk into the cottage without checking it out." Harry's voice was firm. King shrugged and mumbled.

We walked up the driveway hand in hand, relishing the additional contact. The back steps sounded hollow under our boots. Harry turned the knob and pushed the door open.

"Joan, I'm back. You'll never guess who's with me." No answer.

Harry stepped ahead of me and motioned for me to stay put. He walked quickly from room to room, easy to do in the small cottage. "No one is here. Where would they have gone?"

"Could the women be involved too? Would they condone murder as a means to a better life for all of them? I won't believe it of Joan, but I don't know the others that well. Maybe they forced her to go with them. We have to tell King."

Danny King listened and grew impatient. "I don't know if I have one man out of control, a conspiracy of two, or a whole damn gang at work here." The frustration in his voice spread to his hands. He jerked his hand through his hair and rubbed the back of his neck. "Get in. We'll leave her in the car, there's no time to go back."

"Call Marty on the radio and tell him to come here. I'll wait inside with the door locked until he gets here."

"I don't like…"

"Good idea…"

Harry and King spoke at the same time. I knew Harry didn't want to leave me, but they needed to get moving. King's radio crackled. His man back at the hall responded. He relayed the message to my brother. "He's on his way, Chief, but George ain't back yet."

King finished the conversation and got out of the car. He looked at the ground on the road and the driveway. "This doesn't make sense." He motioned to tire tracks in the soft gravel road. "This is George pulling in and him pulling out, but he's headed south. Should be going that way." He jerked a thumb over his shoulder indicating the way we'd come. "And no radio contact to tell me he changed his route. Not good."

"You think your deputy is in trouble?"

"Yes, Mrs. Marsden, I do. Apparently, the safest place for you is in this cottage. No one else seems to be within miles of it." He shook his head and keyed the radio calling for George to respond, but got only dead air. "Let's go. They can't all leave the island at once, unless they made plans for a larger boat to meet them at Bar Spit Point. It's tricky bringing a big boat in that close, but if they paddle out in canoes it could work. I'll radio Metro Water to alert them."

"Get inside now before we pull away." Harry kissed the top of my head and gently shooed me toward the steps, then reluctantly climbed into the car but wouldn't close the door until he saw me step inside. I locked the door and listened to their vehicle leave.

Alone until Marty arrived, I walked into each room looking for clues to where they'd gone. No notes, no knocked-over lamps. Lamps. The lamps were on when we'd left, it was early light but still gloomy in the cottage and the lamps were on. If no one turned them off, does that mean they left shortly after we did? Did someone leave them on as a clue? To what? My head ached with stupid questions. I ran water into the coffee carafe and set up the pot for six cups.

The doorknob rattled and I nearly dropped the toaster I'd pulled out of the cupboard. Three hard knocks, two soft, three hard knocks again. The childhood signal eased my mind. I let in my brother.

Marty stood on the doorstep bent over at the waist, panting with exertion. He limped past me, collapsed onto a sturdy kitchen chair, and took a couple of deep breaths to regulate his breathing. "Whew, that was rough. I am totally out of shape."

"You ran? Are you nuts? Get your boot off and put some ice on your ankle before it looks like part of the Michelin Man's leg." I retrieved the frozen peas and removed my belt to secure the packages around his ankle that looked dangerously swollen. "You didn't have to run, I wasn't going anywhere."

"They told me you were alone and I know Harry wouldn't like the feel of the whole thing. I wanted to get here fast." Marty's eyes shone with the same prideful light that I'd seen countless times when he completed a task or merit badge. It was the 'I done good' look of a kid. How could this great guy have screwed up his marriage? I guess I saw and remembered the great kid. I rumpled the top of his head.

"You done good." He took my hand between both of his.

"I appreciate that you invited me up here with you. Hasn't turned out like the brochure said," he grinned, "but I've had more time to think about Eve and our marriage than I ever did before. I can't find one fault with her behavior. I messed up on my own and she had the good sense to back off before I dragged her and Katie into my problem. Anyway, I'm telling you this because I'm not going back."

I jerked my hand out of his grasp. "What? You have to go back. You can't stay here. Marty, it's like when you were little, every vacation we took you wanted to live there."

"Grace, I'm not a little kid. I've talked it over with Dave. He'll sponsor me until I find a job. I'm going back to school."

"I know, your MBA–"

Marty shook his head. "Nope, archeology. I love this area and all of the history and secrets of its early people. I want to uncover the past." His eyes gleamed with an expression I'd never seen. My experiences with the past lately hadn't been pleasant, and I wasn't even looking to uncover anything.

My heart was torn between bestowing a blessing and dashing the notion. "What about Katie? What about the house, the bills?" Maybe the practicality of life would get through to him.

"Eve and I had talked about downsizing to a townhouse once Katie left for college. She's decided on Western Michigan; that puts her four hours away from Eve and about five hours from me in Midland. I've taken stock options with the company for years. Whatever Eve wants to buy should be covered by the sale of the house and I can sell some stock for my education. Katie's college and spending money are already set aside."

His plan seemed flawless except for one point.

"I'm not going home alone to tell Dad I left you here. You'll have to come home to face him."

"Who do you think suggested I look deep at what I wanted to do with my life?"

"He didn't mean run away to the first place you visited."

"I went to med school because I wanted to make a lot of money. I took the sales job because I wanted to make a lot of money. I screwed up because–"

"Because you made a lot of money," I finished for him.

His annoyed look stopped me. "I screwed up because I hated what I did and felt stuck. I almost made the same mistake by thinking an MBA would fix things. It's not the money."

I sensed it was important that I approve or at least condone this paradigm shift. When would I see him if he moved here? I'd miss him, we all would. Marty blew life into the Morelli gatherings with his incandescent smile and exuberance for life, an exuberance that had waned in the last few years. I held on to that thought.

"Okay, but you still have to come home and tell Dad."

He hugged me. "Thanks, big Sis, you're the best."

I patted him on the head. "Yeah, you say that now."

The door slammed back against the wall. I'd meant to lock it. Shoulda, woulda, coulda…

# Chapter Thirty-six

I whirled toward the sound. Marty jumped to his feet. I heard his sharp intake of breath.

Bob and Ken stopped stock still when they rounded the corner. We stared wide-eyed at each other. I could have seen the humor in the cartoon type confrontation except for the gun tucked into the waistband of Bob's jeans.

He casually laid his hand on the grip. "No one is supposed to be here. This isn't in our plan."

The calm, patient tone I'd associated with him had no connection to this hard voice. His fingers curled around the gun.

Marty hobbled forward a step to put me behind him. "Better be careful, you might shoot off something important, maybe." Marty's droll observation infuriated Bob.

"Marty, be quiet." My admonishment died on my lips when Bob burst into laughter. Not the happy tones of a friend, but the high-pitched trill you associate with a madman. Even Ken looked uneasy.

"Marty, be quiet," Bob mocked me. "Listen to her. As much of a nuisance as you've both been, she makes a good point. Sit down and don't think about being heroes."

I nudged Marty back to his chair and sat down next to him. My brain rocked with thoughts. One pegged Bob as a murderer, another pictured him killing to protect himself; one Bob stumbled into a way out of his financial problems, another Bob planned this excursion to appear casual. I felt confusion and anxiety jump from my brain to my arms, the tingling that signaled a self-preserving shutdown. My breathing slowed, my anxiety lessened. The room grew colder, clearer, until the glass and metal surfaces gleamed with bright light. I heard mumbling around me, snatches of phrases…no way to know if they were now or then voices.

"*Père, père.*" Father, father. Whose father? I struggled to force my consciousness to follow my lead. I wanted to rejoin the *normally scheduled broadcast*, not some loop in my head.

"We overlooked the significance of the capital 'P' on the carving," Bob explained. "The bone in that box is worth millions to religious zealots who collect relics and don't care how they do it."

The room warmed slowly and the once-shiny surfaces dully reflected our distorted images. He continued, "I want that box."

"Is that what you were looking for in their bedroom? You didn't care about the documents like Garry did."

"That fool. He almost ruined the deal a month back going on about historical significance and preservation rot."

"Did you put him in the trunk?"

He nodded. I looked at Ken. "You knew he was in there," I stated more than asked.

"Bob managed to tell me during all the confusion that morning. I told you I'd found your light on the bumper."

"I found it on the deck right before your brother came stumbling out. Your little book light came in useful for working the keyhole in the trunk; I must have left it on the bumper."

Bob spoke calmly about his attempt to silence Garry. It couldn't bode well for us, Marty and me, if the guy with the gun didn't mind telling us how he *did it*. Marty squirmed and drew Bob's attention.

"I wasn't sure if you saw me circling back when we were on that blasted search for him." Bob motioned toward Ken. "Fool got lost."

"It was a blizzard, for God's sake. I missed the turn. It's not like I've roamed the island like you and Dave," Ken whined.

Dave. Oh, no. Was he really involved too?

"Oh, shut up." Bob looked at Marty. "It seemed you stared right at me at one point. When you looked away and tugged on the ropes I circled behind you and waited until you were walking to cover the noise. I figured you'd blame the Band members."

Marty shook his head slowly. "I remember thinking I saw movement, but I couldn't make out anything in the snow."

That high-pitched bark burst from Bob's mouth again. Goosebumps rose on my arms and I rolled my shoulders against the creeping shiver moving up my spine.

"What is it that you really want, the development, the treasure, or the relic?" Marty's voice held no accusatory tone, only curiosity. Only one Morelli succumbed to the usually awkward and occasionally dangerous sin of excessive curiosity more than I did. I waited for the answer.

"Yes," Bob's eyes gleamed with an out-of-control expression. "I'm having it all." I wanted to warn Marty to keep quiet.

"That's impossible now. The police know you're involved. You can't get off the island with the treasure. Your best bet is to turn yourself in. You didn't mean to kill that man, it was self-defense. You haven't hurt anyone else. Bob, think about Debbie. She'll be devastated."

At the mention of Debbie, Bob grew angry. "She'll be devastated? How would you know, or do you know her better than either of you let on?"

I didn't like where this was going.

Marty's natural rashness kicked in. "What the hell is that supposed to mean?"

"I saw you flirting with her, we all saw it." He looked to Ken and me. Neither of us moved. "Telephone charges to the U.S., trips to Toronto. I knew she was involved with someone, just didn't know she'd be bold enough to invite him up here under my nose."

Oh boy, this couldn't go another second. I stared open-mouthed at him. "Marty never met Debbie. I invited him; he didn't even know about this trip till two weeks ago. I'm sorry if your wife is cheating on you, but it most certainly is not with my brother."

"No matter. Where's the box?" His calm tone bothered me.

"That's right, no matter. You won't make it."

"Marty, please." I wanted to duct-tape my brother's mouth.

Ken looked at his watch. "She'll be here in ten minutes. Forget the box, let's go."

The 'she' could only be Colleen. Was she involved from the beginning?

Marty tried a different tack. "Ken, do you want your wife brought up on charges? Why are you involving her?"

Ken looked sidelong at Bob. "She's only bringing a boat across.

Bob told her who to contact on the mainland. The plan got messed up when King arrested me."

"It got messed up when the blasted storm hit. The weather bureau doesn't know their arse from a Tim-bit. The plan was for me and Ken to take the canoes out again and paddle past Bar Spit Point and into the cave. Pete had shown me the entrance and he'd been moving the gold from the grave to the cavern. That's part of what you saw when you were in there."

"Grave, whose grave?" I had a feeling I knew–the markings at the base of the tombstone. "Did the inukshuk in the pit point the way for you?"

Bob's harsh laugh startled me. "I planted that one to confuse the lot of you. I don't recall which of you thought the reddish brown color on one rock could be old blood. I about bust a gut trying not to laugh."

"Did you plant the cut-up photo showing that same spot?"

"No, it didn't make sense until Pete told me where the treasure was buried. I realized that the picture was intended to send the viewer to the cemetery to find the grave with the same markings. You were close there."

"The person who died a few days before Havilland? Who was he? I didn't understand the inscription."

"Ah, the *Trêsor d'Ile*–the island treasure. The dead man was Lissette's brother, Laurent. Somehow Havilland learned of the treasure; maybe he explored the tunnels beneath the lighthouse. From reading the history, I think the Indians, bidden by the good Father to hide the treasure, hid it under the altar stone. He may have recognized it and knew to look for an entrance. Laurent probably found it and was in the process of bringing it out where he could wait for the water to be low enough to ferry it out by canoe. Must have been a falling out between thieves, and Havilland killed Laurent. One of Amelia's letters mentioned the death attributed to poison from deadly wild poke accidentally mixed in with island greens. That did and didn't make sense. I love a good puzzle, don't you, Grace?"

I hated the sound of my name on his lips. I shivered in revulsion.

"Cold? No matter."

I liked that comment even less. He'd gone round the bend and there was no reasoning with him. All Marty and I could hope for is that Harry and King would think to check on us. If they were okay. A horrible thought occurred to me.

"You must have been one step ahead of King. He left for the lighthouse to arrest you and Dave."

"Dave? Oh, that's rich. Do-gooder Dave. I left him in the tunnel after I persuaded him not to turn me in."

My heart lurched at the number of conditions the words 'left' and 'persuaded' could cover.

"I'd heard King brought in reinforcements from Midland. By now they should have spotted the two canoes–one sunk in the clear water off the point, the other smashed on the treacherous rock with enough gold to lead them to the conclusion that we perished in our attempt to escape with the gold."

"But you have the gold and you're leaving by motorboat." Marty's comment left the logical conclusion for us hanging in the air. Ken apparently hadn't thought his part in all this through to the end. His face registered the realization of what must happen to us if they were to get away to some Cayman Island to escape detection and/or extradition. Ken's eyes grew wider and he stepped away from Bob, an unconscious movement that I hoped indicated he'd chosen sides.

"What's wrong, Ken?"

"I never thought, I mean…"

"You were right the first time, you never thought. That's why you let me do the thinking for both of us." He turned to face Marty. "This plan wasn't executed the way I put it together, but the sign of a great mind is the ability to shift and compensate and develop new plans on the run. My preference, of course, would have been to avoid collateral damage."

"Why are you talking like that? This isn't a war game. They're right, we need to stop now before anyone else gets hurt. We'll lose the money, Bob, but we won't go to jail."

I thought his plea made sense except for the part about no jail time, but then I didn't know Canadian law. Ken fidgeted with the strings on his hood–pulling one, then the other, in a see-saw pattern.

The movement mesmerized me and I felt an increasing urge to do the same. I inched my hands up to my hoodless collar and rubbed my thumbs back and forth under the fabric. Marty had leaned down to adjust his sliding ice packs. Our combined movements annoyed Bob. He pulled the pistol from his waist.

"Ken, you're just too decent for your own good. We're ruined without this development. Your home, Colleen's trust, everything you signed will be gone. We need this gold, at least I do. There are all sorts of jail; I'm not settling for any of them." He motioned Ken to move over toward us. "We're going to walk down to the water to meet Colleen. Once we're under way, these two will have an unfortunate accident. You and Colleen can choose your fates.

"As Ken said, she should be out there. She'll be coming ashore up the beach. Time to move."

"Bob, please. Think about what you're saying. You can't do this," Ken pleaded with him.

"I must. The only question is how many of you will have unfortunate accidents." He jerked the gun up and down indicating for Marty to stand. "Slide those off," Bob pointed to the ice packs. "You won't be able to walk with them slogging around your foot."

Marty fumbled with the frozen peas, wincing as he lifted his foot through the belt, shifting the buckle behind his heel. His fingers closed over the metal and he groaned.

"Can't you see he's hurt? It might be broken…Debbie said it could be a slight fracture. Debbie told him to stay off it." I hoped saying her name would give him pause, make him rethink his plan. I prayed if that didn't work, then the diversion might help Marty with what I suspected he planned. One more shot. "Debbie was unconscious when we found her. What did you give her?"

"Unconscious? No, I…" He took his eyes off Marty to stare at me. "Is she…"

Marty snapped the belt up and caught the back of Bob's hand, slamming the hard metal buckle against the thin skin and small bones.

The gunshot pulsed through the room a split second before the gun jerked from Bob's hand and hit the floor. Marty launched himself at Bob, knocking him off his feet and up against the cabinets. As Bob slumped to the floor with my brother scrambling to avoid getting pinned under his dead weight, Ken picked up the gun. He held the pistol in front of him, arm extended, staring at the weapon.

Marty stopped squirming and lay still, partially covered by Bob's upper body. I froze watching Ken's hand turn from palm up to a shooting position. The fractional movement matched the pounding in my head. Had he made his decision to help us or would he save his friend? I wanted to cover my ears and press my fingertips against my temples; I didn't move a muscle. More pounding, louder.

"Drop the gun. Don't move."

King's voice came from behind me, filling the room with authority and demand.

Ken reacted by swinging his arm toward King, putting me between them.

"Drop the gun. Now!"

I didn't believe he meant to shoot, but they couldn't know that. My throat closed up and only a pop of air moved over my lips. My mouth slacked open; the air across my bottom teeth tingled. The tension pricked at my skin.

"Put the gun down." King lowered his voice. Maybe he'd noticed the vacant look in Ken's eyes. "You can stop this. Put the gun down."

Ken's vision seemed to sharpen as he took in the scene. Marty and Bob still sprawled on the floor. Walter moved to King's left side, effectively blocking that escape route. Harry stood off to my right, poised to spring, his eyes fixed on Ken's hand.

"Kenny, honey, please put down the gun."

Colleen walked up behind me and stepped in front of me. "Kenny, we'll work it out. Please."

Ken lowered the gun to his waist, then slowly down until it pointed the length of his leg to the ground. No one moved.

"Put the gun on the floor and step away," King's voice coaxed. "Put the gun down and come to your wife. She needs you."

The dull thud released the stifled movement of the past few minutes. King picked up the gun and passed it behind him to his deputy. Harry pulled me into his arms. I felt the tension in his arm around my shoulder. The sharp click of the handcuffs securing Ken's hands sounded final. Colleen rushed to his side and slipped her arm through his while the deputy led them out.

King helped Marty to his feet and motioned him away from Bob. He lay two fingers against Bob's neck, then lifted an eyelid to check further.

"I think he's just out cold. I slammed him as hard as I could; he hit the edge of the counter." Marty nodded to the Formica top. A smear two inches long wasn't spaghetti gravy.

King rolled Bob over onto his stomach. Blood from the gash at the back of his head seeped into his collar and onto his shirt.

Marty's face paled. "Is he dead?"

King looked up. "No; looks worse than it is. He'll have a 'Halifax headache' for sure."

I didn't know how much a Halifax headache hurt, but I hoped a lot. My head still pounded, not quite the same intensity, but bad enough to make me feel nauseous. I rolled my neck against Harry's arm. He took the cue and began a gentle massage of my shoulders.

"Good Lord, you've knots the size of walnuts." He leaned closer and kissed the back of my neck.

King spoke to Marty. "Wet that cloth. Shame to let him bleed all over Joan's floor." Marty soaked the cloth and handed it to King. "I'm not in trouble for this, am I? I mean excessive force or something."

King's rich baritone laugh comforted me; a wonderful departure from the harsh bark I'd heard earlier. "No trouble, unless a few forms in triplicate and a review with the Metro people bothers you."

Marty shook his head and smiled, "No bother at all."

"If you were a Band member we'd dispense with the Metro side, but you're not one of us, and technically I don't have jurisdiction over you. Heck, you're not even one of them." His laughter filled the room.

Bob groaned and lurched from his stomach to all fours. His head hung below his shoulders. He slowly shifted to a sitting position and focused immediately on King. Bob leaned his head back against the counter inches below the now brownish stain. He closed his eyes and his body language reflected defeat.

"Need a hand getting him to your vehicle?" Harry offered.

King shook his head. "No need. Jack's on his way back. We'll haul him off." He looked at me. "Looks like you've a job to do here."

I snuggled under Harry's arm. "How did you know to come here? I thought this would be the last place he'd show up."

"We did too until we found the wrecked canoes."

"He said you'd think they capsized and drowned trying to get the treasure out of the cave."

"Officer King spotted the charade. The canoe wreckage didn't match the 'wrecking' material."

I looked at King, who easily lifted Bob up by his shoulders and leaned him against the counter. He expertly pulled his prisoner's hands behind his back and snapped on handcuffs. He motioned him toward a kitchen chair. Marty moved out of his way.

King stretched and rolled his shoulders. "The waters on the point come around the spit and cause an undertow. Those canoes had no business smashing up on the rocks where we found them. If they'd gone down coming out of the cave those canoes would had to have been sunk darn near in the entrance. If they'd made it past the undertow and then hit the rocks, the natural wave pattern would have pushed the canoes around the spit."

"When King called it bogus, we knew they'd come to the one part of the island where they could meet a boat. The ferry landing was too public and the police were conveniently at the other end of the island. We spotted Colleen and it didn't take long to get the plan from her." Harry tightened his arm around me. "I don't believe she knew Bob's entire plan. She knew about the treasure."

I nodded my head. "Ken didn't go along with Bob's plan to dump me and Marty in the bay. Bob all but told him if he and Colleen didn't see it his way, they'd be sleeping with the fishes too. I don't think he was going to hurt anyone, I think he was in shock."

"I consider that out of control and dangerous. He could have killed one of you or just as easily taken his own life. Shock is tricky…it's hard to read the eyes, see the decision."

Footsteps announced reinforcements. King's brother stepped quickly to Bob's side. "Metro coming off the ferry. Dad's meeting them and taking them to the Center." He slipped his hand under Bob's arm and guided him up. "His wife wants to see him. That okay?"

King nodded. "Keep him close is all." We watched them leave. Marty asked King, "Should I go with them to make my statement?"

King and Harry laughed. I looked from one grin to the other. Marty's face hardened. I knew that look. Harry stopped laughing and pointed to my brother.

"It's not fair, King. This bloke saved the day."

Marty immediately puffed up. Praise from Harry meant the world to him. Marty had been a teenager when I first brought my English boyfriend to a Morelli party. He'd been in awe of him from that day forward.

King put his hand out to Marty whose confused expression didn't stop him from taking the offered hand. "I don't understand."

King smiled and clapped him on the back. "You stand up to a madman, stop him from shooting your sister, risk your life to jump him, and you think I'm going to turn you over to Metro?"

Marty's grin spread across his face. "When you put it that way…" He grinned again.

"Just having a bit of a prank. Police humor, you know." He turned to Harry and extended his hand. "Thank you for your assistance. I hope you'll let them know how it turned out." King said the last bit more quietly.

Harry shook hands with the island constable, as Harry referred to him. "Indeed I will, although it seems you would have handled it with your team."

King smiled. "Backup is always appreciated." He turned to leave, then stopped. "Your friends will be here shortly, except the ones we're keeping." He dipped his head toward us and left. His footsteps preceded the start-up of an engine.

The tension eased now that the crisis had passed. No one else had died, that was enough for now. "Harry, what did King mean when he said he hoped you'd tell 'them' how it turned out?"

"I had to call in a favor for transport for me and Walter and permission to come over with this." He opened his jacket and revealed a handgun snugged into a shoulder holster.

"Good thing you knew somebody," Marty said.

Harry smiled. "Yes, well, if not I would have had to ask

forgiveness, wouldn't I? Couldn't not be here if you two were in trouble." He clapped Marty on the back. I understood better than my brother that no one could have stopped him. If not through proper channels, he would have found the shadier side of humanity to accommodate him.

"How's that ankle holding up?"

Marty shrugged. "Won't keep me from getting off this island. In fact, if one of you will hand me that walking stick, I'll start packing."

I laughed at his eagerness. "I thought you were going to move here, become one with nature. What happened?"

My brother's ears flamed with embarrassment. "You were right, Gracie. Vacation is over and the grass is definitely not greener on Christian Island." He took the stick from Harry and limped into the bedroom. Walter offered to help and followed him.

"What was that about?"

I waved off the question. "Just Marty being Marty."

He pulled me into his arms. My heartbeat synced in with his and I melted against him, reveling in his closeness and praying the physical bond reflected the spiritual and emotional connection.

"I love you, Grace, so very much," he whispered. I stood still, letting the words wash over and around me.

Angry voices and thumping up the steps tore us apart. Harry pushed me behind him and drew his gun, holding it down at his side.

# Chapter Thirty-seven

Dave burst through the door, followed by the remaining cottagers not under arrest. He caught sight of Harry and stopped abruptly. "They told me you were here. Didn't see you when they got me out. We were 'detained' at the Band Center until King gave the all clear. We walked, said they were short on manpower at the moment."

Walter stepped out of the bedroom and stood quietly, his arms crossed over his brawny chest.

Dave thumbed his hand at the 'fireplug'. "Who's he?"

"Walter Stahl. He's with me," Harry explained.

I looked at the group. "Where's Deb? Isn't she with you?"

Joan shook her head. "She's waiting at the Center for Bob. We were told he was in custody and on his way there."

Harry's face sharpened. "He hadn't arrived by the time you left?"

"No, why?"

"Is there another road to get to the Center?"

"Just the one, loops around most of the island."

Harry walked to the phone and lifted the receiver. "Have you King's number?"

"Phone is out. Bob saw to that." Dave's voice grew angry again.

"Have you a radio?"

"No, what's wrong?"

Wrong indeed. Harry's concern made me nervous. He only worried for good reasons. He looked across the room at Walter, who understood the silent communiqué. He nodded and zipped his jacket. I wondered if he carried a gun under the bulky parka. Dave stepped aside to allow Walter to leave.

We all watched his back and listened to his steps on the wooden stairs. Dave turned to Harry. "What was that? Where's he going?"

"To the Center to find King. Something is wrong."

"I don't know what you mean, but I'll tell you what's wrong. That crazy Band Council has pulled my lease. I can't sell the cottage because the land lease has been revoked." Dave's face blotched red and he slammed his fist against the wall.

"Can they do that, I mean legally?"

Joan stepped around her seething husband and calmly removed another package of frozen veggies from the freezer. She pulled Dave's hand up and not so gently placed the hard package on his bruised knuckles. Dave winced and held the pack against his hand. His breathing calmed and the beginning of embarrassment colored his face. He sat down in the kitchen and took a deep breath. "They can revoke the lease if 'the lessee is deemed to have used the property for illegal or immoral purposes' or some rot to that effect." He lifted the veggies from his hand and wiggled his fingers. "Can't hardly blame them, I suppose. I invite a nutcase to the island who kills two people and steals national treasure. We were counting on the sale of the cottage to build new."

"I love our house. We don't need new. I can't believe this is happening, and for what?" Joan pulled over a chair and sat next to Dave, laying her head against his shoulder. "Nothing is worth what's happened to us." She spoke for everyone.

At some point someone had plugged in the kettle and now a low whistle attracted Laurie to the counter. She poured the boiling water into fresh mugs waiting for takers. We sidled up to the bar one by one, tired and slow in our movements. Marty pulled the anisette from the cupboard, uncapped it, and placed it next to the honey jar.

Joan, always the hostess, stood to lend a hand and clear off the papers we'd left strewn on most flat surfaces. We had pieces of the puzzle, but nothing fit properly.

I remembered what Bob said about the relic. Was he right? Should I even mention it and add more confusion to the mix? Joan handed me a sheaf of papers.

"Can you put this in the white box on the table? These are so mixed up; I'll sort through them later. I want to get them out of the way and back to the historical society on the next ferry."

"You may not be able to return those that easily."

"Why in heaven's name not?" Joan challenged Harry.

"I don't know what's in all of this, but King may need it for evidence." Harry spread his hands out, fingers splayed. "It's a distinct possibility."

"It doesn't matter, we've been through most of it and what we have is that we suspect Joshua and his sister Amelia had a long-term affair which produced at least one child. We suspect that Joshua married Lissette to quickly account to Pentaq society for an infant while convincing his new bride to save his sister's reputation by accepting the newborn as their own. I got the impression that the wedding was eagerly accepted by Lissette's people, so maybe he'd already gotten her pregnant. There was an earlier child born to Amelia, supposedly her husband's but who knows? After his untimely death, she moved into her brother's home to be his housekeeper. It would be easy to explain that child, but certainly not the next one."

Garry spoke up. "Had I known what this would stir up, I would have let it go." He pressed against his temples with his fingertips. "I started helping my sister catalog the letters and establish our family tree. She became interested when her son worked on his scouting badge in genealogy. She thought it fun, and frankly got me hooked too. I spotted the birth dates and checked further with the Office of Records. That led to more digging until I found my great uncle's blood type and compared it to Lissette's. She couldn't have been his biological mother. The child with the surname of Havilland had no claim on anything, and yet the accounts we read always referred to him."

"He was just a kid. Maybe they wanted him to feel part of the family?"

Garry nodded. "They did indeed. I found an adoption record making him one of the eleven Pantiers. It didn't give him inheriting rights, but it gave him the same name, which confused my nephew when he was plotting the family line. Speaking of same names, there were two Joshua Pantiers."

"Let me guess, the boy Joshua adopted and the baby Lissette gave birth to a scant seven months after her wedding."

Garry smiled. "Ostensibly, the children were named for their uncle and father. I'm convinced they were named for their father."

"What would this change?" Harry asked.

"The pecking order of the entire family," Marty answered succinctly. "Garry may very well be king of Christian Island." Marty's humor fell flat. No one cracked a smile. "Sorry. I'm too wound up."

"It's okay. I admit I didn't think myself king, but maybe magistrate of all I see." He grinned and opened his arms wide. "It was stupid of me to talk about it to so many people."

"You couldn't know it would cause this. It's not your fault. Bob set all this in motion." Laurie consoled her husband.

"According to King, with his investigation only started he's found out that Bob's been on island several times since October–meeting with different Band Council members and promising them opportunity, jobs, money…whatever they wanted most. He'd already smoothed the way for the son of one of the Band members to attend university on a scholarship. He found a quick ally in King's cousin, Pete. Apparently Pete had figured out the clues pointing to where the Jesuit treasure was buried.

"Pete planted other clues to cause confusion. The inukshuk in the pit had nothing to do with anything. He also convinced those boys to harass you with the dummies and costumes. One of them finally told King that three of them had been hired to prank the cottagers.

"Apparently, Bob's alliance with Pete and two other Band members gave him the cover he needed to move around and shore up votes. Right before we left for the lighthouse, King received a call from the mainland telling him they'd detained the young man who went off island pretending to be a cottager."

"That would mean they planned to lock me in the trunk and that's not logical. How would they know I'd be out there?"

"They didn't, and if it makes you feel any better I don't think the plan was to kill you either. At that point, I don't think Bob had lost touch with reality. You were tucked deep into the trunk and covered with heavy blankets as I heard it."

Dave nodded. "That old Chevy has a deep trunk, and you were at the far back. As I think about it, I believe Ken didn't spot you because to tuck you back there most of the other gear had to have been pulled forward. The snowshoes were right there and my trunk light hasn't worked in years. Ken was anxious to get information about the inheriting line. He remembered something he saw in the boxes and wanted to get back to it. I thought he knew the route."

"Did Colleen know what Bob intended?"

Harry shook his head. "We spotted her offshore and waved her in. She told us about the phone call from Bob telling her that Ken was released, but that the ferry had restricted trips due to mechanical problems. He intimated that it would be for the best if Ken got off island before the locals changed their minds. He directed her to a small marina where he had left a deposit on a charter."

Joan interrupted. "Wait a minute. Bob had a boat ready to go? I thought he mapped out the old canoe route to use for his escape with the treasure."

"That might have been Plan A. We don't know when he scrapped that in favor of the motorboat, or maybe the canoes were a red herring. Colleen told us she expected to pick up only Ken. Bob told her to motor to the cottage instead of the landing."

"I think King will find that Bob had another vehicle on standby somewhere close, perhaps the car park at the landing. He must have planned to take the gold off island this week. Remember, he had Ken hooked on the gold and he had several accomplices on the island."

"I can't believe all this was going on around us. I had no idea," Joan said. "I feel responsible in a way for dredging up all this historical stuff." She waved her hand at the papers and boxes.

"You've no cause to feel responsible," Garry continued. "I'm the horse's arse that kept digging deeper to confirm my theory. My grandfather was the first issue of a blessed union, but that means my great-grandfather had an incestuous fling with my great-great aunt…not once, but at least twice. Who knows if some of the later Pantiers are from that union? I don't, and I'm dropping the whole thing. A Band Council check every month would be nice, but not at this price." Garry pulled Laurie closer to him. "Not worth it." Laurie's face reflected a calm that hadn't been present all week. She laid her head against his chest. He continued, "I'm thankful it's over."

A hard rap announced a visitor. King reached our sides in quick strides. "They're gone!"

# Chapter Thirty-eight

His face reflected anger and frustration.

"Your friend and my brother. They never made it to the Center."

"Do you think Bob overpowered your brother? I mean, he was handcuffed and wobbly when he left."

"I don't know what to think." King looked at Harry.

"I suspect it would be difficult for someone in Bob's condition to tackle a young man and win. The other option is that your brother is in cahoots with him; perhaps the other accomplice."

King's eyes sparked under furrowed brows. His expression twisted, and the pain displayed caused a lump in my throat. How would I feel if Marty did something despicable? Maybe he hadn't.

"Could Bob have been faking? Would your brother uncuff him if Bob seemed to be in distress?" The words popped out before I'd thought them through. I didn't understand why it was important to throw King a lifeline. He grabbed at it.

"She's right. It would be like him to release him if he thought he'd taken a turn. I've told him he's too good-hearted for this job."

Harry's manner changed abruptly. "Until we know for certain what happened and why, we need to proceed with caution. Would Bob come back to the cottage for any reason?"

I'd forgotten the geef box. "Yes. I mean, maybe. He insisted the bone in the geef box was a relic, an actual bone of one of the Jesuits. He demanded the box, said he could sell it for a fortune. I don't see how without the provenance," I mumbled the last bit to myself.

"Unless he found something in the boxes or letters," Marty said. He shifted quickly from one foot to the other, explaining as he rocked in place. "He could have found reference to it or reference where to find the provenance."

"If the relic fell into Havilland's possession, would he hide it in the lighthouse? Why not turn it in to the Church? Would he know the value of what he had?"

"This is all supposition, and we don't know if we're looking for two criminals or one criminal and his victim." Harry's comment stopped us cold. "If indeed Bob thinks he has provenance for the relic, he won't want to leave without it. The relic is priceless to the Church, but could bring a half million dollars from the right buyer. If he's as snapped as you say, he won't leave without it. Where is it?"

"I'll get it. Why didn't he look for it before? There aren't too many places to hide anything around here."

Garry spoke to King. "I hate to burst your bubble about your brother, but he may have made the call to the deputy you sent to bring me in. At first, he asked me to come with him, but as we were leaving he got a call telling him to bring all of us in. Tight squeeze, but he managed. That cleared the way for anyone to search the cottage."

I set my duffle bag on the coffee table and unzipped it. My *ditty bag* bulged with more than cosmetics. I held the crudely carved box with reverence in case the content was truly a holy relic. "Right next to my toothpaste." Harry and King both reached for the box. I knew King was in charge, but I also knew Harry loved history. King took hold of my wrist. His firm grip didn't hurt, but it did stop me from extending my hand. Harry bristled at the contact. "No need to manhandle her, King. Let her go." His voice rang with authority and a smidgen of accusation. King looked at me and smiled. "No offense intended." I jammed the box into his waiting palm, and fussed with repacking my duffle.

King slid the top open and lifted the thin bone from its resting place. He turned it this way and that like he knew what he was looking for. Showboating is all! He replaced the bone and carefully slid the box closed. He used it like a pointer when he spoke. "I'll call mainland and get this to the right people. You stay put." He nodded toward Harry. "He's armed and can protect you until I can get someone out here." He tucked the geef box in his inside pocket and zipped up his jacket.

"Where's Walter? Why didn't he come back with you?"

King turned his head quickly. "I didn't see him. Was he coming to get me?"

"The hell you say," Harry's voice startled us. "You must have passed him on the road if he didn't get to the Center before you left. Where is he?"

A collective gasp filled the cottage. King stared at Harry.

Harry's eyes never wavered from King's face. In the end I think his steady piercing stare convinced King that there would be nowhere he could hide from Harry if he wasn't telling the truth.

"I don't know." King relaxed his arms. "Maybe someone stopped him; maybe my brother and Hastings." King ran his hand through his hair. "Holy Jezzie, what the hell is going on?"

Harry looked at Dave. "Is there somewhere close to the water that Bob would know about, might hide in until dark?"

"He seemed interested in a shed near the Center." Dave looked at King. "The one half mile north of the Center, down that fire lane."

King was already moving for the door. He stopped and turned back to me, pulling the geef box out of his pocket. "Hang on to this for me."

I took the box and stepped back.

"I'm going with you." Harry slipped his arm around my shoulders and squeezed. "I'll be back in a bit with him." He smiled and left.

I was worried about Walter, but with Harry on his trail I felt he'd be found—I hoped safe.

A sense of normalcy began to replace the tension. Garry offered to make sandwiches. I wet a towel and went to work on the mud we'd tracked on the floor. The repetitive motion let my mind wander.

Who had won? A family secret revealed, a woman's shame exposed, a brother murdered for treasure…more murder, more treasure on the island. *Trésor d'Ile!*

I stopped rubbing and sat back on my heels. My elbow grease had not only lifted the mud, but also a fair amount of old dirt so that the dinner plate-size spot on the floor gleamed compared to the remainder of the wood. A fleeting thought hoped I wouldn't feel compelled to make the floor match the clean spot…I cringed at the thought and pushed it out of my mind before it could take hold.

My toe pushed against the rug. I heard a crinkle and swiveled around to lift the edge. I felt the parchment thickness under the fringe. This hadn't been there before. I remembered this is where King stood when he pulled the geef box from his pocket. It must have fallen out. I closed my fingers around the parchment. I knew in my bones that this letter would have answers. No one saw me find it. I tucked it in my pocket and stood. My brain screamed 'hurry,' but my motions remained cautious and steady. Replace the cleaning solution, wrap the rag, toss it in the trash, smile, wash my hands, smile, nod at Garry's question, accept the steaming mug of tea, smile, make small talk, walk into the bedroom, close the door. Yes!

I carefully placed the mug on the floor and pulled the letter from my pocket, taking care when I unfolded the thick, cream-colored paper not to stress the already deep creases that divided the letter into six uniform panels. I recognized the loopy, childish handwriting. My eyes devoured the words, reading them through twice. I noted the date, the signature. How did King get this letter? From his father? No, from his uncle made more sense. He had to have taken it after his death. Did he kill his uncle for this? Did he get it from his cousin? We may never know. Did it matter who had this hidden? Did it matter that it would become public information now? Too many people had died, were still dying. The back of my throat itched with tears as I thought of Walter. Had he died for this ugly secret?

A light knock at the door startled me. "Just a minute." I slipped the letter under Marty's pillow.

Joan stood in the doorway holding the kettle, poised to offer a refill. "Thought you could use a bit more water." She glanced at the still full mug on the floor. "Guess not."

She sat on the bed and leaned against me. "Dave and Garry are trying to reconstruct this horrible mess, trying to pinpoint when Bob went off his rocker and pulled Ken with him. Laurie is reading a book. Can you believe that? All that's happened and she's reading a bloody book."

Though American by birth, Joanie had adopted some of the more colorful expressions of her new homeland. She even called napkins 'serviettes' and diapers 'nappies.' Her blue eyes brimmed with tears; she looked on the verge of a meltdown. Who would blame her? I wanted to distract her.

"I know where the treasure has been since Havilland found it. He buried it with Laurent, Lissette's brother. One of her letters home mentioned the epitaph. He must have told her."

Joan's eyes widened and I saw her anguish replaced by curiosity. "Why would he tell her? I thought he killed her brother."

"I don't think Havilland killed him for the treasure. I think it was self-defense because Laurent went nuts when he found out about him and Lissette."

"Him and Lissette?"

I pushed the door closed and lifted the edge of the pillow. Joan read the letter, stopping twice to look at me. "Oh my God, do you know what this could mean?"

I nodded and returned the letter to its hiding place.

"We should tell someone."

Dave pushed the door open. "Hey, what are you two doing conspiring in here? We're about ready to start packing up to get off this island. Any takers?" His tired smile was reminiscent of a more jovial expression.

"We can't leave without Harry and my brother, and Walter," I added, quickly praying I hadn't jinxed him.

"I figured we'd meet them at the landing."

"I think we should wait here."

Dave seemed to make a decision. "Okay, we'll wait. Let's at least be ready to go."

"We're supposed to empty the cottage by next week. I don't want to stay, but…"

"No one is staying. I don't care if we have to pay the new owners a disposal fee. I want to get you home."

Joan's eyes sparked. "David Hamilton, I am not leaving my things for other people to toss like garbage." Joan's Midwestern middle-class sensibility reared its frugal head. I'd been raised the same way. 'Waste not, want not' was the operative phrase.

I scrambled off the bed and stood between them. "Let's leave as soon as we can and set a date to come back next week and haul out what you want. Sound reasonable? I mean, we need a break from this island. I promise I'll come back with you to help."

They accepted the terms and left to pack. I checked the freezer to make sure I hadn't left any historical packages inside, folded the letter in half, and tucked it into my journal. My duffle packed easily since I hadn't had time to collect more than the few rocks I planned to use on building my very own inukshuk with authentic Christian Island rocks for Harry's flower garden. He had the green thumb in the family. I contributed unusual garden art that I found at garage sales.

Marty's duffle was easier still. He lived out of his Adidas 'double wide' as I referred to it–dirty clothes one side, clean clothes other side. About now it looked as though the clothes had co-mingled and only the sniff test could separate them correctly. I zipped his bag closed with no interest in discovering the difference.

I scanned the room and crawled halfway under the bed to make sure all we'd left were resident dust bunnies. 'Leave no trace' was our outdoor code, a good one for visitors too. A quick tour of the bathroom netted Marty's shampoo and my razor, which he had not asked permission to borrow.

The back door opened; Harry and Marty slowly entered the kitchen. My stomach churned at the sight of Harry's face…his red-rimmed eyes glimmered with a fear I'd never seen. I reached for his hand; his icy fingers barely acknowledged my touch.

Marty cleared his throat. "Walter wasn't there." He swallowed hard. "We found rope and his jacket in the shed; some blood on the floor. We don't know whose." He stopped and stared at the floor. My arms flew around Harry's chest and I bit my lip to keep from sobbing. I needed to be strong for Harry. Slowly he lifted his arms to hold me.

His flat voice filled us in. "The island is in an uproar. King's younger brother is missing. Bob has escaped. King has attached half the Indians to him."

I wondered if that meant 'deputized,' but didn't want to interrupt.

"We came back to get you off the island. King is holding the ferry for you. Can you be ready to leave in ten minutes?"

"Better than that, we're already packed."

"Excellent." Harry let go of me and assumed the leadership role. "They loaned us another vehicle. Load up, we should all fit."

Dave looked at Joan. "I'll take one car to the dock and get them on the ferry. I'm staying to help you look for Walter."

"Same with me," Garry said.

Laurie's head snapped around. "You're not well enough. No."

He shook his head. His eyes held a sorrowful expression. "Much of this started with my selfish determination to find the truth. I owe these people." She didn't like it, but I knew she wouldn't fight it.

A sense of resignation followed us down the back stairs, and an uncomfortable prickling of the skin on my arms overcame me. I felt the temperature drop from one stair to the next.

# Chapter Thirty-nine

He stood in a shimmering light a few paces beyond the road. I squinted at the brightness, trying to see the shadowy image clearly.

"Got something in your eye?" my brother asked.

I blinked and the aura disappeared. Marty stared at me. I breathed deeply and exhaled slowly. "No, I'm fine."

I rode with Harry, Dave, and Joan. Marty had Garry and Laurie with him. At the landing I held back until the last possible moment. My voice came out squeaky when I grabbed at Harry's hand. "I want to stay and look for Walter."

"I know you do. I can't allow it. We don't know how many conspirators are still at large. It's too dangerous; I couldn't bear it if anything happened to you."

I had to try. "I love him too. Please let me help; at least let me stay here and work a radio or something." Harry crushed me to his chest and I felt more than heard the sob he'd been holding back. It broke my heart to feel him shudder with fear. He breathed in and held it for a calming moment...when he exhaled I knew he'd decided. He released me and walked toward Joan. "It seems my headstrong wife will be staying behind, at the Band Center," he said over his shoulder more to me than anyone else, "So I need to ask a favor of you." He waited until Joan nodded. "Walter's fiancée, Gertrude, and my son, Will, are staying at the Highland Inn in Midland. Please go to them directly and do your best to explain to Gertrude..." Harry's voice cracked. Joan took his hand between hers.

"I'll talk to her."

"Tell her...tell her I won't come back without him."

The finality of his words and the ones he didn't speak, *alive or dead*, sent a chill slithering up my spine. Joan swallowed hard and nodded. No one spoke as Dave and Garry escorted their wives onto the ferry. It pulled away minutes later, chugging into the bay and slowly disappearing into the purple-gray dusk.

We made our way to the Band Center, looking for the Midland police. A tall, rangy officer approached Harry when we entered and motioned him aside for a private conversation.

"There's coffee and tea back in the corner. Let's get some."

Dave grinned. "Already found the beverage center, eh?"

"When we were here earlier looking for you, they had a meeting going about the development." I nodded to Dawn and smiled. "She told us that Bob was with you. King said at the time he thought you were in cahoots with him."

Dawn turned her back to us. Jack King was a popular guy…handsome, single, from a powerful family…and he was still missing. It dawned on me that the Band members could be angry with anyone connected with his disappearance. I filled a cup and passed it back to Dave, repeating the process until we all had steaming mugs. Dave and Garry doctored their drinks with sugar and cream.

Never being one to leave well enough alone, I approached her. "Dawn?" She turned and looked astonished that I'd speak to her.

"Dawn, I'm sorry for all this. I don't understand why these things happened."

Her eyes filled with tears and a deep blush crept up her neck. I thought she would turn away again, but she stepped toward me. I sensed only sorrow and stayed my ground. She motioned me to sit down at the small table near the coffee service. Dave, Marty, and Garry wandered toward Harry.

"Jack is so different from his brother. Many people found…" she swallowed, "…find him cocky and stubborn. But that wasn't him most of the time."

I suspected she had deeper feelings for Jack, and her sudden blush confirmed it.

Dawn lifted her eyes and stared out the darkened window framing our reflections from the lighted hall. She changed the subject.

"They're saying Jack is protecting the cottager. I know one thing for sure–Jack would never have thrown in with a cottager." Her voice rang with sincerity.

"I know that to be true about Danny, I never hung around with

Jack." Dave moved closer. "I've known Danny since I was a teen and spent summers on island hunting, fishing, and exploring. As much as we went around together in the summers, he never 'threw in' with me. It was understood that if push came to shove, he would always side with Band members and I'd be on my own. I found out about the room under the altar stone, but I didn't know there were tunnels all the way to the lighthouse. I knew there were caves; I'd paddled out there with Danny. Again, I didn't know they went in far enough to hit the tunnels. It's like I knew only what I needed at the moment, but no one, least of all King, ever confided in me about island secrets. I'd been tolerated, allowed, but never accepted."

Dawn's eyes cleared. "I wish I would have known them then. My parents moved back to Christian Island when my father lost his job. We moved in with my grandparents. When they passed we stayed."

Harry called out to Dave. "We've a lead on Walter. Let's go." Dave jumped up from the table and grabbed one of the lanterns lined up near the door. Garry and Marty pulled on jackets and gloves and each picked up a lantern. Harry's eyes, still full of fear for his friend, searched the room for someone. His glance fell on a short Indian who, by the looks of him staring straight at Harry, had been waiting to be noticed and summoned. A quick nod and the Indian joined the search team. Harry looked at me. I knew that look–'stay put and wait for me.' I smiled, trying to convey hope that Walter would be found alive.

Only the short Indian remained after the hurry of their departure. He stood near the door, leaning against the wall. I realized that Harry had found a 'Walter' to guard me.

"Who is that man?"

Dawn smiled, and her eyes reflected her expression. "My dad." She stood and brought a cup of coffee to him.

The hall had emptied except for me, Dawn, and my bodyguard. "Why doesn't he sit down?" I asked when she returned.

"Not his idea of standing guard."

My eyes widened. "Does he plan to stand there all night?"

"If necessary. My father entered into an agreement with your husband to protect you. Whatever that takes."

"And you?"

"I'm keeping an eye on my dad and keeping you company. If that suits you."

"That suits me fine. Are you absolutely certain Jack would be opposed to joining forces with a non-Band person?"

She looked up in thought and slowly answered. "He's always been in Danny's shadow…school grades, sports, police academy, but he's never wanted to be anything except a policeman–the family business, so to speak."

I nodded that I understood.

She shrugged. "Anyway, I know he wanted the development. He thought if the island boomed, he'd have a better chance of doing more police work than just as a 'go-fer' for Danny. I don't know if he'd side with outsiders to get that chance. I'm not sure of anything. I don't know which would be worse for Mr. King, to lose a son to violence or to lose him to treachery."

Dawn's words rolled through my mind. Two brothers, two motives? How many Indians threw in with Bob for their own motives? A thought popped into the mix in my head.

"Is your family in the inheritance line from Lissette Pantier?"

"We prefer to refer to her as Banlieu, but no, I am not in that line. Lissette Banlieu is quite the legend on the island. She managed, even though under scrutiny from her sister-in-law, to provide the island with school books, farming tools, and construction materials from her husband's holdings."

I didn't know how to frame my next question. "Does the legend say it was love at first sight? You know…young outsider, island daughter; that could be quite the romance."

Dawn didn't bristle at the insinuation. "My grandmother said she always preferred white men." Her voice held the remembered 'sniff' from her grandmother's accounting.

I chanced it all and asked, "Do you think she could have loved someone before Pantier, maybe the lighthouse keeper?"

Her expression hardened. I'd pushed too far. Dawn stood abruptly and walked away. Had I blasphemed against the island legend or hit the mark dead on? Or both?

No matter, Dawn kept her distance. I sat with my chin in my

hands letting my mind sort out the flotsam and jetsam swirling inside.

Marty burst through the door and nearly collided with my bodyguard, who'd stepped forward to block his path until he recognized him.

"They found Jack King down at the water. He's unconscious, but alive. The shed Walter was held in is nearby. They've taken him there. Where's Mr. King? I was sent to get him."

"He went to gather men from the other end of the island."

"I need to find him. I mean, Jack's hurt. He should be with him." Marty turned to Dawn. "How do I get there?"

Dawn's father spoke. "You'll never find it in the dark." I saw the concern on his face.

"You go and get Mr. King," I said. "My brother will stay with me until you return."

His face was a study in conflicting emotions. He'd promised Harry, but he knew this might be King's last chance to be with his son, in case he didn't make it.

"I'll square it with my husband. He'll understand, he has a son."

He sprang from the room, grateful for his release from duty. I suspected he and Mr. King were old friends.

"That was good of you." Dawn's gaze had softened. "I know you mean well, but island pride is important to us and we almost revere Lissette Banlieu for all she did for the people."

"I never meant to denigrate Lissette. Love is colorblind and, after reading some letters from Amelia and Havilland and Lissette, it seemed possible that Havilland and Lissette had found love together. I think when Lissette found out she was pregnant by her married lover, she initiated a relationship with the only other white man whose genes would explain her baby. I don't think she cared beyond protecting the double shame of being pregnant by a married man.

"What she couldn't know is that Amelia and Joshua had committed incest, and the child Amelia bore was not Havilland's, but Joshua's."

Dawn's eyes widened and her mouth turned down in disgust.

"Exactly. Joshua needed a wife as much as Lissette needed another white man. I don't know when they all realized the truth about who begat whom, but I'm sure it was a twisted secret they all kept. I don't know which of the Pantier children were Joshua's and Lissette's or Joshua's and Amelia's or Lissette's and Haviland's. I suspect that Lissette stayed because of her children and what she could siphon for her people on this island.

"Joshua apparently moved between both bedrooms, but I think his diseased mind thought of Amelia as his wife."

"She had to be sick herself. You have to wonder about the kids they had together. You know, the gene pool."

"I don't think one generation of incest produces idiots or hemophiliacs."

"Still disgusting and doubly confusing. I think it would take a team of inheritance lawyers years to sort out who inherited."

"I don't know if they could without DNA samples to prove who came from whose loins. Blood types alone aren't always conclusive," Marty shrugged. "Maybe this is one secret that should be shelved."

"Fat chance now." I counted off, "Bob's on the loose, Ken's in custody, two people are dead, Walter is missing, a treasure is missing, and there's something glowing outside the window."

Marty turned in his chair, and jumped up. "Something's on fire. Cripes! We are."

As quickly as he spoke, the window burst and hungry flames reached toward us sucking the oxygen in its path. Dawn and I ran for the door.

"Wait," Marty screamed. "Touch it first. If it's hot, don't open it. The flames will fry us from both sides."

I hated his choice of words, but reached out to feel the wood.

"It's hot. What'll we do?" I screamed when flames licked under the door.

"Wet your jackets. Stuff the bottom of the door to buy us time."

Dawn reacted faster and had her jacket dripping wet and blocking the gap. I emptied the coffee on the spots that had started to burn on the wall.

"Good," Marty shouted. "Let's get these walls wet. The metal sides and roof will hold up longer. We can't let the fire get a hold on the stuff in here. Throw water against that door too. We have to buy time until someone sees this and sends up the alarm."

Marty swung toward Dawn. "You have a fire brigade or something, don't you?"

Dawn coughed and nodded. She pulled pans from the cabinet and filled them for me and Marty to use. The flames seemed under control–nothing inside was burning, but the real danger came from the smoke. We'd soaked dishtowels and wrapped them around our faces, but the smoke penetrated the flimsy protection.

The temperature in the room had risen until sweat poured from our bodies. I could only imagine how hot the metal must be. *Pop, pop.* I looked for the source of the noise. *Pop, pop.* The walls were bursting into flames...small punches in the wall, then spreading. The room would be an inferno in minutes.

"The light," Dawn called out. "Go to the light."

I couldn't make out much in the smoke, but it did seem brighter at the far end where the meeting had been held.

"No," Marty yelled. "If it's brighter, there's fire."

"No, it's a light. I know it. It's Havilland's Hope. Go, go."

Dawn pushed me ahead of her. I lost Marty in the smoke. "Marty, listen to me. Trust me. Go to the light."

His voice came from behind me. "I don't see a light, can't see anything." A coughing jag cut off anything else he said.

Dawn kept pushing me over my objection. "Stop. I can't leave him. Go. I have to get him." The heat sucked my breath, and I feared I'd collapse before I found him.

"Hold my hand and stretch out. We'll feel for him." We locked hands, and within a few feet tripped over Marty. He was on his knees, staying low and trying to find us. It was dangerous to stand upright, but we could move faster. We turned and rushed through the room...knocking into chairs, pushing them aside, and holding tightly to each other. The light grew brighter and, for an awful instant, I thought my brother was right and we were rushing into the fire.

Rather than hungry flames, we saw the outline of a small door. The mural had covered it earlier. The door was cool. "When we open this door the flames behind will rush us. When I open it, I'll open it wide and stand off to the side. The flames should shoot through after you. Run off to the sides if you can. If you catch on fire, drop and roll. I'll shut the door as fast as I can to cut off the fire."

"Marty, no. You have to come with us." As hot as it was, my body chilled with what I understood my brother was doing.

"None of us will have a chance that way. Don't worry, once the door is shut and the flames back off I'll squeeze through quickly. Might get a little singed, but it'll work. Trust *me* now."

I knew he was right, but I couldn't leave him. My throat ached with smoke and tears. Dawn touched my hand. "We need to leave now to give him time to make it."

That thought spurred me to action. Dawn and I lined up and planned she'd run left, me right, out of the door. We weren't sure if the door went to the outside or another room, in which case we might be trapped by the fire. Might be trapped was a better option than definitely trapped.

"Ready?" Marty grabbed the knob. "One, two, three!" The door pulled open in one easy movement. "Go, go, go," Marty screamed. The roar of the fire chasing us out the door drowned out Marty's voice. I felt the sharp pain of burning skin on my shoulders, but ran a few more feet before I dropped and dragged my back in the snow. I rolled over and over for good measure and relished the cold. I heard Dawn screaming. She stood yards from me, flailing at her hair. I ran toward her and brought her down in my best Morelli tackle. She hit the ground, and I immediately rubbed her head and face into the snow until the flames were squelched, then patted her down to make sure nothing else burned. Red welts already oozing appeared on her forehead; I gently packed snow over the affected area. She moaned. "Don't move. Lie still for a minute. I have to find Marty."

My heart broke, knowing that he should have been out by now. The door we'd escaped through was covered in flames. I moved as close as I could, searching the ground for any sign that he'd made it through, but I knew in stunned awareness that I'd lost him. The tears slipped down my cheeks–precursors to the sobs that would follow. I slumped to the ground a few yards from the burning building, the heat radiated to where I sat and melted the snow around me.

"Sit there too long, and you're liable to melt too."

"Marty!" I spun around to see my little brother crawling toward me. "Oh, my God. Marty. I thought…" I burst into the sobs that had been building. He reached me in time to cradle my head against his chest. He smelled of smoke, burned hair, and coffee.

"I told you I'd make it." He patted my back. "Shh, I'm okay."

He stood and lifted me with him. "Let's back off. We're too close if that wall buckles."

I let him guide me back to Dawn, who had managed to sit up against a tree. She held a clump of snow against her forehead; I saw her face plainly in the glow from the flames.

"Thank you." She swallowed hard. "Both of you."

A mixture of shouts and commands filled the air. Finally the fire brigade had arrived. We heard the powerful stream of water hitting the metal building; the sound of sizzling water squelching fire causing a cloud of steam to rise above the structure.

A new series of shouts went up when they spotted us. Dawn's dad and Mr. King ran forward, skidding to a stop and dropping to their knees. Dawn looked the worst, but I hadn't had a chance to check out Marty.

"Dawn, oh my God. Oh, my God." Her father held her at arms length, taking in her burned face and clothing. She patted his arm.

"I know I don't look it, but I'm okay. My hair caught fire and I panicked. I ran and then stood there trying to stop the flames." Dawn's voice faltered and her dad tightened his grip on her arms. She nodded toward me. "She saved me. Knocked me down and rubbed snow into my hair. What's left of it," she added as an afterthought. Her sense of humor eased her father's concern.

I turned to Mr. King. "How is your son?"

He helped me to my feet. "He's still unconscious." He looked at Marty and extended his hand to help him up. "Are you burned?"

Marty didn't answer; his eyes didn't focus. King saw the problem immediately. He shouted for help and two men materialized from the perimeter. They each took one of Marty's arms as directed. "Take him to the clinic for now. There is an ambulance coming on the ferry." They turned and helped Marty, who stumbled between them. His tattered clothing lay melted to his skin or hanging loosely in strips of skin and cloth. I screamed, and felt strong arms lower me to a sitting position, where I struggled to recover my common sense. "Please, please, take me with him. Please."

King nodded, helped me up, and we walked slowly after them. Blessedly, the darkness away from the fire covered his injuries from my sight as we gained on them. I knew I had to steel myself to be strong for him.

I heard the ambulance siren and felt relief. Mr. King called to the two men with Marty to stop, and he walked into the lane waving the lantern he carried. The ambulance stopped and rolled out a gurney.

"There is another one at the clinic. This one has severe burns on his back. I think he is in shock."

The emergency medics lost no time in assessing Marty's situation. They started an I.V., cut away extraneous clothing, and covered his burns with saline compresses until they could get him to the burn unit in Midland. There wasn't room for me in the ambulance, since they had another patient to pick up.

"Please take me to the dock. I want to go across with him."

"Are you all right, not burned?"'

I thought about the pain across my shoulders. "A little, but not like Marty and Dawn. I must have chosen correctly when I ran to the right. The flames came out more to the left of the door."

"When we arrived, the door was burned open. How did you make it out?"

"Not that door. The one behind the mural. We got out there because it was still cool to the touch. Dawn saw the light, and we found the door." I didn't think I made much sense.

"Impossible. That door has been locked for years. We put up the mural to stop people from trying to use the door."

He didn't catch me in time.

# Chapter Forty

"Grace. Gracie, can you hear me?"

Harry's voice pushed aside the dense curtain of white noise in my head. I struggled to open my eyes.

"Hiya," squeaked through my parched throat. Harry's face split into a grin. I felt his breath against my cheek and reveled that amidst the smoke I smelled Colours. I reached for his hand.

"Easy, Gracie. We're waiting for one of the medics to check you out." I looked around and realized I was in the back seat of a car. I must have looked confused.

"Mr. King wanted to get you out of the weather as quickly as he could, and this was the closest place. He told me about the fire. My God, sweetheart, I almost lost you. I thought you'd be safe here. That nutcase picked this one building to cause a distraction. He got clean away in a powerboat he stole from up the shore a bit."

"Walter?" My heart ached to ask and almost broke at the answer.

"Still nothing. I came in when I heard about the fire. King is still out searching further up the coast. Someone reported a stolen canoe."

I struggled to sit up. "Marty, I have to find Marty."

"Take it easy. Marty is already in the ambulance. He's stable. They're loading Jack King now and they'll be here soon to make sure you're right as rain."

I shook my head. "No, don't bother. Send them across now. Don't waste time on me, I'm fine."

"I'll make that decision, ma'am." The young medic who had approached King on the road switched places with Harry. He lifted my wrist and asked a few innocuous questions to determine if I was in the here and now. "I'm going to check your pupils and make sure they're dilating properly. Looks good. Tilt your head back a bit so I can get a look at your nostrils. Looks fine. The other two were okay as well. You were all lucky, that fire looked intense."

"We had wet towels around our faces."

"That saved you, but you got out just in time. Are you burned?"

"My neck and across my shoulders hurts."

He gently maneuvered a look. "I've used all my saline compresses on the man. Your burns are more surface than deep tissue. Still going to hurt like the deuces. Get over to the mainland and they'll fix you up at hospital."

He backed out of the car. Harry immediately reclaimed his seat. He kissed the top of my head and the side of my neck. "Let's get you off this island and into a proper hospital room." He helped me sit up and went round to the driver's side.

The dock area glowed with emergency generator lights. The ambulance drove up the ramp and parked. No other vehicles boarded. Harry helped me out of the car and walked me on the ferry.

"Darling, please understand I can't come across with you."

I nodded my head, afraid to speak. The chances that Walter was still alive were slim. I knew Harry wouldn't leave until he found him.

Harry took off his jacket and wrapped it around my shoulders. "I'll come to hospital as soon as I can." He pulled me to his chest and carefully hugged me. "Grace, I wouldn't want to live without you. I love you, darling."

A little voice in my head wanted to remind him he had Will to live for, but my heart gripped the sentiment and filled with joy.

"We're pulling in the lines, sir," one of the ferrymen said.

"Yes, thank you." He lowered his mouth to mine and, too quickly, backed away to leave. I watched him walk off the ferry and onto the island, where Dave stood waiting for him. He pointed up the coastline and I wondered if the news was about Walter.

We pulled away until the shore lights glowed like smudge pots and I thought of the room beneath the altar stone. Had it been prepared for a ritual? Had it taken place or had the death and destruction of the past twenty-fours hours caused a halt?

I opened the door to the large cabin area in the center of the deck. Warm air enveloped me and drew me in. I chose a bench toward the back so I could lean against the wall. The warmth of Harry's jacket and the cabin air lulled me to a light sleep. It felt wonderful to relax and drift.

The door opened and voices preceded two people into the cabin. I recognized one as the medic. "Shh, let's move over there. She needs to sleep."

I listened to their voices droning in and out of the engine's hum. Nothing made sense, but nothing mattered except Walter. The gold, the vote, the rightful heirs had added up to nothing. Dawn had told me the vote had been 'yes.' The Indians wanted development, just not where New World wanted it. They had agreed to meet with New World to discuss developing the island's north end at Daly Point, leaving the southern end untouched. The development might not go through, but it had a chance.

Did it mean anything that there was a dispute on the rightful inheritance line? Who could prove anything after all this time? If the development went through, it was with the proviso that each and every registered Band member and their descendents would receive a stipend from the proceeds.

That left the gold in Bob's possession. Where could he run? Could he make it to the Cayman Islands or would he head into the Great North to escape? How could he spend the money? Do you fling gold coins at bank tellers and ask them for fifties? My thoughts fell off one by one until I slowly tumbled to sleep.

I don't think I slept long. Shouts woke me. I jumped up and ran out of the cabin onto the deck.

"Holy St. Marie, there must be a freighter out there. Where's the light coming from? She's got to be coming from starboard." The pilot and first mate swiveled their heads from port to starboard, aft to stern, searching for the ship shining a powerful beam on us.

"There, off the port." The medic was gesturing. "A small boat. Stop, or you'll run it under."

The captain acted quickly, the ferry slowed, and changed course. The mate and the medic moved to the port side with a long pole that had a big, heavy hook on the end.

"Easy, easy. It's drifting right into us. Let her hit the hull, and we'll reverse to give us a shot at snagging her."

The loud scrape and whine of the engines were almost simultaneous. The powerful beam blinked off and left the rescue mission to continue in the low lights from the ferry.

"She's hooked. Hold her steady. Holy cripes, there's a man in the bottom. How we gonna' get him up here? We can't stay dead in the water."

The paramedic ran to his rig and returned with two harnesses, one that he slipped into, strapping it securely around his body; the other he hung over his shoulder. His partner ran a line through the ring at the front of the harness and secured the standing end to the portside cleat.

The tied-off medic climbed over and walked his way down the side of the ship until he dropped into the motorboat. All the passengers hung over the rail, watching the dangerous rescue and knowing that the paramedic was risking either being crushed against the ferry hull or lost at sea if the hook gave way. The engines revved and drew down, keeping the boat in this position.

"He's alive." A cheer went up from the rail. I realized a life is a life and precious at that, but it pained me to know Bob had made it possibly at Walter's expense.

He tried to start the engine. We saw him using his penlight to search for something. "Won't start!" he called out. "I'll stay with the boat. Send for help."

"Too risky. You're liable to drift out to a shipping lane."

"I'll send him up. Get ready to haul the line in."

The paramedic bundled the unconscious form into the harness and tied his line to him. He looked up and shook his head. "I need a board," he shouted. "He's unconscious, he'll be smashed against the hull."

"No time," the first mate answered. "I can't hold you much longer. Tie the line to the boat. We'll tow you in as best we can. Use the bumpers to absorb some of the shock and pray you don't break apart before Metro can reach you or we get ashore."

In minutes the line was secured and the captain had a decision to make. He was closer to Christian Island, but he had an ambulance filled with injured people. He called down to the medic on deck. "Can those people wait or are they critical?"

"Two can wait, burns but nothing life threatening. The third is a head injury. There's always the risk of swelling."

"It's your call, you're the doc."

The paramedic looked from his friend to their rig. His Hippocratic oath won. "I gotta get him to hospital. Can't risk it."

The captain set his course and inched across the bay. We all stayed at the rail watching the scene below as if our collective thoughts could change the tide or at least the waves that pushed the small craft against the large vessels. The medic had hung four bumpers. The danger now was if the motorboat moved out too far from the side and missed the wave, it could tip against the side of the ferry. The conversations were hushed.

"It was Havilland's Hope. He reached out to save him."

"You're crazy, old man. It was probably some kind of aircraft crossing above us."

The older man sniffed his skepticism. "We woulda' heard an airplane."

"Then maybe a freighter turning around the point and hitting us with its light for a few minutes. I know one thing, it weren't no ghost lighthouse keeper and his phantom light." He crossed his arms over his chest and moved off.

I believed in angels. I was coming to believe in lighthouse keepers.

The sounds of the small boat hitting the side jarred my teeth, each scrape sounding louder and more destructive. How much longer could the boat and its human cargo survive?

The captain had radioed ahead explaining his emergency, and we heard the sound of another powerful engine. Metro Water had reached us. They slowed to avoid creating a wake that would further jeopardize the small boat. Relief spread through the crew and passengers. The search beam mounted on the cruiser picked out the boat bobbing and bucking in the murky cold waves.

The loudest scrape yet grated in my ears and I heard the emergency siren on the cruiser blast three times. The change in wave action tipped the boat and pushed the toe rail under water, causing the cabin to smash into the hull. Both men disappeared under the shattered wood. The blasts came again; the penetrating sound throbbed in my head. The captain shouted orders and the constant vibration in my legs from the machinery below decks ceased.

The scene in the water was chaos. Divers from the cruiser had gone into the water, immediately swimming toward the wreck. The first mate and medic worked quickly to retrieve the towline, hoping the men were holding onto that bit of boat. Nothing but the cleat itself and a three-foot piece of the railing still attached came out of the water. Smaller pieces of the wreckage drifted passed the stern and on to wherever they would wash up. Were the men clinging to it, or had they been sucked under by the wash of the ferry?

The cruiser's light played across the area, picking up the bobbing headlights of the two divers and the myriad of debris: cushions, bumpers, the vee deck…my mind shut down and my lips moved in silent prayer.

"There! There, over there," one of the passengers shouted, waving madly at the water. The crewman aimed his handheld light in that direction and the cruiser followed suit. A tiny pinpoint of blinking light signaled weakly.

"More to the stern," one diver shouted. "We see them!"

We saw them too from the deck; sprawled across part of the hull barely visible bobbing at the edge of the light spreading from the two boats. In minutes they would have drifted into total darkness and certain death. The cruiser changed course and slowly moved toward the rescue operation. Our captain engaged the engines. The deck surged with power and the familiar hum filled my ears. We moved away from the scene resuming course for the landing and hospital.

In all the excitement I'd forgotten that Marty might be awake. I hurried to the ambulance and climbed in the passenger side to peek in on the patients. Marty heard the door and lifted his head. "It's about time," he whined softly so as not to wake the other two. "What the hell is going on out there? If I could have reached these straps, I would have been out there," he hissed between clenched teeth. Dawn stirred in the cot next to his. Two gurneys and one borrowed cot were jammed into the back of the rig. Dawn, triaged as least injured, had the cot.

"They found the boat with Bob unconscious in the bottom. The paramedic rappelled down the side of the ferry to help him, but the boat couldn't withstand the pounding against the hull and it broke up. Metro Water had divers in the water, and they found them on some of the wreckage. We've just pulled away to head for the landing."

"Geez Louise, I missed everything."

"Get some rest, we'll be docking soon. You'll feel better in a real bed. Does it hurt a lot?" I noticed some of the compresses had dried.

Marty shrugged, then winced. "Oww. Only when I do that." His raised voice woke Dawn. I left Marty to explain recent events to her. I knew I'd have to find a way to reach Harry with this news.

\* \* \*

Joan met me at the landing. "Any news? We heard the cruiser put out with lights and sirens."

"Will it come here?"

"No, it'll go up to Midland. Why did an ambulance cross from this side? Usually the Anishinabek ambulance makes the crossing and transfers to a waiting one."

"Don't know. Marty's on this one. I need a lift to the hospital."

"Marty? What happened? In fact, what's that smell and you don't look so good yourself."

I waved my hand to stop her. "Can we get in the car first?"

"Sure, sorry."

I reached for her hand. "I'm sorry. It's just that they found Bob alive in the boat Metro went out to rescue." I shook my head. "No sign of Walter." My throat pinched with tears and I gratefully slid into the front seat of her car. The pain of leaning back against the soft cushion lessened after first contact and the comfort of the car seat soothed my aching muscles. I explained about finding Jack, the fire, and the rescue on the bay.

The ambulance, with lights and sirens, beat us to the University Health Network, but not by much. Joan and I followed through the emergency entrance. The lone medic spotted me on his way out pushing one gurney and then another before him to his ambulance. He'd already brought in his charges. He paused and pointed me out to the triage nurse. "Her too," I heard him say and motioned me over.

I knew I needed something for the pain that prickled my shoulders now that my adrenaline had leveled out. I walked toward the nurse, stopping to ask the medic if he'd heard about his partner.

"They're bringing him in to Huronia District. I'm on my way there now."

I thanked him for his help, and he left wishing me luck.

I submitted to an exam and treatment, nearly nodding off when left alone for a few minutes. I knew I needed sleep, but I also needed to see Gertrude and then get back to the island.

We tucked Marty in for the night, promised to be back in the morning, only six hours away, and drove to Joan's house.

"After I met with Gertrude I invited her and Will to stay with us until…"

I nodded and swallowed, realizing I'd be seeing Gertrude in a few minutes. What could I say? Will would be there too. I hoped he was asleep, one less explanation.

*No, one less confrontation is more like it. Somehow, I'll be the bad guy.*

*That's not fair. He helped save your life.*

*A moment of weakness I'm sure he regrets.*

*You're the one with the problem.*

*I know.*

We sat in the driveway on Russell Street. "We have to go in. I'm sure she's up."

I nodded and slowly climbed out of the car. Whatever they'd slathered on my shoulders worked like a charm. Gertrude opened the door before I reached the bottom step. The lamppost light illuminated my eyes and she saw the answer before I spoke. Her shoulders slumped and her chest heaved with the effort to not cry out. I rushed to her side.

"We haven't found him yet, but there's hope. There's always hope." I put my arm around her shoulders and guided her inside. Her thin shoulders moved in time with the sobs she couldn't contain. Joan brought out three glasses and filled them with honey-colored liqueur.

"Drink this." She pressed one into Gertrude's hands, who I thought needed water instead of alcohol. Gertrude sipped and then drained the small glass. She cleared her throat and took a deep breath. "*Danke*, Missus Joan. You are nice lady."

I sipped at my drink which slid down my throat. The soothing effect came immediately.

Neither Joan nor I brought up the rescue; that information would destroy any hope she held. Gertrude leaned against the couch, slips of her light brown hair loosened from her bun lay against her cheek. Her breathing became slower and smoother. Joan and I tiptoed away to the kitchen.

I couldn't find sleep, and we talked the night away. The secret of the treasure, the mysterious inukshuk, Havilland's Hope…we covered it all until we'd rid our systems of the long-ago tragedy, better to meet and handle current affairs.

We talked and drank the honey liqueur until we agreed to close our eyes on our folded arms. It would be dawn soon.

# Chapter Forty-one

We didn't hear them enter because Dave had his key. I stirred at the sound of footsteps across the wooden floor.

"Here they are," Dave said. That we heard. Joan's head popped up like a cork, and she rushed around the table to hug her husband.

"Are you okay?"

"I'm fine. Come with me, I've an errand to run."

I smiled at Dave, then spotted Harry in the hallway. Oh, God. He said he wouldn't come back without Walter. They'd found his body. I choked out the words, "You found his…him?" I wanted to be strong for Harry to comfort him and Gertrude, but I felt a gash in my heart and wanted to feel Harry's arms comforting me.

Harry reached for me and I rushed into his arms prepared to be his rock, but his body language was all wrong–strong and bursting with energy. He held me away from him and I saw him clearly. "We found him. Actually you found him, but didn't know it. He's alive, Gracie, he's alive."

Harry held me until my breathing calmed. He released me and held me at arm's length again. "I guess none of us looks too rested. Sit down and let me make us some tea. Dave and Joan have taken Gertrude to see Walter. He's a tough old bird; needed sutures and a bone or two set, but he's a survivor."

"You've seen him? How, when?"

Harry set a cup of hot tea in front of me and laced it with honey. He picked up the empty bottle and arched an eyebrow at me in good humor. "Surprised you heard us at all."

"It was for medicinal purposes," I grinned. "Tell me."

"When we heard about Bob's rescue, we told Debbie and she hopped the next ferry across. By that time they'd brought the paramedic and unconscious man to hospital, only not the one you were at or you might have known first."

My eyes widened. "It was Walter in the boat." I clapped my hands together then sobered as I remembered the unkind thoughts I'd sent to the man in the bottom of that boat when I thought he was Bob.

"When Debbie rushed into hospital expecting to see Bob, she brought down the ward with her screams."

I rejoiced at Walter's life being spared, but understood how devastated Debbie must have been to have her hope cruelly snatched away. Harry understood. "The nurses calmed her as best they could until a doctor was called to administer a sedative. I think Colleen and Laurie are with her."

"Colleen is in Midland?"

Harry nodded. "The police brought Ken across in their squad on the same ferry that Debbie took. Colleen sat with Debbie and they heard the story of the rescue from the crew."

"How awful for her to find…"

"It was terrible for her. After they settled her, one of the nurses noticed that Walter was awake, groggy, but awake. She called in the policeman standing guard outside the room who'd been trying to make sense out of Debbie's accusations. Walter identified himself and told the copper the most bizarre story about working his way free of the shed, but running into Bob and the young deputy. Bob had tricked Jack King and was using him to get off the island with the gold.

"Bob forced Walter to steal the boat and walk it down, up to his thighs in water, to the spot where he'd stashed the backpacks filled with gold. He didn't want to risk starting up the motor until he was ready to leave. He tied off the boat and brought both of them back to the shed. He bashed Walter with the barrel of the gun. When Walter came to Jack was gone. We think Jack managed to crawl out and down the shore before he passed out. That's why they found him but not Walter; they'd already searched the shed. Walter spotted the fire and surmised that Bob had started it as a distraction. He took off to intercept Bob. He ended up jumping in the boat to stop him. They fought while the boat zig-zagged through open water. Bob slammed Walter's arm in the hatch while they struggled over the gun. It went off and must have hit the engine block through the decking. The gun slipped out of Bob's hand. The engine stalled and the waves started tossing the boat about.

"Bob had strapped on one backpack and stood near the transom trying to feel for the gun with his foot. A wave hit the drifting boat broadside and Bob lurched into the water. Walter rushed to the side shouting for him to drop the pack and swim for the boat. He watched in amazement as Bob began swimming for the shore carrying the burden of the treasure on his back. Walter said he sank beneath the waves within four strokes. He could have made it back to the boat, but he chose to take his treasure with him to the bottom. Another wave toppled Walter, and that's the last he remembers until he woke up in hospital."

I shivered and sipped at my tea.

"Wow, that's a great story." Will stood in the doorway still wearing his pajamas. "Is Walter going to be okay?"

Harry held out an arm to his son and Will wrapped his arm around Harry's waist. Harry kissed the top of his silky blond head. "He'll be right as rain in a short time."

I stared at the two of them, so alike in features and now, the more time they spent together, so alike in demeanor. "Hello, Will." I didn't know what else to add.

"Hi." He looked up to his dad. "Are we going to the island today?" his little-boy excitement apparent in his voice. Harry and I exchanged glances and I turned in my chair to contemplate my tea. I doubt anyone had any interest in going to the island. I wondered if we were even allowed back on the island. I'd miss some of my clothes and the lovely rocks I'd collected for Harry's inukshuk, but I'd rather leave them than return.

"Your neck. It looks burned. Did you get hurt too?" Will's voice held concern as well as curiosity.

I turned to face him and nodded. "I was in the building with Uncle Marty and an Indian woman when Bob set fire to it. It was supposed to be empty; I don't think he knew anyone was inside." I shivered and swallowed. "If it's all the same to you, Will, I don't think I can go back to the island." He didn't like me already; I might as well be the bad guy. My eyes filled with tears and I pretended to press them because of fatigue.

He touched my hand. "I get it. Guess I wouldn't want to go back either. Let's just go home. I'm gonna' change. I'm already packed."

The glance that Harry and I exchanged expressed hope to our fragile threesome.

"You heard the lad, darling. He wants to go home."